For Josh with the good wishes

THE VAMPIRES OF JUAREZ

Alan / Dec-2017

ALAN SCARFE

SMART HOUSE BOOKS

Heidi von Palleske/Smart House Books
100 Bain Ave, 35 The Oaks, Toronto, M4K 1E8
www.smarthousebooks.com

Cover design - Aaron Rachel Brown
Cover concept - Barbara March

The Vampires of Juarez/ Alan Scarfe -- 1st ed.
ISBN - 978-0-9689718-5-7

This is a revised edition of the novel previously published as The Vampires of Ciudad Juarez by Clanash Farjeon (Trafford Books, 2010) and *I vampiri di Ciudad Juarez* (Gargoyle Books, Rome, 2010). It is now the only author-approved version.

Also by the same author:
The Revelation of Jack the Ripper
The Demons of 9/11
The Mask of the Holy Spirit

Praise for The Vampires of Juarez

"This book is a masterpiece. As an investigative criminologist I have interviewed over thirty of the world's most heinous serial killers. I have sat with them as they relived and gloated over the torture and suffering they brought upon their victims. I have seen the results of their gruesome work firsthand, butchering, flaying alive, every way one can imagine of destroying an innocent living human being, but nothing, I stress nothing, I have ever witnessed compares with the content of *The Vampires of Juarez*. To write such a magnificent, blood-chilling work such as this one has to plunge into the bottomless abyss of pure evil. Alan Scarfe *is* 'The Abyss' for he terrifies the living daylights even out of me."

- **Christopher Berry-Dee,**
former Editor-in-Chief *The Criminologist* and Director of the Criminology Research Institute, Portsmouth

"Fast-moving, eloquent, funny and at the same time profoundly violent and distressing . . irony saves it from insupportable sadness and instead creates a fresh and captivating story. Another terrific novel from Alan Scarfe."

- Susanna Raule, *Cut-up*

"Scarfe's vampires are nothing like the classic literary and cinematic archetypes. They are neither romantic nor troubled spirits. They are pitiless, arrogant and vulgar, without immortality and unafraid of the sun."

- Vito Tripi, *Word Shelter*

"The violence is not supernatural but a direct result of the brutality that occurs every day in Ciudad Juarez yet Scarfe's novel is by no means exclusively a denunciation. The complex plot is easy to follow, the characters are instantly clear to the reader and the narrative is fluent and laced with wisdom and humor."

- Il Catafalco

"This book is simply stupendous and I say it as a reader, not a reviewer . . a beautifully told punch in the stomach . . a masterpiece half way between Scarface and a 1980's B-movie with a result that leaves you breathless . . Don't waste time reading this review. Go straight out and buy it and then you can thank me."

- Valerio Bonante, *Ca' delle Ombre*

"Witty and hilarious throughout thanks to the liveliness of its central character yet so disturbing it makes your hair stand on end . . an eloquent indictment of the corruption of power."

- Giovanni Scalambra, *Stradanove*

"I sincerely hope this novel will reach a wide reading public . . It is impossible to speak or write enough about Ciudad Juarez."

- Simone Scataglini, *Horror.it*

"This review is a shout-out to everyone who appreciates books that jolt us . . whether we want it or not . . into some new understanding. Scarfe wants us to reflect on the horror and terror of places such as Ciudad Juarez, a field of nightmares not a field of dreams. Precious little media attention is paid to what has been taking place there and Scarfe asks us to consider the extent to which we are all culpable, not only for the tragic circumstances of Juarez but the endless saga of bloodletting that is the dark side of our legacy as a species. But he tells stories, he does not lecture."

- Eric Ross Green,
Awash with Blood, an Awake and Arise Call to all Goths

"The First World and the Third World
are the bread in this sandwich
and we are the baloney!"

So a resident described the sprawling industrial war zone on the U.S.-Mexico border that is Ciudad Juarez, the epicenter of the drug trade, where the Third World comes to make what the First World wants. Hundreds, perhaps thousands, of young women have been abducted, raped and murdered here yet the mystery of *las desaparecidas* has been only superficially investigated and remains tragically unsolved.

This book is dedicated to them.

"Drinking when we are not thirsty
and making love at all seasons, madam;
that is all there is to distinguish us
from other animals."

Pierre-Augustin Caron de Beaumarchais
The Marriage of Figaro (1778)
Act Two, Scene 2

PROLOGUE

At 4:22 AM on Sunday, March 16th, 1997, something decidedly mischievous was taking place in a small private clinic in Mexico City.

A night nurse on the third floor of the Hospital of Our Lady of Santa Monica, situated discreetly behind wrought iron gates and high bougainvillea smothered walls in the exclusive Polanco district, had been alerted by a flashing light beside the number 407 at her nursing station and was hurrying down a polished hallway to enter the recovery room of a wealthy patient named 'Florio Bastida Morales'.

An ominous insistent buzzer greeted her ears. Two men were standing by the curtained window smoking, dressed in dark suits and shirts with open collars, quite apparently unperturbed by the noise. The nurse eyed them suspiciously but said nothing.

A large shapeless masculine lump lay on its back in the bed attached to a bewildering array of life support equipment. The face on the pillow was horridly swollen and covered with a painful crisscross of hastily wrought sutures. The livid bristled cheeks and lips were caved as though dentures had been removed. Vacant eyes stared upward with an eerie look of betrayal and discomfort as if the soul were frozen and unable to make progress. Above the man's head the green screen of the cardiac monitor displayed a calm flat white line.

A doctor was summoned to take the pulse. A mere nurse was not qualified to confirm something as mysterious as death. He shut off the buzzing alarm and informed her quietly that they had been temporarily unable to complete the facial surgery due to a circulatory problem. It was a common reaction with cocaine addicts and the early liposuction phase of the procedure had evidently caused too great a strain on the patient's system. They had first siphoned off over three and a half gallons of subcutaneous fat from his torso, belly and buttocks and had already started on the second phase when complications arose and the unfortunate man had been shifted for a few hours to this solitary room under heavy sedation to see if he might stabilize sufficiently for them to continue.

Evidently he had not.

The doctor cast the briefest of veiled glances at the two men by the window but knew well enough not to do more. Then he sighed and finished his notes, went to the door and gestured to the nurse to follow him.

Once they had gone one of the men dialed his cell phone and spoke.

"El Señor ha muerto."

As they left the room the other dropped his cigarette butt in the dead man's gaping mouth.

§

At precisely the same moment, disregarding the illusory confusion of 'time zones', Michael Davenport awoke in his flat in the Chalk Farm area of London to the horror of a savagely inflamed throat and thus, for him, the depressing portent of weeks, if not months, of sinus catarrh.

Michael was English, or as he was proud to say, Saxon, and as obsessively fond of cats as he was of desert landscapes, and of capturing both through the lens of his gigantically old–fashioned video camera, so it was not really surprising that ninety-nine hours and fifty-eight minutes later, while making his way by bus from Miami to Los Angeles, he would find himself without his passport in Mexico having waded absent–mindedly through the pre-dawn light across the shallow demarcation of the Rio Grande from the effusively hospitable grin of El Paso to the impassively threatening scowl of Juarez while filming an enormous white male Siberian tiger.

His beloved tabby sat patiently purring on his chest as he cautiously teased open caked and itching eyes and stared in accusation at the ceiling dreading a first swallow and coming to terms with the awful truth. 'I knew I shouldn't have left it so long,' his semiconscious mind groaned sluggishly, 'I knew I was on the verge. Christ damn this sodden climate.'

"Death or sunshine. No alternative. I simply must get away," he had told his boss at the magazine. The sun was Michael's god and beckoned annually. "I'll find something interesting in America to report back about. Wherever I go I always do."

He had an informal relationship with an obscure publication called 'Enigma' which was dedicated to the rational examination of all irrational phenomena. He had asked his boss to pay for his flight to the States and John had reluctantly agreed to fifty percent as long as Michael sent two cracking good stories within the month.

Then he and Marta had gone down to the local pub and celebrated a little too energetically over his imminent departure given their age, enjoying each other's company for a change, even sharing a quickie for old time's sake. That was three nights ago.

'Shit and derision,' he realized with a jolt, 'It was her! Why didn't I think?!'

Slowly, painfully, he gathered sufficient saliva in his mouth, reached over to the nightstand for the last sip of mineral water remaining in the glass tumbler he always kept by his bedside and, taking courage, forced himself. The muscular contractions of the pharynx necessary for ingesting the now faintly acrid liquid were more excruciating than even he had been prepared for and were accompanied by an ominous popping of already clogged Eustachian tubes.

'Wouldn't you just know it. Jesus bloody Christ!'

He turned his head to the alarm clock. 10:27. His flight from London to Miami was not until late afternoon and the previous day had been entirely spent in meticulous last minute preparation. Two ancient, stickered and perilously overstuffed suitcases stood eager and bulging with everything conceivably requisite to his journey in the hallway. 'Travel light' was all very well as a motto but it was beyond Michael's skill to achieve it. No, readiness was not the problem, no, bugger it, but it was a bloody Sunday and he knew he must suffer the immediate devastation of antibiotics in order to have any chance at all of kicking this bug, this phagocytic wage of ill–considered luxury, before it ruined his holiday and where the hell was he going to get them?

'What a prospect! Trying to maintain fruitful discourse with some smiling dentine–bleached druggist in Florida.'

This terrifying thought finally impelled him to sit up. Flossie foresaw the impulse and jumped to the floor, miraculously spry and agile for a semi-blind cat of seventeen, stalking round the corner of the door to her empty dish in the kitchen twitching a threadbare tail.

Michael's younger sister Helen, with whom he shared the cramped but cozy flat, was on a week's holiday on the Costa del Sol with some workmates. She was more reliable in the feeding department. She was an art lover not an art doer and, after the break up of a frustrating marriage with an ambitious bisexual American art dealer, had used her knowledge to secure a position as personal secretary to the director of the Central St. Martin's College of Art and Design so she was used to organizing things.

Michael slid his classically formed feet into slippers and stood. It was his custom on rising to stretch and objectively scrutinize his reflection in the mirror of an old Victorian dressing table that had belonged to his grandmother. He couldn't really say why except that, as long as he could remember, he had been amazed that other people seemed to take the daily continuities of their existence for granted.

Since there was less than twenty-four inches separating the side of his bed and the dresser he could only observe himself from the knees to the neck without crouching or jumping which was frowned upon by the landlady.

He still cut a fine figure though he would vehemently demur, he considered himself sway–backed. Firmly muscled legs, he could give a much younger man a run for his money and often did, tight buttocks, well–formed and ample scrotal appendages which Marta had once fondly described as 'velvety', perhaps a shade undernourished of arms and torso except of course for the intransigent little paunch but, taken all in all, not too shabby for a much–traveled specimen of forty–seven. He grimaced and turned away in disgust.

Having relieved himself, washed his eyes, brushed his teeth, gargled for a full two minutes with strongly salted water and reversed the hanging of a still damp pair of rinsed knickers on a string line above the tub, he opened a fresh tin of Whiskas Tuna Casserole for Flossie, put the kettle on to boil, then went and sat down at his desk in the spare bedroom Helen allowed him to use as a study.

The room measured perhaps eight feet by eleven and was crammed from floor to ceiling with the unbearable to be trashed flotsam and jetsam of a lifetime of eccentric creativity. Primarily pile upon pile of dog–eared papers, folders stuffed with unpaid bills and unanswered correspondence, mountains of uncompleted manuscripts, plays, novels, stories, poems, essays, theories on everything from the cosmological constant to fish and chips, carefully worked out plans for rebuilding the Crystal Palace on the Sussex coast of his boyhood as the surround for a heated sea water spa resort and a detailed design for the internal renovation of a disused Victorian power station in South London as a state–of–the–art film studio. All unquestionably fine ideas but the power brokers of this world lack the perspicacity to heed one whom, with the inbred instinct of all such gimlet–eyed vermin, they dismiss on sight as a penniless crank.

Yet even more dominant in the room were the videotapes, thousands of them, a loving and artful, albeit from a strictly rational viewpoint a trifle obsessive, compendium of the infinitely beautiful and at once infinitely ugly experiences of a life, shot from every imaginable angle, framed to catch every conceivable nuance, critiqued time and again late into the night, edited and re-edited, inching endlessly toward a final distillate masterpiece.

As well as the desk, the boxes and buried bookcases, there was a single armchair by the window with an open area of table beside it just sufficient for an elbow or a meal and set neatly with a placemat on which sat six remotes facing no fewer than four dusty television sets of assorted sizes and three blinking video players only one of each still operable.

Michael lifted the phone to his ear and dialed. The receiver crackled with such malignant ferocity as to render any communication virtually inaudible but he persevered. British Telecom had been persistently pestered to fix the problem. In high dudgeon Michael had once even lugged the entire unit to a friend's home in Canterbury where to his immense satisfaction it most assuredly did not crackle, and he had signatory witnesses, but the various beleaguered telephone company representatives had equally stubbornly maintained that the source of the offending static lay in his out–of–date equipment. Once a summoned technician had been so rude as to intimate that the noise might be linked in some fashion to the 'state' of his digs. The young man found himself lucky to escape with an eloquent, though mercifully to him quite incomprehensible, tongue–lashing. Such boring and seemingly forever to remain insoluble impasses were the desolate common denominator of modern life and were a good part of the reason, Michael was obdurately convinced, that with each succeeding winter the colds to which he had been prone since a child became more and more menacing and intractable.

A female voice with a hard to place middle–European accent answered.

"Hallo."

"You've given me a bloody cold, you inconsiderate cow!"

"Oh, no," Marta responded with an admirable show of sympathy given that she knew very well what was coming, "It wasn't my idea."

"Go on. You'd have thought I was being moody if I hadn't."

"I mean going back to my flat."

"Well, whose idea was it then?"

"We both had it at the same time as I recall."

Michael despaired of parsing the matter further.

"Look, for god's sake, have you got any pills? I can barely speak, you can hear it. I can't face trying to wheedle them out of some tanned smiling dolt in Fort Lauderdale. I'd rather drown myself in the Everglades. I'd rather be fed to a great white . . "

Marta cut him off.

"I'll have a peek but I don't think so. You took the few I had left over in January."

"Never mind. Can you please, for the love of heaven, try and get some tomorrow and send them on."

"How? Who from? Where to?"

"Anyone. I don't care. That Himalayan, New Age, fruit–bat doctor friend of yours! I'll let you know where to. You've got to try. It's your bloody fault."

"Now look, Michael . . "

"Just try. Please. For me. Pretty please. My throat is a necklace of fire! I'll ring you. Ach, Christ, I'm dying. I can't talk any more."

"Alright. Have a goo . . "

Michael replaced the receiver gently and hung his head exhausted on his chest.

Marta was originally Hungarian. She was his wife though they had never lived together. He had married her twenty–five years previously to get her a visa. A romantic student gesture after a drunken weekend on the island of Hvar on the Dalmatian coast of what was then Yugoslavia where she had been working as a waitress for the summer in a small seaside hotel which catered primarily to overweight and overbearing German tourists.

'Why? Why? Oh lord, please tell me why?'

He tried revolving his jaws to ease the pain. The viral gremlins were setting up a ruthless tattoo on his larynx. Placing a finger and thumb gingerly on those sore and throbbing glands, rock hard beneath the stubbled skin of his throat, he sighed with not so patient resignation, then managed a small rusty chuckle and growled, "Oh well, fuck it."

CHAPTER ONE

Sixty–eight hours and twelve minutes after his arrival in the welcoming subtropical balm of Miami Michael was sitting at the rear of a super-chilled Greyhound bus zooming across the dry expanse of West Texas with a disheveled array of camera equipment, maps, juice bottles, sandwich wrappers, tanning lotion, decongestants and analgesic lozenges spread out across the plush tartan upholstery of the broad bench seat to either side.

Against the driver's surly remonstrations he had opened the window and balls of used Kleenex were blowing about his bare toes like dust devils in the desert heat. He was also higher than a kite on the Percodan that Marta had borrowed and, all–forgiving angel of mercy that she was, brought round to his flat just ten minutes before the cab came to take him to Heathrow airport.

In a further boundless gesture of generosity she had even offered to drive him there herself and he had gallantly declined saying, "No, no, sweet thing, you've done enough." But, in the end, he relented. Well, it was a saving of more than thirty pounds.

The new driver had taken the wheel in Dallas at eight that morning. He was definitely a no shit sort of fellow and it hadn't taken him twenty seconds to spot a troublemaker. Before the bus reached the outskirts of Fort Worth he had pulled over.

"You want to keep the window closed, sir, please?" he drawled, turning his massive frame with obvious discomfort part way out of the driver's seat.

Michael had quickly obliged but the process had repeated itself several times with Michael surreptitiously inching the window open until the driver would notice and scowl at him with growing ferocity in the mirror. Finally, at a rest stop in Abilene, just when it appeared that the great ox might lose patience altogether and eject him, Michael took him by the horns.

"Look here," he said with a carefully calculated forthrightness of manner, confronting the huge man at a vulnerable moment as he relieved himself in an adjacent urinal, "I understand all about rules and regulations, believe me, but I suffer from an awful asthmatic condition.

Your bus is far from full and I'm freezing and my lungs won't take it. If I can't have the window open beside me at least a tiny little bit I'm likely to have a serious attack and start gasping and wheezing and writhing on the floor. It happens, I promise you, and it's not a pretty picture. I can feel it coming on. I might die, then where would you be? You can't possibly want the aggravation of upsetting your timetable, to say nothing of the other passengers, with an unscheduled and unnecessary detour to the nearest hospital, now can you? They don't seem to care. They all want to sit near the front anyway."

Three men with deeply weather–wrinkled faces, Michael assumed them to be ranch hands of Mexican descent, passed behind them smiling affably.

The driver was clearly fed up and mentally fatigued by the whole business. He stared vacantly at the wall and seemed quite unable to sustain the effort of comprehending such an argument. Something about Michael's accent appeared to be giving him a headache as well and, at length, after a true Method actor's pause and a long ruminative shake of his porcine member, he had grunted, shrugged in dyspeptic acquiescence and stalked off twitching his head in baleful dismay.

It was true the other passengers had long since despaired of rectifying the matter and had been trying to doze away their boredom while giving the 'crazy Englishman' a wide berth. Michael was delighted. The three rows now empty in front of him gave ample freedom to range about with camera in hand capturing the desiccated beauty of the passing landscape.

Mile after mile of nothing but desert, glorious desert. The middle of March, not a cloud in the sky and eighty degrees Fahrenheit at half past two in the afternoon. Simply and utterly magnificent.

§

An old man sat rocking himself in the sunshine on the peeling porch of a rundown farmhouse on the outskirts of Sweetwater, not more than eight hundred yards from where the Greyhound was speeding by just twenty–seven minutes after Michael's artful placation of the still inwardly grumbling driver, staring blankly in the direction of the freeway with watery eyes.

In the living room a younger man was watching the news slouched in a half–collapsed armchair with his boots up on a cluttered coffee table, a bottle of Dos Equis beer hanging from his calloused hand. He was heavily muscled and tall and tanned but perhaps more than anything else it was his thinning curly brown hair that had led him once or twice to be mistaken for Gene Hackman.

"The authorities in Mexico City will only confirm that the man, who was registered at the Our Lady of Santa Monica Clinic under the alias 'Florio Bastida Morales', died from heart failure after extensive plastic surgery to change his appearance. But General Larry McWhirter, President Clinton's newly-appointed Director of National Drug Control Policy and Loomis Consterdine, the head of the DEA, stated at a press conference this morning that, if the body is indeed that of Amado Portillo, the disruption in the flow of cocaine into this country will be significant and will give them added leverage in their pursuit of the remaining Mexican drug cartels . . "

The man heard a car pulling up outside, snapped off the television with the remote and hauled himself to his feet.

"More bullshit," he muttered contemptuously and walked into the kitchen past a sink piled high with unwashed dinner plates and out onto the porch as a woman got out of the arriving car. She was his age more or less, pushing fifty with streaky blond hair and not looking any too pleased.

"Chuck, I don't think I . . "

"Look, Laurie, thanks for doing this. I appreciate it."

"How long are you going to be gone?"

"I don't know. Four or five days maybe. It's the best chance I've had for quite a while. It's necessary."

"Is that so? Necessary to who?"

"Me. And pop. For Christ's sake, Laurie, you know damn well."

He held up the full coffee mug that was sitting on the gray wood of a table beside the old man and helped him take a sip, then put his hand gently on the old man's shoulder.

"You take care of yourself, papa. Laurie's here now. You two'll have a fine time."

The old man turned his head and looked up at his son. There were no words but deep inside the look Chuck knew there was understanding.

He grabbed a half-empty duffel off the table, trotted down the parched wooden steps to his sister and brushed her cheek with a kiss, then tossed the bag in beside the driver's seat of a battered mud-streaked 1985 Ford Ranger.

"You're going to get yourself killed."

Chuck grinned, acknowledging the possibility and his indifference to it.

"Enjoy," he said.

"If they don't do it maybe I will."

As he blew her another kiss and the truck bounced away down the dirt lane the old man's veined eyes watched him go.

§

A mere twelve seconds after Chuck's pickup had lurched out of sight of the silent old man, Cecilia Portillo Perez, tight–lipped and wearing impenetrable designer sunglasses, was standing in the shade of a rose-covered loggia outside her family's sprawling blue stucco ranch house not far from the dusty village of Guamuchilito in the sun-baked farmland of Sinaloa in northwestern Mexico, lapping up her fourth large martini of the afternoon.

She would have been staggeringly attractive were it not for the oddness of something about her mouth.

Beside her on the gargantuan stone patio on a high-backed white wicker chair sat her mother Doña Aurora, a stocky plain–faced *campesina* in her late sixties, decked out in incongruous heavy gold jewelry and an overly frilly black gown, looking totally forlorn and out of place.

Four long black limousines and an ostentatious array of Ramchargers, Grand Cherokees and Lincoln Continentals were parked inside the gates of the ten acre compound on the tree-lined oval drive and many more cars and trucks and farm vehicles were straddling both sides of the flat gravel road beyond where a squad of uniformed soldiers and policemen with video cameras were making a nuisance of themselves filming and frisking selected attendees.

Dozens of wreaths, some bigger than refrigerators, were scattered across the sweeping lawns and a long line of mourners, mostly peasant women with baskets and farmhands holding their sombreros and cowboy hats, were shuffling slowly through the gates and along the drive and, after traversing an immense rose garden, up the curving steps to the patio to offer their condolences.

"He always said they would not take him alive . . "

"Believe me, Doña Aurora, we will not rest until . . "

"He built our chapel, the Lord will welcome him . . "

"Gracias, muchas gracias . . "

When they had said their few words the uninvited straggled back down to the gates and drove away. Those that had already preceded them, the men and women dressed in dark glasses and expensive clothes, were now split into separate groups, the women for the most part entering the cool of the house, the men staying outside to light cigars and speak in somber tones.

Cecilia's older brother Amado, the second of Doña Aurora's ten children, had been born here forty–one years ago. His now deceased father, Ramon, had been a hardworking, and some would say hard spirited, farmer and landowner who grew winter vegetables. The house was much less imposing then, a third the size and the stucco was adobe brown not blue.

At age thirteen, having attended school only until grade six, Amado had run away from home to live with an uncle in the highlands of Chihuahua where marijuana and opium poppies were being cultivated in abundance, declaring to his siblings, "I'm not coming back until I'm rich."

Twenty–four years later, after a ruthless and much-publicized sequence of rival assassinations, Amado Portillo Perez became the undisputed kingpin of the Juarez drug cartel, arguably the most powerful in all of Latin America, and was rapidly amassing a personal fortune estimated at twenty–five billion dollars. He had politicians at every level of government and many law enforcement officials on his payroll, keeping them and himself in power by the ingenious method of helping them eliminate his competitors while making them look like anti–drug crusaders in the process.

He was fabled as 'the Lord of the Skies' and beloved as a latter-day Robin Hood by the local people.

And it was known that he used the alias 'Florio Bastida Morales'.

§

Now it so happened that a national election was gearing up in Mexico in the spring of that year amid a rapidly proliferating money–

laundering scandal which concerned both the current and previous president's respective brothers and their alleged close ties to the drug cartels. An ambitious young lawyer named Hernano Salvador Medina had recently prosecuted one of the brothers for murder and been instrumental in the arrest for bribery and corruption of a high-ranking army officer named Jesus Gutierrez Rebollo and had just been appointed, after being rigorously tested himself for drug abuse, including the humiliation of urine analysis, to the equivalent position of General McWhirter south of the border and the headquarters of the United States Drug Enforcement Administration in Mexico City was a wee bit more than the usual hive of activity that afternoon.

Sam Wanless, the station chief, separated by a glass door from the chaotic hubbub, lunchtime sandwich and glass of milk still unfinished on his desk, was pacing, phone in hand, in excited anticipation of promotion and reprieve from what his wife considered to be despite its size and sophistication little more than a corrupt Latino backwater, talking to his boss in Washington.

"Medina's dropped everything. He's heading to Culiacan right now to examine the body. He suggested we come along. What do you think, sir, are we starting to smell decoy?"

There was a brief pause.

"Let's not jump to that conclusion, Sam," said the deep voice of authority from Washington, "The general and I don't want to jump to that conclusion. But go with him to Culiacan and make damn sure. There's more riding on this than you know."

§

The bus roared past the Highway 17 exit to Fort Davis at that moment and Michael was able to record for his future compendious masterwork a billboard, with the words set against a background of the Lone Star flag, proclaiming 'Fort Davis, Capital City of the Republic of Texas, 67 miles SOUTH!!!'

As luck would have it there were several army vehicles, including a tank, parked on the overpass and Michael guffawed volubly as he immortalized them and barked out of the side of his mouth in a hammy, horribly inaccurate Texan drawl.

"Whoooeee! Sure as shootin', it's a war zone out there, kids!"

The words caught the back of his parched throat causing him to sneeze mightily and he was forced to lower the camera and blow his nose. A scrawny little man in a Stetson a few rows forward fingered the handle of a concealed Colt six–gun and winked at one of the Mexicans sitting across the aisle. They both grinned at the idea of putting an end to their hyperactive companion.

Beyond the entrance ramp on the other side of the overpass a sign read 'El Paso 179' and, as Michael gingerly wiped his cracked and flaming nostrils and turned to consult his map, a light green Ford Ranger zipped by the windows of the bus at ninety miles an hour with the radio blaring.

Chuck was only half listening to an up–and–coming Mexican folk group called *Los Tigres del Norte* singing their latest hit *'Jefe de Jefes'*, 'Boss of Bosses', soon to become the title song of a new album.

" . . Muchos creen que me busca el gobierno,

Otros dicen que es pura mentira,

Desde arriba nomás me divierto,

Pues me gusta que así se confunda . . "

Which, roughly transformed into a functional English lyric, might become, 'Many think they're after me, others say it's a lie. It pleases me to confuse them. I'm smiling from the sky.'

Chuck laughed quietly to himself.

"No kidding."

CHAPTER TWO

It was dusk as the bus arrived at the central station in El Paso and there was a flashing sign above it that alternately gave the time and temperature, 6:39 PM and 74 degrees, eighty–seven hours and fourteen minutes since Michael had awoken so miserably in Chalk Farm, and he filmed that too. Heat, glorious heat, was going to rescue him from the dark microbial curse of the English winter. He could already feel his corpuscles thawing.

This was the end of the line for the bus. Michael had a separate ticket for Los Angeles in the morning where his old Hamburgian friend Gottfried and his Polish wife, Anna, had at last been granted full membership in the Screenwriter's Guild of America after years of frustrated and demeaning dog-work and were waiting to celebrate with him in their modest home in Silverlake.

The vertical neon sign for a hotel was visible down the first grubby street from the station. It was appropriately named the 'Republic' though the gas was not flowing properly through the first three letters. Nonetheless 'ublic' made a perfectly acceptable word Michael mused with a smile as he made his way rather awkwardly towards it, two stuffed bags in one hand and a satchel slung round his neck, yet somehow managing to film the entire progress. Might be Hungarian for 'oblique' or possibly 'cunnilingus', though perhaps that was stretching it a bit. To his shame he had never absorbed more than a few syllables of anything Finno-Ugric over the twenty–five years of his marriage.

The hotel was undoubtedly a fleapit but the name was irresistible and he went in. He made a mental note to capture the atmospheric delapidation of the facade in daylight as well.

The concierge was fat and white and of indeterminate femininity and eyed Michael coldly as he diligently squiggled the required information on a register card. Her voice was a grating wheeze.

"One night. Thass all, y'said."

Michael nodded and enquired pleasantly enough, "Is there a bath in the room or just a shower?"

As with the bus driver his very British accent seemed to give the woman an instantaneous migraine.

"Juss a whaaaat?" she drawled.

"A shower," he repeated.

"What in hell's a shah?"

Michael suddenly felt overwhelmingly fatigued and demonstrated with broad impatient gestures.

"Is there a baaaath in the room or just a show–er. I like a baaaath."

"Well, there ain't one. Juss a shower. You sure you want the room?"

"Yes, I'm shore. I shore am shore."

With that she decided he was crazy and to ignore it.

"That'll be twenty–six fifty."

"Good lord," Michael said, both stunned and pleasantly surprised by the price. He pulled out his billfold and struggled to extract a credit card.

The long British-style wallet was made from aging black leather and had the letters 'MAD' engraved in cracked gold Gothic script on the front. It had been a present from his parents to mark the occasion of his leaving home a few days after his nineteenth birthday. The 'A' stood for 'Anderson', his deceased mother's maiden name, and ever since he had been a child Michael had always thought of the initials as a unique gift.

"No credit. Strickly cash," the concierge rasped.

This was starting to be irritating. Michael replaced the card and counted out twenty-seven dollars. He hated the always puzzling sameness of the bills.

"I don't suppose there's a telephone in the room," he said as the waddling behemoth put the money away in a cash-box and tossed two quarters in change on the desk.

"Yup. Local calls only."

"Ah, and if I want to make an international call?"

"Koo Koo Roo on the corner by the station or there's Pantera's further on down the street. They got payphones at both."

Michael smiled benignly and nodded as the woman pushed his room key toward him.

"Number nine. Upstairs in the rear."

"Thank you, I'm shore. No, no, I'm shah it'll be lovely."

The concierge mouthed insults at his disappearing back.

Michael arrived at the asylum gray portal of number nine and before attempting the lock readied his camera for the entrance. Infuriatingly enough it refused to cooperate and he had to put the camera down and fiddle with the key for at least half a minute until it finally succumbed to his touch. Not to be deterred, once the bolt was released he picked up the camera and held the door closed again with one hand until he was ready to film then swung it open with a flourish and fumbled for the light switch. The naked overhead bulb revealed exactly what one would expect for twenty–six fifty a night.

Michael also liked to record the soundtrack of his life and once again launched full–bore into the apish drawl.

"Well, well, well, and here we is then. Yessirree there, Bob. A fine little ol' room in the fine little ol' Reepublic Hotel in the fine little ol' Reepublic of Texas. Lordy, lordy, ain't it juss sweet. Good Book by the bedside and love juice on the walls. But no baaaath, can you believe it, no fucking baaaath."

Having filmed all the minute tacky details, Michael brought the camera slowly to rest on his pallid sweaty reflection in the cracked mirror above the bathroom sink, zoomed ever so slowly in to linger for a long moment on a single bloodshot eye and then switched it off.

"Bloody hell, you poor old thing, you look a hundred and forty. Well, never mind. Despite the suet dumpling in the lobby you are now on the road to recovery."

He retrieved his luggage from the hallway and took out two neatly folded linen sheets and pillowcases from the large valise, stripped off all the existing bedding, rolled everything into a ball and tossed it into a vacant corner with a gesture of extreme distaste, then began deftly remaking the bed.

"Koo Koo Roo or Pantera's. Holy geewhillickers, Bobbo-jobbo, a positive sumptitude of choice there, wouldn't ya say? A chicken farm or a bakery, d'ya suppose? What the Sam Hill more could a young feller want?"

Another gigantic sneeze interrupted the characterization.

"Damn," he muttered as the inevitable feverish shiver shot through him like an electric current, "How could I have been such an idiot? You'd better be in when I call this time, sweetie."

Having recovered sufficiently to finish with the bed, Michael took off his clothes and hung them over the back of the single wooden chair that inhabited the room, put his feet into tan suede slippers and his body into a silk bathrobe, found his toiletry bag in the side flap of the valise and went into the bathroom.

Once he had finally unraveled the mystery of the shower tap and made it function, lo and behold, miracle of miracles, there was actually hot water and pressure as well, he doffed the slippers and robe, unwrapped his shower gel and a still damp flannel from their protective plastic bag, pried off the top of his soap dish and stepped in.

After enjoying the warmth for a few minutes he lathered himself all over, applied some shampoo and began to sing at the top of his lungs. It was one of the great crosses of his life that he had always been hopelessly tone deaf and the painful rendition slid quite unmagnificently from key to suffering key.

"Oooooh, as I walked out in the streets of El Paso,

As I walked out in El Paso one day . . "

Almost immediately there was a vicious hammering from the other side of the wall. Michael stopped singing and shouted at the invisible protester.

"I know it's Laredo, you fool! Who cares?!"

He sneezed again.

"Damn."

He blew his nose in his hands and rinsed them thoroughly, then cupped them together and took a big snort of the gathered shower water. He blew it out again loudly and repeated the process several times.

"Damn. Damn all fucking purists to hell."

He began to sing again but quieter. He had been raised by a beloved mother who firmly and patiently instilled in him a kind consideration for his fellow man. The sound was now a tender mournful croaking.

"I spied a young cowboy all dressed in white linen,

All dressed in white linen and cold as the clay . . "

§

At that moment in a suburban square in Culiacan, the shambling state capital of Sinaloa, a long black limousine with darkened windows was slowly drawing up outside the city's sole fully equipped funeral home amid a scene of raucous pandemonium.

A dozen heavily armed bodyguards were shoving the paparazzi roughly aside, making a passage to the car, as the driver pushed his way out and another bodyguard from the passenger door and both hurried to the rear to help Cecilia and her mother step down and then accompanied them along a plush carpeted walkway into the chapel through a barrage of flashbulbs and shouted questions.

At the door to the chapel Doña Aurora turned to the crowd tearfully with anger in her voice.

"Sí! Es mi hijo! Déjennos en paz!"

'Yes! It is my son! Leave us in peace!'

Cecilia took her arm gently and they were ushered inside and across the foyer into a large ceremony room crowded with mourners and down the center aisle past ten rows of chairs to an ornate golden altar, brilliantly illuminated by a thousand candles, where a very heavily built man, dressed in an immaculate blue suit and white shirt with an open neck, lay propped amid the plush pale silk interior of an open burnished silver coffin entirely carved with flowers.

His face was an eerie purple pink, even thick makeup couldn't hide the awful swelling and the Frankenstein crisscross of sutures. The livid hollow of his mouth had been repaired with pristine white piano key false teeth that peeked through the tautened lips to form a thin mocking simpleminded grin.

The two women mounted the steps of the dais to look and Cecilia leaned in and kissed the man on both cheeks but the horror of the sight was unbearable to Doña Aurora and she fell to her knees beside the coffin and wept aloud and all others in the room were silent.

Beyond the momentary serenity of the chapel, however, the chaos was taking a rapid turn for the worse. Thirty police cars had entered the square and encircled the building and it hadn't taken the bodyguards more than a second to see they had little chance and they raised their hands away from their weapons and backed off as forty officers wielding submachine guns swarmed into the funeral parlor.

They burst through the doors of the ceremony room and, heedless of the screamed protests of Doña Aurora and other members of the Portillo family, they quickly cut a path to the altar, slammed down the coffin lid and carried it from the chapel to a waiting armored van which raced away into the night with a six car escort in front and six behind, all with sirens blaring.

The rest of the police stayed to block the streets and prevent anyone from following, even the tiny scooters of the paparazzi who were catching the whole thing on camera for the world to see, and despite howls of abuse no one was allowed to leave the area for more than half an hour.

An inconsolable Doña Aurora remained with the family inside the chapel but Cecilia stood silently in the doorway smoking a thin Cuban cigar with a hard smile etching the curiously indented corners of her lips. She could have been Ava Gardner if her famous dimples had slipped forward out of place.

CHAPTER THREE

As the crowd was finally allowed to disperse in Culiacan, Michael came out of the Republic Hotel looking surprisingly elegant in a fresh button down plaid shirt, light brown corduroy jacket with elbow patches, brown slacks and closed toe sandals, hair still damp and nattily slicked back, camcorder in hand and satchel of necessaries casually slung over one shoulder. He knew he stood out like a very sore thumb in what was at second glance, or even first, without doubt the El Paso red light district but such things only added to Michael's zest for, and appreciation of, life's endlessly fascinating little nooks and crannies.

He peered up and down the dimly Hadean street and saw a neon sign flashing 'Pantera's' just as the pudding had foretold. He sniffed and made toward it. A tired neon panther, outlined in pink, adorned the window and Michael was unable to resist getting it on tape before he went in.

A muted basketball game shone blindingly from a television set mounted high above the bar and the troglodytic denizens stared with a mixture of innate menace and blank-brained disbelief as Michael entered. The bartender, a young Mexican barely in his twenties, smiled but otherwise showed no reaction.

Just as Michael was opening his mouth to speak he was caught helpless by another colossal sneeze. The sparse assemblage found it mildly amusing.

"Gesundheit," the bartender said but somehow it seemed natural.

Michael carefully blew his nose and wiped it tenderly.

"Thank you."

"What'll it be?"

Michael's mind was still recovering from the shudders.

"Oh, yes, ah, um, well, I don't suppose you'd have a draught Guinness? No, well, no, of course you wouldn't, would you. I'll have a large, um, bourbon whisky, Jack Daniel's, yes, that's it. But no ice please. Thank you."

Chuck was watching him from the far end of the bar, nursing a Dos Equis.

The bartender took down a fresh bottle of Jack Daniel's, placed a six-ounce tumbler in front of Michael and started to pour.

"Say when."

Michael, without any sense of why himself, launched momentarily into an excruciating imitation of John Wayne.

"Gimme five dollars worth, pardner."

The bartender didn't seem to find it all that strange and filled the tumbler to the brim as Michael extracted a five-dollar note from his billfold.

"I'm told you have a payphone."

"Yup," said the bartender, "Right back there by the john."

Michael nodded and drained the tumbler of bourbon in one gulp. He had the whole bar's attention now, particularly Chuck's. He didn't seem to be much aware of it as he walked back to the phone but then his mind at that moment had other fish to fry.

A drunk of indecipherable racial origin was slumped unconscious in a chair under the phone beside the john door and the stench of stale beer rising from the man was even strong enough to penetrate the mucoid clog of Michael's nasal membranes.

"Good lord," he sniffed.

He needed somewhere to put the camera but thought better than to place it on the man's lap and the floor looked damp so he held it awkwardly over his shoulder as he rummaged in the satchel for his address book. Once he had found it and fumbled open the page to Marta's number it was next to impossible to dial the phone. "Fuck it," he said and put the camera into the bag and half zipped it and plopped the whole package down on the drunk's obligingly spread–eagled crotch. The man's hands jerked upwards from their hanging position and cradled it gently.

"Good boy," Michael said, turning the zero hard around with a forefinger.

"This ought to be fun."

He had a phobia about telephone communication and could be easily flustered which was why he needed Marta's number open to the page though he knew it perfectly well. Experience had shown how even time-tested knowledge could evaporate on such occasions.

The operator answered.

"Number please."

"Yes, hello, I'd like to place a call to London."

"Would that be London, England, sir?"

"Yes, yes, of course, and I want to reverse the charges."

"You want to what?"

"Reverse the charges. Oh, I see, no, no, hang on, I want to make a collect call, yes, that's right. Silly me."

"A collect call. Will that be person to person?"

"Yes. I hope so. It's from me. I'm a person. My name is Michael. It won't matter who answers."

"A collect call from Michael. To what number please?"

"Ah yes, the number is, well, once you've got the overseas operator, the code for England is 44 and then London is 171 and then the number is 683 2179."

"171 683 2179."

"Yes, 683 2179. That's it. Well done. Thank you. And it's from Michael. The archangel."

"What was that, sir?"

"Nothing, no, please, just forget I said it."

"I'll try that number for you now, sir."

"Oh, would you be so kind? Thank you."

The agony of the exchange had made Michael start to perspire heavily. His impatient, over–enunciated and patronizing tone was idiotic, and as always he was painfully aware of it, but it was an atavism beyond his control.

"Bloody hell. New world bloody disorder," he muttered quite unfairly, "Come on, sweetie, be a good girl."

Chuck was watching and listening with growing amusement.

Marta's sleepy voice answered and accepted the call.

"Thank god."

The connection was distorted by an infuriating static.

"Michael? Are you there? It's four o'clock in the morning. God, this line is nearly as bad as yours."

"Yes. I'm here. In a callbox, of sorts." Michael was almost shouting to compensate. "Where the hell were you yesterday? I called you every time we took a pee stop."

"I had to go to Birmingham. Where are you? Are you all right?"

"Yes. I'm fine. I'm in Texas. In El Paso. Listen, I've tried everywhere but I can't get any of these grinning nitwit druggists over here to break down and give me some fucking antibiotics. 'Sorry, sir, but I couldn't do that without a prescription from your doctor'." It was a passable imitation of Jerry Lewis doing his cross-eyed goonie act and followed by a rattling sniff. "Reasoned argument doth not prevail. Can you please get some and Fedex them to Gottfried's address in Los Angeles? I'm never going to shake this bugger without them. Can't stop sneezing. Been driving the fellow passengers round the bend."

"I got some from my Himalayan tribesman yesterday."

"Aaah, bless you, you're a sweetie. I arrive tomorrow night so if you send it first thing the package should get to LA the day after and that will work splendidly. It's Gottfried and Anna Herzler at 137 Hidalgo Avenue. Los Angeles or Silverlake, I don't imagine it's of any great consequence which. And the zip code, as they call it, the postal code in California is 90039. Have you got it?"

"I've got it."

"Ta, my darling, I'll call you from there. Love you. How's Tigger–cat? Is she moping?"

"No."

"No? Little bitch. Well, she's an Egyptian goddess in feline disguise. She wouldn't let on no matter what. Tell her meow. Helen's back tomorrow, I think. Thanks for looking after, darling. Bye, darling, bye."

"Bye."

"Oh, how are you by the way?"

Marta laughed. She was used to being an afterthought.

"I'm tired, Michael. Do try and take note of your time zone when you call. Or make sure it's between midnight and noon. Have fun in El Paso. Bye."

After she rang off Michael kept the receiver to his ear for a moment, letting his relief settle, then put it back on the hook.

"Thank god, thank god, thank fucking god."

He retrieved his bag from the drunk's hands which seemed to flutter ever so slightly with some unconscious vestigial regret at parting with it and, after he had taken out the camera again and captured the man's innocent childlike pose for posterity, walked back toward the bar exit.

"Hey, mister Englishman, let me buy you another 'large' one," Chuck said as he passed by.

Michael turned to observe him and thought, 'Well, he looks pleasant enough, not totally besotted like the others, quite an interesting subject in fact.'

"Sure. Why not? The name's Michael. Michael Davenport."

They shook hands.

"Chuck Bowman. Pull up a stool."

Chuck motioned to the bartender who smiled and nodded in return.

"You here for any particular reason?"

"No," said Michael, "A brief stop on the way to Los Angeles. From Dallas this morning. From Miami to start with. I love the American southwest. Well, deserts anywhere anytime really."

The bartender brought another Dos Equis for Chuck and another tumbler for Michael and once again filled it to the brim with Jack Daniel's.

"You an actor?" Chuck asked.

Michael stared at his new acquaintance in mock horror.

"Good god, no."

"In the movie business?"

"Well, not as you might think. But I'd love to get a shot of the two of us in the mirror there behind all those rows of bottles. It's classic. That is, if you have no objection."

Michael started to raise the camera to his eye but Chuck put out a hand to restrain him.

"I wouldn't take pictures of anyone in this neighborhood if I were you."

Michael glanced around the bar.

"Yes, I do see what you mean. Ah well. You live here, do you?"

"Not any more. Used to though. Worked here for fifteen years."

"What at?"

"That'd be telling."

"Yes, I suppose it would."

Michael sniffed and said, "Well, bottoms up."

They clinked glasses and once again Michael downed the bourbon at a gulp. Chuck grinned broadly and took a sip of beer.

"You're kinda thirsty."

"No, I've just got a bloody awful bug and I can't get any pills. But I'm feeling better already."

"Bourbon'll do it every time. But if you still need pills you can get all you want over the border."

Michael looked at him with surprise.

"Really? Where?"

"Juarez. Any little *farmacia.*"

"And you don't need a prescription?"

"Nope. Drug companies ship them their leftovers. Mexicans often take the wrong stuff and get sick from it. Some even die. It's a horror show. You want to film something, film the border in the morning. You're a man with a sense of humor."

Michael began to feel there might just be a story in this tall quiet–spoken cowboy and he waved again to the bartender for another round.

§

At 11:30, as Michael and Chuck decided to call it a night, Michael having consumed all but three ounces of the bottle of Jack Daniel's without betraying the least sign of what ordinary mortals familiarly recognize as inebriation, and left Pantera's with the agreement that Chuck would pick him up at the Republic at 5 AM and show him the border, Hernano Salvador Medina and several aides and local police officials were walking out of an examination room in the morgue at Culiacan, followed by DEA bureau-chief Wanless and his deputy deep in hushed discussion.

"It's him. I'd bet my badge on it," Wanless whispered.

"Sure looks like it," said the deputy.

The corpse of 'Florio Bastida Morales' had been removed from the silver coffin and stripped and was laid out naked on the examination table in all its ghoulish glory. Massive bruising from the liposuction was evident on the torso, buttocks and upper thighs and the coroner and his team covered the body with a sheet, lifted it expertly onto a tray, slid it into a refrigerated drawer and locked it. Then they switched off the lights and left by a rear door, locking the whole room behind them as well.

From the corridor, the two DEA agents entered a small bare private office where a telephone was waiting with a call from Washington and the chief picked up the receiver.

"You're gonna be glad as hell to hear this, sir . . "

"I'll get him. Hold on," said a female voice.

Wanless raised his eyes to the ceiling and drummed his knuckles on the white metal tabletop. After nearly a minute he heard someone sitting down with an audible sigh at the other end of the line.

"So, Sam, do we smell decoy?"

"I can't say about that, sir, but we got a perfect match with Portillo's immigration prints from '85. Absolutely one hundred percent."

"What about his face?"

"It was pretty much a mess from the plastic surgery but there's no doubt in my mind it's the same guy in the photographs."

"Unfortunately that doesn't prove anything if he's a decoy."

"No, sir. My concern all along."

"Hard to believe though. We've had him under surveillance for over twelve years. He's been identified a hundred times. Mostly by his enemies."

"I know. And why would a decoy need plastic surgery?"

"Did you go over the dental records?"

"He must've had dentures. Or been getting them. There were no teeth in his mouth."

"Did you look at his gums?"

"They were raw as hell. Could have been a recent extraction. Maybe even part of the whole change of appearance."

"What was Medina's reaction to that?"

"Nothing much. Just said he was satisfied with the examination so far. But they're not gonna release anything down here until they fly the body to Mexico City for DNA tests tomorrow."

"Sounds like they know something we don't."

"Could be. They were trying hard as hell to hide it but they've definitely got a case of the jitters."

There was a moment of silent rumination on the other end of the line.

"I don't want to start thinking that sonofabitch Bowman was right."

"I can understand that, sir. But I guess we have to allow for the possibility."

There was another pause.

"Did Medina say anything else?"

"Just that he needs to go real careful because of the election. Well, he's new on the job. Doesn't want any mistakes."

"Neither do we, Sam. Neither do we."

The chief swallowed nervously. He could feel not only his promotion but his marriage slipping away.

"I'll keep right on it, sir," he said but the only response was a dial tone.

CHAPTER FOUR

At thirty–seven minutes past noon the next day London time, as Michael's baby sister Helen returned suntanned from her Spanish holiday and walked into the flat in Chalk Farm to be greeted by a subtly sulking Flossie who was hiding behind the tea towels in the cabinet above the washing machine in the kitchen, Chuck and Michael, with camera in hand, were standing in the pre–dawn light on the north side of the filthy knee-deep thirty–foot–wide trickle that remains of the Rio Grande once it reaches El Paso and Juarez after the double puncture of the Caballo and Elephant Butte dams that straddle the sleepy resort of Truth or Consequences, New Mexico, have siphoned off the last flush of its youthful glory and the high Colorado promise of its birth under the Continental Divide and the Slumgullion Pass.

The area surrounding Truth or Consequences was blessed with mineral spas and until 1950 the little town in their midst had been known more simply as Hot Springs but the quick-to-react city fathers, looking to gain wider notice and boost the local economy, had rechristened it after an irresistible offer of national publicity from a popular radio quiz show of the same quaint name.

"Here they come."

Chuck pointed to a group of *indocumentados*, twenty or more, who were beginning to creep one by one through a ragged tear in the twelve–foot–high wire mesh fence that ran along the Mexican side of the gently sloping concrete containment channel in either direction as far as Michael could see.

"Mexicans call it the *Rio Bravo del Norte*," Chuck told him with obvious irony, "There are places with stepping–stones upriver where they don't even have to get their feet wet. Men carry women across for a buck."

"Fantastic. What happens if they get caught?" Michael asked, filming it all, the whole right side of his face avidly clenched to the eyepiece.

"Nothing much. They know it's just a game."

Suddenly there was the sound of a woman's muffled scream from beyond the fence and several more illegals squirmed through the gap and dashed across the river and two men even came tumbling right over the top where a section of the razor wire had snapped off and ran and fell and got soaked in their panic and then no more people came through.

Chuck and Michael couldn't see what was causing the commotion because the thick green canvas attached to the fence obscured their view but they could still hear a few sporadic shouts and screams.

Then, just as the last of the Mexicans splashed to safety on the American shore, the cause appeared. An enormous Siberian tiger slithered like white silk through the hole and padded majestically down to the murky river to lap up a morning drink.

Michael actually dropped the camera from his eye in amazement, turning to Chuck, thrilled to the core, laughing and speechless, but only for a fraction of second.

"Fantastic!" he whispered.

Even Chuck could hardly believe what he was seeing.

"Jesus H. Christ," he said quietly.

Michael was again immortalizing every moment.

"Have you ever seen anything so beautiful?" Michael went on, his voice shaking, "So utterly, totally magnificent? I love cats beyond all other animals. It's impossible! And a white! Where on earth can it have come from?"

"It's happened a couple of times before. Mexicans believe it's a ghost."

The tiger finished its drink and the great yellow eyes stared hypnotically into Michael's lens for a long moment before it turned and went back toward the hole in the fence. The uncaring gaze of a god and it made him shiver with joy.

"Fantastic," he repeated.

And, as foretold, he couldn't resist and without a thought for the consequences started splashing across the river after the tiger filming all the while. Chuck laughed.

"Hey, come back Englishman, you'll get yourself killed!"

"Nonsense! Don't worry!" Michael shouted, "Cats love me! I've got a way with them!"

"You're entering another country, you madman! What the hell do you think you're doing?"

The tiger was no longer in sight but Michael ran up the opposite bank dripping from the thighs down and stopped briefly by the fence to wave.

"Back in a jiffy! Surely if they can do it, so can I!"

"Come back now, you fool! It's not what you think!"

But Michael was too excited to listen and ducked quickly through the hole into the unknown world of Ciudad Juarez.

The sun was just tweaking the horizon, painting the dismal trash-strewn gravel expanse beyond the fence a dingy polluted red, and the tiger was only a hundred feet ahead of him but moving faster now. People were everywhere in motion, some still running to hide, some who had noticed the crazy gringo with the camera pointing and laughing, many more using the opportunity to slip through the hole behind him as Michael followed the glorious beast, trying his best to keep up and at the same time not to trip and fall. He was zooming in and out and swinging the camera around in wide panoramic arcs in his frantic desire to capture absolutely everything.

The tiger had crossed the open space and started along a drab store-lined street and sirens could be heard approaching in the distance. Some people had lost their fear and were following it, running and shouting encouragement to Michael who had somehow miraculously managed to narrow the gap. A car with no doors ground to a jerky halt at an intersection as the tiger trotted calmly through it with Michael a mere twenty feet behind. Three old women dressed in black coming out of a peeling wooden church fell to their knees screeching and raising gnarled hands to beseech heaven's forgiveness as the ghostly apparition and its madcap entourage swept by.

The crowd was growing ever larger and the mood was turning festive as two battered and honking police cruisers made their way slowly down a cross street. The policemen in the cars were too frightened to get out and switched off the flashing lights and sirens as they joined in the procession. Michael had to squeeze tight to avoid being crushed as they passed close on either side but he never took the camera from his eye. It was becoming rather like the running of the bulls in Pamplona and before long he went almost unnoticed amongst the holiday throng.

They came to a small plaza with a dry cracked fountain in the middle, a relic of former days, and the tiger began to circle it looking at the crowd. In an instant there was silence. The wordless spectators spread flat along the shabby shop-fronts and a long white limousine could be seen coming from the opposite direction scaring up bits of blown paper from the dust as it approached. No one blinked or dared to breathe as it entered the square and came to a stop on the far side of the fountain.

The rear door of the limousine opened and the tiger padded round the sad stone statuary and languorously wound itself into the car without a backward glance but before the door closed again Michael stepped abruptly forward from the protective camouflage of frozen onlookers and, with maximum zoom but a minimum of thought, captured a shadowy presence inside. A slender manicured hand adorned with rings, a flash of pale silk pajamas, bare ankles, gold slippers and the dark outline of a face.

It took several seconds after the limousine drove away for the assembled crowd to regain their voice and animation. Some threw strange fearful looks at Michael as they began to return to their daily business, some were still smiling and called out what could have been words of threat or admiration or warning but the words themselves were unintelligible to him and anyway it didn't matter. What mattered was that he had caught without doubt the most extraordinary footage of a lifetime and he finally lowered the camera and sat down exhausted at the fountain's edge. He checked the battery and saw with relief that it was not quite spent.

"Thank god," he said out loud and chuckled. What a rush!

One of the police cruisers took a couple of turns around the square before it too drove away and the broad faces within gave Michael careful scrutiny at each passage. He was wise enough to leave the camera where it was for a change but looked steadily back at them, wiggling the fingers of one hand, winking and mouthing 'toodaloo'.

Beads of sweat were standing out on his forehead. The sun was shining brightly now and he had to sit for a long time to catch his breath and try to get his bearings. The little plaza was architecturally nondescript Michael observed ruefully, depressingly decayed and charmless, all slapdash and careless haste, a far cry from the equally impoverished yet still proud and picturesque *borghi* of central Sicily that he had walked through with Marta twenty years ago and as his previous excitement was dissolving in this more somber mood something even less pleasant began to nag at the corners of his consciousness.

'Where the hell am I?' he wondered with alarm and sneezed.

The procession had covered nearly half a mile and the river was nowhere in sight. He consulted his watch. 6:44. Not once in the last thrilling hour had he given thought to his illness. But, however needful at the time, the Jack Daniel's had provided only temporary relief and he suddenly felt feverish again and overtaken by a blazing thirst.

"Damn and bugger," he croaked as he blew a blotchy nose on his hanky.

Another lifelong cross that Michael had to bear was a decidedly hazy sense of geographical direction together with an almost supernatural talent for finding dead ends. The chase had taken many twists and turns and Michael had not the faintest clue how to find his way back to the river and the border. There were rocky treeless hills visible to both north and south but he didn't recognize any of them for the obvious reason that he had never been there before and for him to head directly north, which of course he knew was the general idea if you wanted to find the United States when in Mexico, could be somewhat misleading from this old section of Juarez where El Paso was more like northeast.

As he was puzzling over his next move, and wondering if there was still the slightest chance of making it to the Republic in time to retrieve his luggage and catch the 8:12 departure for Los Angeles at the bus station, a small man walked crisply by the fountain, crossed the remainder of the plaza and unlocked the door of a shop.

After a few moments Michael's bacterially fogged faculties focused on the sign above the door - *Farmacia* - and its meaning slowly penetrated.

'Ah, brilliant,' he thought, 'Positively cosmic. Why not?'

He gathered up his shoulder–bag and jacket and the camera and followed and tried the door but the man had locked it behind him.

"Damn, wouldn't you know it," he growled.

He peered in through the murky glass, a light had been turned on at least, and knocked on the door. Nothing. He knocked again. After a third attempt, more like pounding than knocking, the man came and looked at him. Evidently he had just relieved himself somewhere in the rear because he was still buckling his belt. He had pleasant aquiline features and a gentle demeanor.

"We are not open yet, *señor*," he said, "Come back in ten minutes."

Michael was amazed at the man's excellent and unaccented English.

"This is an emergency," he said, "I've got a bus to catch in El Paso."

The man relented and opened the door.

"Thank you very much," Michael said and sneezed, barely managing to cup his hands in time to prevent spritzing the kindly druggist's face.

"You are welcome, *señor.* Come in please. I see you have a bad cold. What can I do for you?"

He retreated behind the counter rubbing his hands together. It wasn't in any way a gesture of either malice or avarice, merely an habitual indication of readiness for service. Michael instantly appraised him to be perfect casting for the apothecary's role in Romeo and Juliet.

"It's more than a cold. I always get an unbearable sinus infection as well. I'd like to buy some tetracycline if you have it."

Michael, being somewhat more than a borderline hypochondriac, was very well able to diagnose the many and varied symptoms of what he knew to be his ineluctably disintegrating immune and metabolic systems. His grim response to Helen's accusation of paranoia was, "You wait, ducky. It happens to us all."

"Tetracycline. Of course. How many would you like? Fifty? A hundred?"

'Good lord,' Michael thought, 'This is paradise.'

"How strong are they?" he asked.

"These are strong. I will show you."

The man took a large white plastic container from a shelf and turned it so Michael could read the stick–on label. 'Tetrasiclin 500 mg' had been written with a ballpoint pen but nothing else. No logo, nothing. The druggist unscrewed the top and emptied a few of the pills into his hand. They were large and ovoid and shone like opalescent blue rugby balls.

"You're sure those are tetracycline?"

"Of course, *señor,*" the little man assured him with a smile, "They were just received last week."

"All right," Michael said, calculating the days, "I'll take thirty of them."

"You could take a hundred. More. They are not expensive."

Michael thought about the possibility of future need but said, "No. Just the thirty, thank you."

The druggist turned his back to count out the pills. Michael looked around the tiny shop, more like a newspaper kiosk really, and took up his camera to film its Lilliputian austerity. The man was aware of it and kept his face away.

When he had counted the sapphire capsules into a stainless steel beaker, an object Michael considered might have been used for cream in some yesteryear American wayside diner, the mild-mannered apothecary poured them into a small pinkish plastic bag and said, "That will be one dollar and fifty cents please, *señor.*"

"Good lord," Michael said and stopped filming, "That's less than a pound."

The druggist grinned at the confirmation.

"Ah, you are English English, *señor.* I thought so."

"You take dollars? I wondered if you might want pesos."

"It is no problem to take dollars in Juarez, *señor.*"

"No, I don't suppose so. Of course. Probably better for you. Rather silly of me."

Michael was able to find the necessary sum from coins he had neglected to remove from his pockets the night before and, at the same time, gesture around the little store.

"Where do all these pills come from then?"

"Germany, Switzerland sometimes, but mostly America."

"Fantastic," Michael said, carefully depositing a handful of change into the man's patiently obliging palm. Three dimes, three quarters, eight nickels and five pennies.

The druggist didn't bother to check Michael's accuracy but grinned again and, having secured the little pink bag with a twist tie, gave him the pills.

"May I be of any other service to you, *señor*?"

"Well, um, yes," Michael replied, "You may find this rather odd but I'm, ah, not sure that I can find my way back to the border crossing, you know, where the U. S. customs are and all that. I'm sure it's perfectly simple but could you direct me?"

"Of course, *señor.* As you say, it is very simple."

He told him that it was just five short blocks one way and then two to the left and Michael couldn't believe it was that close and quickly thanked the man and hastened off in the direction he had indicated.

After about a hundred yards he came upon a stall with four high-backed wrought iron stools with torn red cushions standing in front of the counter. A rough hand painted sign hanging on a nail beside the open wooden canopy read '*Hamburguesas*, Burritos, *Tortas*, Sodas' in descending order. Michael's thirst had become quite desperate and he was finding it increasingly hard to swallow so he stopped and looked around without success for the proprietor. He could see several tins of something new to him called Cactus Cooler on a shelf which he divined must be the 'Sodas' component. They wouldn't be cold but that was probably all to the good he told himself. His stomach was empty and gurgling and there were some quite appetizing–looking meat–and–bean–and–chili–filled flatbread things sitting available to the use of sign language beside the tins. Whether they were the *'Hamburguesas'*, 'Burritos' or *'Tortas'* he neither knew nor cared but where was someone who could sell them to him? He was about to call out when an old woman's voice asked, "What do you want, *señor*?"

Michael nearly jumped out of his skin and was astonished to discover a tiny wizened face peeking over the worn and weathered countertop. She had obviously been sitting there the whole time but had blended somehow into the shade of the canopy. She could not have been more than four foot eight.

"Oh, ah, there you are," Michael stammered, "Good lord. Yes, well, well, well, what do I want. Um, I'll have two tins of the, um, Cactus Cooler and two of those what–d'you–call–thems."

"Burritos, *señor.* They have *chile.*"

"Splendid. No problem," Michael said.

The woman shrugged and put the two burritos in a paper bag.

"Quanto per tutto?" he asked idiotically. The fever was causing his brain to freewheel out of control. Was that Spanish or Italian? Or neither? And then he managed more sensibly, "How much?"

"One dollar, *señor.*"

"For the whole lot? Good lord."

He had only a few coins left in change but rescued a crumpled dollar bill from another pocket and paid.

"Gracias señor," the old woman said mildly and sat again.

Despite his inbred English reserve, and a natural reluctance to eat while being observed by strangers, Michael decided to pause and avail himself of the convenience of the stools. He balanced his various bits and pieces precariously on the soft torn cushions and flipped open the first can, downing half of it in one mouthful but only with mixed relief. It flushed the agonized inflammation of his tonsils with the sting of a toilet brush. But it was liquid, blessed liquid.

'Cactus Cooler, hm,' he thought, 'Not half bad at all, at all.'

He launched into the first chili burrito. The taste was surprisingly good and, as he swallowed, it clumped through his narrowly swollen glottis with a fiery whittling purge but nothing could be too spicy for

Michael. In his student days in London curry was the favorite and the hotter the better. He and both male and female aficionados of the sport would have competitions as to who could ingest the most sulfuric vindaloo.

The old woman was staring at him.

'Damned if you'll see this Englishman's eyes water,' he thought, then chuckled, realizing the absurdity of it. Why on earth should he care to impress her?

Having consumed the first burrito with relish and taken another glug of Cactus Cooler to wash it down he deemed he had taken on sufficient ballast to try one of the pills without upsetting his ever-unpredictable digestion. He untied the plastic bag and fidgeted one out. The heat had made the soft gelatin coating slightly sticky to the touch. 'Odd,' he thought and then said to himself, 'Oh, what the hell, why not?' and, as the old woman's eyes widened further, he retrieved a second glistening football and disposed of them both with another draught of the scourging fizzy fluid. What such a pleasant drink had to do with cacti he couldn't fathom. It was sweet orange soda pure and simple. He belched with satisfaction and rose to his feet.

"Gracias señorita," he said.

As he gathered his things, checked up and down the street to be sure that he was still going in the right direction and hurried on, the old woman's eyes were twinkling.

By the time he reached the left turn that the smiling druggist had told him would lead straight to the border he had managed to munch away all but a bite of the second burrito. It was a broad avenue and he halted momentarily at the corner. He could see the rear of a double line of cars waiting in the distance.

'Made it,' he congratulated himself as a scarred and filthy black Mercedes 4x4 came roaring up beside him and squealed to a stop. Before he had time to realize what was happening two burly Mexicans jumped out and threw him to the ground quite literally spilling the last morsel of his beans.

Michael was no pansy pushover and began to struggle but one of the men put the business end of a pistol hard to his forehead which made him think better of it while the other grabbed his shoulder-bag and camera.

The second thug unzipped the satchel and rustled through it and found a spare videotape which he put in the pocket of his denim jacket. Then he found Michael's passport and looked at the picture and grinned a gap–toothed grin that was both exceedingly malicious and perverted and pocketed that as well.

"You can't take that!" Michael objected but the man instantly gave him a ferocious slap across the face and grinned again.

Then he popped open the video camera and removed the tape inside and the two of them jerked Michael to his feet and frisked him and, having assured themselves that he had nothing else they wanted, tossed the bag and the camera back into his arms. He had to juggle desperately to prevent the camera crashing to the ground as the men ran back to the car, wheeled round in the intersection raising a cloud of dust and debris and raced away. Two minibuses jammed with Japanese sightseers were forced to swerve uncomfortably to avoid sideswiping them.

Michael stood thunderstruck, gasping in impotent rage.

"I don't fucking believe it! Who the fucking hell were they?!" he spluttered at a young Mexican woman who happened to be passing by pushing a child in a rusty stroller. She looked at him with sympathy but said nothing.

Michael suddenly noticed that a police cruiser was parked on the street directly opposite and the two officers inside had undoubtedly watched the whole disgraceful felony unfold.

"Are you just going to sit there and do nothing?!" he bellowed and started running through the traffic toward them, "I've been robbed! Mugged in broad daylight! Don't you care tuppence for your fucking tourist industry?!"

The officers saw him coming and the driver put the cruiser in motion and sped off past the line of cars toward the crossing.

"I'm an Englishman, not a fucking dog!" Michael shouted, trotting a few more futile paces after them, "An Englishman, do you hear?! We don't give up without a fight!"

But, alas, it was useless, the cowards were gone and so was the tape of his masterpiece. And his passport. His fucking passport!

He looked at his watch. 7:27.

"Shit! Shit! Shit! Shit! Shit!" he moaned, rocking back and forth on his heels in an agony of frustration like some manic worshipper before the Wailing Wall.

Then, in an instant, his mood changed, his mind hardened and he hitched up his trousers which were still rather damp and muddy from the mid–thigh down and strode with decision for the border.

§

At that moment, from a brightly lit boardroom in downtown Mexico City, a spokesman for the Mexican Attorney General's office was being interviewed by remote feed on Good Morning America. He was tense and trying very hard to hide his irritation. He spoke in mentally fluent English though his lips had some difficulty getting round the words.

"No, of course we do not disagree with the general's assessment but in the final analysis it is our government that has the exclusive responsibility of making judgments in a case like this, not a foreign agency. We have no confirmation as yet that the patient 'Florio Bastida Morales' was, in fact, Amado Portillo, though we know, as do the American authorities, that it was one of his many aliases. We have taken the body into custody for detailed examination, including the most up–to–date DNA testing. We will make an announcement when we have gathered all the facts. In the light of this, we think that the press conference held yesterday in Washington by General McWhirter and Director Consterdine was somewhat premature."

"Would you go so far as ill–advised?" came the quick-fire query.

"No, assuredly not," the spokesman replied with clipped emphasis, yet still managing an impeccably polite tone, "Merely premature."

CHAPTER FIVE

Michael had reached the pedestrian crossing and was standing seventh in line in the passport queue and finding it very hot and smelly in the crowded room and the customs official was taking his sweet time with the Mexicans in front of him. He was also beginning to feel exceptionally unwell, nauseous, dizzy and seeing double.

'Damn,' he thought, 'The chili things,' and then, more alarmed, 'Or the big blue pills.'

Without knowing it was going to happen he found himself blurting out in a loud, theatrical, almost disembodied command, "Oh, for heaven's sake, come on, I'm going to miss my bus!"

The officer looked up with pale blue eyes but didn't seem at all perturbed by the outburst. He motioned Michael to come forward.

"Thank you," Michael said, once he had squeezed past the uncomplaining Mexicans.

"Y'say you got a bus to catch, sir?"

"Yes, in less than half an hour," Michael replied urgently.

"Can you show me some ID please."

"Look, that's the problem, you see I had my passport not five minutes ago but it was taken from me. Stolen, do you understand?"

The world was beginning to swim in wobbly circles about his head.

"I was thrown to the street and robbed by two men and the police simply watched while it happened. I'm telling you the gospel truth but I don't have any documents and I have to catch a bus so can you please just let me through."

The officer scratched his double chin.

"You have anything at all that can prove who you are?"

"Well, yes, of course, if you insist. I've got a credit card or two and my business card and some other things."

He laid them all out impatiently in front of the man.

"Nothing with a photograph? No driver's license?"

Michael had lived in London all his life and had never found it necessary to obtain one. He enjoyed the relaxing freedom of public transport.

"Astounding as that may seem, alas, no."

"Nothing at all with a picture?"

"I've told you. They took it. It's gone."

Michael sneezed and burped at the same time and an incredibly painful pulse of stomach bile shot up into the back of his throat like a Stygian blowtorch.

The officer sighed.

"When did you enter Mexico, Mr. Davenport?"

"Only this morning. Look, I'm English and, as you can surely see, I don't reside in Mexico. I've just eaten something that isn't making me feel at all well. I'm middle–aged and a law-abiding citizen of the realm and I'm telling you the truth. I've been beaten up and robbed so can't you please get on with your job and process these other good chaps here and let me go through."

The officer pushed a buzzer under his desk.

"I'm going to call in my supervisor, Mr. Davenport. I don't know if she can help you with this but . . "

"Of course she can help me! She can go and find the men who robbed me! She can go and arrest the two pissing policemen who sat and watched! She can drive me to Los Angeles if I miss my bus if she wants to help me!"

Michael was aware that he was becoming delirious and completely losing control of the situation and another threatening geyser of up-rushing bile choked off the nonsense he was speaking as he started to hiccup in great noisy wracking spasms.

The summoned supervisor came in through a door behind the officer. She was mid–fortyish with a prim unappealing face and despite his fever-fogged retinas Michael mused rather cruelly that she must have dressed that morning in the expectation of lunch with some gigolo because she was coiffed and prettified and her light yellow suit and fluffy lemon blouse still held their dry-cleaned press.

"We got a little problem here, Millie," drawled the officer.

"Oh?" she said, leaning over his desk and looking at Michael sternly.

He was swaying back and forth in agony as he had on the street, trying desperately to calm the rebellion in his body.

"Yes, Mr. Davenport here . . "

Michael cut him off.

" . . has been robbed of his passport and violated and has to catch a bus!" And then blundered on in jagged syncopation with each bilious heave. "I'm English and a jolly decent sort of fellow and you have to let me go through! I'm not some suicide bombing terrorist or vampire or extraterrestrial! I'm Michael Anderson Davenport and I . . "

But the heathen hordes in his stomach were readied for a final assault and before the officer or the supervisor could duck the whole massed barbarian army of tortilla, chili, ground meat, beans, purple pills and Cactus Cooler, the whole stinking enchilada one might say, came spewing from Michael's mouth all over them in a foaming volcanic stream spackling the poor woman's suit and blouse and face and hair with an acrid scalding carrot–colored porridge and temporarily blinding the officer's milky blue eyes.

One errant wodge of the glutinous eruption scudded across the desk onto the floor taking some paperwork with it but the gods were smiling and somehow not a drop of the offending magma besmirched the humble arrangement of little cards, the only things that might still assure the meddlesome world of Michael's fragile identity.

"Jesus! Shit! You sonofabitch!" the woman shrieked, nearly tripping as she staggered backward two goggle–eyed unbelieving paces, "Goddamit, it's all over my suit! Shit, what a stink! Goddamit, Carver, get off your fat ass and clean this shit up!"

Then she stopped suddenly and reached up, fearing and feeling the worst.

"Shiiiit!" she wailed hysterically, "It's got all in my haiiiir!"

Great globules of unapologetic orange goo were in pyroclastic flow and atomically bonding with her hairspray.

"I could kill you, you, you sonofabitch!" she screamed, "Get the stinking sonofabitch out of here!"

The officer was whimpering, fumbling frantically to find some Kleenex in a drawer, something, anything to cleanse the stinging daub of gastrointestinal napalm from his pearly blues.

Michael, on the other hand, was feeling mightily relieved, if only for the moment, and mentally recomposed enough to gather his documents from the desk and return them to his billfold as the poor woman dashed for the door with defiled fingertips outstretched.

"Get out! Get him out! Filthy sonofabitch!"

"Sorry," Michael offered, "Thank you. Something I ate. I did inform your man here that I wasn't feeling well. Bad pills. Sorry."

But she was gone.

"You heard the woman. Fuck off out of here, you fucking pig!" hissed the officer, tenderly wiping his burning eyelids and still not daring to prize open his field of vision more than a timorous crack.

"Thank you. I did warn you. So sorry," Michael repeated.

But he knew not to look this particular gift horse in the mouth and lost no time in pushing open the swinging glass doors and dodging through swiftly to the other side.

At least seven smiling Mexicans took the opportunity to follow him.

The city that greeted Michael as he walked beyond the immediate scoured sanctity of the American border enclave was if anything even grubbier and more garbage strewn than the one he had just left.

'First World, what a joke,' he thought and tried to straighten up a little.

He smiled weakly and said aloud, "Well, that was a piece of cake," but the attempt at levity was short–lived. Another shuddering ripple of nausea caused him to grimace and he muttered, "Man alive, what have I done to myself?" and lurched off along the scabrous street in what he hoped was the vague direction of the Republic.

§

As the Trailways coach for Los Angeles eased out of the El Paso central bus station onto West San Antonio Avenue right on time at 8:12 that morning the temperature was already 75 degrees Fahrenheit but in the much higher valley of vanished Lake Texcoco, where once stood the island metropolis of Tenochtitlan, built by the Nahua in the fourteenth century following the commandment of their god Huitzilopochtli, son of Coatlicue the earth mother, from the central square of which, with its great temples, blood–soaked sacrificial platforms and racks of grinning skulls, four broad causeways spread outward across the shallow brackish waters of the lake like the rays of the sun, it was only a chilly 59 and a large yellow and white helicopter could be seen descending, if anyone had cared to look, over the tranquil verdure of modern Mexico City's Chapultepec golf course, site of the springs which had once supplied fresh water to the Aztec capital via double terracotta aqueducts more than four kilometers long, and landed, without apparent fuss or fanfare but amid rigorous security precautions, at Military Camp #1, a stone's throw from the aptly named Avenida de los Conscriptos and an equivalent distance due west of the snarled traffic in the city center as the teeming bustle of Benito Juarez International Airport is due east. It had covered the seven hundred miles from Culiacan in less than three hours.

Hernano Salvador Medina, his two dark-suited deputies and the three forensic specialists who had accompanied them, came down the steps to the still blustery tarmac and watched with tired eyes as the silver coffin containing the corpse of 'Florio Bastida Morales' was carried from the chopper by six soldiers, placed on a trolley, wheeled to a waiting van, slid into the rear cargo space, all as efficiently as a flag-folding at a military funeral, and driven four hundred meters to a specially prepared laboratory.

After exchanging a few words with the others, Medina and one of his aides got into a black Lincoln Continental and drove toward the guard post and the high gates of the camp exit.

The second deputy quickly ushered the doctors aboard another van which sped after the corpse.

§

It was 8:21 as Michael puffed the last few paces up the hill to the station despite the fact that, by the grace of Saint Cosmas or Saint Damian or the twined serpent staff of Asclepius or all three at once, he had managed to walk straight there from the border without further gastric mishap nor even once having to enquire the way. However, the time was no longer of consequence. He could see the refuge of the Republic beckoning in the distance down its pitted side street and he had long since decided on his plan of action.

He walked inside to the ticket office and was grateful that it took less than a minute for the young Mexican couple in front of him to request and purchase their passage to Chihuahua.

'Good lord, was that a place name? Of course. Of course those ridiculous mutant rodents so doted on by the pampered ermined offspring of oil tycoons had to be created somewhere,' his bruised manhood mused sourly, 'Wherever it was it had doubtless gone to the dogs like everywhere else.'

He chuckled and, with ticket in hand, approached the booth. At least he was not so discomfited by his loss that he couldn't make up an awful joke.

The clerk behind the glass was a large unsmiling black man masticating a wad of bubble gum and Michael, who was fully prepared for a pitched battle, didn't wait for him to initiate their dialogue.

"I have a ticket for the 8:12 coach to Los Angeles."

"It's gone."

"Yes, I'm sure, but that doesn't matter. I know you won't credit this but I was robbed an hour ago by two Mexican hooligans and it was quite impossible to get here in time. I want to make an exchange."

He thrust the ticket through the semicircular hole beneath the window expecting the worst.

"When for?"

"Well, let me think, what's today?"

"Thursday."

"Yes, of course, Thursday. March the 20th, yes. I'd like to exchange it for Saturday."

"Morning or afternoon?"

"Oh, ah, well, let's see, when does it leave and, even more importantly, when would it arrive in Los Angeles if it leaves on Saturday afternoon?"

"Leaves at 4:20. Arrives 9:50."

"9:50 when?"

"Sunday morning."

"Yes, yes, of course, well, that won't do."

Too much nighttime traveling and therefore too much scenery missed.

"When does it leave on Saturday morning?"

"7:45."

"Oh, I see, a slight difference from today. I'm sure there's some reason for that, is there?"

The clerk made no response.

"Or perhaps not. And when does that one arrive?"

"11:17."

"In the evening, of course."

"You got it."

Gottfried and Anna were expecting him tonight at 11:40 so that would likely be all right with them too. He would have to let them know the change of plan.

"And it's a wee bit faster than the afternoon departure. Good."

He thought better of testing the poor man's patience further and enquiring why one trip should take one hour and fifty–eight minutes more than the other, though the question was on the tip of his tongue.

"All right. Yes, that will be fine."

The monosyllabic clerk immediately ripped up the first ticket, punched the new schedule into his keyboard, tore off the second as soon as it emerged from the printer, kept the first half, flicked the second half without another word under the window and folded his hands.

"There's no extra charge?" asked an astonished Michael.

"Nope."

It was hard to believe his ears.

"Christ," he said, "I take it all back. God bless America."

The clerk shrugged one side of his mouth in begrudging agreement and said, "Hey, man, why not?"

Michael would have liked to engage this delightful fellow with a further moment or two of drollery but he could sense the impatient breath of another customer over his shoulder and just waved the ticket in farewell.

"I can't thank you enough. Truly. Thank you."

He could see that the clerk was no longer paying attention and chuckled. Then he put the new ticket carefully away in the billfold in his shoulder-bag and walked off whistling down the street toward the hotel with his corduroy jacket slung nonchalantly across his back. Life had its downs and it had its ups and what else could one do about the former but plot to avenge oneself ruthlessly on one's trespassers.

The pudding was nowhere in sight as he entered the lobby and he had to ring the hand bell to rouse her. She emerged eventually from a door at the rear and waddled toward him eating, of all things, a breakfast burrito. Small drops of red sauce dribbled from the corners of her lips and Michael didn't find the vision easy to contend with. He had developed a nasty headache and was still feeling decidedly unsettled.

"Checking out?" she said, her flaccid cheeks bulging.

"No. I've had a change of plan. I'd like to stay two more nights and I'd like the same room if at all possible."

She looked more aggravated than pleased as she consulted the register with greasy fingers. Her labored breath wheezed in and out like a bicycle pump trying to inflate a tractor tire.

"I'd like to check out on Saturday morning if that's all right."

"So you want tonight and Friday?"

"That's the idea," he said, winking in that insufferably patronizing British way he loathed without being able to stop it.

"Same room?" the behemoth asked, sucking her ketchup-colored teeth.

"I'd like the same room, yes. If possible. I believe I have mentioned that already. There's no need for a maid. I don't require fresh towels or sheets or anything like that."

"You wouldn't get 'em anyhow!" the female Pantagruel exclaimed and the wittiness of her repartee made her burst into a cackle and a little spatter of chili and spittle flew from her mouth onto Michael's shirt which only made her cackle all the more.

"Oooops, sorry mister," she said in a girlish unrepentant voice, placing the fingers of her free hand to her mouth.

"I've seen worse," Michael told her.

She reached out the same fat greasy paw to wipe the splotch and Michael jumped back, he knew well enough to leave the stain untouched, but he could see that his action had in some bizarre way rebuffed and offended her.

"You don't service the rooms every day then?" he asked.

"Nope. Weekly or change of client is all."

"I see. Well, that's perfection in my case. I suppose you'd like cash in advance as before?"

"Hotel policy."

She began scribbling a sum on the register pad and mumbling.

"Let's see, two more nights is, no, no, wait a minute, no, weekends is twenty–eight fifty, so that's twenty–six fifty for tonight and twenty–eight fifty for Friday . . "

Michael was already counting out the notes from his billfold, two twenties, a ten and a five. He couldn't understand why the bandits hadn't taken his money as well.

"That's fifty–six dollars."

"I think you'll find it's fifty–five," he said, his nostrils pinching slightly, another pompous mannerism that he found, alas, impossible to control though he despised it mightily in others of his race, and put the money down in front of her.

"Oh yeah, you don't say."

She repeated the calculation twice more, pudgy fingers retracing the figures each time with the nib of her thick ballpoint pen. Michael could read the blue letters along the pen's length, 'El Paso – Los Angeles Limousine, 720 South Oregon Street'.

'Good lord, what would that cost?' he thought and laughed inwardly, 'Oh, well, if all else fails, ha ha.' At least he still had his credit cards.

The pudding had at last found her error and put the bills away one by one in the cash register while chawing off another juicy mouthful of burrito and then added sullenly as though her arithmetical difficulty had somehow been his fault, "Checkout's noon on Saturday."

"Thank you, my dear. I'll be off long before that."

As he walked away, she called after him, "Hey, I forgot, you took your key. Next time you go out leave your key here on the desk. Hotel policy."

"I'll do that little thing," he replied without turning, "It's a good idea."

Her sunken accusing eyes followed him up the stairs as though he were an alien refugee from outer space.

CHAPTER SIX

Michael had flopped straight into bed the moment he reached the barren yet blissful solitude of his room and had slept for a solid twelve hours so it was after ten in the evening by the time he had showered and shaved and dressed and walked down to Pantera's. The worst of the nausea and headache had gone but his stomach was still a trifle ginger.

Chuck was at the bar sipping a Dos Equis and laughed as he came in.

"Thought you had a bus to catch."

Michael gave him a sour look and the young bartender asked without a trace of sarcasm, "Same as last night, *señor*?"

"No, just some bottled water and an empty glass, thank you."

The bartender obliged and watched with amused interest as Michael took a small paper packet of powder from his satchel, tore off a corner and poured the contents into the glass. Then he half–filled it with water, swirled it around and, as the powder frothed wildly toward the top of the glass, downed it. He stood motionless for a long moment, leaning on the bar, and then his eyes opened wide and he reared back and let out a tremendous protracted prizewinning belch.

Everyone in the bar clapped and Chuck laughed again.

"One for the record books."

"I've done better," Michael said modestly and released a second eructation almost as lengthy as the first. "Bicarbonate of soda. Remedy from home. My old mother used to swear by it. God, what a relief."

He dabbed his lips dry on his sleeve.

"So what happened?"

Michael moved close to Chuck.

"You wouldn't believe it," he said quietly, "Everything was perfect. I had the most fantastic footage, utterly fantastic, and then just as I was coming back two little bastards drove up in a Mercedes and threw me on the pavement and stole the tape! I'll tell you the whole thing but I've got to make a phone call."

§

As Michael was informing Gottfried and Anna that something had come up and he would not be arriving on the 11:40 as planned but instead the 11:17 on Saturday a short slim casually but expensively dressed man stood perfectly still at the side of a private airstrip in the hills above Juarez. A small executive jet was rolling to a stop.

The man watched with cold narrow eyes as the door of the plane opened and the ladder swung down and two bodyguards in black suits helped Doña Aurora the three steps to the tarmac. When she saw the man coming towards her she burst into fresh floods of tears. He kissed her on both cheeks and wiped her eyes and led her gently to a waiting limousine. Cecilia followed and the man opened the door. He held Doña Aurora by the elbow to steady her as she got in.

"*Tenga cuidado*, mama," he murmured softly.

"Be careful."

Cecilia flipped a cigarette from a gold case and lit it as she reached the car. She looked at the man with hatred but he returned her gaze without apology.

"Asesino!" she hissed and blew smoke in his face.

§

It took just an hour and twenty minutes of, for the most part, admirably restrained conversation in Pantera's that night for Michael and Chuck to lay the foundation of fast friendship, giggling like schoolboys on occasion at Michael's abundant depiction of the details and if he lapsed into an excessively emotional and theatrical mode from time to time it was quite understandable because they each knocked back half a dozen double Hornitos tequilas with Dos Equis chasers in the process.

By the tale's end Chuck had put two and two firmly together and laughed a long bitter laugh and said, "Come on, I'll show you," and they had hopped in the old Ford Ranger and taken Rim Road Scenic Drive to a high viewpoint under Comanche Peak from where Chuck knew there was an unobstructed panorama of the river, the lights of El Paso and Juarez and the stony hills beyond.

They tumbled from the truck into the cool mesquite-laden air and realized with sophomoric glee that they were both pretty smashed.

"You can see it from here," Chuck proclaimed loudly as he walked over to the guardrail, "Not more than three fucking crow fly miles away."

He pointed across the twinkling valley and held Michael by the shoulder so he could follow his finger.

"Take a line straight up from the cathedral. You see it? The dark slope and the mountain above. The whole thing's his private compound. Airstrip, wildlife park, you name it."

"The tiger came all that way?"

"Why not? It was night. Who was gonna stop it? You see the bright cluster of lights at the top of the first ridge? That's his mansion. Forty fucking rooms and a fucking Olympic swimming pool. He just sits over there laughing at us."

"And you think he's there now," Michael said, stifling a resurgent hiccup. Minimal compared to the pneumatic horrors of the morning but he had eaten nothing since and hadn't exactly been treating his empty stomach well.

"No doubt in my mind. That was him you saw this morning. And he saw you, that's for damn sure. Why do you think they took your tapes?"

Chuck pointed again.

"You see way in the far distance in the valley where that big mother of a plane is coming down? That's Juarez airport. He flies the stuff in from South America in fucking 727s."

"Fantastic."

"No kidding. He's got business holdings all over El Paso. Calls himself Amado Barragan. Launders the money through Texas and California banks. Plenty gets funneled into political donations. Both parties, what's the difference. And the CIA. And Wall Street, oh, you bet. I've got photos of him buddying up to Junior Bush at his ranch and the Clintons at the White House, for Christ's sake! He comes over here to his hotel whenever he needs a bit of peace!"

Chuck roared with laughter.

"Fantastic," Michael agreed, "And no one stops him. Of course not. Why would they? How could they? The whole pissing global economy would probably collapse."

He had to pause while he held down another uncomfortable reflux.

"Oh god. Perhaps that last tequila was a trifle unwise."

"Fatal after what you told me most likely," Chuck concurred with an ironic smile.

"Almost certain, I can feel it."

"You've stopped sneezing though. That's a good thing."

Michael realized with surprise that he was breathing more freely and the endlessly protracted and normally unstemmable suppuration from his sinuses that he so dreaded hadn't troubled him much since he had awoken.

"Yes, quite amazing." He inhaled deeply through his nose as though to convince himself of the matter. "I told you, I took a pill. Well, two pills, but I feel sure they parted company with me at the border before they could really have done much good."

He hiccuped more forcefully and something that tasted awful backed up into his mouth and he made a face and they both laughed.

Once Michael had this latest esophageal revolt momentarily under control he asked, "So who was the poor chump who had the plastic surgery?"

"The one he supplied them with photographs of all along. His sad dumb brother Vicente. I told them for years it wasn't him."

"Told who?"

Chuck didn't reply and Michael guffawed at his sudden silence.

"What were you for god's sake? Don't tell me, a narc? A faithful foot soldier in the War on Drugs? Deep cover? Cops and robbers? All that macho stuff? Good lord, does no one in this parochial little country read the Greek myths? This prick is just one head of a Hydra."

He tried a hammy visual demonstration of the legendary beast, burbling like the Jabberwock, flapping and flailing his arms and waggling his fingers.

"Catching him wouldn't make any bloody difference to anything. You said it yourself. It's like changing governments. Nothing happens. You just have to put up with a new lot of corrupt idiots in place of the old ones."

Chuck's mood had become somber. Michael noticed the pain in his eyes and they stared at the vista without speaking for a moment.

"It makes a difference to me that's all," Chuck said finally.

Michael looked at him, puzzled.

"Why?"

There was another even longer pause.

"He killed my son."

Michael felt instantly regretful for his glib commentary and couldn't think what to say.

"Anyway, if you want your film back, Mr. Englishman, that's where it is," Chuck said and turned abruptly and walked toward the truck.

On the way down the hill Michael discovered Chuck had indeed been an agent of the DEA but that his son had somehow fallen in with the wrong crowd and got himself killed. Chuck wouldn't say how, only that he was certain Amado Portillo had ordered it. And now that Michael understood who the owner of the tiger was and why the thugs had robbed him he was nonplussed to know what, if anything, he could do about it and his previous rather simpleminded plans for revenge evaporated depressingly.

It came upon them as they drove that they were both ravenously hungry. Chuck knew an all night takeout not far from the Republic and they ordered four hamburgers with four orders of French fries and two large cokes and sat in the truck stuffing themselves.

"I suppose there's nothing for it," Michael sighed, after having polished off the first burger in three bites which surprisingly enough had quelled his hiccups, "I'll just have to forget it ever happened and go on to LA." And then he added, "I imagine there's no point calling the police," at which they looked at each other and both burst into gales of laughter.

"Well now, I don't know," Chuck reconsidered, "Reporting it might help you get a new passport faster."

"Oh god no. I don't think I could face dealing with a police station here. I'm sure there must be some sort of British embassy or consulate in LA. I don't care about the passport, I just can't bear losing the tape. Bastards! Dirty filthy thieving bastards! I'm telling you, it was gorgeous. Absolutely irreplaceable. And I was only a few seconds away from the blasted border!"

Chuck nodded in sympathy and thought for a while, chewing silently.

"Oh, what the hell," he said with sudden decision, "I know someone who might be able to help you get the tape back if it's that damn important."

Michael looked at him blankly.

"If you really want to risk your skinny neck."

CHAPTER SEVEN

Michael had listened to what Chuck had to say with mounting excitement and it hadn't taken him more than a minute to decide and by five o'clock in the morning after three pointless hours of tossing and turning he had found his way to the river again and was wading across, this time unabashedly stripped to his undershorts and barefoot, holding his trousers, socks and sandals high.

Chuck said that he didn't really need a passport to get into Mexico, only to get out, but nonetheless this had seemed the safer course. Chuck had also told him that today was a national holiday, the celebration of the birthday of Benito Juarez, so few *indocumentados* would be coming from the opposite direction.

As he inched carefully forward through the current, pressing his feet into the cold muddy bottom of the channel and at the same time feeling with his toes for sharp objects, he experienced a keen appreciation of their plight.

Benito Pablo Juarez Garcia was a Zapotec Indian, born on March the 21st, 1806, and rose from illiteracy to become a respected lawyer and judge. He was the only full–blooded indigene ever elected to the presidency, no less than five times between 1858 and 1872, the period now known as *La Reforma.* He fought to curtail the power of the Catholic Church and the military and for his liberal views and honest effort to create a modern civil society he is rather misleadingly called the Abraham Lincoln of Mexico. Of course, *La Reforma* was soon followed, as always seems to happen in the bloodthirsty back and forth of human affairs, by the corrupt thirty–five-year autocracy of Jose de la Cruz Porfirio Diaz Mori. However, Juarez had sowed the seeds of the Mexican Revolution, a twenty year struggle that eventually succeeded in overturning the Diaz oppression and which was at once both unquestionably noble and deeply confusing. Despite the fact that Michael considered himself a bit of a history buff he could never make heads or tails of the plot of 'Viva Zapata!' even at the umpteenth viewing. He was well aware, nonetheless, how quickly that hard won victory had been betrayed by the Institutional Revolutionary Party, the name in itself he felt should have seemed sufficiently worrying, and the nearly seventy years of shameless crony capitalism that then flourished under their mendacious care, a regime that was only now beginning to show signs of implosion due to the courage of men like Hernano Salvador Medina.

Much of this had been known to Michael for many years but it certainly wasn't at the forefront of his mind as he stopped to dry himself on the sloping concrete embankment, no, it was the thought that he was stark staring bonkers to have even considered what he was about to try, the thought of Flossie and Helen and their quiet existence in blessedly post–imperial Chalk Farm, the sense that his mother's ghost was looking down fretfully at this rashness, those were the things that began to intrude like the strident notes of an off-key choir in his still alcohol bedazzled brain.

Chuck had unearthed a dog–eared map of El Paso-Juarez in the glove box of the pickup and in the semidarkness outside the hamburger joint had drawn on it, with a woolly–tipped red marker, a complex sequence of lines and directions which would hopefully allow Michael to find the 'someone who could help him' whose name was Fernando Rios.

As he sat among a tickle of encroaching weeds in the pre-dawn glimmer, rubbing silt from between his toes with a frayed hand towel from the Republic which he had popped into his satchel at the last minute, he was overcome by the distinct feeling that he had been cast, for the sin of incorrigible pigheadedness no doubt, into some bad 1940's film noir.

§

At that precise moment, Cecilia Portillo's naked body was being thrown onto the stuffed silken coverlet beneath the canopy of her bed. A hand grasped her by the hair, first pulling her head violently backwards and then plunging her face–forward into the pillows. She had said all that she wanted to say and more and knew if she screamed or complained now she would be dead in an instant.

She could feel the sharp cold tip of a knife touch the lips of her vagina and tried to relax as the long thin blade was slowly inserted to the hilt. She could feel it cut into the muscle of her cervix but no real sensation of pain filtered through the haze of drugs and liquor coursing in her veins, only a strange electric tingling that made her want to urinate.

"I'll feed you to the wolves," a male voice said quietly.

She felt the knife being turned inside and winced involuntarily and then it was equally slowly withdrawn and a few heavy drops of blood came with it and soiled the creamy whiteness of the bedclothes.

The hand traced the point of the stiletto up the curve of her backbone to caress her neck depositing fine threads of gore and painting the luminous pallor of her flesh with a lurid web of crimson filaments.

"But only at the last, I promise you," the voice purred.

After a long moment to let the threat penetrate the hand tossed the knife on her back, nicking it under the right shoulder blade and flecking the skin with tiny red dots and she could hear the soft sound of slippers crossing the tile floor and then the solid thud of the door closing.

She didn't rise or move to cleanse her wounds but drifted tearlessly away into a torpid slumber.

§

Everything was also gravely silent in the forensic lab at Military Camp #1 and Hernano Salvador Medina sat perched disconsolately on a corner of the examination table surrounded by his team drinking a cup of lukewarm morning coffee from a Styrofoam cup.

"They know we know they know," he said finally, staring down the length of the corpse at the once more dentureless and sunken mouth, "They know it isn't him but they want us to keep quiet about it."

The team waited for further explanation.

"The president phoned me personally at eleven o'clock last night and told me to make the announcement this morning. He wants me to confirm to the world that it *is* him. That it's him and that he's dead."

"Why?"

"You all know why. The American Congress is about to take its annual vote on our so-called 'certification'. He knows as well as I do it's a joke but with his brother implicated in the money–laundering, Rebollo's arrest and seven other generals indicted, he needs something that looks good. And the Americans fed him some nonsense about them not wanting Portillo to know that they know."

"What good will that do?"

Medina raised his palms and shrugged.

"What can I tell you? It's bullshit."

"Did Wanless know all along?"

"I don't think so. He's just a patsy. But McWhirter and Consterdine knew. They don't care that people die. To them it's a game. The only thing that really interested them was how we knew."

"Did you tell them?"

"Not the truth. Nothing about the dentist. I don't think even they know about that."

"Didn't they ask when we knew?"

"No. That doesn't matter to them. They've never cared what we think."

The room fell quiet again.

"So I thank you," Medina said finally, "But there's nothing more for us to do here. They want the body ready for transport by this afternoon. As far as I'm concerned it's ready now. Go home to your families. Enjoy the day."

§

By ten o'clock Michael had followed the lines on Chuck's torn map past the glorious twin baroque towers of the city's 17th–century cathedral and the Franciscan mission to *Nuestra Señora* of Guadalupe, Spanish explorers had first set foot in the area in 1581 and named it *El Paso del Norte*, the north pass, but it took another quarter millenium for the Treaty of Guadalupe Hidalgo to formally create the border and forever divide the growing settlements on either side of the great river, and he had now entered an industrial zone well beyond the half mile radius of knickknack stores, pottery and blanket stands, strip joints, restaurants, nightclubs, bars and brothels that cater to the world's tourists.

The walk had thus far been pleasantly uneventful. He had kept his clothes dry, he had a fully recharged battery in the camera, the churning in his stomach had eased, his clogged nasal passages were feeling miraculously clear despite a sleepless night, it was blissfully warm, the sun was shining, he had purchased and consumed another two tins of Cactus Cooler and he had been freely able to film streets filled with smiling people who were simply enjoying their holiday and didn't take much notice of him. Several who did recognize him from the day before had even called out a friendly greeting.

But here the city had become eerily deserted and Michael continued on, puzzling at the numbers which, as well as being few and far between, seemed to range up one side of the street and down the other in no particular order. He was rubbing his sweaty brow in exasperation and just about to give up the search when his eyes happened to fall upon the sign he was looking for, nailed to the side of a nondescript two–story clapboard building.

'Nada Que Ver', it proclaimed, 'Nothing to see'.

The sign had a curved arrow pointing to the rear and Michael followed it through a narrow garbage-strewn passageway and found a door sandwiched in between an auto-body repair shop and an outlet for superfluous sporting goods, both of which were closed, with another sign *'Nada Que Ver'*.

It didn't look promising but he tried the door and was surprised to find it open. The gloomy hall beyond led to a flight of wooden stairs with no visible end and Michael was torn between proceeding upward or turning on his heels and running all the way back to the river but some buried indomitability in his Saxon genes propelled him to the former course.

'Saxon be damned, this is pure idiocy,' he thought.

The dry wood beneath his sandals set off a symphony of melodramatic creaking as he ascended the stairs but he could now see a faint light at the top and then to his astonishment he recognized the unmistakable distant soundtrack of a Roadrunner and Coyote cartoon.

"Hello," Michael called out hopefully as he came into a large whitewashed room. Suddenly the lights were switched on and a bare gallery with high ceilings and a dark polished floor and every wall covered with a myriad of photographic blow–ups was revealed to his still-adjusting eyes. A young man was sitting at a table in a far corner with a small girl about four years old on his lap watching television but the display of images was so overwhelming that at first Michael couldn't speak. Nothing in the street outside could possibly have led anyone to expect what was here.

There seemed to be at least a hundred portraits of women, many just faces but some taken at full length. Not one was tawdry cheesecake, as perhaps an adventuring tourist might have hoped, but young healthy fully–dressed Mexican women in a wide variety of poses with expressions ranging from the demure and gentle to angry and rebellious. Innocent hardworking honest faces accompanied on every side by the most gruesome counterpoint.

Relatives holding derelict pieces of tattered clothing, shoes and handbags, limbs and gnawed bone. One blankly staring mother standing in the desert sand holding an eyeless severed head. Policemen pulling a barrel from the river and an almost unbearable to look at close-up of the half–dissolved remains inside it. Dozens of photos of the seedy nightlife of Juarez, loitering punks with cigarillos dangling from slack mouths, prostitutes of every conceivable size and shape and gender, transvestites, drug addicts, shootings, robberies, kidnappings, rapes, the sullen unrepentant mugshots of murderers and the dusty downcast eloquence of the dead. Broken mothers and fathers and brothers, numbly forlorn or weeping over the tortured bodies of daughters and sisters, those few at least that had the good fortune to be found intact.

Michael stood shaking and dumbstruck in the center of the room as the young man came up to him and said softly, "The jungle is on fire, is it not?"

Michael was still too moved to manage a reply.

"And the fire screams."

"Yes," Michael agreed, finding a husky voice at last, "Yes, it does."

"You are English. I knew it before you spoke."

"Yes, English English," Michael replied almost absently, blinking his wet eyes, "Someone else defined me that way. Just yesterday, I think it was." He had to stop and clear his throat. "These photographs are, um . . well, it's rather hard to find an appropriate word . . extraordinary. Did you take them?"

"Some of them. The one you are looking at now. The dead girl. I took that."

"Incredible. I couldn't quite make out what it was at first."

"After she was raped and tortured someone poured diesel fuel on her and she was burned alive."

"Who?"

"It is under investigation."

The adjacent image was a smiling young woman in a wedding dress and Michael absorbed it with difficulty.

"Are you Fernando Rios?" he asked.

"Yes."

"I'm Michael Davenport."

They shook hands.

"I have a message for you."

Michael took out his billfold. Chuck had written a brief note with the red marker on the back of one of Michael's 'Enigma' business cards and he handed it to Fernando who looked at him curiously.

"Would you mind if I filmed some of this?"

Fernando shrugged his shoulders and gestured 'be my guest' with his hands and there was a brief silence as he read the card. Michael was busy with the camera and didn't notice him glance back at the young girl and frown.

The message said simply, 'Help this guy if you can. Kiss Juanita for me. Chuck Bowman.'

"What is 'Enigma'?" Fernando asked, looking at the front of the card.

"It's a magazine that I write for sometimes. Occult and supernatural stuff but taken with a large grain of salt. And we flatter ourselves that it offers more in-depth analysis than usual. *'Nada Que Ver'* means 'nothing to see' Chuck told me."

"That and other things. Nothing to do. No one is looking, perhaps."

"I think it's brilliant. Tell me about the pictures."

"What would you like to know?"

"Who are they all? What happened to them?"

"They were girls. They were killed."

"From Juarez? Killed by who?"

"Yes, from Juarez. From Chihuahua. Some from further."

"Is Chihuahua an actual place?"

"Yes, a place."

"Forgive me, but I only know it as the breed name of a very silly–looking little dog. A tortured creation of meddling mankind. Sorry. I prefer cats."

"Don't be sorry."

"Does the dog come from there?"

"It was sacred a thousand years ago but I agree it is very silly. The Aztec called it *'techichi'*. 'Chihuahua' means 'dried ground' in Nahuatl not 'dog'. And now Chihuahua is both a city and a state. Juarez is in Chihuahua state. Chihuahua city is the capital. Over 200 miles south through the desert. But more than half the people in the state work in Juarez. In the *maquiladores*."

"What are they?"

"Assembly plants."

"For what?"

"You name it. Anything and everything for the rich world. Nothing stays in Juarez."

"Who killed the girls? Why? How can there be so many?"

"The first was in January four years ago. Since then there have been many more than the hundred you see here. Some bodies are never recovered."

"Is it gangs, do you think, or a serial killer?"

"You mean like 'Jack *el Destripador*'?"

"Is that what you call him in Spanish? I believe they use something like 'Jack *lo Squartatore*' in Italian. Some of these are horrifyingly reminiscent of the photographs they took in London at the time."

There was an image of a legless woman lying in a cotton field with her belly ripped open from the groin to the breastbone.

And then his eyes came to rest on the photo of a naked girl partly buried in a sand dune whose corpse was quite whole and there were two close–ups of her torso and neck beside it and the flesh was covered with what appeared to be deep double–pronged bite marks. Michael couldn't quite believe what he was seeing and moved in to study them more closely.

"Are those what I think they are?"

"The police said it was done by coyotes or wolves but the girl was not eaten and coyotes and wolves are always hungry."

Michael had known as soon as he came into the gallery that he had stumbled upon a hell of a story but could it even be one for Enigma? He took the camera from his eye and turned to look at Fernando.

"You think it was done by a person?"

Fernando returned his look with an expression that undoubtedly meant 'yes' and Michael took up the camera again.

"Incredible. Just incredible."

"Who and why we don't know. We only suspect."

"Who?"

"It was also four years ago that a different group of *narcotraficantes* took control in Juarez and decided to make it their base. Whether that is the reason or not no one can say. But the date makes us wonder. And the fact that the local authorities have done almost nothing."

"You're talking about Amado Portillo."

"And his family. They bought the mountain above the cathedral."

"Why would they want to kill young girls? People like that only want the money that comes from killing millions at a distance."

"That is true. I can't prove what I suspect. It is only rumors."

"How many are there in the family?"

"There were three that came here. Two brothers and a sister. And their mother. And many cousins and servants and many, many bodyguards."

"What happened to the father?"

"He was a small landowner in Sinaloa. Not wealthy. I think most likely he is dead."

"Chuck said that the younger brother, Vicente, was the one who died in the hospital in Mexico City. The one they are saying is Amado."

"I do not think they believe what they say."

"No, neither does Chuck. What's going on there?"

"Many years ago Vicente applied for an American immigration visa using his brother's name. All the photographs in the newspapers of 'Amado Portillo' since then have been Vicente. To look at them, you wouldn't have thought they could be members of the same family. Vicente was big and fat and hairy with a beard and pale skin and you couldn't miss him and Amado is short and thin and bald and clean-shaven and looks like the *mestizo* that he is. It was a clever plan and convenient for Amado."

"Convenient for a lot of people maybe."

"Maybe."

"Not so convenient any more for Vicente. Did he die or was he killed?"

"Who can say?"

"What about the sister?"

"Her name is Cecilia. I do not know how she fits except that in age she is the middle one."

"Are there pictures of any of them here?"

Fernando smiled.

"No. They are like the whitewash on the walls. The background noise we cannot touch or see."

"I understand that very well now. I made the mistake of taking one. I was filming his tiger. It was loose in the street yesterday morning and I caught a glimpse of him in his car when he came to fetch it. Well, Chuck is sure it was him. It must have been because two of his thugs drove up and wrestled me to the ground an hour later and stole the tape. I know it seems ridiculous but I'd love to find a way to get it back. I don't care about him. It's just the footage of the tiger I've got to have. It was utterly fantastic."

"You are a film maker also?"

"In my own eccentric way. Chuck said you could help me. That you could show me where to find him."

Fernando laughed out loud.

"Everyone knows where to find him, Mr. Davenport, but even I am not crazy enough to go looking."

Michael joined in the laughter. His camera had come to rest on the photo of a Mexican policeman standing in front of a very thorny many-branched cactus holding up a high–heeled shoe.

"It is a good image," Fernando said.

"Simple, eloquent and fantastic," Michael agreed and moved on to the next. "Chuck told me that Amado Portillo killed his son but he wouldn't tell me how or why."

"Chuck is a good man. Honest. He worked many years for the American government against the *narcotraficantes*. But his son got involved. I don't know how much, but enough. Chuck blames himself. That could have been part of it also. It's hard to know."

"How did it happen?"

"Like all of them, I only know how it ended."

Michael had nearly completed a full circuit of the room and was filming at the back near the table and the little girl by the television.

"How?"

"They found his bones in a barrel of acid in the river. Like many others. It seems that is almost their favorite way."

Michael shut off the camera and was silent for a moment. He looked quickly at the little girl but her dark brown eyes remained fixed on the cartoons and her face betrayed no emotion.

'Perhaps she hasn't been listening or can't understand English,' he hoped.

The painful and always frustrated quest of Wile E. Coyote had changed to the eternal cat and mouse of Tom and Jerry. Michael loved animated shorts of any kind and it was weirdly wonderful hearing one of his favorites dubbed into Spanish.

"When?"

"About two years ago. Chuck quit his job a few weeks later and left El Paso. It was the last time I saw him."

"Jesus."

"How do you know him?"

"We met in a bar called Pantera's two evenings ago."

"What is he doing in El Paso? Did he tell you?"

Michael hadn't given the subject a thought.

"No," he said, "He didn't. It never occurred to me to ask."

He turned the camera on again and moved to capture the last few images.

"If you are interested in the occult there are some photographs that I do not dare to display," Fernando said, opening the drawer of a metal filing cabinet, "That are even beyond what you have seen."

Michael shut off the camera and looked at him.

"Please," he said.

Fernando took out a thin plastic folder and said, "You will see them better in the light of the windows at the front," and gestured Michael to follow him away from the little girl.

"I cannot bear that she should see these," Fernando said quietly and laid out a sequence of eleven photos on the floor, "It is also too dangerous for me. No one has seen them and the police do not know I have them."

After the first glance Michael could feel every hair on his body stand on end, his mind was reeling and he knelt on the floor staring at the images.

"Where were these taken?" he said, almost whispering.

"In the Samalayuca. A vast area of nothing that starts twenty miles south of the city. Some Dutch university students had lost their way and took them."

The eleven photographs were different angles of the same appalling scene.

Three tall wooden poles with double crossbars stood upright, half buried in the desert sand, beneath a rocky outcrop on which an ancient petroglyph had been carved untold centuries ago of three recognizably male figures all greater than human height appearing to face straight forward though they were only a featureless sequence of lines with rough circles for heads at the top.

Below the petroglyph the naked corpses of three women were impaled on the poles. Sharp objects had been forced through the bodies at different angles. One had been staked twice through the lower belly, another upwards through the armpits and a third through both knees and elbows. They had been roped by the neck to the poles and dangled six or seven feet above the ground. Most of the women's flesh from the waist down had been torn away by animals. Two had nothing left at all below the knee. Another's arm was missing from the shoulder. One had both breasts cut off or wrenched away perhaps though it was hard to imagine any wolf leaping so high. Another's face showed hollow blood–rimmed eye-sockets, whether the natural work of ravens or the inhuman cruelty of the murderers it was impossible to say. All three had similar double puncture marks covering what remained of their desiccated windblown skin.

"One can only hope they were dead before it happened," Fernando said.

Michael stayed kneeling for a long time. If he had not been so transfixed by what Fernando had laid out before him he would have been amused by the cadence of a Spanish Mister Magoo coming from the television.

Finally, he raised his camera and filmed the images in silence.

CHAPTER EIGHT

From the windows of the Director's office in the DEA headquarters at 700 Army Navy Drive in Arlington, Virginia, it was still possible to see flecks of snow on the bare branches of the maple trees and General Larry McWhirter, trimly dressed in a dark blue suit and matching striped tie, skewered neatly in place with a silver tie pin thrust through the starched collar of a light blue shirt, was looking out and listening with only half an ear as DEA Director Loomis Consterdine finished reading the transcript, hastily but expertly translated from the Spanish by an employee in the Office of Codes and Encryption three floors down, of what their new counterpart Hernano Salvador Medina had said that morning according to their wishes at a press conference in Mexico City, that he could confirm after extensive tests, including the examination of blood samples, dental records, scars, ear shapes, fingerprints and DNA, that the body of the man named 'Florio Bastida Morales', who died of heart failure in the early hours of Sunday morning, March the 16th, at the Hospital of Our Lady of Santa Monica following radical plastic surgery to alter his appearance, was in fact Amado Portillo Perez, the most powerful of Mexico's drug barons, billionaire *jefe* of the infamous Juarez cartel and high in the top ten of the global War on Drugs' most wanted list.

The drug lord's plastic surgeon, Pedro Lopez Saucedo, had been cleared of any responsibility in the case and rumors of lethal levels of Dormicum sedative in the body had been categorically proved untrue. His death was the result of massive coronary failure due to shock or a malfunctioning respirator, or both in conjunction, and that was the end of it.

Consterdine had sauntered over to join the general by the window as he read the last few words and folded the transcript and slipped it into the breast pocket of his blazer.

"What do you think, is Medina trouble?" McWhirter asked laconically.

There was a constant slushiness in the general's diction that had always irritated Consterdine. It reminded him of Sean Connery and made him want to tell him to get better fitting dentures.

"He's green but I think we'll get him to play ball," he replied instead.

"Zedillo's scared as hell about the certification."

"I would be too. It's worth a shitload of money."

They both chuckled. Ernesto Zedillo was the current president of Mexico and the American Congress had a big stick to beat him with. Their annual vote to certify that his government was fully and diligently participating in the global War on Drugs and the money pipeline that either flowed or didn't flow south because of it.

"A shitload," McWhirter concurred, "Yeah, he'll play ball."

"Did just fine this morning."

"And whaddya hear about that fella Bowkin, Bowlen, Borden, what the hell was his damn name?"

"You mean Chuck Bowman?"

"Yeah, that's him."

"Not surprised he's come to mind."

McWhirter cleared his throat and swallowed a mouthful of spittle.

"He was trouble."

"Might still be."

"Where's he at now?"

"Still out there in Texas. Near some podunk place called Sweetwater. Got himself a cattle ranch. Strictly penny ante stuff."

They both gazed down at the bare branches of the trees and the rapidly melting snow glistening in the spring sunshine.

"Sure is pretty," McWhirter slurred, "Think we need to do anything?"

Consterdine twitched his chin sideways and a vertebra at the base of his skull shifted with an uncomfortable click.

"Not if the dumb sonofabitch keeps his mouth shut."

§

Chuck was chewing on a wad of tobacco so his mouth wasn't completely closed at that moment as he parked his rusty pickup half a block down the street from the entrance to El Paso's elegant Barragan Hotel. He got out and spat in the gutter and stood for a while leaning on the truck taking a good look.

The Barragan had been built in 1912 and was listed in the National Historical Register. It was known until three years ago as the Camino Real but its famous name had been altered, amid loud and acrimonious local controversy, after its abnormally whirlwind purchase by the real estate tycoon, international philanthropist and rumored clandestine moneybags to the world's political elite, Amado Barragan, and there was still much heated disagreement as to whether the extensive interior remodeling had truly returned it to its former glory as the 'Jewel of the Southwest' and made it the centerpiece of what everyone who was anyone in 'Sun City' hoped was going to be El Paso's new vibrant and revitalized downtown core. Many long time guests were quoted as preferring the old style and some had gone so far as to label the new decor 'pure kitsch'. A storm in a Texas teacup, one might well say, since there had been little alteration to either the grand staircase or the Dome Bar, with their famous crystal chandeliers and handcrafted Italian marble, and the original red brick and terracotta facade had been left entirely unchanged except for a thorough cleaning and the huge white–on–black sign on the roof above the seventeenth floor which now read 'The Barragan'.

As Chuck walked toward the massive drive–through arches at the entrance he saw a tiny dust-coated rental car arrive and judder to a stop outside and a young Hispanic valet come swiftly forward to open the driver's door. He was close enough to see an old woman's hand slap the valet sharply on the wrist and slam the door shut again, barely avoiding the severance of the poor boy's thumb, and heard an indignant piping voice similar in cadence to the British comic actress Margaret Rutherford and every bit as peremptory.

"What do you think you're doing, young man?! How dare you?!"

"You want to park? I park it for you," replied the confused valet.

Chuck was just passing in front of the car and couldn't help noticing an elderly red–faced gentleman in the passenger seat fussing and fumbling with a map and a camera and other assorted travel paraphernalia and trying to pack the whole awkward jumble away into an antique green canvas rucksack with newly re-stitched leather shoulder straps.

"What's he saying, Dickie?" the woman demanded, clearly quite unable to penetrate the mystery of the young lad's very mild accent.

"Give him the keys, Ethel. He wants to park the car," the man muttered, stating the obvious in a manner only a lifetime's sufferance can attain.

Chuck didn't linger but followed two ostentatiously wealthy middle–aged Texan matrons, who had drawn up behind the splattered rental car in a spotless powder-pink Cadillac convertible and wasted no time dropping their keys into the waiting hand of another young valet, through the gold revolving doors into the hotel and it was impossible not to overhear a snatch of their conversation as well.

"Her older sister just graduated SMU with my LuAnn," the first woman drawled, "But that wasn't for her, oh no, not since she got made a beauty queen. Cute as a button and cold as a dead man's pecker."

"Why not if she gets to be the richest woman in Texas," opined the other.

"Texas shit, in the whole damn hemisphere," countered the first, dabbing a fleck of slaver from her lip with the knuckle of a jeweled finger.

"Where the heck did he get it all?"

"Who cares where, honey. Betcha never ask your sweet little Bobby Joe."

Mercifully for Chuck their invidious cackling was quickly drowned by the ambient clamor of the crowded lobby.

He passed through the bar, pausing to glance up at the world-renowned twenty–five foot wide Tiffany cut glass dome, and noticed four young men at a table laughing and speaking Russian. They looked curiously out of place but he just clocked it and continued on to the Grand Ballroom where everything was in busy preparation for 'the guaranteed highlight of the year's social calendar', tomorrow evening's finale of the annual Miss Texas Scholarship Pageant. There was a broad stage with its backdrop still far from completion with a multi–tiered bandstand for the orchestra on one side, a raised platform for the judges on the other and a long runway leading from between them to the center of the colossal room. A crew of delivery men were setting a dozen upholstered dining chairs around each of sixty-six large circular tables and electricians clambered high above the floor on catwalks focusing a barrage of lights and follow-spots.

Chuck had seen posters and billboards all over town announcing the gala. Last year's Miss Texas, the bleached blonde bombshell Beverley McIntyre, who had later been third runner-up to Miss USA, would, of course, be in attendance to surrender her diamond tiara. Tanya Tucker, back on top of the charts again, was coming to thrill everyone with some of her old time favorite country classics and being a good fun–loving kind of gal she had also graciously agreed to be one of the judges. Joining her on the podium would be the pageant's sponsor Amado Barragan and none other than Texas's own First Lady Laura Bush, high school sweetheart, ever–smiling helpmeet and beloved wife of the state's increasingly popular governor.

Chuck had been told that there were three remodeled and ultra–luxurious suites on the seventeenth floor that were always reserved for the owner and his family and special guests and could only be accessed from the hotel lobby by a private elevator that was guarded at all times but he was hoping his informant had been wrong and he could find another way.

§

After what Michael had just experienced he realized full well that scaling the ramparts of the Portillo mountain fastness and demanding his tape back was obviously idiotic and quite certain suicide yet he had still not entirely dismissed the idea.

However, the cartoons had come to an end and the little girl said she was hungry and so was he and Fernando had taken them in his car, a retired New York taxicab that he had rescued from the scrapheap and lovingly repainted and restored, to a local *taberna.* It was noisy and cramped and the furnishings didn't match but the smells wafting from the kitchen at the back were wonderful and Fernando seemed to know almost everyone who was there.

Michael had discovered on the way that the girl was Fernando's daughter, the Juanita referred to in Chuck's message, and her mother was called Marta, the same as his Hungarian wife, which Fernando and he agreed made it a very small world.

They had made their way through the crowded *taberna* to a large table at the rear and Fernando had made introductions and an older man with a long graying ponytail named Enrique had taken Juanita in his arms and hugged and kissed her and she was now sitting happily on his lap. There was a younger man also named Rafael but Michael didn't catch the names of the others.

They had all shaken hands and before Michael had uttered a syllable Enrique said, "You are not American," and everyone laughed.

"It's that obvious, mm?" he said with a mock downturn of his mouth.

"Michael is English," Fernando told them, "He is a film maker," and then added, "Everyone here is a film maker," and they all laughed again.

"What else? You're in Hollywood!" Rafael offered loudly.

"Michael was at *Nada Que Ver*. Now he has seen everything."

"It was brilliant. Stunning."

"It is our life," Enrique said with a shrug, "Soon it will be everyone's."

"Welcome to the future, Michael Englishman!" shouted Rafael.

They ordered beer, a good dark beer called Indio that Michael liked, and fajitas for Fernando and Juanita and Michael thought his stomach could use a good dose of protein and Fernando suggested *carne asada* with beans and rice and guacamole and *pico di gallo* and Michael was amused to find out that it was just salsa with a colorful name. The origin of 'rooster's beak' was hotly disputed and Enrique made the little girl laugh by holding the fingers and thumb of one hand closed and clucking and pecking up scraps of his food with it.

"We like to say Juarez is a sandwich," Enrique went on, "The bread is the First World and the Third World and we are the baloney."

The laughter around the table was more subdued this time.

"The food will make your cold feel better," Fernando said.

"I think I've already kicked it," Michael replied and confirmed his miracle cure with a dry sniff. "I was sick as a dog yesterday but I bought some pills in one of your *farmacias*. They made me throw up all over two custom's officers at the border, poor devils, but they must have worked."

The others chuckled though they were sure such a fantastic story could only be gringo exaggeration and were too polite to question further.

"Let me see them," Enrique said.

Michael found the pink plastic bag and handed it to him.

Enrique untied the bag and looked in and smelled it and then made a big show of carefully removing one of the shiny blue pills. Everyone was grinning. Enrique put the capsule down on the table and cut it in half and a thick clear oil oozed from it. He touched the oil gingerly with the end of his finger and tasted a tiny drop on his tongue.

"I will tell you why they made you sick, my friend," he said, "These pills are to clean out your ass!"

"Good lord," Michael said and joined in the laughter until he cried.

"Anybody care to try one?" he added finally, offering the bag around the table and wiping his eyes.

There were no takers.

"Hey, if it works don't knock it," Rafael said, to which Michael proposed, "I should bring them home with me and patent them," and they all laughed some more.

The food arrived and they tucked in and the mood changed and after a few delicious mouthfuls Michael turned to Fernando and asked, "Have you tried to get the photos shown anywhere else? Even in El Paso?"

Fernando was taking a bite of fajita and shook his head silently.

"No one wants to look," Enrique replied for him.

CHAPTER NINE

The sun had long since set behind the mountain when Cecilia woke herself from the grip of a terrifying dream in which Vicente had been laid out on his back under the bright lights of an operating room and was crying like a great white baby because she was tearing away his intestines with huge fangs and the assisting doctors and scrub nurses in green masks and gowns were shrieking for her to stop but their gloved hands seemed somehow impotent to reach her and she became aware of the searing soreness in her own lower belly.

Memories of the night before came flooding back. She had not slept after the aborted funeral and started on cocaine early the next day and by noon she was washing it down with more double vodka martinis. By the time the jet took off from the ranch over the darkening cornfields of Guamuchilito she had lost all perspective. During the flight she had tried to convince her mother of the truth of Vicente's death but Doña Aurora had closed her ears and wouldn't listen.

As soon as they arrived at the villa above Juarez she had launched into her brother with a vicious harangue. She accused him point blank of having ordered Vicente's murder and called him a 'loveless, chickenshit, brown–nosing assassin' who only did it so he could go on sucking up to the world's elite with impunity and her mother had started to scream.

"You should have respect for your brother! You have a sick imagination! It is you who are the murderer! You are killing me! You are killing yourself! Why? Stop her, Amado. Why does she keep saying these terrible things?"

Amado had told Doña Aurora to calm herself and come to bed and took her arm to help her up the great winding staircase.

"What right did they have to take him?" she wailed as they were climbing, "Why did they do it? He was always a good Catholic. They had no right!"

"They like to show their power, mama."

"You should not have stayed away. They would not have dared to take him if you had been there."

Cecilia was staring up at them in fury from the vestibule, still dressed in knee–length furs, swaying drunkenly back and forth while trying to kick off her heels across the marble floor.

"Ha! Tell her the truth about how much power you have! Tell her the real reason you weren't there, you cowardly fucking weasel!" she had yelled but they ignored her.

"Do not worry, mama. We will have the funeral as you want it."

"When?"

"On Sunday, mama. Do not think about it any more."

"Speak to her, Amado. Why does she say these things?"

"I don't know, mama. Come and rest. I will speak to her."

Doña Aurora had turned at the top of the stairs and looked down.

"He loves you," she said in tearful admonition, "He pays for your life and what do you do? It is you who are the murderer."

"You don't know anything! Everything he tells you is a lie! He doesn't love anyone! He killed his brother and he doesn't give a damn!"

Doña Aurora stood silent for a moment as if she were giving the words some thought but she had only the Catholic Church and her eldest surviving son left to believe in and it was impossible for her to show her back to either.

"It is you who are the liar," she had said with sad finality and had turned away and gone to bed.

Cecilia had not seen Amado for hours after that although she slammed around the villa looking for him but she had been too tired and drunk to search the grounds and besides it was too cold so she had gone up to her suite to snort some more cocaine and had watched videotape after videotape of Vicente and their time together.

At about five o'clock in the morning, as she was at last sinking beneath the waves of her addiction and finding sleep, Amado had walked into her bedroom and snapped off the television. There was blood on his hands and mouth and shirt and without a word he had dragged her to her feet and ripped away her nightclothes and thrown her on the bed. She knew exactly why he had done what he had done and what it meant.

Now she was lying naked and uncovered and shivering. She tried to stand but the pain was bad and the inner walls of her vagina were stuck together with congealed blood. She did not want the servants to see her so she couldn't call for help and forced herself to roll off the bed onto her hands and knees. Holding a torn piece of silk nightgown to her violated groin she managed to crawl into the bathroom and run a bath.

§

By the time Cecilia had cleansed her wound and risen from the soothing water Michael and Fernando were not more than a kilometer in a direct line and six kilometers by road below her boudoir.

They had bade farewell to the convivial company at the *taberna* late that afternoon and after having taken Juanita home to her mother they had gone to another one and had more beer and now they were parked in Fernando's antique yellow cab on a busy street of clubs and restaurants in the tenderloin of Juarez.

At the far end of the block they had driven past a marble–faced building with huge brass doors that looked like a bank. It was set back from the street about twenty yards and a lot of expensive cars and a long white limousine were scattered under the palm trees in front of it. There were a dozen dark–suited men lounging on the steps below the brass doors and more were strolling around among the vehicles. There was no sign but Michael had easily guessed what the building was.

"Don't tell me. It's a bank," he said.

It had made Fernando smile.

"What does he call it?"

"Barragan's. It is another name like Bastida. Now that Bastida is dead he will be Barragan."

"Tell me the two again."

"The man who died was a fiction named Florio Bastida Morales. The one who owns the nightclub calls himself Amado Barragan Fuentes. Bastida was only a drug lord. Barragan wants to be a god."

"Do you think he's there?"

"He's there. You can tell by the number of jackals outside."

Fernando had turned and stopped the car facing back in the direction of the building but far enough away so that it would not arouse suspicion if the guards saw them sitting there. He grinned and lit a cigarette.

"OK, I showed you. Now what? This man kills hundreds of people every year, Michael. I think you should forget about it."

Michael knew Fernando was right but it was too late. The beer had added fuel to his natural stubbornness and the theatrical intensity of his situation had fired the absurd delusion, if such a perfectly self–aware state of enjoyment may fairly be called delusional, that he was the latest incarnation of Philip Marlowe, Raymond Chandler's unflappable private detective, and therefore invincible. Personally Michael had always preferred Mitchum to Bogart in the role though he realized he was in the minority.

"What can they do to me? I'm just a stupid British tourist, aren't I?"

"The way you're dressed they won't even let you in the parking lot."

"One can but try. I promise you if they don't I'll give up."

"What if one of his men recognizes you?"

"I shouldn't think that's very likely. There were only two who stole the tape. He's got thousands probably."

Fernando sighed.

"Leave your bag and camera with me then. If you're carrying something and they don't know what it is they'll shoot before asking questions."

"Michael Davenport, the suicide bomber."

The joke fell flat.

"They might anyway. No one walks up to those steps. Everyone has a chauffeur."

Michael made another attempt at levity and looked at Fernando as if to say, 'Well, what about doing just that?' but it didn't work either.

"Right then," he said, summoning his nerve.

He took a deep breath and got out of the car, leaving his satchel on the seat with the camera wedged behind it for safety, then closed the door.

"Wish me luck."

"Don't forget who you're asking for. Amado Portillo is officially dead."

Michael stuck his head back in the car window and said in an atrociously inaccurate imitation of Speedy Gonzales, "*Buenas noches, amigos*, I bring *mucho* eemportant message for Señor Barragan. I think he ees here, no?"

This time his efforts elicited a tiny grudging smile.

"I'll wait for you," Fernando said.

Michael nodded gratefully and stood upright. He looked down the crowded holiday street and hesitated, feeling somehow incomplete and denuded without his accustomed baggage, then took the plunge and crossed through the slowly moving traffic toward the big brass doors.

As he walked along the other side of the street he was startled by a male falsetto voice calling out behind him.

"Hey, John Wayne, looking for me?!"

He turned and was astonished to behold a pair of fantastically attired African–American transvestite prostitutes in white makeup and heavy purple lipstick bearing down on him.

"What? Oh. Good lord. No, thank you."

They both screeched with laughter at his accent.

"Shiiiit, he ain't John Wayne."

"Noooo, he's Boney Prince Charlie!"

Michael was mesmerized by their appearance and didn't try to escape and they caught up, towering over him like two androgyne Watusi tribesmen in their six-inch stiletto heels and bouffant wigs.

"Sorry, your Highness, Carmela only likes cowboys," the first one trilled, "They have such little pricks. Me? I've got room for the whole Royal Family!"

Their painted talons were all over him.

"How much?" Michael asked coolly.

"How much can you stand, Princeypoo?" warbled the second.

"Twenty for me. Ten for Miss Carmela."

The second screwed up his face in a babyish sulking pout.

"Twenty–five for a double scoop," the first added, caressing Michael's scrotum with the long artistic fingers of his slender black hand.

"Dollars?"

"We don't work for pesos, brother," Carmela said in a sudden sarcastic basso drawl, "We're way too good."

"Good lord. For how long?"

"How long can you wait, your Nobbykins?" said the first, rubbing harder.

"Charming."

Michael decided it was time to extricate himself.

"Well, it's been fun girls but, alas, I'm promised forth," he said, nodding toward Barragan's, "My dancing partner Amado is expecting me."

The prostitute's hands leapt backward as if they had touched a snake.

Michael smiled innocently at them and whispered.

"Si. Amado Portillo. *Mio grande amigo.*"

The weird sister's eyes went instantly cold and they turned on their spikes without another word and wobbled away.

"Good lord."

Michael could see Fernando watching from the cab and shrugged as if to say, 'Oh well, to everything there is a season,' and Fernando really did laugh this time. Indeed, the brief encounter had had its fascination. Michael waved gaily and walked on.

He paused on the street outside the club. Beyond the palm trees he could see two magnificently sculpted tigers burning bright at the bottom of each ornate marble balustrade beside the steps. Six men in black suits stood smoking in the reflected light below. Michael knew very well that he could be taking his life in his hands entering this particular forest of the night and even fancied he could hear the tigers' snarl of warning but despite everything his feet began to propel him as casually as they knew how toward the doors.

Before he was a third of the way through the cars a guard moved swiftly out from behind one of them and accosted him, clamping a firm hand on his shoulder.

"Members only, *señor.*"

"How do you know I'm not a member?" Michael said indignantly. He was genuinely miffed at the man's assumption.

"You are not a member, *señor.*"

The guard's face was humorless as stone.

"Well, all right, but suppose I'm thinking of becoming one. How can I tell if I want to join the club unless you let me take a look inside?"

"Only members can go inside, *señor.*"

"But don't you see how ridiculous that is?"

The guard gave him a small push backwards.

"Steady on, old chap. All right then, I've come to see Señor Barragan. He has something of mine and I'd like to get it back."

"I have never heard of this man. Now move."

The guard pushed him again.

"What do you mean you've never heard of him. He's your boss. He owns this nightclub, doesn't he? That's his limousine, isn't it?"

"This building is owned by the mayor of Juarez, *señor.*"

"All right, well, will you take Señor Barragan a message at least and let him know I'm here."

"I told you I have never heard of this man. You have five seconds to move, *señor*, before I shoot you."

The guard was pulling a nasty–looking sidearm from his shoulder holster.

"Good lord, you don't want to do that, old chap. I can assure you

you'll regret it if you do. How do you know I'm not . . ?"

Michael was suddenly grabbed from behind by an elbow tight around his throat and a powerful arm yanked his left hand backwards and upwards into a painful lock.

"Well, well, if it is not the foolish gringo," his unseen assailant said into his ear and a waft of stinking beer and chili breath puckered his nostrils.

Michael knew without looking that Fernando had been right.

"You stole my tapes," he said, hoarse from the choke-hold but nonetheless accusatory, "And my passport. I want them back."

The thief turned Michael roughly around to face him and grasped him by both cheeks. Alas, it was the same gap–toothed perverted grin he had seen when the man slapped him.

"You want them back, *señor*? Of course. Come with me. It is no problem. I will get them for you."

He gestured with his head to the first guard who rammed his pistol into Michael's right kidney and the two of them frog-marched him towards the club.

Michael had a fleeting moment of optimism that they might actually be going to take him inside but before they got to the steps he realized it was naive. Instead they swerved past the other guards, who stared with silent malevolence but said nothing, and took him around to the rear of the building where it was almost pitch dark.

'Christ,' Michael thought, 'Is this how it ends? Mother, don't look.'

To his relief they didn't stop to shoot but hustled him straight down a flight of metal stairs and through a door into the cellar, then along a clean bright polished hall to a small windowless storage room, crammed with disused odds and ends of nightclub furniture, where they dumped him unceremoniously onto a hard wooden chair.

The gap–toothed pervert switched off the light, a single bare bulb in the ceiling that was operated from the hallway, and they both went out and locked the door. Michael assumed from their conversation that the stone–faced one had been told to stand guard.

CHAPTER TEN

Once her bath was running Cecilia hauled herself to her feet by the taps, found a bottle of codeine pills and swallowed four with an unfinished mouthful of vodka, then lowered herself slowly into the warm water and after about fifteen minutes of soaking the pain away she made a call.

"I want a new one. Now. Tonight," she said tersely and hung up.

After another hour, when nothing remained of the sting in her belly but a faint throbbing tenderness, she rose Phoenix–like from the tub, threw on a loose black shift over her still dripping nakedness, pushed moist bare feet into a pair of laceless black sneakers and, carrying her fox–fur coat over one arm, slipped out into the hallway.

As she passed her mother's suite she could hear voices and stopped to listen at the door but it was only the soundtrack of some old sentimental movie playing on the television. Doña Aurora had probably fallen asleep in front of it as usual.

Cecilia left the villa and looked to make sure Amado's limousine was not there, then took one of the golf carts the family used to get around the six hundred acres of their mountaintop estate and drove out through the wildlife compounds. The tiger's cage was nearest to the mansion and it sensed her even before she started the motor and, though it could not see her from the deep grotto where it liked to spend its nights, it got to its feet and began pacing back and forth.

The drowsy herbivores in the grassy paddock beyond calmly raised their heads to watch the passage of her headlights but, farthest away, the wolves ran to accompany the golf cart the full length of their enclosure, loping hopefully along and stopping barely an inch before their moist snouts touched the corner of the high electrified fence, whining softly with frustrated desire, their yellow eyes following her out of sight as though parting with one beloved.

Two hundred yards more along a rutted track, surrounded by a scrub of low trees at the disused end of the property, there was a scatter of tumbledown barns and sheds and pens that had once been part of a pig farm.

Since their arrival the Portillos had made little alteration to the outside but inside it was a different matter. Cecilia and Amado and Vicente had divided the area equally between them and each refurbished a separate building according to their taste. Access was strictly barred to everyone else by the security system but the three siblings knew each other's codes. In the early days they had on occasion indulged their pleasures together when the mood took them and up to now had left well enough alone when it did not.

Cecilia stopped at Amado's building first. There were always two guards and helpers waiting in the anteroom of each section night and day but they never asked questions of the family. Cecilia motioned one of them to follow her as she placed her right eye to the retinal scanner and punched in her override code and a great oaken door swung slowly open revealing a dark pentagon of empty space thirty feet in diameter. In the mahogany floor a huge star pentagram enclosed in double concentric circles with a golden goat's head at its center shimmered like a pool of brimstone. There were four other smaller but otherwise identical doors leading from it.

"Where does he keep her?" Cecilia demanded.

The helper took a bunch of heavy keys from his belt and unlocked one of the doors and Cecilia could hear the sound of someone stirring.

"Turn on the lights," she ordered and the helper did so.

The room was entirely furnished in the tasteful semblance of a Victorian parlor and a young woman, decked out in a very low cut mauve ill–fitting floor length satin evening gown, was cowering in a far corner. She was panting with fear and had clearly just risen in panic from a stuffed leather couch because the quilts that had been covering her were now lying in a heap on the carpet.

Cecilia judged that the girl could not be more than fifteen and was at least three–quarters Indian, most likely of Tarahumaran descent, but her brown skin was flushed beneath the surface with a strange mottled purplish pallor. Her eyes betrayed extreme exhaustion and were red with weeping. Her once black hair had been carelessly stained bright orange and stood out from her head in wild matted curlicues. There was blood thickly-caked around her choker.

"I'll need both of you," Cecilia said quietly.

The helper with the keys went to call the other guard and Cecilia stood in the doorway until they returned.

"Muzzle her and hold her down."

The guards quickly did as they were told. They caught the girl as she tried to run and jammed a rubber ball into her mouth and taped it shut. Then they half carried her to an antique walnut dining table and laid her on top of it and pinned her by the arms, one holding her tightly by the throat to still her.

Cecilia lifted the bottom of the girl's dress and held it out to them and the helpers pulled it up until all that it covered was her face. She was naked beneath it and there was more dried blood on her breasts. On her torso and buttocks and upper thighs were dozens of bite marks surrounded by massive bruising, not the twinned puncture of cuspids but deep semi-circular indentations made by what can only have been a complete set of ordinary human teeth, as though the flesh had been mercilessly squeezed to encompass the clench of an entire jaw. The tips of both nipples had been chewed away and the wounds were now scabbed over.

Cecilia prodded the girl's stomach. It was swollen and a fatty ripple rose below her out-popped navel.

"Give me the razor," she said and the helper obligingly placed the handle of an old-fashioned barber's cutthroat in her palm.

Without a second's hesitation Cecilia grasped the soft belly flesh firmly in her left hand and made a deep slice with the blade straight down from the navel to the clitoris. The girl moaned and writhed violently but the men held her fast and despite the buffet of wildly flailing legs Cecilia went on making cut after cut, higher and higher and deeper and deeper, until the spine was laid bare from the sternum to below the coccyx.

The girl had long since lost consciousness but her heart was still beating. Blood was spurting into the peritoneum, emptying her brain and filling the livid cavity with irregular dying gurgles. There was a clump of foetal tissue clinging to the punctured balloon of her uterus, barely discernable as a human form, and Cecilia wrenched it free and brought it around and lifted the gown from the girl's face. Her head was lolling over the end of the table and Cecilia ripped off the tape from the girl's slack mouth, fingered out the rubber stifler and stuffed the foetus in. Then she carved the blade down through the grimy creases of her neck and the heart stopped.

"Leave her just like that," Cecilia said, dropping the razor on the floor and wiping the worst of the gore from her hands on the girl's dress.

She went out and the now terrified men left the corpse exactly as she had instructed lying spread-eagled in an overflowing jumble of guts on the table and followed, turning off the lights and locking the great oak doors behind them.

By that time Cecilia was already half way around the sheds to Vicente's section. Or what used to be. There were no apprentice torturers on duty here and hadn't been for many weeks and the entry was open to an anteroom similar to the first. Cecilia brought a flashlight from the cart and repeated the same security process but this time instead of oaken doors two broad concealed panels rolled aside and an iron drawbridge fell clanking outward across the ordurous water of a moat and a portcullis set in an old stone archway rose beyond with a deafening squeal of hidden cogs.

All modernity ended at the gate. Nothing had ever been made convenient or comfortable. Nothing was clean. It was a charnel house.

One huge octagonal chamber with great rafters angling up into the gloom. The walls were rough–hewn planks lined with rusting rings that once had held the flame of oil-filled cressets. The earthen floor was covered in straw and the putrid stench of rotting flesh filled the air. Chains and ropes and manacles and a sinister array of medieval torture instruments poked from every sepulchral nook and cranny.

The broken bodies of three unfortunate young women, in various stages of decomposition and decay, were revealed one by one in the indifferent beam of Cecilia's torch. All were naked.

The first was little more than a shrivelled husk and hung suspended from the ceiling by the arms. The wrists and elbows had been knotted tightly together behind the back and then pulled upwards on a chain until the weight of the body had dislocated and torn loose the shoulder joints. Fractured ribs jutted from the torso and the skin from head to toe was covered with twin punctures precisely the width of eyeteeth but such had not been the cause. A branding tool shaped like a pitchfork dangled from a cord nearby, the thick tines of which had been filed to a lethal point and heated in a forge before being plunged unmercifully a hundred times to perforate and shock the delicate flesh. The staring holes were burned black and flaking round the edges.

A second was arched over a giant wheel where stout cables had stretched the tiny fragile body beyond breaking. The joints of the legs and arms and neck were completely separated but for ghastly strands of vein and tendon and gristle and on the surface of each segment there was the same horrendous piercing. But the third was the most difficult to behold if such inhuman sights may in any sense be comparable.

On a gigantic chopping block, grooved and splintered by the thwack of countless fearful blades, a once smooth and voluptuous young body lay twisted on its side. The hands of the corpse had been fixed motionless behind the back with curving double–ended nails, the ankles were held fast in the same manner and an enormous rusty spike had been driven sideways through both swelling young breasts and deep into the table destroying all vestige of their form in the process. Another skewered a ripe bulge of stomach in like fashion. Another had once riven the cheeks but, most horrible of all, the whole miraculous glory of the eyes and ears and face had been seared with flame so that nothing could be seen now but teeth clutching the spike and glistening charcoal bone.

One might hope that even someone so cruel as Cecilia would have been appalled but it had merely whetted her appetite. As the drawbridge rose again to hide the monstrous scene her only thought was that tomorrow she would have to reprimand the handlers for not cleaning up and taking out the trash.

She raced the golf cart around to her own domain and breezed cheerily in. She looked at her two helpers and they nodded 'yes' and she motioned them to follow. She put her eye to the retinal scanner and the third portal of the Portillo's hellish playground swung open. No override code was necessary here. This was her space, a private sanctum of her very own, something she had longed for since she had been a little brown–skinned *muchacha* sitting alone and lonely in the Sinaloa sun and at exactly the same second that Michael was being deposited on the chair in the storage closet and left to sweat it out Cecilia was closing in on her new prey.

She was a pretty well–formed bud of thirteen with red ribbons braided in her hair, wearing a light hand-knit pale pink cardigan over a simple flower–print knee-length dress, white ankle-socks and polished black shoes that fastened with a buckle. The handlers had already gagged and bound the girl against a wall but she was sobbing despite the gag. Her head hung forward looking at the floor and tears were spattering her shoes.

In contrast to the others the room was airy and bright and gaily decorated with dozens of Cecilia's paintings. Bold shiny monochrome depictions of her and her brothers' manifold crimes, not good, not even mediocre, overdone and naive by any standard but undeniably vibrant in their coloring and chillingly graphic.

It was the perfect cliché of a studio, comfortably furnished with sofas and stuffed armchairs and cut–glass lamps and all the atelier equipage so needful to a productive and dedicated artist but there was also an entire wall fitted with an elaborate entertainment system and a separate area with a well-stocked gourmet kitchen and state-of-the-art appliances.

The sight of the young girl stirred Cecilia to the boiling point. She went to her immediately and kissed away her tears and ordered the waiting assistants to untie her.

"I won't hurt you, you'll see, my pretty one," she purred but it was hardly reassuring. Perhaps she had forgotten that her shift was wet and slimy, her face still flecked with blood and her arms smeared crimson to the elbows and the girl began to shiver in uncontrollable panic as Cecilia began to undo the little pearly buttons on her sweater. She watched the stained fingers work with terrified eyes and brought up shy hands to try and stop her but Cecilia's intensity was far too powerful and the attempt was unavailing.

"Sssssh, my sweet one, I'm not going to hurt you. I love you. I'll love you and you'll love me and then I'll let you go. I promise I won't spoil you. Sssssh."

Cecilia tugged down the sleeves of the cardigan and pulled the dress off the girl's shoulders and let the garments slip to the cold tile floor, then snipped through her brassiere and thin white cotton panties with a pair of scissors.

"Now take off your shoes and socks, my darling."

The girl was shaking so violently she could barely keep her balance as she obeyed. When at last she stood upright she placed her hands over her breasts in a gesture of hopeless modesty but Cecilia brought them gently to her sides and bent to brush the stiffened nipples with her lips.

"There now, do as I bid you. I'll love you, you'll see."

She twirled the soft shred of panties into a makeshift blindfold and tied it around the girl's eyes.

The pain in her groin was returning and she took her shuddering acolyte by the hand and hurried her to a long trestle table covered with pots and tubes of paint, hundreds of brushes soaking in spattered cups, mixing boards, notebooks, sketches and all the varied paraphernalia of her avocation.

The swarthy henchmen hovered beside, waiting for their cue.

"Hold her," she said and they clasped the girl's soft helpless quivering skin with callused hands.

Cecilia was hyperventilating and nearly passing out in anticipation. She too was trembling as she selected a thin sculpting gouge from among the clutter and then swept the rest to the floor with a fierce unintelligible howl.

The girl's terrified body convulsed at the noise and Cecilia stepped quickly out of her loose black gown and lay down on the table on her back.

"Put her on top of me," she said, panting for control.

The girl still didn't struggle as the men lifted her high by the elbows and forearms and brought her down on the table like the statue of a supplicant with her knees straddling one of Cecilia's legs so they were groin to naked groin.

"Keep hold. Gently," Cecilia murmured, bringing her free hand round to caress the girl's vulva.

"I'll love you so."

After a brief moment of tenderness the other hand touched the chisel's tip just below the fresh young folds.

"Hold tight now!" she gasped and rammed the gouge with all her might into the girl's inner thigh. She lurched violently and let out a frightful strangled yelp but the gag was still in place and she was choking on it as Cecilia ratcheted the chisel viciously back and forth inside her, pivoting the curved point on bone, until it severed the femoral artery and blood suddenly spurted from the wound in a relentless horrifying stream.

"Hold her still!" Cecilia screeched, tossing the chisel away and thrusting upward with her hips, opening her labia wide with her fingers and reaching to suck every drop of healing fluid that flowed from the young girl's crotch into her violated womb. Their bodies bucked and writhed in unison as Cecilia wound her legs tight around the girl's thigh and rode it, struggling frantically to ingest each precious vital gush.

The girl's throttled gulping had slowly dwindled as she lost consciousness but Cecilia was insatiable and went on squealing and squeezing until the pulse of her evacuated heart gave a final erratic spasm and jolted to a stop.

Cecilia lay in ecstasy for a full seven minutes until her breathing calmed. She could feel the thrum of the life force flooding her loins and replenishing her inmost being in blessed molten waves as the two expressionless accomplices held the girl's sad limp beauty dutifully in place above her and amorphous coagulant puddles spread slowly outwards below the table, staining the porous clay of the tiles and enveloping the heedless objects of her art in a corrupted sticky mass.

At last she motioned them to lift the corpse and rolled to a sitting position on the edge of the table.

"Chop her into roasts and wrap them in the freezer," she said with a smile, "And clean all this shit up afterwards."

She got to her feet feeling thoroughly rejuvenated and stooped to rescue her gown from the encroaching ooze then tiptoed playfully over it and went out through the door to her shower room dribbling rivulets of virgin blood from her vagina and happily naked but for her black sneakers.

CHAPTER ELEVEN

Chuck waited until after midnight in Pantera's for Michael to show up but as he drove back to his motel he told himself it was too soon to start getting worried. Fernando could talk sense into the crazy Englishman if anyone could and they were probably just getting drunk together in some *taberna.* Chuck sure as hell didn't want to have to go looking for him. Fernando, however, was still sitting in his cab fearing the worst.

After two solid hours of cursing his stupidity, pacing three steps forward and three steps back, doing knee-bends and deep breathing exercises to try and stay calm, Michael had given up and decided to pretend the whole thing wasn't happening. He lay down across three perishingly uncomfortable hard-backed chairs using his jacket as a pillow in a stubborn attempt to get some sleep.

He had heard voices in the hallway from time to time and hammered on the door and yelled to be let out. He did genuinely have to pee and had even intimated that he might be forced to release his bowels on the floor but still no one had responded and, to make matters even worse, the copious quantity of beer he had consumed with Fernando was making him furiously thirsty.

But despite his discomfort and the grim shudder of impending doom Michael was at last able to drop off, he had taken little real rest of any kind the night before, and he was just in the middle of a delicious dream in which he was making love to a leopard–faced princess and somehow cooking goulash at the same time when suddenly the light switched on and the door opened and a man chuckled and spoke.

"Wake up, Mr. Davenport."

Michael sat bolt upright and rubbed his eyes.

"You are British. Are you on holiday?" the man asked politely.

Michael focused and looked at him. He was short and slender and balding with piercing black eyes and very dark skin. He appeared to be more Indian than Hispanic. A kind of Zapotec Charles Boyer. An unflattering cross between Benito Juarez and the Canadian pop-singer, Paul Anka. Michael had stumbled upon the monument to Juarez in the city that morning and Fernando had shown him a fifty peso banknote with the great president's portrait on it at the *taberna* and he had the briefest idiotic sensation as he stared at the man standing before him in his dinner jacket, mod wing collar and black bow tie that he had entered some kind of hallucinatory time warp.

"Yes," he replied in a feeble croak and had to spend several embarrassing seconds clearing the phlegm from his vocal chords before he could continue.

"Sorry. Excuse me, yes. Yes, English."

"And you want your tapes."

Michael could barely believe his ears.

"Oh, um, well, yes, yes I do. Well, I'm trying to complete a film you see. A film about cats, all kinds of cats, and, ah, the extraordinary way they seem to know what's going on. Beneath the surface of our little human world. And, well, I don't care about, um, anything else on the tape. I'm sure you understand. I'd just like to, well, I really have to, you see, get back the footage of the tiger. I'm assuming it was yours. Well, of course, I don't really know who you are, sir. But, as I say, if there's some way just to get that footage back I'd be very grateful. It was truly sensational."

The man smiled.

"Have you visited Juarez before?"

"No. No, never until yesterday. Well, two mornings ago now."

"How did you know where to find me?"

"Ah. Yes. Well, I, um, just happened to see the limousine parked outside and put two and two together and thought you wouldn't mind if I . ."

He had to stop and clear his throat again.

"Would you like something to drink, Mr. Davenport?"

"God yes, thank you. And, ah, I'm sorry to ask this just as we're getting on so nicely but I desperately need to go to the bathroom."

"Of course, Mr. Davenport, I apologize for keeping you waiting."

The man turned and spoke in Spanish to the two guards.

"My friends here will see to your needs. Would you do me the honor of spending the night at my villa, Mr. Davenport? It is the least I can do. We will be able to discuss the situation at more leisure. And you can meet *El Tigre* in person if you wish. Ah, but I see you are without your camera this evening. What a pity."

There was a certain ominous overtone to the invitation and Michael could see he had little choice in the matter.

"Of course. That would be delightful. Thank you."

"Good. Once you have made yourself comfortable my friends will bring you. I will greet you in twenty minutes, Mr. Davenport."

"Splendid. Thank you very much. Most kind of you," Michael said but the man had already disappeared down the polished hallway.

§

Cecilia stayed in the hot shower cleansing herself for nearly an hour and by the time she emerged her two faithful helpers had chopped up and packaged the young girl as they had been instructed and were in the anteroom again with several large white buckets filled with intestinal organs and bones and hands and feet, all the leftovers unsuitable for *haute cuisine* including the unfortunate maiden's head. A human being is very different from a cow or pig and not many truly attractive portions can be obtained from a cadaver.

"I'll take them," she said and they loaded the offal onto the back of the golf cart and she drove away.

These torturer's assistants were the most loyal of the loyal. They had to be otherwise their life expectancy would have been very short. Normally they were unmarried volunteers but a few were family men. And the job did have its perks. Not only the joys of voyeurism but sometimes an opportunity arose to take their own sadistic pleasure on a victim after the threesome had played through. This last had not been one of those occasions.

Cecilia stopped beside the fence where the wolves still waited patiently and as soon as she reached in the glove compartment for the remote that opened the double gates they began dancing with excitement and leapt around the cart in a wild frenzy as she entered. She told them to be quiet and closed the second gate and got out, calling them each to her by name and caressing them individually and then tipped the buckets in separate mounds and let them feed. She might easily have been one of them in her fox-fur coat.

The leader of the pack took the head for himself and trotted twenty yards off with it. He lay down in the spring grass holding it between his forepaws and began to lick it with the tenderness of an attentive lover. Cecilia knew that by the first light of dawn not a scrap would remain.

"Feed me to them? Fuck you, you creepy bastard," she murmured.

§

She had changed and was warming herself by the great stone fireplace in the main living room, smoking a thin Cuban cigar and sipping a second martini, when Amado came into the villa with Beverley McIntyre on his arm.

The soon to be deposed twenty–year–old beauty queen was dressed in an extremely low cut white knee–length sequined silk sheath and a chinchilla coat that almost trailed on the floor. From a distance she bore a faint resemblance to Marilyn Monroe but close up the illusion vanished. 'Shallow as a pool of dog piss' was Cecilia's unkind phrase.

They were greeted by Doña Aurora who arrived in the marble hallway as they entered. She had roused from her catnap in front of the television and been busy in the kitchen cooking her son a midnight snack.

"Come, Amado. Eat. *Tamales de camarón*. I made them myself," she said cajoling, "Just the way you like them."

Beverley rolled her big blue Texan eyes impatiently.

"It's way too late for me, honey," she drawled.

Her voice, if one could call it that, was a tinny throttled bray produced by some anatomical maladaptation far behind her molars. It was not uncommon to the area but hers was an acute case.

"Does she always pull this shit? I need my beauty sleep."

The two women had loathed each other on sight. Amado brought his new young companion to the villa for the first time just a month ago and they had seen each other only twice since but Doña Aurora knew in her maternal bones that if the McIntyres were Mexican they would be hoeing her potatoes.

"Come, Amado. They're your favorite," she said.

"We're not hungry, mama. There is another guest on the way. He will eat."

Cecilia's ears pricked up.

"You said this was my party," Beverley pouted, "I don't know where you got off inviting him."

"I told you we have a business proposition to discuss."

"But why now? It's the middle of the damn night."

"It is not your concern and would only bore you. Go to bed. You have a big day tomorrow."

"Okay, buster," she snarled, "If you're not there in ten I'm locking the fucking door," then instantly turned on a perfect winning smile and threw her arms around Amado, kissing him and pressing herself against his groin in an unsubtle bump and grind, after which the choicest flower of the Lone Star State flounced off up the great curving staircase and stuck her tongue out at Doña Aurora's back as she passed by.

"Our guest will be with us in a few minutes. Set a place for him on the *terraza*, mama. We will talk there," Amado said.

Doña Aurora held her peace and nodded and returned to her preparations in the kitchen. Since she was a tiny girl she had seen many times what happens if a woman dares to raise her voice in protest and she understood well the benefits of silence.

Amado had been aware that Cecilia was listening because he could smell her cigar and stared at her coolly as he walked into the living room.

"We agreed you would not smoke in here. Put it out."

Cecilia smiled and tossed the half–finished cigar into the fire.

"What good is the little bitch to you? You look like a fool."

§

Michael was shown to a surprisingly spotless convenience just two doors from the storage room and relieved himself as quickly as he could under the henchmen's gaze and quenched his thirst from the tap.

They led him out of the basement, reasonably politely this time, and put him into the rear of a sleek Mercedes sedan. He wished there were some way to let Fernando know. He hoped they might drive past his cab but the tinted windows of the Mercedes were quite impenetrable so it would have been to no avail.

In any case they took a back route away from the club and in minutes they were beyond the city streets and climbing rapidly up through the darkness on a winding mountain road. Michael could see glimpses of the lights below through the trees and several times as the stone–faced driver slowed a little to negotiate a hairpin curve he thought of rolling from the car and taking his chances in the underbrush. He even tried the handle surreptitiously but the lock didn't respond. Yet still there was the slimmest of possibilities that he might retrieve the tape and even live to view and edit it in the privacy of his study in Chalk Farm, though that beloved haven seemed far away indeed.

Suddenly the pale expanse of the villa appeared above them. The whole colossal edifice was bathed in the soft glow of hidden floodlights and Michael stared up at it in awe through the misty window. The lower levels were carved into the precipitous rock of the mountainside and topped with an endless marble balustrade overhung with cascades of bougainvillea and once the car had wound its way along beneath it and turned to climb the last few hundred feet he could see that it formed an immense semicircle with the outside of the arc facing the valley. Then three more floors became visible above and behind the balustrade with a broad curving terrace sweeping majestically around the entire building's length in front of them. From the terrace and spacious balconies protruding from almost every window it was clear an unobstructed panorama of the city must spread out below.

The main entrance was tucked away behind the inner curve of the villa and was as grand as that to any Roman emperor's *palazzo*. Michael could see the white limousine and a variety of other flashy vehicles in the parking circle. As at the club black–suited guards were stationed at the bottom of marble steps but the atmosphere was far less sinister here. An imposing fountain in the bull's-eye with four playful bronze dolphins leaping upwards and outwards and glistening in the water's splash completed the attempt at classical design.

The Mercedes stopped beside it and Michael's door was opened and his grinning nemesis came round and marched him over to the other men and up the steps. He told him to wait by one of the pillars and went inside, presumably to make sure it was opportune to admit him, and Michael turned and caught the look of the stone–faced driver still standing by the car and winked and wiggled his fingers at him cheekily. He could sense they were at the very top of the rise. Beyond the brightness of the immediate area the terrain appeared flattish and receded into the starlit shadows.

The gap–toothed crony came out again and took him by the elbow into the hallway past the magnificent curve of the staircase to the living room. Cecilia had just sneered at Amado for looking like a fool when the guard entered and they were both more or less in the same place except that Cecilia was now sitting by the fire on a seventeenth century chaise with her lovely bare legs folded demurely on the brocade beneath her.

The guard nodded to his boss and went back through the vestibule.

"Welcome, Mr. Davenport. Come in. Are you feeling better?"

"Yes, yes, much better, thank you," Michael replied.

It was a lie. He was sweating and his eyes weren't focusing too well either, a syndrome that often troubled him when he felt alienated. In the circumstances it was more than understandable. The unreality was overwhelming. The villa, inside and out, was impossibly like a movie set. How the devil was he supposed to act? The dapper little man welcoming him so suavely was a mass murderer with no trace of human compassion and he had not the slightest idea why he had been invited here. And who was this gorgeous creature lolling there like Cleopatra?

"Come in," Amado repeated, "We won't bite. Would you like something to drink? Come and say hello to Cecilia and then my dear mother has prepared a special repast. You must be hungry."

"Thank you. You're very kind," Michael said and managed a few unsteady paces toward them.

"Cecilia is my sister," Amado continued with a smile, "But she is a very wicked person and if I were you I would have nothing to do with her."

"There is an English expression," Cecilia purred, "About the cooking pot calling the frying pan black. I'm sure you know it."

She raised her hand languidly and Michael found himself stooping to kiss it and saying, "Enchanted."

Good lord, was this some fire-lit netherworld of ceaseless cliché?

"And do please call me Michael," he went on, unable to stop himself, in an egregious dripping tone that sounded like a bad parodist's imitation of George Sanders.

"Perhaps you will have time to get to know each other better tomorrow," Amado said, "But now we must have a little talk."

He began walking briskly toward the terrace, gesturing Michael to follow.

"It was a great pleasure to meet you, Miss . . ?"

"Fuentes," Amado cut in quickly, "Señorita Cecilia Fuentes."

"Ah yes. So sorry. *Buenas noches, señorita*," Michael said, instantly regretful of what his foolish apology might have revealed, but completing the absurdity with a gallant little bow.

There was no reply and as he turned over his shoulder for a final nod of farewell he saw that the woman's eyes had gone stone cold.

CHAPTER TWELVE

As they walked through the house to the terrace Amado gave Michael a brief and quite unnecessary rundown on the history of Mexican naming order and the confusing muddle of patronymics and matronymics. He told him their mother's *apellido paterno* had been Fuentes, that their birth names had been Perez Fuentes but they had not liked their father and he and Cecilia had for that reason chosen not to call themselves Perez but had gone their own way and she now used only Fuentes and he had taken Barragan because when he was a student at the university in Mexico City, though he was too young to have taken part personally in the so–called 'night of Tlatelolco', he had been inspired by the social activism of Daniel and Philip Berrigan, the Catholic priests who were jailed for protesting against the war in Viet Nam by pouring blood and homemade napalm on some draft cards and accused of plotting to kidnap Henry Kissinger.

Michael came out onto the terrace with the further worrying conviction that his host was not just a homicidal maniac but totally insane. What a strange load of nonsense he had spoken. Fernando had told him that Amado Portillo had a sixth grade education at best and was forty–one years old. He would therefore have been twelve in that revolutionary summer and autumn of 1968. Michael himself had only been eighteen but he remembered about the Berrigans and at the time of the tragic student massacre in Mexico City he had just begun his not very distinguished stint at the Rose Bruford School of Dramatic Art in London. His father was a lover of Shakespeare and the director of amateur productions of the Bard in the seaside village of Worthing, Michael's birthplace on the south coast of England. It was he who instilled in Michael the pride of being a Sussex man, a Saxon, and also moulded him, rather unwillingly, into a child star of sorts portraying Ariel and Launce and the young Macduff and the Fool to his Lear, all of which had led to Rose Bruford and the occasional acting job thereafter though the offers had eventually dwindled to nothing.

The terrace curved out of sight in both directions. It was lavishly adorned with exotic plants and marble tables and upholstered furniture and a swimming pool, beautifully fashioned from desert stone and floodlit from beneath, bubbled like a cauldron at its center.

Under a covered portico near the kitchen door a table with candles and wine had been elegantly set for two and a young woman in a white blouse and dark skirt was standing by to wait on them.

"I will return your tapes," Amado began, motioning Michael to sit, "But I am going to ask a favor in return."

'Ah ha, now we're getting to it,' Michael thought.

"Anything. Assuming it's within reason," he said.

"Would you care for some wine?"

Michael was feeling reckless after the idiocy of the story he had just heard and was bold enough to demur.

"I'm afraid I've got a bit of a dodgy stomach for wine just now. Do you think I might have some beer instead?"

"Of course, what kind would you prefer?"

"Well, if anything's going, I don't suppose you'd have a Guinness?"

"Chilled or room temperature?"

"You're pulling my leg . . "

"On the contrary, Mr. Davenport, I feel it is you who are pulling mine. I love Ireland. I have a country estate near the mouth of Galway Bay. It has a wonderful view of the Aran Islands."

Michael laughed out loud. He must surely have passed through Charles Dodgson's looking–glass without noticing. 'Curiouser and curiouser' were the only words to describe it.

"Good lord. Room temperature, in that case!"

Amado spoke in Spanish to the waiting girl and she gave a tiny nod and disappeared without a word into the kitchen.

"You have a certain theatrical flair, Mr. Davenport. Are you an actor?"

"People often seem to ask me that. No, I'm not. Well, not any more. Never have been really. In any serious way."

"What do you do?"

"Oh, yes, well, um, a variety of different pursuits."

"What occupies you the most?"

"Well, ah, that would be writing, I would say."

Amado's eyes narrowed.

"Are you a journalist?"

"Oh no, no, not in the sense you mean. I've never written for any of the major newspapers. No, no, I write for a magazine."

"What magazine?"

"Oh, an obscure little English thing. You would never have heard of it."

"What is it called?"

"Enigma."

"But of course I have heard of it. Its subject is occult phenomena."

Michael nearly fell off his chair.

"It is often diligent in its analysis," Amado went on earnestly, "Though, if I may say so, it has been rather blind about one subject in particular."

The young girl returned and put a pint of Guinness down in front of him and Michael took a long swallow before speaking. It was astonishingly perfect but the madness was getting deeper and darker and he didn't know whether to have a fit of the giggles or bolt and fling himself off the terrace.

"Lord, that was good," he said with genuine satisfaction, wiping a thin line of foam from his upper lip on the linen napkin, "I can't thank you enough."

He could see Amado was waiting for him to take the bait.

"And which subject is that?"

"Vampires."

Suddenly, a voice cut into the quiet of their conversation coming from one of the more distant upper balconies. Was it female? Michael couldn't say.

"I can hear y'all down there," it cooed in a bizarre strangled drawl, "There's a whole lot more party in the party girl if you wanna come up an' get it."

Amado made no comment.

"Come on, Amado," the voice continued with a whine of impatience, "You know you said this was my night. You know you did."

There followed five seconds of silence and then the voice exploded.

"OK, that's it for you bubba if you're gonna play games! I'm going to bed! I'm locking the fucking door and you can take your little Mexican dick and stick it!"

Something made of glass smashed and a door slammed shut and Michael could feel something black and ominous close inside his host but after a moment Amado took up where they had left off.

"What is your personal feeling about vampires, Mr. Davenport?"

Michael swallowed another long draught of the thick delicious liquid.

"Well, I think I have an open mind on the subject."

"What would you say if I told you I were one?"

This time Michael had to struggle with all his might to keep from jumping right out of his skin. Were they doing some kind of wacko peyote dance? But wait a minute. There was a rational explanation. The American press had called Portillo a vampire. Of course, of course, Chuck had mentioned it.

'Thank goodness,' Michael thought and found his voice again.

"I would have no reason to disbelieve you," he said calmly and smiled.

"Or believe me?"

"Yes, either. As I said, I think I have an open mind."

"We will see," his host said.

The kitchen door was opened and Doña Aurora came out followed by the young servant girl. They were both carrying covered tureens and the girl put one down in front of Michael and Doña Aurora put the other in front of Amado.

"I told you I was not hungry, mama."

The two women lifted the lids from the tureens and revealed four tamales wrapped in corn shucks with fresh slices of mango on each side.

"Eat a little, my son. You work so hard," Doña Aurora said gently and bent to kiss Amado on the cheek. "I am going to bed now. I will see you in the morning."

"*Buenas noches*, mama," he said and kissed her also.

As she went out the door again and the servant girl closed it behind them Michael thought how strange it was that the old lady had not once looked at him nor did she seem to expect any introduction.

"Eat, Mr. Davenport. My mother made them herself. They have shrimp and peas and delicate spices. I know you will like them."

"Are they a local specialty?"

"Yes, where I was born. The Sea of Cortez provides a rich harvest."

"Ah yes, the *Baja*," Michael said smoothly, as if from some profound well of knowledge that he didn't possess, "They smell wonderful."

"That is what you call it but California will be ours again, Mr. Davenport. It is only a matter of time."

Michael was sympathetic to the assertion and would have been interested to pursue it were he not already treading such uncertain water.

"Would you care for another Guinness?"

"Thank you, yes. It was amazing."

Amado got up and went to the kitchen door and spoke through it in Spanish to the unseen girl.

"Now for the favor I need," he said as he returned and sat again.

He did not touch his food but explained to Michael as he ate and drank the gist of what he wanted. His host was expected in El Paso the next evening. He had foolishly agreed to be one of the judges at the gala finale of this year's Miss Texas Beauty Pageant along with the lovely wife of the present governor of Texas who was also a good sport. The event was to take place at a hotel that he owned and had recently refurbished. The woman whose horrid voice they had just heard was his current girlfriend Beverley McIntyre, last year's queen who had subsequently been third runner-up to Miss USA, but the tiny involuntary shrug he gave as he mentioned her name gave Michael a strong sensation that the young woman's blood was the thing now foremost on his mind. It was very hard not to look for a glimpse of teeth as he spoke.

Amado then said he wanted Michael to accompany him but not to the gala. He had another meeting to attend before the pageant in his private suite. It was the real reason he was going. He needed Michael to be there dressed in a particular manner, nothing embarrassing or outlandish he assured him, merely a well-tailored business suit that he would, of course, provide. He didn't want Michael to speak at the meeting. He just needed his presence there and when it was finished he would return the tapes and his passport and Michael would be free to go. He offered no further details.

Michael was all ears but took a moment to finish the tamales and wipe his lips. He had left the mangoes.

"That was wonderful," he said, "Please thank your mother for me."

"You do not like mangoes?"

"Oh, is that what they are. I didn't quite recognize them."

"We grow over thirty varieties in Sinaloa."

"Really. Well, ah, no, of course I love mangoes. But I think I'll leave them if that's all right. They might have gone down with wine but . . "

He raised his glass and took the last taste of the Guinness, feeling much more settled now that he had eaten something. He had consumed nothing but beer since lunching with Fernando and his friends at the *taberna.*

Amado's coal-black eyes stared at him in silence, awaiting a response to his proposal.

"Yes, well now, regarding the favor, um, is it really in the nature of a favor or would you say it was more like a demand?"

"It is both, Mr. Davenport," Amado replied without a trace of irony.

Michael weighed his host without speaking for a moment. It was easy to imagine in the candle-lit flicker that he had been transported to Transylvania and was dining with some Mighty Mouse version of Count Dracula. But the man's lack of stature wouldn't make him any less venomous, probably more so Michael told himself, and besides now he knew without doubt that the well-spoken little reptile before him was completely off his chump.

"Then I have no choice but to agree," he said pleasantly.

"We all have choice, Mr. Davenport."

"Some may have more than others," Michael countered, "But nonetheless, I will be happy to oblige."

"Excellent," Amado said, pushing back his chair and rising to his feet. "And now that your more primitive appetites have been satisfied I'm sure you would like to meet *El Tigre*."

§

There were six separate suites on the topmost level of the villa that flowed through from a plush connecting corridor on the mountain side of the semicircle to their own private balconies overlooking the terrace and the broad valley of Juarez beyond, four in the center for the family and one at either end for special guests, and Cecilia watched from a window in the hallway near her door and was directly above them as Amado and Michael walked down the steps from the front entrance and got into one of the waiting golf carts and drove out past the bull's–eye and the gaily leaping dolphins into the darkness. There was no danger that he would take the one she had used because she had told the guards to have it cleaned and she knew it would now be in the maintenance garage that was used for the purpose, an outbuilding that also housed Amado's prize collection of seventeen vintage racing cars on the second floor.

She needed to know Amado's movements. It was the reason she had been waiting for him in the living room and why she had been pleased to hear the announcement of an unexpected guest. It was only a matter of hours before he would discover the revenge she had taken for his outrage and she had to be well prepared. The alternatives were fight to the death or flight but which she hadn't yet decided.

Like Beverley she had been listening to their conversation on the terrace from her balcony. She had the advantage because Beverley's suite was at the far end of the building while hers was in the center so she had been able to overhear nearly every word and she knew what her brother had asked of his guest and where he was now taking him. She couldn't believe that Amado would visit his paramour in the pig barns tonight so she was pretty sure she had at least until after the stupid beauty pageant in El Paso and possibly even Vicente's funeral in Guamuchilito on Sunday to choose her course of action.

She stood behind the curtains peering out at the mountaintop and three hundred yards distant in the shimmering moonlit shadows she could see that the lights of the golf cart had stopped by the tiger cage and she waited until Amado had shut them off before returning to her suite and mixing herself another large martini.

She had a shrewd idea why Amado needed the new arrival and wondered if she might not also find some way to use him to advantage before her brother killed him.

CHAPTER THIRTEEN

In the ninety seconds it had taken them to get from the villa to the tiger's cage Michael and Amado had not exchanged a word. If nothing else, Michael was fairly certain that he was not about to be fed to the great beast, well, not until after the meeting tomorrow in El Paso anyway, and he had enjoyed the warm night air rushing past and the approaching smell of the animals.

They got out of the golf cart and walked around the grotto's perimeter and he could hear the tiger pacing back and forth in expectation of his master and he could see ghostly flashes of its movement through the foliage below.

The grotto was roughly circular and had been excavated to a depth of twenty–five feet and was perhaps a hundred and fifty feet in diameter at its widest. It had a deep moat surrounding a large central island which had been thickly planted with a rich variety of native trees and shrubs and there was even a stream with a waterfall cascading through it. The whole area was bounded by a double tier of twelve-foot-high mesh fencing topped with coils of razor wire though it seemed quite impossible that the tiger could swim the moat and scale the sheer concrete walls to reach them.

"In the middle of the city it's the best I could do," Amado said.

They arrived at an elevator and he turned a key to open the doors.

"My associates in Colombia have an entire island of four square miles with elephants, rhinoceros, lions, herds of wildebeest and buffalo. Beautiful. Like the Garden of Eden."

They descended to the grotto level and emerged in a concrete room that was used for storage. The doors did not open directly into the tiger's lair but through some bars beyond Michael could see its shadow waiting.

"How often does he eat?" Michael asked with not so mock apprehension.

"Do not worry, Mr. Davenport, Tamur is very well fed. Unlike his wild cousins he eats twice a day."

"That's a lot of gazelle."

"Yes. But he is too lazy to kill himself. I have had him since he was a cub of one month. They must be trained by their mothers to hunt or they will never learn. I have tried. I keep a herd of grazing animals for the purpose. Red deer, sika, goral. I have tempted him with our little native javelinas and even a great northern moose but he is hopeless. The cooks slaughter his food and chop it up in big pieces for him like a baby."

"How did he get out?"

"My sister. She drove him to the river just to annoy me. It was not the first time. I told you she was not to be trusted. He sleeps in the house during the day. He likes the air conditioning. But he prefers it out here at night. Dreaming of another reality."

"I understand just how he feels."

"He knows what we have done to his world. But he is patient. Like God."

Amado opened the barred gate to the grotto.

"Come. Don't be afraid. I can tell he wants to meet you."

They went in and the tiger came to Amado and rubbed up against him like any household tabby and Amado stroked the gigantic beast gently about the head and ears and whiskers.

"Tamur, this is Mr. Davenport. He likes cats."

The tiger came to Michael and sniffed him and Michael was thrilled to the very bottom of his soul and though his knees were shaking violently he crouched in front of the enormous head and gazed in rapture at its moist pink nose and limpid yellow eyes and smelled the glorious feral musk of its breath and reached out with an adoring hand to touch the salivate fur beneath its massive jaws and the tiger let him stroke him too.

"How about a little walk with me round Primrose Hill?" he murmured.

He caught a brief glimpse of its huge fangs as the tiger gave him a friendly lick on the face and then turned and padded away into its ersatz jungle. Never in his life had he been so close to a deity. He had difficulty regaining his standing position and Amado put out a hand to steady him.

"Just like the one I've got at home," he said.

The tiger lay down under a tree and looked back at them, then started to wash its paws.

"He is unspeakably magnificent," Michael went on, unable to take his eyes away, "The biggest I've ever seen. Tamur is a marvelous name. Where did you get him? Is he Siberian? I didn't think whites could be. He's not snow-white I know. His stripes are too dark for that."

Amado looked at him with interest.

"They have become darker living here where it is so warm. I see you are well informed about tigers, Mr. Davenport. He comes from a long line all born in zoos. I can trace him back to Kubla, a registered Siberian but not white, born at Como Park in St. Paul, Minnesota. His parents had been captured in the wild and were thought to be brother and sister. Kubla was the grandfather of the famous Tony who was, of course, three–quarters Bengal. At a later date Kubla was bred to another pure Amur named Katrina from Rotterdam and it is little known that they began a line of whites at Center Hill in Florida though neither were white themselves. This would have been impossible had they not both possessed the so–called 'chinchilla' gene. An extremely unlikely occurrence as I'm sure you know. So yes, Tamur is very special. A pure white Siberian. He was a gift from a colleague in the Ukraine who obtained him by bribing an official of the zoo in Wroclaw, Poland. You will meet this person tomorrow but unfortunately you will not be able to speak with him about it because, as I've told you, you are to say nothing."

"How old is Tamur now?"

"It will be his fourth birthday in one week's time."

Amado opened the gate again and they went out but the tiger didn't raise its regal head to look nor stir from its ablutions.

As they ascended to ground level Michael asked, "Do you have other animals up here on the mountain besides the deer and, what was it you called them, Havana Gilas?"

It was a very lame attempt at a joke and Amado didn't smile.

"We do not need to keep javelinas, Mr. Davenport. They are common to the desert. Both in the United States and here."

"What kind of animal are they?"

"They are small wild pigs."

"Really. For some strange reason I've never heard of them before. So you have nothing else then besides the herd of tiger feed?"

"Only wolves. I keep a few wolves," Amado replied and they drove back to the villa in silence.

§

The gap–toothed guard showed Michael up to a private suite on the third floor, the second one for special guests at the opposite end of the long curving carpeted corridor from the glottal-clogged beauty queen, and, after unlocking it, handed him the key with a malevolently challenging smirk.

It was now ten minutes past two in the morning. Amado had told him he should enjoy a swim whenever he awoke and take breakfast on the terrace or in his suite, whichever he preferred. A tailor would come to take measurements at noon and they would leave for El Paso at three.

Despite its obvious pointlessness Michael locked the door behind him. He was almost beyond fatigue as he took in the palatial unreality of his new quarters and walked through to the bathroom for a much–needed piddle.

"You realize you're not going to get out of this alive, you fool," he scolded his reflection in the gilded mirror as he washed his hands.

It was habitual that he talk to himself aloud in such moments.

"What the devil did you think you were doing? This is not a movie! That humorless little shit is not Al Pacino! He said he was a vampire for fuck's sake and I'll bet he's a hell of a lot worse than that!"

He noticed a phone jack in the wall between the toilet and bidet but there was no phone attached to it and he went into the other rooms to look and found they all had jacks but nothing else. Well, of course, it was to be expected.

"You're a stupid bloody arsehole," he muttered, "You always have been. Gottfried and Anna will call Helen and then she'll call Marta and none of them will have a clue where you are. They'll never be able to find out what happened. How could they know about Chuck or Fernando? No, no, wait a minute, Chuck knows my name, he'll figure out how to contact them. But to do what? Look for my remains in a barrel?"

He was standing in the center of the sumptuously–furnished living room and suddenly became aware that there was a bowl of fresh fruit on the antique coffee table and six bottles of Guinness and a large bucket of ice filled with an assortment of tropical juices and sodas stood beside them with plates, napkins, two pint mugs and smaller glasses and, thanks be to heaven, the all–important church key. What angel had been thoughtful enough to place it there?

He whistled appreciatively though his nerves were so jangled he could without doubt have torn the tops off the bottles with his teeth.

"We who are about to die salute you."

He flipped open a bottle of the dark ambrosia and, after decanting it into one of the mugs, raised it high and made a toast.

"To the consolations of being offed with class."

He was actually desperate to sleep and thought this last nightcap might do the trick despite the overwhelming experiences of the day and the certitude of coming horror. But, as he took a grateful swallow and belched, a breath of wind caught the curtains at the balcony doors and an apparition wafted through them wearing only a red silk pajama top and dangling a bottle of green viscous liquid from a gold-bangled hand.

CHAPTER FOURTEEN

Cecilia put her fingers to her lips to silence him and closed the doors. She was also holding two videotapes. A strange coincidence but the floral design on the covers proclaimed, alas, they were unlikely to be his.

"So he couldn't resist telling you he was a vampire," she said scornfully.

'Well, well,' Michael thought, 'To die, to sleep no more, indeed. Vamp is more like it from the look of you. An eavesdropping dipso vamp.'

"Yes, ha ha, I assume he meant metaphorically," he replied.

What he had taken as an initial hopeful glimmer of warmth from her eyes went instantly frigid.

"No, Mr. Davenport, he did not mean that he is a vampire because he is a criminal who sucks money out of innocent drug addicts. That is a stupid idea. He is a vampire. We are a true family of vampires. Even our saintly mother though she does not know it."

'What can I possibly say to that?' Michael thought, 'A family of nutcases. Fantastic story though. Pity I won't live to write it.'

"All right, why not," he said, "OK, you're a true family of vampires. How nice."

"I will show you it is not a joke."

"Wonderful. I'm thrilled. No really, I need a good story."

"Yes, I know you are a writer. Your magazine is foolish."

"If you say so. I'm gob–smacked you both knew of it."

"We didn't. My brother likes to play games. He stole your passport in case you have forgotten. Since yesterday he knows everything about you."

Michael hadn't thought of that. Further reason to curse his gullibility.

"I have brought some proof. You can watch and then you can tell me if you still think what I say is just a story."

Cecilia walked over to a console containing a massive television and put the tapes on the video-player beside it.

"But first you are going to have a drink with me."

"Look, um, I'm quite tired actually and . . "

"You are going to die tomorrow, you silly Englishman," she said with cold finality, "Do you want to sleep away your last hours on this earth?"

Michael swallowed hard.

"Your brother said he would let me go after the meeting."

Cecilia grunted in derision.

"Don't be naive. He won't let either of us go."

"What do you mean?"

"He is going to kill me too. Maybe not tomorrow but soon enough."

"Why?"

"That is too complicated to explain. Maybe after you have seen the tapes you will understand something. Maybe there is some way that we can help each other."

"I'm all ears," Michael said.

Cecilia was pouring two stiff drinks from her bottle. Whatever it was it looked positively lethal.

"And what is that?" he asked.

"It is called Damiana. It is special to the area where we were born."

"Hm. Do I have to? I mean, it looks delicious but I'm quite happy to join you with another of these," he suggested, holding up his glass.

She took the half–finished beer, emptied it in the ice bucket and thrust the glass of opaque green liquor into his hand.

"There never seems to be much choice with you lot does there."

"You will like it," she said, "I am doing you a favor."

Michael took a trial sip. She was right. It was unique but wonderful.

"Mmm. What is it made from?"

"There are many varieties. This one is half mescal."

"Like in Under the Volcano? Hallucinogenic worm and everything?"

"Just drink it," she said dismissively, "There are more important questions you must want to ask me."

She lay back on a couch, tucking her bare feet under her in just the same coquettish way he had seen before. This time, however, she was wearing a great deal less. And she was stunningly beautiful there was no arguing that.

"Yes, indeed, I've got quite a few," he said.

"Don't be shy. I have nothing to hide."

She seemed quite genuinely oblivious of the irony. A humorless family of murderers and mad people, what luck!

"All right then, how old are you? I mean, if you're a vampire."

"If you are going to be stupid I will leave. True vampires are nothing to do with legends. We do not live forever. We are born and die like everyone else."

"OK then, were you born a vampire or did you become one?"

"I was born the way I am."

"Why are some people born vampires and not others?"

"I have no idea."

"When did you first know then? Surely you can't have known when you were a baby or even a child."

"I did not really know or understand until four years ago. Until we came here. None of us did."

"Who do you mean by 'us'?"

"Amado and Vicente. My brothers. The three of us."

"You say your mother is one also?"

"She must be."

"Because she is your mother?"

"I told you not to be stupid."

"All right then. Did you have any brothers and sisters besides Amado and Vicente?"

"Yes, seven. Four are dead."

"Are the other three vampires?"

"Maybe or maybe not. What does it matter?"

"Where are they?"

"They work the farm for us in Sinaloa."

"That's where you're from?"

Cecilia nodded and took a slender cigar case from the pocket of her shirt and lit up, inhaling deeply.

"Would you mind if I have one?" Michael asked.

He didn't normally indulge but the liquor was already making his head swim and he was starting to feel very much like the Consul in Lowry's novel. He remembered the film of it he had seen some years ago at the Piccadilly. It wasn't good at all. Even Helen could tell it wasn't the actor's fault. No, no, such things were never the poor old actor's fault though too often they take the blame. It wasn't anybody's fault really. No, as he was fond of saying, the simple fact is you have to trash any great novel to make a movie of it.

Cecilia lit a second cigar from the first and handed it to him.

"Thank you," he said and took a slightly off-balance puff.

"And what about Vicente then? Is he here at the villa?" Michael asked.

The question was disingenuous and though Cecilia couldn't be sure of it she gave him a searching look.

"No. He is dead. Amado killed him. His funeral is on Sunday."

"Good lord. Yes, I can see you're right about things coming to a head. Why would he want to kill his brother?"

"It was useful to him. He tells himself it was because Vicente had gone too far and become dangerous. You will see some of this on the tape. But the truth is he is an ambitious little shit."

"Can you explain please?"

"He wants to rub shoulders with the high and mighty."

"And Vicente was somehow in the way of that?"

"Amado is a snake trying to shed his skin. Vicente was the skin."

None of this was making much sense to him and Michael could feel the Damiana, or mescal or whatever she had called it, starting to seriously affect his hearing as well as his sight. And, despite all comfortable notions of having better judgment, he found himself leaning over the back of the couch and replenishing their glasses and thinking that this woman, humorless as she might be, perhaps a natural trait of vampires, really did look awfully tasty.

"All right then, OK," he said, "What's your real name?"

"Portillo."

"Not Fuentes."

"That was bullshit. Our mother's name was Aurora Perez Fuentes and she kept it after marriage. Our father's name was Ramon Portillo Morales. In Mexico children take the names of their grandparents so . . "

"So he is Amado Portillo."

"Of course."

"Amado Portillo Perez."

"Yes."

"I'm not sure it's good for my health to know that."

"It won't make a damn bit of difference. All right, it's time for me to ask a question."

"Please."

"What the fuck are you doing here?"

Michael gave a wry chuckle.

"Yes, yes, very good question. Well, um, actually, as I now understand it, if I'm really to believe him, it's all your fault."

Michael proceeded to tell her the story of the tiger and what Amado had said about her taking it down to the river and the tape he had made and why he wanted it back so badly and for the first time she laughed.

"It's your fault for being a stupid Englishman! Where did you think you were? By the duck pond in Hyde Park?" she scoffed, still laughing.

Michael could certainly see her point.

"So what do you think he wants me to do tomorrow?" he asked.

"Pose as someone else."

"Who?"

"I am not part of his business. I just do drugs, I don't deal them," she said and this time her laugh turned into a cough.

"And why will he want to kill me afterwards?"

"He kills everybody afterwards."

Well, all right, that was apparently the end of that line of discussion.

"OK, so try and tell me again how you know you're a vampire."

She must have been getting as squiffy as he was, he thought, because she got up and came to the armchair where he was now sitting and leaned over with her face close to his and opened her mouth wide with her fingers. She had only four front incisors in both upper and lower jaws and then there were four huge inch-wide spaces where her canines and premolars should have been. The gaps crevassed far above and below the gum lines of her other teeth and still looked extremely tender. He could now see why her mouth was so peculiar. The odd forward indentation in her cheeks had been caused by the recent excavation of a large quantity of bone.

"Take a good look," she said clumsily through tight spread lips.

"Did you just have some sort of accident?" he asked.

She closed her mouth and leaned her hands on the arms of the chair.

"You enjoy being stupid, is that it?" she said almost nose-to-nose and then pushed herself upright.

Lord, but she smelled good. The sweet perfume rising from between her breasts had overtopped her boozy ashtray breath.

"Vicente and I had beautiful fangs. Amado was jealous because he didn't and two months ago he drugged us and had them removed."

"Good lord. They look more than just removed."

"He wanted to be sure they could not grow back. Then he had the rest of Vicente's teeth yanked out when he killed him."

"Good lord, why?"

She sat again after topping up their glasses and this time he was sure she was intentionally letting him see everything between her legs. What a pity the room was spinning!

"It's time for you to look at the tapes," she said.

"Just one thing more. Did you always have fangs? I mean, when you were in school and all that?"

"No, they grew in much later."

"At what age?"

"More or less when we started to know who we were," she said.

Michael caught a welcome unsteadiness in her enunciation but the liquor was also undermining his ability to question her cryptic answers.

"OK, shoot," he said, gesturing at the screen, "What's the movie?"

She got up and went to the television and took quite a little time figuring out how to get the first tape working.

"Vicente was a film maker. Like you," she said as she was fumbling.

"Let me guess. Home movies of his romantic exploits?"

"If you like. Mostly the one Amado pretends is such a problem. He's a hypocrite. An ass-licking brown–nosing liar and hypocrite."

"But you love him."

"I don't hate him or love him. That's not what vampires do. I'm just going to try and kill him before he kills me, that's all."

She finally got the tape rolling and came and flopped down seductively on his lap and they watched the whole thing that way together. It was by far the weirdest and most disjunct experience of his life. The unbelievable horrors being revealed on the screen and the unfathomable chasm that lay between that reality and the soft warm sensual beauty of their perpetrator.

"This was nearly five months ago," Cecilia said.

In brief, it was the whole sickening event that Michael had seen depicted in Fernando's still photographs. The secret ones he had laid out on the floor at *'Nada Que Ver'*. It began in Vicente's sector of the pig barns.

Vicente and Cecilia, with a dozen or more of their helpers, all with white clown makeup on their faces and hands and dressed in the long hooded priestly robes of the Spanish Inquisition, mercilessly torturing the three young women, tearing their clothes and binding them, burning off their hair, prodding their ears and the lips of the genitals with glowing pokers and inserting them deep into the anus, drawing rivulets of blood with bites into the naked flesh, proudly showing off their huge vampire fangs and mugging for the camera as they did so.

Then the broken bleeding bodies trussed up and carelessly tossed into the back of three windowless vans and a nightmare procession of the vans and other vehicles in a pitch black desert landscape with long eerie hand–held close-ups of the terrified women unable to scream in pain through their choking gags as they bounced along and the laughing faces of their tormentors sniffing cocaine by the handful and swilling mescal.

Then the motorcade's arrival below the eyeless petroglyphs, the lighting of hundreds of flaming brands, the laying out of the crosses on the sand, the lashing of the women to them by the neck and a ridiculous Medieval ceremony with sprinkled holy water and gently swaying thuribles and the thick smoke of burning incense wafting in clouds around them as Vicente and Cecilia went on with their unbelievable savagery.

They began by slowly impaling the women one by one, taking great care not to kill them in the process. The first with two thin spikes driven straight through the lower belly inside each hip, the second upward through each armpit with short stout swords that separated the shoulder joints, the third with heavy nails through both elbows and knees. Incredibly, though their pain must have been beyond bearing, they were all still conscious. Then Vicente took a sharp knife and fell upon the first and pinned her weakly flailing arms and sliced away her breasts and flung them on the ground. Cecilia tore out the eyes of the second with her thumbs and held them up to the infinite starlit sky like a prize and they each swallowed one. Then Vicente drove the sharpened handle of a broom up into the vagina of the third and maneuvered it slowly and carefully through her blank but still staring body until the tip emerged from the superclavicular fossa on the right side of her neck and occasioned wild congratulatory ululation and applause.

Then the whole screeching blood-soaked mob lifted the third cross high and carried it to a deep hole below the expressionless petroglyphs and buried the lower half in the sand. They completed their grotesque parody by erecting the other two poles slightly lower to the right and left and then danced and howled like rabid wolves around Golgotha.

There the first tape ended and Cecilia got up and put in the second. It is an understatement of galactic proportion to say Michael was utterly aghast and sickened but the liquor had numbed his true emotional response and he felt strangely calm as though he had been hypnotized.

"About six weeks later a group of Dutch university students looking for a back route into the *Zona del Silenzio* stumbled across it and called the police. Amado was furious with us. It put him in danger he said. He uses it as his excuse for killing Vicente. But he doesn't give a shit about the police. Why should he? They love his money. He was just afraid it might affect his sad little ambitions."

"What ambitions are those exactly?" Michael asked.

"I told you. The elite world. He'd give his eyeteeth to get into it."

Michael was amazed she never seemed to get her own jokes. Either that or she would have made a very good card player.

"You mean he was worried, whoever the elite are, they might not approve of such activities?" he asked incredulously. The preposterousness of the question was intentional but again she seemed oblivious.

"I told you it was pathetic," she answered and continued earnestly, "As far as I know they'd love it."

What in the name of holy hell was she talking about? A secret coterie of ghouls? Were such creatures yet living on this planet? Impalement? Crucifixion? An elite world of what? Super-vampires?

"And what pray tell is the *Zona del Silenzio*?" Michael asked, not certain if he was actually changing the subject.

"It's in the desert south of Chihuahua. People think it has magic. You know, like Atlantis or the Bermuda Triangle. UFOs land there. Water runs uphill. People disappear. The usual crap."

"Ah yes, now I remember. The magazine did a piece about it."

"It kills me the nonsense some people will believe."

It was all Michael could do to refrain from shrieking. How was it possible she still maintained a straight face?

"Amado doesn't know I have this," she said as the second tape started to play.

Michael wasn't sure he could take any more but the liquor had glued him to his seat and paralyzed his will. Cecilia didn't sit with him this time but filled their glasses and paced back and forth smoking as they watched.

"After the little sonofabitch had us drugged and his surgeon chiseled out our beautiful teeth Vicente set up some hidden cameras. This was put together from bits and pieces taken over a whole month."

What he had captured took place almost entirely in the model Victorian parlor at the pig barns though Michael had thus far no clue to its existence. When the sequences began the young Tarahumaran girl who Cecilia had just murdered had already been in Amado's clutches for at least two months.

At the beginning he was decked out in a cheesy vampire costume that any child might wear on Halloween and the first fifteen minutes were only of him and the girl. Sometimes she wore the satin gown but mostly she was naked and being whipped across the breasts or on the shaved skin around her labia with a thinly-strung black flail or hung upside down by the feet with an electrified pessary jolting her frail body or being nipped about the neck until blood flowed or being choked with white gloved hands until her eyes bulged wide and her face went purple or bent double over a wing–backed chair while a full bottle of tequila was decanted into her anus or on one occasion deeply violated there with a sculpted crucifix and any number of other revoltingly infantile pranks. It was often difficult to tell exactly what was happening because of the static positions of the cameras but the girl was never gagged and her screams on the soundtrack were eloquent testament to her suffering.

There followed another brief sequence in which Amado was dressed in the modern attire of an ordinary Catholic cleric and a dozen other men were in the parlor gang–raping the girl in the mouth as he watched. And then another in which Amado brought the tiger to the room and left her alone with it, naked and bleeding and chained to a wall. The great beast showed little interest other than an initial sniff of her loins but the girl's terror was so overpowering as it padded back and forth examining this new territory that her breath stopped altogether and Amado had to come in again and slap her on the face to revive her.

In the final sequence there was no sound for some reason and the room was different. During it Michael noticed that Cecilia stopped her own pacing and was paying close attention. Amado was in everyday clothes. The girl was in her awful dress again but tied to an ordinary chair and forced to watch as a group of Amado's black–suited henchmen dragged in two male victims who were already bleeding about the eyes and mouth. The men were stripped, gagged and trussed like sausages then raised on pulleys and slowly lowered feet first into barrels of acid. Every time the girl turned her head away from the sight of their helplessly struggling bodies Amado would beat her viciously about the temples and hold her eyes open with his fingers.

"They were two Russian drug dealers," Cecilia said as the tape ended and she pressed rewind, "Amado thought Vicente had bribed them to kill him but he found out it wasn't true. Now he is in trouble with the Russians. He wants to make a business deal with them but he has some explaining to do. Maybe that is why he wants you at the meeting tomorrow."

Michael didn't really feel like discussing Amado's problems after what he had just seen. He was yearning with all his heart to be back at the flat in Chalk Farm having a quiet cup of tea with Flossie on his lap and never to go out again.

"I'm sure I couldn't say," he said in a tired distant voice.

She came and looked at him.

"Did you find it shocking?"

He glared back at her.

"Oh, a wee bit more than that."

"What in particular?"

"Nothing in particular. All of it. You are unspeakably vile."

"I know," she said as if it were a compliment, "So now, how would you like to have your big English cock sucked by a vampire?"

God, it was appallingly true. He had got an erection as she was sitting on his lap during the first tape. He had tried to stop it happening but it had stayed hard for a long time. He told himself it was a natural reaction to the warmth of her femininity but he knew if he were to be totally honest he couldn't deny that the cruelty he was watching had also been something to do with it. There was a revolting vicarious pleasure buried deep within the pain. An atavism that lurked beneath the cobweb veil of civilized conscience powerful enough to subvert the sense of horror and vaporize compassion.

"Christ Almighty," he exploded, "I just saw you eat a woman's eyeball!"

"I cannot help what I am. Vampires do not feel sympathy. We enjoy what we do. We are having fun. What about you? Don't you want one last touch of a woman before you die?"

She unbuttoned her pajama top and let it fall to the floor, then got on her knees before him and unzipped his fly.

"I promise I won't chew it off," she said.

Much as Michael would have liked to pick her up and throw her out the door he didn't and succumbed as she coaxed his penis from its hiding place and kissed it until it was fully engorged with blood and then put it in her mouth.

'For god's sake don't watch me, mother,' he said to himself, 'I've joined the soulless ranks of the undead.'

As Cecilia sucked him to a powerful orgasm and hungrily swallowed each ecstatic spurt an endless stream of horrid images from the tapes flowed through Michael's reeling mind.

What is humanity? What are we all? Soulless carnival tricksters who make morality appear and disappear at will like a white rabbit from a top hat?

She let their excitement ebb and then got up and sat naked on his lap and put her arms around his neck and kissed his ear.

"Vampires do a lot of things," she whispered, "Now I'm going to bed."

He found himself stopping her by the hand as she got up.

"Don't you want one last touch of a man before you die?"

"I'm indisposed," she replied matter-of-factly.

He could only assume the obvious and let it drop but drew her glorious body close once more and kissed her breasts.

"What about helping each other not to die then? What about that?"

"I'll see you in the morning," she said and pulled away and picked up her nightshirt from the floor. She draped it over her shoulders and went to collect the tapes, then walked to the door and listened and opened it a crack and, satisfied no guards were stationed outside, disappeared into the silent hallway.

Michael stared at the door in a daze and took a last sip of the green liquor, fascinated by the swirl of its different densities and shades. What the hell was it? Some ancient aphrodisiac as well as everything else? He picked up the empty bottle and tipped it and shook a fat dead larva into his palm. He knew what it was. This was hardly his first experience with tequila. Tequilas are mescal. Mescal is made from agave cactus. It was a 'maggie' worm. What did they call the good ones, red goose-somethings? Goose-anuses, was it? No. He held the worm between his fingers and gazed lovingly at it for a few moments.

"Gone pale with death, my girl?" he enquired tenderly.

He popped it into his mouth and swallowed and sat motionless with the room whirling round his head wondering if the whole phantasmagoric evening had been real.

CHAPTER FIFTEEN

At just about the same time that Cecilia left Michael's suite Fernando was awakened by two policemen tapping on the window of his cab. He had been dozing on and off for hours and a faint dawn light was in the eastern sky. The streets were nearly deserted now and they told him to move along.

It was only a few minutes drive to the tiny second–floor apartment where he and his beloved Marta and Juanita lived and when he tiptoed in he found them asleep together in the bedroom.

"Where is the Englishman?" Marta whispered.

"I don't know. Sssh. Go back to sleep. Wake me at seven."

He crawled beneath the covers in his clothes and kissed Juanita softly on the forehead and fell into a deep dreamless slumber.

Marta woke him at seven as he asked and he went immediately to the phone and made enquiries about the number for any Charles Bowman in Texas. He called ten or more that were wrong but finally found Chuck's sister Laurie at the farm in Sweetwater.

"Has something bad happened?" she asked before Fernando had a chance to find out if he was talking to the right person.

"No, nothing," he reassured her, "He sent someone to my gallery in Juarez with a message but he didn't know where Chuck was staying. We are old friends and I would like to see him again. Do you know where he might be?"

"He didn't tell me. But I know he doesn't have much money so it's gotta be someplace cheap."

"What kind of car does he drive?" Fernando asked.

"A dirty old Ford pickup," she replied.

"Do you know the plate number?"

There was silence for a moment as she thought about it.

"No, sorry, I don't. And I can't ask our dad 'cause he doesn't talk no more. But I'll tell you what, it's light green and covered with mud. There's a great big old dent in the driver door and another in the rear. And, oh yeah, the steering wheel should have a cowhide cover. I gave it to him last Christmas. I hope that's some help."

"I hope so too. Thanks," Fernando said.

"If you find him tell him to come on home and not to do anything stupid, will you please?"

"I will. Do you know why he came to El Paso?"

"Has to be something to do with the bastard that killed his son that much I'm sure. He hasn't set foot there in the two years since. I'm worried about him so please, if you find him, you tell him to come home."

"I will."

"What was your name again?"

"Fernando Rios."

"Did you work for the damn DEA too?"

"No, I'm a photographer," Fernando replied, "I used to take pictures for him sometimes when he was in Juarez, that's all. That's how we met."

"Well, nice talking to you, Fernando. Will you at least tell Chuck to call me if you find him?"

"I will."

"And tell him I love him."

"I will."

"Good luck."

"Thanks."

"Oh, yeah, one more thing. You probably would have figured this anyway but he'll be in a motel. He doesn't like hotels where he can't park his truck right by the door."

"Yes, I remember that, thanks," Fernando said and hung up the phone.

He grabbed a coffee from the stove in the kitchen and a bite of cold quesadilla and told Marta that he had to go to El Paso.

"You can both come if you want but we have to leave now."

Marta did not have to go to the *maquiladora* because after working there diligently for over fifteen years reassembling and reconditioning used outboard motors she was allowed both Saturday and Sunday free. The minimum wage in Mexico at that time was twenty-five pesos a day but you could make fifty pesos a day in the *maquiladores*. It was why half the people of Chihuahua state had come to live in Juarez. Marta was now making two hundred and seventy-five pesos for her five-day, fifty-hour week. It would buy thirty–one dollars at the bank.

"I have to find Chuck Bowman."

Juanita said she knew who *Tio* Chuck was even though she had been only two years and a few months old when she had last seen him and she got excited about seeing him again and they decided to go together. They thought it wasn't bad because it took less than an hour at the border crossing and while they were waiting Fernando told them about Michael and why he now had to find their old friend.

First they went to Pantera's where Fernando asked if anyone knew where Chuck was staying. Of course no one did but after a couple of unsuccessful tries at the Super 8 and the EconoSuites on South Mesa they had driven out South Desert Street to the Days Inn and got lucky. They spotted the pickup under one of the three tall palm trees in the otherwise barren parking lot right in front of the door to room number 105.

Fernando knocked and when Chuck answered he could tell right away from the expression on his old friend's face that he hadn't been able to talk any sense into the crazy Englishman either and that it was time to get worried. When Juanita saw him she got out of the cab and ran to him and he lifted her in the air and gave her a bear hug and kissed her mother on the cheeks and said, "It's been too long, *amigos*," and they all went into his room and Fernando told him what had happened.

"I think Señor Davenport has found himself some big trouble," Fernando said in conclusion.

"Sure does look like it," Chuck concurred.

"I've got his camera and wallet and everything in the car."

"He just couldn't stop obsessing about that damn tape. I thought once he took a look at the stuff in your gallery he'd give up on the idea."

"I tried to talk him out of it, believe me, but he wouldn't listen."

"Well, maybe he'll be needing them and maybe he won't. It's a son of a bitch but I've got a feeling he just might be wacky enough to get out of this the same way he got himself in. If he's still alive Portillo will be wanting to get rid of him that's for sure."

The two men grinned.

"It's hard to imagine them together," Fernando agreed.

"But we don't know if Michael got that far."

"No."

The ugly possibilities were all too obvious.

"Well," Chuck sighed, "There's not a whole lot we can do right now."

"What about the El Paso police?"

"They won't lift a finger either. They stopped listening to me a long time ago. But Portillo will be over this side tonight. He's judging the latest Miss Texas beauty thing at his hotel."

They both grimaced at the irony.

"Along with Laura damn Bushwhacker no less. Scheming bastard. What a sick joke. We'll just have to keep an eye on it and see what happens."

"You think he might bring Michael with him?"

"I doubt it but it's possible."

There was a brief silence. Chuck stood by the window looking out.

"Why are you in El Paso, Chuck?" Marta asked with concern.

She had overheard the end of Fernando's conversation with Laurie.

"Nothing special."

"Your sister was worried about you."

"She wanted you to call," Fernando added.

"Yeah, I'll do that."

"Please tell me, old friend, you are not here to do something stupid."

Chuck turned and looked at them squarely.

"I'm not. I promise. Maybe the best thing will be for you to take Marta and Juanita home and then come back yourself later if you want and keep watch at the entrance of the hotel. There's a helipad on the roof but he probably won't turn up that way. He likes parading his phony identity."

"Will you join me?"

"I'll try. I'm kind of busy tonight but I'll try. If there's no sign of Michael maybe we can figure out something else tomorrow."

"Like what?"

"I don't know. Call the British embassy?"

§

As Chuck suggested they all go and get some breakfast there was a knock on the door of Michael's suite and after a second knock a maid came in. It was exactly ten o'clock and Michael was fast asleep on the floor beside the armchair where he had swallowed the worm. He made a disgracefully disheveled sight lying there on his back with his belt undone and his fly still open, an empty bottle on the carpet by his hand and snoring away like a grampus.

The maid walked to the balcony doors and opened them wide and then came and shook him gently by the shoulder. On the third shake he stirred and peered at her through red-rimmed eyes.

"Señor Davenport," she said politely, "Señorita Perez asks if you will have breakfast with her by the swimming pool."

It took Michael several seconds to grasp where he was and the phrase that involuntarily escaped his lips, "Thou art a soul in bliss," didn't make any sense at all to the puzzled maid but as the full horror of his situation came crashing back upon him how apt the words were. He was about to die!

"Oh," he murmured and was just on the verge of saying, 'Good lord, no,' when, of course, he remembered that at some point during the unreal sozzle of last night the wonderful dreadful monster of a vampiress, ogress, tigress, if any words at all were adequate to describe her, had talked about them helping each other to survive and instead he replied, "Oh, yes, um, give me a minute, yes, tell her in fifteen minutes. Where did you say?"

"The *señorita* is waiting for you on the *terraza*."

"Oh, yes, thank you, tell her I'll be there as soon as, um, possible."

"I will tell her," the maid said and went out the door.

Michael lay still for a few minutes gathering himself and became aware of a monotonous drone, the sound of a plane getting closer and closer.

§

Amado and Doña Aurora were standing on the runway as the executive jet carrying Vicente's body from Mexico City for the second time in four days landed and came to a stop and the flower–embossed silver coffin was unloaded.

"What if it is not him, Amado?" she said, "I do not trust them."

"We will bring him to the villa and I will look."

"We must be sure."

"Do not worry, mama, I will make sure."

Doña Aurora started to sob.

"I cannot bear to see what they have done."

Amado put his arm around her and wiped her tears with his thumb.

"I know, mama," he said gently, "We will take him home tomorrow."

§

Michael was just passing the front entrance of the villa on his way to the pool, having relieved himself with understandable difficulty, taken a quick hot and cold shower and brushed his teeth and shaved. He had found everything he needed for the purpose laid out neatly in the bathroom, another miracle he had been too preoccupied to notice the night before.

A black windowless van with the coffin inside came slowly around the bull's–eye into the parking circle followed by the white limousine and drew up by the steps. Michael lingered for a moment and watched through the door long enough to see Doña Aurora and Amado get out of the limousine and the casket being removed from the van but he was well aware that in his present decidedly tricky situation the less he appeared to know the better and before they all came in he walked briskly through the vestibule and out the other side of the building onto the terrace. He was barefoot and had donned the thick white bathrobe that had been provided, leaving his own soiled and sweaty clothes in the suite. The whole place was so much like a five star hotel he assumed the maid would find them and have them cleaned.

Cecilia was sunbathing by the pool, stretched out on a cushioned chaise with a large straw hat covering her face, wearing only the lower half of a golden yellow bikini thong. Michael stopped to look. How was it possible that someone so ravishingly beautiful could be so remorselessly cold and cruel at the same time? Ah yes, he thought glumly, the inscrutable paradox of our maladjusted species.

"Don't start getting ideas, Englishman," she said without looking up and without a trace of coyness.

It startled him from his momentary reverie.

"Did you rest well?"

"Yes, too well probably," he replied, "Good morning. Stunning day."

"We have a lot of sunshine here."

"Yes. Marvelous for me. Wonderfully hot. In London at this time of year it's always gray and gloomy. That's why I like to get away."

"And how is your vacation going so far?"

"Hmm. Not exactly as planned."

He was about to comment that, from his understanding of the literature, vampires were not supposed to thrive in sunlight but just then the same young woman who had served him the night before came from the kitchen door with a breakfast tray and laid out the contents on a table near Cecilia under the shade of a broad umbrella.

"It's for you," Cecilia said without removing the hat from her eyes, "I never eat in the morning."

"All I really want is a cup of tea."

"It's there. Yuccch. I can smell it."

"Can you? Good lord. I can't."

Michael walked over and examined the table setting and indeed there was a teapot and a jug of fresh cream and cubes of sugar in a bowl with silver sugar tongs and a good size cup and saucer and silver cutlery and a napkin in a silver napkin ring and six slices of toast in a silver toast rack and butter in a tub of ice and a heaping dish of marmalade and, wonder of wonders, an unopened bottle of HP sauce. A silver warming-dome glistened in their midst and Michael lifted it and his astonishment grew even more. Beneath it lay a platter with three steaming fried eggs sunny side up and English sausages and thick rashers of lean bacon and baked beans and fried tomatoes. It looked so impossibly delicious that it almost made him vomit and he put the lid back on.

"Good lord."

He poured himself a cup of tea and stirred in plenty of cream and three lumps of sugar and sat in the sunshine on a deck chair beside the imperturbable devil–goddess with the hope that his stomach would soon settle enough for him to enjoy a valedictory breakfast.

"Aren't you hungry?" she asked.

"I'll just have the tea first."

"Take a swim. It will refresh you."

He wasn't wearing anything beneath the bathrobe and she read his mind.

"Go naked. What do you care?"

"Well, I don't really. My friends in Los Angeles, the ones I should be staying with tonight if I weren't going to be dead, belong to a naturist resort called the Elysian Fields. I used to go there with them. Rather funny actually."

As usual she didn't get the joke and he took a long swallow of tea.

"Yes, well," he began in a low voice after clearing his throat, "I don't think we've got a lot of time to think about this so I would be very interested to know what you meant last night when you said we might help each other?"

Cecilia got up and walked into the shade by the table in order to scan the house and make sure Amado wasn't anywhere in sight, then turned to Michael.

"I have dubs of the two Russians being killed," she said quietly, "On small cassettes. We will both take a copy. If we are meeting who I think we are meeting they could be very useful."

"Are you coming? I thought you said you weren't part of it."

"He doesn't tell me anything but sometimes, if the people are important enough, I serve his purpose. He wants me there today."

"So, what?" Michael asked, "You mean they could be Russian bosses who would like to know how their men really died?"

"Perhaps, if we play our cards well, they will kill him for us," she said and disappeared without a splash into the pool.

Well, it was a ray of hope at least, however minuscule. He finished his tea and thought 'Why not?' and just as he dropped his robe and was diving in after her that hideous voice rang out.

"Hey, skinny party, skinny party, wait for me!"

Michael caught a glimpse of blonde hair and huge red butterfly sequined sunglasses before he hit the water. Three seconds later he surfaced and Beverley had already thrown off her clothes and was jumping up and down stark naked on the diving board. Her perfect skin was much fairer and her body considerably more voluptuous than Cecilia's though it lacked the supple feline grace and for some obscure reason Michael had never been a big fan of pink nipples.

'Good lord, can this one be a vampire too?' he wondered before it dawned on him who she must be.

"Cannonball!" shrieked the beauty queen as she took a last soaring bounce and folded her knees tight into those delightfully bobbling bosoms and propelled herself into the pool right on top of him, nearly breaking his neck and drowning him in the process. When they came up again they were face to face.

"Gee, I sure hope I didn't hurt you," she giggled, "I'm Beverley."

"No, no, of course not. What fun!" he spluttered, choking on the water, wiping his eyes and struggling not to curse.

"Oh, I know who you are!" she exclaimed, "You're the fucking Englishman who ruined my party. But I forgive you coz you're so cute."

And with that she popped him on the end of the nose with her forefinger and swam away and all he could think of was signing her up for voice lessons. Cecilia was already out of the pool and drying herself as Michael became aware that Amado had arrived and was sitting in the shade by the breakfast table. He was dressed in a white sport shirt and tailored slacks and wearing dark glasses.

"I see you have made each other's acquaintance," he said coolly.

'Brilliant,' Michael thought, 'Now he's going to kill me twice for messing with his girlfriend.' Beverley was splashing up and down the entire length of the pool with a powerfully professional backstroke. "Come on in, sugar, the water's fine!" she yelled, knowing full well her Latin lover hated swimming.

Cecilia had covered herself in a golden yellow robe and was returning to the villa without a word. There being no alternative Michael put a brave face on it and hoisted himself out. He could feel Amado's eyes enjoying his discomfort as he picked up his dressing gown.

"Leaving so soon, honey pie?" the adenoidal siren sang from behind him, "Aw, and we were having such a good time."

Michael turned toward the voice but made no response, then wrapped the gown around his waist in as casual a manner as possible and came to sit at the table. He poured another cup of tea, lifted the silver lid again and began to eat.

"There is another thing I should mention," Amado said.

"Oh yes?"

"Yes. As well as the suit of clothes and shoes we will have to dye your hair. It will be temporary. I hope you don't mind."

Michael's own hair was light brown and graying at the temples.

"Would it make any difference if I did?" he asked.

"Come now, Mr. Davenport, I find it is always best to be civil."

What in blazes could he say to that?

"So you want me to impersonate someone in particular then?"

"It is not necessary for you to know who it is. You will hear me introduce you to my clients with a name. It will not mean anything to you. You will nod politely when I do. When I say *'si'* you will repeat the word as if you agree. When I say *'no'* you will do the same as if you do not. And in both cases only if I turn to look at you. That is all. If you attempt to say or do anything else you will be killed. But if all goes well I promise

I will return your belongings and make generous restitution for the inconvenience you have suffered. It is a very simple bargain, is it not?"

"Very simple."

"My brother arrived this morning," Amado went on pleasantly, "When you have finished your breakfast I will take you to see him."

Michael wondered why on earth Amado would want that, he had never said a word about any brother, all that Michael knew about Vicente had come from either Chuck or Fernando or Cecilia. Perhaps he had some obscure need to prove they really were *'nosferatu'*, the mythical 'plague–carriers' that they seemed so genuinely to believe. Or was it something even more sinister?

"Is your brother coming to the meeting too?" he asked innocently.

Amado stared at him for a moment as if he didn't believe the pretense.

"My brother is dead."

"Oh, is that so, I'm sorry. Yes, I thought I saw a coffin in the courtyard this morning."

"We will bury him at our home in Sinaloa tomorrow."

"May I ask why you want me to see his corpse?"

"It may be instructive," came the terse reply.

Beverley had tired of cavorting like a mermaid and was coming up the steps. The word that occurred to Michael as they watched her was 'Rubenesque'. It was surprising she had become a beauty queen. Not that she wasn't beautiful, she was and she knew it standing unabashedly in front of them drying herself, but in an age of manufactured fads and marketing and the witless worship of the super-skeletal female she seemed altogether too curvaceous.

'Thank god she isn't sporting an extra nipple,' he mused, 'But why should she if the bitch–goddess wasn't. No outward signs nor new moon births, defects or cauls betray these bloodsuckers, no, only damn big teeth. And in the head honcho's case no obvious clue at all. Or could he be the seventh son of a seventh son?'

When Beverley had finished drying she sat down at the table beside him. She was still completely naked and was clearly trying to annoy Amado because she gave him a sly smile and stole two pieces of bacon from Michael's plate and sat there nibbling on them like Bugs Bunny with one heel up on his chair so he couldn't avoid admiring the pale pink parted lips of her honey pot.

'Not exactly the beginning of a beautiful friendship,' Michael thought, 'But then you never know.'

"God, it's going to take them for fucking ever to fix my hair," Beverley groaned, pulling idly at her damp straggly locks.

"A car is waiting to take you when you're ready," Amado said.

"Aw, sugar, couldn't they bring my people here?" she whined, "Don't you think it's important everyone sees us coming in together?"

"Normally yes, but not today."

There was a growing iciness in his voice. She looked at him and pouted and Michael thought he caught her wondering whether or not to turn on the tears but instead she dipped her fingertips into the butter dish and flicked a few drops of ice water in Amado's face. Then she got up from the chair and bellowed at him like a fishwife.

"Well, I don't know what the fuck is wrong with you lately, Amado, but I swear you seem just determined to piss me off!"

The rosy peach of her cheeks had turned fulminous red and Michael was perfectly positioned to admire a spectacular rear view of swiveling *glutei* as she stormed away.

He took a final forkful of baked beans.

"I've been thinking about what you said yesterday," he ventured once he had chewed and swallowed, "Do you mind if I ask a few questions?"

"It depends on the subject."

"Are there any other vampires in the family besides yourself?"

"Yes. Both my brother and sister."

"Anyone else?"

"Not as far as I know."

"Are they . . well, I should say 'were' in your brother's case . . aware of it?"

"Of course. When you are a vampire you know it, believe me."

"Yes, I'm sure. Rather silly in retrospect. And how may I ask, if it's not too personal, does this vampirism manifest itself?"

"It is not too personal but it is our secret."

Michael nodded while methodically wiping up the smears of egg yolk and bean sauce from his plate with a third slice of toast.

"How old was your brother and how did he die? Forgive me but most people think vampires live forever."

"We don't," Amado said curtly, "We are as fragile and mortal as everyone else. My brother was very fat and very vain. He died because he was too lazy to diet and stupid enough to insist on plastic surgery instead. The doctors told him his heart might not be able to withstand such invasive procedure. Liposuction to remove four gallons of tissue that was nothing more than the deserved result of his selfish overindulgence. He was only thirty–six. It has caused great sadness for our mother. He was a beautiful boy."

Michael started to wonder if Amado was asking him to impersonate the newly evacuated Vicente at this meeting. Was that the reason he wanted him to look at the corpse? Was Amado going to lay the blame on him for the Russian hit men's death? Was he being set up as a sacrificial offering? Was that why Cecilia had mentioned the cassettes? In such perilous circumstances he could surely do no further harm by trying to find out.

"I'm getting a strange feeling it's him you want me to play. Am I crazy?"

Amado gave him another odd look.

"It is both crazy and ridiculous. He is dead."

"Ah yes, quite ridiculous, I do see that. I suppose I thought you could be meeting some, ah, clients who you wanted to make believe he was still alive."

"You think too much."

Amado rose to his feet.

"I am just a businessman, Mr. Davenport. I told you never to listen to my sister."

Michael nearly choked on his last sip of tea.

"I've only spoken with her for a few minutes this morning," he said, "And I promise you she didn't say anything about the meeting."

"She is a liar and a witch. You are a fool if you believe a word she says."

Michael dabbed his lips with the napkin, then rolled it and replaced it in the silver ring and stood also.

"Will I be all right like this?" he asked, pulling the white gown on fully and tying the belt, "Do I need to get my shoes?"

"You will find an adequate pair of slippers in your left pocket. We won't be long."

Amado turned and walked briskly toward the villa. Michael did his best to keep up, hopping awkwardly to pull the slippers on at the same time, and he thought he caught a glimpse of Cecilia looking down from her balcony as they went in.

As they crossed the vestibule Michael was thrilled to see four enormous furry paws and a long striped tail sticking out from either end of a twelve–foot couch in the cool air of the living room.

'Only vampire women and mad English men go out in the noonday sun, dogs and tigers have more sense,' he sang to himself, rubbishing the old Noel Coward lyric, and chuckled.

They took the elevator down to the lowest level of the villa.

"We have a hundred and thirty-seven servants," Amado informed him as they descended, "Most live on the floors we are passing and they live very well."

"I'm sure," Michael responded in a suitably sycophantic tone.

They got out and walked along a red–tiled hallway to a cold storage room that was hewn directly into the stone of the mountain. A guard was sitting by the door and got to his feet as they approached and unlocked it and held it open for them. The room was freezing and a dozen animal carcasses dangled from hooks in the ceiling. The huge coffin lay on a metal butchering table to one side.

"My mother has asked me to make certain it is him," Amado said, "She is very superstitious."

Michael knew he had already asked too many questions for one day.

"Mothers are like that," he agreed.

Amado picked up a thick–sided meat cleaver and used it to prize open the lid a crack. Michael noticed that his hands were trembling. It was damn cold, yes, but there seemed to be more to it than that. He had taken off his dark glasses and his eyes were unsteady. He had the look of a frightened deer. Perhaps his mother wasn't the only one.

"The silver is heavy," Amado said, "Lift one end and I will lift the other."

The casket was perfectly rectangular so it was impossible to tell, except perhaps if you knew the details of the exterior design, which end was which. As it happened Amado was at the head end and stared in ill–concealed horror at his brother's face. He was sweating profusely despite the icy temperature. It was a ghastly sight and the acrid smell of formaldehyde together with a fetid whiff of something like unwashed brothel bed-sheets rose in unwelcome waves causing Michael's always delicate nasal membranes to sting.

To his surprise the corpse had been carelessly thrown back into the coffin. Even the unavoidable jostle of transport could not have created such disarray. It was dressed in the blue suit but what once had been pristine was rumpled and soiled and unbuttoned and there were no shoes or shirt or tie. The hands were invisibly scrunched under the body and the feet were black and blue with jagged ochre toenails unclipped and overgrown. The sutures on the face and belly were leaking an ambrous sticky pus. The cheeks and forehead were chalky purple. The livid crimson mouth was a hideous sunken hollow which lent stark credence to Cecilia's tale of the uprooted teeth. The glass orbs that had been used to replace the originals in a futile attempt to make the visage more presentable had slipped from their gluey moorings and bulged in accusation, one up, one sideways, like a maniacal ventriloquist's dummy. Most strange of all to Michael, who had no way of knowing the reason why, a full set of bright white dentures had been tied around the dead man's neck with a rough strand of brown string. It was evident that someone was sending the drug lord a message.

"I should sue the undertaker if I were you," Michael said softly but Amado was too fixated on the teeth to hear.

He was breathing in and out so violently he couldn't speak and Michael thought to himself how useful it would be for any actor attempting Claudius in Shakespeare's Hamlet to have beheld him. It hath the primal eldest curse upon it! A brother's murder! So often he had seen the desperate horror of that moment undercooked but here was a shuddering *mestizo* vampire with the true guilt of Cain trenching his tawny brow!

Amado could clearly bear it no longer and suddenly looked away, letting go his hold on the lid at the same time and Michael had to do a bit of a dance to avoid losing an arm and twisting his back as it slammed shut. One of his slippers fell off and his foot instinctively recoiled from the chill mongery moisture of the floor and he had to hop like a crippled kangaroo to get it back on as Amado fled from the room.

Michael thought better of trying to catch up and waited until Amado was out of sight around the curve of the hallway and he heard the faint sound of the elevator doors in the distance. There was a constant rythmical thrumming which Michael assumed must be the villa's air conditioning system that nearly drowned out all other noise on the floor.

He looked at the guard and wondered if there might not be some exit on the level by which he could escape. The guard seemed to catch the thought and put his hand to his shoulder–holster threateningly.

"Vámonos, señor," he said, giving him a little shove.

It made Michael angry enough to have hit the man but he didn't and as he was escorted back to the elevator he cursed himself for an opportunity lost. 'Nothing ventured, nothing gained,' he could hear his mother chant, but then she was equally fond of that other old chestnut, 'Discretion is the better part of valor,' and what chance did he have really and who knew if there was such an exit and anyway he wasn't James Bond for Jesus wept's sake. But still it rankled within as he rode all the way to the top floor and returned to his suite. What if? What if he had summoned the courage to knock the guard out and take his gun?

When he opened the door the tailor and his assistant were already waiting for him. They had wheeled in a clothes rack on which hung several sizes of the same conservative medium–blue business suit and a variety of shirts and ties for him to try. Michael was overcome with the nervous helpless feeling he always experienced as a young beginner on those rare occasions when he landed some insignificant part in a play or television soap opera or film and was called in for a pre-rehearsal costume fitting. An emasculated puppet. How utterly depressing. An impotent man of straw.

The two men were friendly enough but could speak absolutely no English and gestured him to his underwear. They were folded on a chair on top of his trousers and his shirt and sleeveless jacket were hanging over the back of it. His sandals were neatly placed below. Everything was freshly laundered and even his undervest and shorts were pressed and as he picked them up and retired to the bathroom he could feel they were still comfortingly warm. Well, good girl, at least he had been right about that.

He looked at himself grimly in the mirror. A pathetic mannequin, an idiot and a coward. Why debate the point? He put on the undergarments and, with the robe closed over them again, returned to face the unavoidable humiliation in the living room.

CHAPTER SIXTEEN

As Michael was unhappily observing his reflection Amado was staring at the eviscerated cadaver of his plaything in the pig barns. He had gone straight there in search of some vampiric solace after the upset of seeing Vicente's corpse and the cryptic message of the dentures.

The helpers who had foolishly trusted Cecilia's authority and assisted in the grisly work of the previous evening were not there. Quite possibly they were already half way to Brazil because as Amado looked down in white-hot fury at the ravaged body of the murdered girl and stalked around the table to observe the fetus of their child stuffed into her mouth he made an instantaneous decision that would have been less than good for their health.

He walked calmly out to his golf cart and opened the glove compartment and took a silenced Beretta back into the anteroom and shot the two handlers whose shift it was unlucky enough to be between the eyes at point blank range before they had a chance to question why or protest their innocence. Then he drove to Vicente's section and found three others cleaning up inside the torture chamber as Cecilia had instructed and killed them all as well. At Cecilia's studio he found nobody so he went back across the moat and ignited his baby brother's favorite Gatling–sized blowtorch and set about burning the whole place down.

By the time he reached his own little fantasy funfair again and was licking the flame at its corners thick columns of dark gray smoke were already billowing from the other buildings into the pale blue sky.

§

The two tailors had chalked one of the suits for alteration and they were just wheeling out the clothes rack as Cecilia came into Michael's suite. He was sitting disconsolately on an armchair in his underwear and a third man was trying to find a pair of shoes from a trunk that would fit his size twelve feet.

One of the tailors spoke to Cecilia in Spanish and asked her with fawning politeness if she would please tell the *señor* they would return with the finished suit in forty–five minutes. She nodded curtly and told the man on his knees with the shoes to get out and come back later also.

When the door was closed she came to Michael and put the promised 8mm cassette into his hand. She was elegantly dressed in a deep wine–colored silk pant and jacket ensemble and he noticed that her usual cool composure was more than a little frayed.

"I have to go," she said quietly, "Hide this well. If he finds it he will kill you without hesitating."

"Are you still going to be there?"

"Maybe. I don't know."

"Has something happened?" Michael asked as she turned on her heel.

"Take a look."

She was already at the door and pointing to the hallway windows.

Michael pulled on his trousers but by the time he saw the huge swirling cloud that was rising over the mountaintop and threatening to blot out the sun she had vanished. The man with the trunk of shoes was a few yards down the hall looking through the window and was quite obviously feeling an urgent need to get on with their selection and pleaded with his eyes and gestured for Michael to let him back into the room.

§

Twenty or more of Amado's black–suited guards had raced to the barns and Amado had ordered them to let the blaze burn itself out. He told a dozen of them to stay and make sure the conflagration didn't spread to the surrounding scrub but he wanted the structures completely razed to the ground. As soon as the fire was cool enough they were to bulldoze the site and have everything the flames did not consume carted away immediately and buried in the desert.

§

Juan Guadalupe Sandoval, the commander of the Juarez *Departamento de Incendios*, was gazing at the mountain through binoculars. He knew the ominous cloud was not coming from one of the city's endlessly proliferating piles of scrap rubber and informed his crews that he could see no reason to interfere.

§

Doña Aurora, however, was wringing her hands in panic as Amado came back into the villa with smears of soot on his face and arms and clothing and he had to reassure her there was no cause for concern. He had been meaning to get rid of the eyesore ever since they had come to Juarez and the men were tending the fire and would make sure there was no danger.

"Cecilia has gone," she said.

Amado smiled at her without surprise.

"Yes, she is meeting me in El Paso this evening."

"Did you look at Vicente? Did you make sure?" she asked.

"Yes, mama," he said.

"He is comfortable? Nothing was disturbed?"

"Nothing. He is exactly as you saw him. Rest, mama. We must leave early in the morning for Guamuchilito."

§

Cecilia was already half way down the hill with the radio blaring from her mauve 1956 Mercedes Benz 190sl convertible and the dry desert wind streaming flails from her long black hair.

CHAPTER SEVENTEEN

Fernando wanted to leave Michael's camera and the rest of his belongings in Chuck's motel room before they went to have breakfast but Chuck said it was better he kept them and he and Marta had driven over to the Denny's on West Gateway Boulevard and Chuck had followed with Juanita in the Ranger because he said he had to go on from there.

Marta hadn't pried any further into why he was in El Paso and they had just reminisced about old times. They spoke about Juanita and then Marta's work and Chuck's little ranch in Sweetwater and his father who was still OK but didn't want to talk any more and what was happening with the gallery and Michael's reaction to the photographs but not about that for too long because Juanita was there and everyone knew it was a sensitive subject.

They shared another good laugh about the crazy Englishman and how he got sick from swallowing suppositories and then got serious because they might never see him again and Chuck said he would find out how to call his family in that case and he knew he had been staying at the Republic so he could collect the rest of his stuff.

When they said goodbye Chuck told Fernando that if he wanted to come back he would try and meet him at the Barragan around seven o'clock which was when he thought Amado would probably arrive but they didn't really hold out much hope that Michael would be with him and if he wasn't they would call the British embassy in New York and also in Mexico City and see if they'd like to do anything about their missing subject.

The family had been sitting for half an hour in the queue at the border when they noticed smoke rising from the top of Amado's mountain.

"It's coming from his property for sure," Fernando said.

Marta suggested that maybe Michael had started a fire in the villa to give him a chance to escape and Fernando agreed it might have been a good idea but probably wasn't what had happened.

Over the next twenty minutes the cloud had grown steadily bigger and darker and by the time they were showing documents to the border guard there wouldn't have been anyone in north Chihuahua who didn't know about it.

After finally being admitted they had traveled no more than a hundred yards along the lineup of cars waiting to proceed in the opposite direction when they saw Cecilia's Mercedes roaring down the express lane toward them. As she passed by Fernando and Marta agreed it must be her though neither had an exact idea what she looked like and Fernando watched her go in the rearview mirror and saw that she was waved through the permit holders gate without stopping.

Seven minutes later they were outside the *taberna* where he and Michael and Juanita had eaten lunch the day before and talking to Rafael and Enrique.

"The story is they are clearing brush," Enrique said.

Rafael snorted with derision and then asked, "Where is the Englishman who ate the shit softeners?"

Fernando told them what had happened as far as he knew it and about their breakfast with Chuck and that they had just seen Cecilia Portillo crossing the border and he was returning to El Paso as soon as he had dropped Marta and Juanita off at the apartment and what were they doing right now and would they like to go with him and they said they would both come and hopped in the back of the cab.

There was a flight of exterior wooden stairs up to the apartment and the three men stood on the rickety landing outside the door looking at the enormous cloud which now seemed to cover half the sky.

"It's too dark for brush," Enrique said, "But not solid black like a pile of tires. More like some old wood building. There's oil in it and creosote maybe and roofing tar."

"And flesh and bones," Rafael added sardonically, "Like from those ovens they used to cook the Jews. I bet he's burning the evidence of his crimes."

"The sheds and barns from the old pig farm that was up there before they bought the place," Fernando agreed.

They all knew that the rumors were more than rumors and were silent for a moment to honor the souls of the dead.

"What is the little turd doing tonight, did you say?" Enrique asked.

"Judging the Miss Texas contest at his hotel," Fernando replied.

"Hot stuff at both ends," Rafael said but they didn't laugh.

§

Amado had decided not to call the hotel and have his men take Cecilia to his suite and lock her in the bedroom when and if she arrived. It was better that he kept her guessing. She was not one to delay the inevitable he knew but if he could fool her into thinking that he didn't care or hadn't noticed or perhaps even that the fire was an accident that had nothing to do with him then he could wait to kill her at his leisure or at the very least until after Vicente's laying to rest in Guamuchilito on Sunday. He didn't want anything more to upset their mother.

Michael had no idea the commotion was anything to do with what Cecilia showed him on the tapes though it was pretty clear the blaze must somehow be connected to the danger she claimed she was in. Why else would she have left so suddenly?

He had allowed the anxious shoe fitter to return and slipped Cecilia's cassette into his trouser pocket as the poor man continued rummaging through the trunk for a large enough pair. In the end he gave up the search and hurried out again communicating with agitated gestures that he would be right back and no sooner had he disappeared than Amado entered with a hairdresser.

He had changed his clothes and was now immaculately dressed in a light tan suit and a dark brown crew neck sweater and seemed completely recovered from his horror at seeing Vicente.

"How are you feeling, Mr. Davenport?" he asked.

Michael was sitting on the chair in his undershirt, trousers and socks with his hands on his knees and getting grouchier by the minute.

"Oh, just tickety–poo," he muttered.

"Is something wrong?"

"Good lord no. What could possibly make you think that?"

Amado chose to ignore the sarcasm.

"We have had a fire in some outbuildings. That is why I was not able to be with you sooner. My sister came to see you did she not?"

Michael briefly considered denying it but he had come to the conclusion that he had better just start playing the stupid game the same way they were.

"Yes. She came to say she would see me at the meeting. I didn't know she was going to be there."

Amado smiled as if he could easily penetrate the deception.

"Chichi is often an important part of our negotiations."

Chichi? Michael's mind staggered backwards in revulsion. Were his ears playing tricks? Chi-Chi and Hua-Hua, why not, the two–headed vampire dogs of Sinaloa! Butchers and bloodsuckers with Christmas card sentiment! How truly sickening.

Amado sensed his reaction and went on.

"A childhood name, Mr. Davenport. I was Mamado and my little sister and brother were Chichi and Shentivi. We were very close. Cecilia and Vicente were inseparable. Do you find it strange?"

"No, no. It's charming. Utterly charming."

"We don't use them much any more."

Amado then spoke to the hairdresser in Spanish. He was a large flaccid man with unhealthy white pockmarked skin and had been sweating and out of breath as they came in. Michael instantly judged him to be homosexual but he obviously felt no need to pay deference to Amado because he flopped down on the couch with a bored look on his face while he waited for them to finish their conversation.

As Amado was giving the man his instructions there was a timid knock on the door and Amado went to open it. It was the shoe fitter again holding a large pair of beautiful black Italian loafers.

There was a long interchange that Michael assumed was about the size of his feet which was a simple enough problem to understand in a country where he stood head and shoulders above most of the male population but the man was clearly very nervous and found it necessary to elaborate at length upon it as his excuse for not having produced a suitable pair sooner.

Amado looked at his watch and cut him off by asking the hairdresser if he had any questions and he yawned and said he didn't and, after the man with the shoes had tried them on Michael's feet and pronounced them to be a perfect fit, Amado told Michael he would be back in twenty minutes and left the room.

Michael was surprised when the hairdresser spoke to him in English. "Come on," he said laconically, "We'll do it in the bathroom."

§

Beverley was gone from the villa in the limousine Amado provided long before he set the pig barns alight. It took only twenty–five minutes for the car to arrive at the Barragan because, like Cecilia, the driver had a pass.

She was much earlier than she had told her public relations manager she would be and therefore no gaggle of autograph seekers greeted her in the lobby which didn't improve her mood and to top it all off as she was trying to enter the private elevator to the seventeenth floor, where she thought her people, the six poor devils whose unenviable job it was to take care of her every need, her daily datebook and appointment schedule, her capricious nutritional requirements, her myriad array of clothes and accessories and shoes and the endless finicky obsessions she had with her appearance, would be waiting to attend her in the luxury of the central suite, something to which she had become very quickly accustomed in the few days since Vicente's death, she had been prevented from doing so rather brusquely by two of Amado's low key muscle in their casual light green suits and politely informed by the hotel manager that on Señor Barragan's orders everything of hers had been moved down yesterday to what she was assured were equally prestigious accommodations on the eleventh floor and her entourage who had been staying on that level all along were now in convenient readiness for her there and she had been furiously dialing the villa from her cell every minute on the minute since.

Amado himself never used a cell phone and had left instructions to leave her on hold permanently.

§

Chuck didn't notice Beverley's premature arrival because before he had gone back to Pantera's the previous night to see if Michael might show up he had returned to the bar in the Barragan where he had seen the four Russians and spent a couple of jolly cocktail hours befriending them while getting pleasantly smashed on draft beer with Stolichnaya chasers and now he was in the bar again playing poker with another group.

Luckily he was winning a little because he had started the game with less than two hundred dollars in his pocket and the Russians tended to bet like they drank but even though no one had ever said anything about why they were there Chuck's instinct and long experience with the irrepressible swagger of all such men, and the fact that the waiters allowed a gambling game in the elegant Dome bar in the first place and never brought a bill or let their quiet Southern manner be ruffled by the occasional raucous outburst of Slavic enthusiasm, and most particularly the frequent changes in the composition of the group and the timing of their recent movements back and forth from the top floor elevator and their almost constant liaison with the men in the light green suits, who appeared to be nothing more than hotel security but who Chuck rightly suspected of being Amado's own personal bodyguards, was giving him the sure sense that these gently guffawing goodfellas were the advance clearing party for someone who was damned important, someone who would be there today.

Chuck knew there was no way in hell they would trust him or let him within a mile of their boss so he hadn't really figured out how playing cards and getting drunk with them was going to help get him any nearer to his objective when suddenly Cecilia walked into the bar.

No one seemed to recognize her except him and he was relieved that his back was to the opposite wall so he didn't have to turn his head to watch her get seated at a table by a distant window and order a large martini.

§

It took the epicene barber a lot more than twenty minutes to give Michael an expert trim and dye his graying hair a dark walnut brown but Amado hadn't come back as he had promised and Michael was now rinsed and coiffed and blown dry and the tailors were ready and waiting with the alterations done as he came out of the bathroom.

The Egyptian blue suit was double–breasted but not at all flashy and once Michael had suffered the investiture he had to agree the cut was extraordinarily flattering. He couldn't put his finger on any one element but the undeniable effect of the whole outfit, the highly polished slip–on shoes, the silver cufflinks, the pearl shirt and lapis lazuli tie, the flowing wave of the hairstyle and the color change, was to subtly metamorphose a scruffy eccentric Sussex intellectual into the elegant embodiment of an Italian banker!

The final touch was supplied by Amado who appeared in the doorway at that moment holding a pair of spectacles with thick black frames in his hand. He was accompanied by his driver carrying a small white duffel bag.

After walking a full circle around his creation and giving every detail of their work careful scrutiny Amado nodded his approval to the two tailors and the hairdresser and told them they could leave and without waiting for them to do so he came and tried the glasses on Michael himself.

"They are tinted but not prescription," he said, "They will not harm your eyes or cause discomfort. You are to wear them at all times."

He turned to the driver as if to ask his opinion of the ensemble but the man made no remark.

"Perhaps you cannot see it, Diego," Amado said, "But it is perfect."

"I wish you'd tell me who I'm supposed to be," Michael grumbled.

"Come now, you were an actor, use your imagination. Diego will bring your other clothes with us."

The driver picked up Michael's sandals, socks, sleeveless jacket, trousers, shirt and vest, which the tailors had not allowed him to wear because its outline would be visible beneath the fine pearl material, and put them in the duffel bag.

As he was being dressed Michael had deftly palmed Cecilia's cassette from his trouser pocket and while making the standard adjustment to his male appendages had secreted it in a rather irksome position inside his undershorts and it was now more or less stuck between his left testicle and inner thigh.

"Please take some refreshment," Amado said, gesturing to the assortment of newly replenished soft drinks and juices on the coffee table, "But be careful not to spill anything. I'm sorry there is nothing alcoholic but it is important that you are sober. We will leave in fifteen minutes. Diego will come for you."

"Ciao," Michael responded with a small wave of his hand.

Amado looked at him humorlessly but otherwise made no reaction and the two men left the room.

Once they had gone Michael removed the cassette from the tacky tropical moisture of its hiding place and finally decided that the most inconspicuous and least bothersome of the poor options available would be to wrap it in toilet paper and wedge it at his back beneath the leather belt and shirt but inside the elastic of his undershorts so that if it became dislodged it wouldn't slither down a trouser leg onto the floor.

Satisfied that there was no better solution to the problem he couldn't resist examining his new persona in the bathroom mirror.

Who on earth did the King of the Vampires want him to be? He certainly didn't resemble any member of the Corleone family from the movie though he did try out a few Brando gestures and puffed out his cheeks. He was nothing in particular, at the same time distinctive and yet nondescript. Maybe a doctor, a lawyer, an industrialist from Torino or Milano possibly, even a politician, but no, when all was said and done, most probably a money man. Yes, someone closely connected to extreme wealth but without the need to flaunt it. Oh, good lord, what the hell did he care!

Michael left the bathroom and opened a bottle of mango juice and went out into the sunshine on the balcony. He looked up at the sky and could see that the smoke from the fire had diminished and dispersed and then down across the broad valley with the city smoldering in its haze feeling more lost and yet more thrilled with anticipation than he had ever before in his life.

CHAPTER EIGHTEEN

It was ten minutes to three when Fernando and Rafael and Enrique pulled up outside the Barragan. Something to do with the time of day had made their passage at the border much smoother and quicker than it had been for Fernando and his family that morning despite the fact that Rafael's dog–eared paperwork caused the customs officer's rather torpid mind some brief confusion. They were lucky and found a parking spot not far from the hotel where Rafael and Enrique could see most of what was arriving and departing through the entry arches and Fernando went to have a quick look inside.

He came into the bar and caught Chuck's eye but could see it was not the time to make further contact. Chuck glanced at Cecilia who was lighting one of her thin cigars and Fernando followed his look and watched the waiter bring her a second martini and after another moment of pretending the person he was hoping to meet wasn't there he turned around and went back out to the lobby.

Chuck had a feeling Cecilia was observing the progress of the game from behind her sunglasses. He didn't think she would recognize him but he knew it was a possibility and he figured he'd give it a few more hands with the Russians and then amble over and speak to her and see what information he could shake loose. He wondered why Fernando had come back so early but in a way he was glad. He would have gone and talked to him outside but the Russians might see them and get suspicious and he didn't want them to think he was anything other than a good–natured barfly enjoying a little friendly diversion. Men of their kind wouldn't suspect him for chatting up a beautiful woman if he did it in the right way. After all, they had shared the typical masculine grin of appreciation when she walked in.

Fernando crossed back over the street and got in the cab.

"Chuck's in the bar playing cards," he told them, "And Cecilia Portillo."

"She's with him?" asked Enrique.

"No, she's by herself."

"Who's he playing with?"

"Three or four men at the table and a couple of others standing watching."

"Who are they?"

"How should I know? But I don't think they're Americans. He said he had things to do after we had breakfast and that he was tied up with something else this evening but he'd try and meet me here at seven o'clock. It's only three so why is he here now? I don't know what's going on."

"He knows Portillo will be here to judge the beauty contest. I think he is waiting to kill him," Rafael offered with a shrug, "We should grab the little prick when he comes and hold him while he does."

"And get shot," Enrique countered.

"He saw me," Fernando said, "Maybe he will come out."

They decided to sit and wait for awhile as Chuck was telling the Russians to keep his place and that he'd only be a minute and with a wink at them to wish him luck he sauntered over to Cecilia's table.

"Mind if I join you?"

She looked at him coldly for a moment and then smiled.

"Please," she said.

Chuck waved at the waiter to bring them a round.

"Have we met somewhere before?" he asked.

"I don't think so, Mr. Bowman," she replied, enjoying his surprise, "But I'm sure we know who we are."

It was Chuck's turn to smile.

"I had a feeling," he said.

They eyed each other in silence as the waiter set another double martini and draft beer on the table.

"Did you want a chaser with that, sir?" the young man asked.

"No. No thanks. I'm fine," Chuck replied.

The waiter walked away and they both took a sip.

"Bunch of Russians," he said and gestured back across the bar at the game.

The men were glancing their way and laughing.

"They're wondering how I'm doing."

"Are you spying on them for your government, Mr. Bowman?"

"No. I quit."

"Why? You were good at it."

"I think you know why."

"But you know who they are."

"I've got a pretty good idea."

She took another sip and smiled again.

"So if you are no longer a spy, Mr. Bowman, why are you here?"

Chuck returned the smile but didn't answer right away.

"There's a ton of security circulating for Lady Bush," he said, "I'd say it looks like a heavy night all round. But that's not why either. It's personal. I quit the whole thing."

"Did you have any other children, Mr. Bowman?"

He looked at her hard.

"No."

"What do you do now?"

"Farm."

"Just that?"

"Just that."

"Well," Cecilia said, stubbing her cigar, "If you are not here to work, Mr. Bowman, I have something I would like you to do for me."

§

The driver knocked on the door of Michael's suite at five minutes past three and escorted him down to the long white limousine in the parking circle. He would have liked to know if Tamur was still taking his siesta on the couch in the drawing room but they didn't pass directly by.

On this side of the villa he could see that some smoke was still drifting up from the outbuildings in the distance and the guards idling on the steps laughed at his costume but as he walked away to the car Michael turned and gave them all the finger. What could they do, kill him?

Amado was already waiting and gestured Michael to sit beside him and when Diego got in the driver's seat he grinned back through the security window and lifted the little white duffel bag and then held up Michael's passport and the two stolen tapes, the spare blank and the one with the tiger footage, so that he could see them. Michael acknowledged the possessions with a grateful nod but inwardly cursed himself. He hadn't the slightest clue how his insanely obsessive pursuit would end. How could any such dubious artistic masterpiece be worth dying for?

"How did the fire start?" he asked as they set off.

"They were old buildings with old wiring. It is good they will be gone. It will make more space for the wolves," Amado answered but

Michael could see he was preoccupied and they rode down the hill without saying anything more.

Michael noticed that the ordinary people on the streets of Juarez did their best to avoid looking at the car as they passed even though it was impossible for them to see anything through the darkly tinted glass.

Finally, as they approached the border, he broke the silence.

"So, will we be meeting any other vampires?" he asked.

"It is an excellent question," Amado replied with no evident awareness of the irony in Michael's voice, "I wonder if you will be able to tell."

§

As the limousine crossed the bridge over the Rio Grande without stopping Cecilia and Chuck were on their way up the elevator to the seventeenth floor. Chuck didn't know whether to think of their chance meeting as good luck or that he was walking into a trap but how could either she or Amado have known he was going to be there and besides something about the way she had asked him for help made it seem like it might just be worth the risk. He had gone back to the poker game and told the Russians the lady required his services and they had a good chuckle about it and he said he'd probably rejoin them but who knew when. None of them appeared to have any idea who Cecilia was.

They had walked together through the hotel to the lobby and Amado's guards by the elevator had looked at Chuck with suspicion but they knew better than to question Cecilia about such things and they had whispered her name to two more Russians who were standing beside them. These young men had also taken their turn at poker and knew who Chuck was and now they nodded to him with a tiny veiled twinkle and a new respect. One of Amado's guards and one of the Russians accompanied them on the ascent.

It took only a few seconds before the doors opened into a plush common area where yet more Russians were lounging but when they saw that the new arrivals were ushered in by one of their compatriots they didn't bother to get up and frisk them and went back to their quiet conversation.

The floor was divided into three suites separated by the common area and two sections of terrace which led out to a communal garden with a swimming pool and a helipad beyond. The incoming guests were now to occupy the central suite which faced south toward the Wells Fargo Bank tower and the valley of Juarez but didn't afford much of a view of either because the garden and the helipad were in the way. Amado's was far to the left and had its own balcony overlooking the hotel pool on the roof of the annex nine floors below and a broad vista of east El Paso and north to Fort Bliss Military Reservation, Biggs Field and the International Airport. Cecilia's was to the far right and its corner windows looked west and north to the Franklin Mountains and at night the moonlit sweep of glittering mansions climbing the slopes of Comanche Peak and the outline of the world famous Lone Star shining brilliantly above them had been known to inspire an almost religious awe.

Cecilia had said nothing more about what she wanted Chuck to do only that it would be better if they spoke privately in her suite because her brother would be arriving at the hotel in a few minutes. Neither of them needed to spell out which brother that was.

"Would you like another drink, Mr. Bowman?" Cecilia asked after locking the door and pressing a button to open the living room curtains.

"No thanks," he said.

"I have put you in great danger by bringing you here."

Chuck nodded. She knew he must be well aware of it.

"I am in danger also," she continued, already mixing herself a shaker full of martini, "Before two days are over Amado will try to kill me."

"Care to tell me why?"

"I'm sure you can imagine why. My brother is cleaning house as you say in America. You know better than anyone what really happened to Vicente and for the same reason I am certain I will be next. I would like you to help me kill him first, that's all. He is the one responsible for the death of your son and I think that cannot have been far from your mind during these last years."

"What, killing him? No. I want to get rid of him not kill him."

"There is only one way to get rid of rats, Mr. Bowman."

"You want me to just walk in and shoot him?"

"Of course not. It would be suicide."

"No kidding."

"We will have to talk quickly. If anyone tells him you are here he will have this suite searched. It is possible that they will say nothing because I have taught them to respect my privacy but I can't be sure and today is a special day. When everything is finished our chance may come."

"You want me to stay in here until tonight?" Chuck asked with a trace of incredulity, "Where did you plan to hide me?"

"Are you afraid of heights?"

"Depends what you have in mind."

"There is a ledge between the windows. It is easy to walk along it. If you go to the corner they cannot see you from either direction even if they put their heads outside. It would only be for a few minutes."

Chuck went to have a look. It wasn't impossible.

"How do I know you aren't the one trying to get rid of me? Or that you'll let me back in?"

Cecilia shrugged.

"You can leave if you don't think I am telling the truth, Mr. Bowman."

She had finished mixing the martinis and poured herself one and took a thoughtful swallow then went into the still curtained bedroom and made a mess of the pillows and bedcovers as if the two of them had just been in there making love.

"If they search I'll say you came but they didn't see you going," she said as she walked back in. Chuck grinned at her choice of words but she didn't smile.

She switched on the television and brought up a static surveillance image of the elevator doors and most of the common area between the suites.

"It will give us thirty seconds," she said.

"Better than nothing."

"You haven't told me why you were playing cards with our guests. Did you think they would help you 'get rid' of my brother, as you call it?"

"No."

"You say you know who they are."

"I'm guessing they work for Vyacheslav Ivankov."

"Perhaps some. I think also higher than that perhaps."

"Didn't your brother tell you?"

"I am not so much a part of this organization as you assume."

"Enough so that he wants to get rid of you."

"Yes. Like Vicente. He believes I am a danger to him."

From the window Chuck could see the angle of North El Paso Street that led around to the hotel arches and what he thought might be the yellow cab and Fernando standing beside it with two other men and one of them was pointing in the direction of the entrance.

"Did you just come from Juarez?" he asked.

"Yes."

"Was a crazy Englishman with your brother last night?"

§

Fernando and Rafael and Enrique had been watching the approach of the long white limousine down South El Paso Street and it had to make a difficult turn to get around the corner onto West Mills and then back under the arches. They saw three men in light green suits come to the car and open the doors and Amado and another man get out but at that distance because of his different clothing and the change in hair style and color and the glasses they couldn't tell if it was Michael and decided to walk over and try for a closer look.

It was exactly twenty minutes to four as Amado and Michael were being ushered through the revolving doors into the increasingly crowded lobby by the three guards and at precisely the same moment the remaining four Russians in the bar stood up abruptly from their poker game and a completely retitivated but entirely unmollified Beverley was just coming out of the public elevator with her entourage on the way to the Grand Ballroom to record a taped interview with the new head of entertainment for El Paso's KFOX TV 14 and co-host for the coming evening's festivities, Cindy Kellerman, a beautiful woman in her own right who secretly loathed Beverley but had been gushingly apologetic to her on the phone an hour before because the live broadcast of their chat had been nixed at the last minute by a previously unscheduled college football game.

There were several reporters waiting for her in the lobby and Beverley had to stop and smile for their cameras. They had also seen Amado coming in and Michael was quite surprised he didn't try to escape the situation.

"Have you set a date yet, Mr. Barragan?" one asked him.

Beverley had been too busy posing for the flashbulbs to notice Amado was there until that moment but as soon as she did her face burst into a radiant smile and she rushed without hesitation into his arms and kissed him. In her heels she was several inches taller than he.

"Is it true you're to be a June bride, Miss McIntyre?"

"Has your Daddy given his blessing?"

"Of course, why wouldn't he?" she cooed and kissed Amado again.

There was a smattering of applause and a few whistles as the kiss went on and on and if Michael hadn't been so amused by this spectacular display of sham emotion he might have realized that he was missing his best and possibly last chance to get away and then suddenly an elderly British voice rang out.

"Ooooh, look over there, Dickie! It's, oh, what's his name . . oh, you know, the young chap we used to like so much on Coronation Street!"

Michael's blood ran cold at the words. Good lord, it wasn't possible! It was over twenty years ago and he had only been on the blasted thing for ten days in a minor part but nonetheless the old bag who had shouted was barging through the crowd toward him with an excited red–faced partner in tow and before either Amado or he could do anything about it they were on top of him.

"It is you, isn't it, Mr. Dagenham? Look, Dickie, it is, isn't it."

"Davenport, Ethel," the man corrected her, "I think you'll find it's Michael Davenport. You'll have to excuse my wife."

"Oh yes, of course, I'm so sorry, Mr. Davenport. Oooh, isn't this exciting, Dickie? Whoever would have thought?"

"Very exciting," the elderly gentleman concurred heartily.

Even though the crowd's focus had shifted away from her, something that normally would have provoked a tantrum, Beverley started laughing when she realized who Michael was.

"Oooh, sugar pie, you are even cuter with your clothes on!" she cried but no one knew what she was talking about and it only added to the confusion.

Amado made a subtle sign to the guards to get Michael in the elevator.

"Are you here to make a movie, Mr. Davenport?" Dickie asked.

"We were hoping your character might become a regular at The Rovers," said Ethel, "We were ever so disappointed when you left."

Two men in green suits stepped up on either side of Michael.

"There appears to be some mistake," one said politely.

"Si," Michael said in agreement and looked at Amado innocently. Well, he was only following orders.

"Oh, come on now, Mr. Davenport, you can't fool us," Dickie said, "Ethel and I would have recognized you anywhere."

"Non sono lui," Michael demurred with a slightly pained Mafioso shrug.

Beverley laughed even louder and Amado had to kiss her to shut her up.

"Excuse us please," said the other guard and they took Michael by the elbows and began guiding him forcefully away.

"Ciao," Michael said, turning over his shoulder with a cheeky little wave to his unwanted fan club, *"Non parlo inglese. Mi scusi. Cin cin."*

Amado caught up and walked beside him and at that moment Fernando, Rafael and Enrique came through the revolving doors and scanned the lobby.

"If it turns out that you are insane," Amado hissed in Michael's ear, "Or have some difficulty perhaps in following instructions, the remainder of your stay on this earth will be very short."

"Si, si. Capito molto bene."

Amado gave him an icy look of final warning and went to rejoin Beverley.

"Well I never, Dickie," Ethel exclaimed, "Whatever has happened to him, do you suppose?"

"Got in with these jet-setters, Ethel. Gone off his chump," said Dickie.

Fernando could now see it was Michael in the blue suit and tried his best to push through the crowd toward him as he and Amado's men approached the elevator. The guards told the last of the Russians from the bar who were waiting for a ride to the top floor they would have to wait for the next one and hustled Michael in and as the elevator doors were closing Michael and Fernando looked straight into each other's eyes but it was too late.

This was not lost on Amado. He would have been suspicious of Fernando and his companions anyway even though he didn't know exactly who they were but he decided he would deal with them later and that he had better accompany Beverley to the ballroom to prevent any further awkward questions from the cavalcade of press that was following her.

He explained to her quietly as they walked that Michael was a famous British actor and now director who was visiting him and who wanted to come to see her this evening because he knew she was going to sing at the contest. He didn't want to be recognized because he was in the final stage of negotiation with some major Hollywood producers and Amado was acting as an intermediary because he was an old friend and possible backer for his new film and if Beverley would promise to shut up about it Michael had told him secretly there could be a juicy part for her.

"Aw, honey," she purred gooily, instantly forgiving and weak at the knees, "Why didn't you say so before I was such an awful bitch?"

"I was hoping to make it a surprise."

CHAPTER NINETEEN

Cecilia finished telling what she knew about Amado's plans for the crazy Englishman and Chuck was relieved that Michael was still alive and there might be some way to save him.

"Who does your brother want them to think he is?"

"I don't know," she said.

"Do you know what the meeting is about?"

"Not really."

"Has he done business with the Russians before?"

"No. He executed two of their foot soldiers by mistake because he is paranoid. I think he has some explaining to do."

"So Michael is the patsy?"

"Maybe."

"What time is the meeting?"

"Now."

Suddenly the telephone rang.

"Be ready, Mr. Bowman," she said and then answered.

Chuck went to the window and made sure the latch was open. He was cursing himself. It was a hell of a long way down if he lost his balance. And he had only one small handgun. He had bigger and better options in the Ranger but his snap decision to accompany her had left him virtually unarmed.

Cecilia said only a few words in Spanish and then put the receiver down.

"They are here," she said, "They are bringing Michael up."

They both turned to the television screen.

"Are they going to search?"

"Not yet."

"Where are the emergency stairs?"

"There are two. One opposite the elevator. One beyond the helipad. But they will both be guarded. There is nothing you can do until the Russians are gone."

"By then Michael will be dead."

"Maybe not. I will do my best to help him but if it is to be him or me what choice do you expect me to make?"

They could see the elevator doors open and the two security men in green suits ushering Michael out.

"Christ, is that him?" Chuck said, grinning in amazement.

The men handed Michael very politely to the care of two others who led him toward Amado's suite. The Russians who had been lounging and chatting when Chuck and Cecilia came through were standing now and walked forward as if they wanted to frisk him but after exchanging a few words with Amado's guards they became deferential and let him pass untouched.

"They're making like he was a *capo*," Chuck observed, still grinning.

"I will try to let him know you are here."

They watched as the two men who had brought Michael got back into the elevator and the doors closed.

"Your brother wasn't with them."

"I don't know why."

"Is there some way to get me in there before he comes?"

"No, it is impossible. They would suspect us immediately. They would find your gun and Amado would recognize you. You must wait here. I will come back after the meeting. What is more important, a foolish Englishman's life or to revenge your son?"

§

Fernando and Enrique and Rafael had walked through the lobby into the Dome Bar and discovered that Chuck and Cecilia were no longer there.

"She was sitting at that table by the window," Fernando told them, "He was playing cards over by the wall with those men you saw at the elevator."

"They were Russian," Enrique said.

"Are you sure?"

"I'm sure."

"Maybe your friend Chuck is not what you think," Rafael said.

"What do you mean?"

"Maybe he has become one of them."

"Never."

"Well, where did he go?"

"I don't know."

"You say the top floor is private. The Russians are going up there and if he is with them what else can he be? Maybe the crazy Englishman is one too."

At that moment they were approached by three hotel detectives.

"Are you gentlemen guests of the hotel?" the oldest one drawled.

"Do we have to be?" said Enrique.

"Today you do. From four o'clock only guests and ticket-holders will be admitted. I don't believe you boys are either of those things now are you?"

"Tickets for what?" Enrique asked.

"There you go," the detective said as though Enrique's ignorance of the coming event was proof, "I'll have to ask you to move along."

Suddenly Amado reappeared from the ballroom with two of his men and gave a brief glance at Fernando as they passed by on their way back to the lobby.

"Señor Barragan," Fernando called out, moving quickly after them before the house detectives could easily prevent it, "Señor Barragan, sir, may I ask you a question?"

Amado didn't stop.

"Señor Barragan," Fernando insisted, "Where is Michael Davenport?"

Amado didn't react at all and the odd procession of Amado and his men with Fernando and Rafael and Enrique hustling behind and the three detectives shadowing them and trying to pretend to any curious onlookers that nothing serious was happening continued into the lobby. Fernando had nearly caught up as they reached the elevators.

"Where is Michael Davenport, *señor*?" he repeated loudly.

The reporters and camera crews that followed Amado and Beverley had remained in the ballroom but there was still quite a crowd milling about and the urgency in Fernando's tone was making all heads turn as the two green–suited guards wheeled around to confront him.

"I must ask you to speak more quietly, sir," one said, "Why do you ask this question?"

Amado strolled back smiling and waved the guards off.

"Who is it you are looking for, my friend?" he asked pleasantly.

"An Englishman. Michael Davenport."

"I do not know this man. Why do you think I would know where he is?"

Fernando looked at him levelly but didn't answer.

"What is your name?"

"Our names do not matter, *señor.*"

"That is very true."

Amado became aware that the old English couple were making their way across the lobby toward him.

"You will have to excuse me," he said and walked swiftly into the waiting elevator accompanied by the guards.

"Now, as I said, it's time for you three boys to be moving along," the chief detective repeated and the other two stepped into position behind them looking as if they were more than ready to force the point but before they could do so Ethel and Dickie came panting up.

"Did we hear you say the name Michael Davenport?" she asked, "Isn't that extraordinary, Dickie?"

"Extraordinary indeed," said Dickie.

"He was just here," she said, "He came in no more than ten minutes ago with the man you were talking to. Did he say he didn't know him?"

"Yes," Fernando replied.

"Well, he's lying whoever he is," Ethel pronounced indignantly.

"We'd know Mr. Davenport anywhere," Dickie concurred.

"I don't mean to interrupt," drawled the detective, "But I'm guessing you two good people are guests of the hotel?"

"We certainly are!" exclaimed Ethel.

"Yes, and it's not an experience we'd care to repeat let me tell you," added Dickie.

"Well, I sure am sorry to hear that, sir. If you have any complaints please feel free to address them to the manager. You'll find Mr. Jordan in his office right over there behind the desk. But I have to tell you kind people that these three gentlemen are being asked to leave."

"Why? What have they done?" Ethel demanded.

"Nothing, ma'am, nothing at all. It's just that from now until midnight only paying guests and ticket-holders are allowed inside the hotel. It's not the hotel doing it, ma'am, we've got orders."

"From who?"

"The government of Texas."

She was singularly unimpressed by his weighty tone.

"Well, we're paying guests and we want to talk to them!"

"Paying through the nose," Dickie seconded.

"Are you suggesting guests aren't allowed to have guests?"

§

On the elevator Amado asked the guards if Cecilia was in the hotel and they told him she was and that she had brought a man who had been playing cards with the Russians up to her suite but they hadn't recognized him and she had refused to tell them his name. He told them to describe the man and they did and he was silent for a moment and then asked if the man was still there and they said they didn't know but they thought so.

Chuck had watched on the television as Cecilia crossed the common area past the Russians who were still standing and generally looking more attentive until she disappeared out of sight and he could now see Amado and the guards coming from the elevator. He was ready make his exit through the window and was a little surprised when Amado walked immediately away towards his suite without a glance and the two guards took up positions beside the elevator doors. No one had made a move in his direction and after a few moments he heard the sound of an approaching helicopter.

Michael was alone by the window in the spacious living room pretending to admire the view, inwardly churning but hopeful that the bizarre coincidence of the dotty octogenarian fan club coupled with the fact that Fernando was at the hotel and therefore possibly Chuck as well might mean he had some slim chance of survival.

When Cecilia came in she didn't look at him and he realized there were too many others present for them to speak. There were four Russians and four of Amado's green-suited guards and also an immaculately dressed but unsmiling black woman who had caught Michael's interest. He assumed she was American and thought she bore an uncanny resemblance to Condoleezza Rice, who was the Provost of Stanford University and little known to the general public at the time but Michael, being a keen student of foreign affairs, remembered well her role as advisor to George H. W. Bush's administration during the fall of the Berlin Wall and the final days of the Soviet Union.

The woman was standing between the double set of French doors that led out toward the terrace pool and the helipad beyond and turned to watch as the chopper came in to land.

Amado entered at that moment and quickly crossed the room toward her and they exchanged a few hushed words.

Cecilia had never taken off her dark glasses and had lit one of her thin cigars and was at the bar fixing herself yet another martini. Amado came to her and plucked the cigar from her mouth and extinguished it in her cocktail. She held his eyes and tossed the contents in the sink and began again.

After the briefest of pauses, in which Michael expected that one or both of them might suddenly begin tearing flesh and eyes and hair, Amado walked over and took him by the elbow.

"It wasn't my fault," Michael whispered, "It's unbelievable they recognized me. It was twenty years ago."

Amado wasn't interested and gestured him to sit on a high–backed Louis XV armchair with ornate golden trim and floral–patterned red upholstery which held a regal and commanding position in the room and after Michael had done so he leaned to whisper maliciously in his ear, "Relax. Imagine you're the Pope if that helps you but say nothing, nothing at all do you understand, nothing except as I instructed and no matter what happens do not react in any way or remove your glasses or get up," then went to rejoin the black woman.

Chuck had turned the television so he could keep an eye on it and was peeking out through the bedroom curtains at the helipad as the rotors slowed to a stop and were silent. Several Russian guards ran to the chopper and wheeled round to face the suite and form a security screen as the pilot jumped down and opened the doors.

There were two male passengers. The first to alight was short and thin with close–cropped graying hair and vaguely oriental features and the second a great lumbering bald–headed bear who sported a bristly H. G. Wells moustache. They stopped for a moment at the bottom of the steps to inhale the warm desert air and get their bearings.

Chuck identifed the first instantly. He had been right. It was Vyacheslav 'Yaponchik' Ivankov, former boss of the Brighton Beach Mafia, now nicknamed 'Little Odessa', the base of operations for the Russian mob in New York. He had been convicted of extortion two years previously and as far as Chuck knew he should still be serving time.

The second passenger he wasn't too sure about but from the descriptions it seemed likely he could be Semion Mogilevich. If so, it was astonishing because he was pretty much the top man of the whole *'organ-*

izatsiya' and what would he be doing here? A Ukrainian–born Jew known as the 'Brainy Don' because he held a degree in economics from the University of Lvov. He now lived in a heavily fortified villa outside Budapest with his Hungarian girlfriend Katalin Papp and it was feared he had acquired legal ownership of the entire Hungarian armament industry as well as running a vast criminal empire that stretched across Europe to South America and Asia. He controlled Inkombank, one of the largest private banks in the new Russia, and was thus able to launder the organization's money through Israel where he had also been granted citizenship. Beside him Amado Portillo was almost small potatoes so why the hell was such a man risking arrest and deportation to come to a meeting in El Paso?

And why had Amado dressed Michael up in this way to greet them? What else could he possibly be but a sacrificial patsy? Chuck thought of trying to use the telephone to contact Fernando downstairs but how and to do what, call the police?

§

Fernando decided there was no point standing in the lobby arguing with the detectives and suggested to Ethel and Dickie that they take a little walk in the fresh air and continue their conversation.

"I don't understand why this man, who you say owns the hotel, would say he didn't know Mr. Davenport when we saw them with our own eyes coming in together," Ethel said after they had made brief introductions and were passing through the revolving doors.

"We thought perhaps he was making a movie," Dickie added, "He spoke to us in Italian. He looked made up like an Italian."

"I don't know why he was dressed like that," Fernando told them, "He was in more ordinary clothes when I was with him yesterday. But you say he is an actor? He told us he was a journalist."

"When we knew of him he was an actor but that was ever such a long time ago now I come to think of it," said Ethel.

"We just remember him so well because he was on our favorite program."

"Yes, Coronation Street. You must get it on the telly over here, I'm sure you must. It's ever so good."

"There's not much in it to interest people in America, Ethel."

"Oh, I don't know . . "

"Well, we all agree he was here in the company of Señor Barragan and that his name is Michael Davenport," Fernando cut in.

"Oh, yes, no doubt whatever," the old couple concurred.

"So what can we do?" Rafael shrugged, "Complain to the manager that he has some Englishman upstairs against his will? He'll just tell the bastard."

"And have us arrested," Enrique added.

It took a moment for Ethel and Dickie to digest their comments.

"Is Mr. Davenport in some sort of trouble then?" he asked.

§

Brewster Jordan, the hotel manager, had been informed by his detectives about the three Mexicans who were standing under the arches harassing a pair of elderly guests and posing a bit of a problem and he was already on the phone to the El Paso Police Department Central Command.

"Harley," he was saying, "I got three wetbacks all worked up over nothin' down here. Maybe you better run 'em off."

§

Amado met the two Russians at the French doors and they shook hands and spoke a few words together which Michael could see being translated by the black woman but he couldn't hear precisely. Cecilia had mixed another martini but refrained from lighting up again.

Michael observed with a mixture of amusement and mounting dread that the new arrivals who he thought resembled Laurel and Hardy in a sinister Slavic incarnation were now looking at him with uncharacteristic ingratiating smiles. They came toward him and in the silence that followed he quickly realized they expected him to outstretch a hand, which he did, and they bent to kiss it one by one. It was utterly weird. Why hadn't Amado made him wear a ring? Who was he? Van Helsing's assumption, 'He must have been that *Voivode* Dracula', made chilling flip-flops through his mind.

They almost backed away like Catholics from an altar and he understood just enough Spanish to glean that Amado was telling them he was an old friend and business partner who happened to be here for an unexpected visit and as the black woman translated Michael was sure he heard the repetition of something like 'Signor Vespucci' in the midst of it.

'Oh ho,' he said to himself, 'Not the dreaded Transylvanian count after all but the eponymous founder of America!'

Amado went on and the gist seemed to be that his chance presence would automatically clear any obstacle to whatever was the nefarious purpose of their meeting. The reason for this was never spelled out as far as he could tell and the Russians clearly needed no explanation because they kept smiling and nodding toward him in the same fawning manner. Amado glanced in his direction several times during the interchange using the informal name 'Bartolomeo'. He tried to catch Cecilia's eye but she appeared to be listening carefully. He sensed she was every bit as puzzled as he.

'OK, you win,' Michael thought, 'It doesn't mean anything. All right then, I'm not Amerigo but Bartolomeo Vespucci. Who in the name of all darkness and demons is that?'

§

Fernando and Rafael and Enrique had a sixth sense which was bred in the bone and knew what the manager was probably doing and before the police or Secret Service or whoever arrived to force them to get lost they decided to make a decoy move and got back in the cab and drove away.

Fernando didn't want to involve the indomitable old couple in Michael's predicament and didn't have to explain their sudden departure because Dickie and Ethel had bustled without hesitation to the front desk and demanded to see the manager. They had brushed aside the clerk's excuses and all weasly attempts by the house detective to delay the confrontation and were now seated in the manager's office facing him like a pair of ruffled partridges.

Brewster Jordan was fifty-five and balding and the continually perspiring flesh beneath his pale flannel suit had been the victim of a lifetime of fast food abuse. However, despite the fact that this had already been a very bad day and was only likely to get worse, experience told him the quickest option for dealing with the undeflectable intruders was the politic one.

"And how can I help you good folks?" he purred.

"We want to speak with Mr. Davenport," Ethel began imperiously.

"We want to be sure he's here of his own accord," Dickie added.

"I see. And is this person a guest of the hotel?"

"We don't know," Ethel went on, "We only know he arrived half an hour ago with Mr. Barbican."

"It's Barragan, Ethel," Dickie corrected her, "His name and the hotel name are one and the same."

"You say this person was with Mr. Barragan?"

"Yes, we saw them come into the hotel together."

"We tried to speak to Mr. Davenport but he was acting very strangely."

"Is this gentleman a friend of yours?"

"No. He's an actor. We used to watch him on the telly."

"The what?"

"Television, Ethel, they don't call it the telly."

"It doesn't matter what they call it. What matters is that we know it was him and that you tell Mr. Barricade, or whatever his name is, that we know he's here."

"If he's here with Mr. Barragan, ma'am, I'm sure that Mr. Barragan knows he's here," Jordan observed, stating the obvious with dry equanimity.

"Don't get stroppy with me, young man," Ethel said huffily, "I know I'm old but I don't enjoy sarcasm. You just tell your Mr. Bargaboon from us to mind what he's up to."

"Well now, I wouldn't worry yourselves," Jordan countered patiently, "If this person is with Mr. Barragan, as you say, I'm sure he's being treated to the finest of our famous southern hospitality. Mr. Barragan is a very wealthy man and known all over the world for his philanthropic endowments and generosity but I'm afraid he's in a meeting right now and I can't interrupt that. And, as you probably know, he'll be tied up later with the Miss Texas final. I can't say I'll have the opportunity but if I do I surely will ask him about your friend . . what did you say the name was?"

They both repeated it and Jordan made a show of writing the name on his memo pad asking them to spell it out for him at the same time just to be sure and as they did they looked at each other and raised their eyes to heaven. Dear, dear, but American education was very far from what it should be!

When he had finished Jordan took a pair of tickets from his desk drawer and smiled his best managerial smile.

"Do you two good folks have seats for the show tonight, by the way?"

§

Beverley was posing prettily on a high stool under the bright lights of the stage as the cameras rolled and Cindy Kellerman, 'the fox of KFOX', began the interview strolling around her casually with mike in hand.

"We're here in the absolutely gorgeous new Grand Ballroom of beautiful downtown El Paso's Barragan Hotel with our very own Beverley McIntyre!"

There was loud applause and whistling from the three hundred fans who had won the state-wide raffle and thus been fortunate enough to attend.

"As you all know, Beverley will be retiring her Miss Texas crown tonight but what you probably didn't know is that she has broken the all time record for personal appearances during the short year of her reign. It's hard to believe but that number is a mind–boggling six hundred and twenty–three!"

More wild applause and hooting.

"Six hundred and twenty–three! Wow! That's nearly two appearances every day not only in our great state of Texas but locations all over America and around the world. Congratulations, Beverley! Tell us how you were able to keep up such an awesome pace."

"Well, Cindy, I believe with all my heart in helping people and my mama and daddy gave me a darned good Southern upbringin' is how."

The fans loved the answer and clapped and hollered for a full half minute.

"And what are you going to fill your time with now?"

"You mean other than cookin' for my husband?" Beverley answered with a consciously exaggerated country drawl.

There followed a burst of approving yuk–yukkery and a jocose nudging of fleshy ribs.

"Well, we have set the date but it's gonna stay our little secret for a while," Beverley continued in the same coy vein, "Anyway, I have to tell y'all Amado has been an absolute sweetheart. When I said to him I needed a little downtime after the honor of my responsibilities and before embarkin' on the joys of matrimony and that I wanted to work with Dr. James Dobson at Focus on the Family, well, he fully supported it. It'll only be for a few months this summer but he knows it'll mean a lot to me and for our whole life."

"So you'll be going to his institute in Colorado Springs?"

"Yes, that's right. It's a very spiritual place."

"Dr. Dobson is such an amazing man."

"Oh yes, he's a genius and, I'm proud to say, a friend."

"And he does good work in this world, praise be!"

"Oh Lord, yes he does, yes he surely does," Beverley said, gazing skyward with tears of humility glowing in her eyes, "He has so much to teach us all."

The three hundred rose in unison and the applause was deafening. Every heart was positively charged with ecstatic electricity and there followed many a righteous homily and a fine upswelling of Jesus-love.

CHAPTER TWENTY

Thick curtains had been drawn in the living room of Amado's suite and all the guards had been dismissed either to the sun–drenched patio or the common area by the elevators.

The Russians had been lavished with stiff drink and helped themselves to heaping platters of caviar, smoked salmon, shashlik, piroshki, pelmeni, golubtsy and roasted sheep's marrow on thinly-sliced black bread toasts and the bear was lounging on a tiger-sized couch stuffing himself and swilling vodka with his eyes glued expectantly to the television.

Michael had watched Amado introduce Cecilia to him as though she were the poppy seed cake and Apple Sharlotka and she was lying full length with her head in his lap still wearing dark glasses and trying not to react to the occasional hailstorm of spittle-soaked chaw cascading down over his belly onto her face.

Amado was standing behind the couch and the black woman was sitting on a hardbacked chair to one side. The smaller Russian stood by the drinks table puffing on a Sobranie.

Amado pressed the remote to begin the show and there was silence.

As they watched, despite the air conditioning which kept the suite at a perfect seventy-two degrees, a heavy sweat began percolating down Michael's back, soaking the tissue paper around the hidden cassette and tickling the fine hairs between his buttocks.

It was exactly the same horrifying event recorded by Vicente's cameras in the pig barns that Cecilia had shown him at the villa, that she had assured him might help them survive and that was now pressed to his spine, but this time the camera was in motion and it had all too vibrant sound. One of Amado's ghoulish assistants must have been filming out of sight of the other lenses.

The two men, who Cecilia thought were 'Russian drug dealers' and whose horrid demise she hoped might cause Amado problems, were dragged into the bare parlor room where the hapless young Tarahumaran girl had been tied hand and foot to the wooden chair. She was never visible on this tape, however, and her sobs and screams could be heard only faintly in the background. There was nothing of Amado slapping her across the ears or ramming his hands down her dress and viciously squeezing her breasts if she dared to look away.

The victims were already staggering from the injection of some paralytic drug and bleeding from the eyes and mouth and five of Amado's black–suited henchmen stripped them naked and gagged them with wads of wet paper towel and duct tape and bound their bodies round so tightly with reels of stout twine that they could do no more than undulate like spiked caterpillars.

Though their agony was played at a lowish volume it was almost beyond bearing but to Michael's utter horror and amazement the two guzzling Russians were roaring with laughter and this macabre mirth only increased as the trussed and moaning men were hooked to chains and lifted high on pulleys above two great bubbling barrels of acid and slowly lowered in. One man's flesh was fully dissolved to the ribcage before he finally expired.

The sight and the smell had evidently made the poor girl vomit. Michael could hear the sound of her hysterical racking spasms and nearly did so himself. He was aware the Russians were glancing at him and trying to gauge his reaction during the whole length of this unendurable sadism but he could barely manage not to faint and sat staring like a stone.

At the end the Russians applauded loudly and shouted their approval and the smaller one came to Amado and clapped him on the back in congratulation. Michael dared to turn his head and noticed with a smidgen of relief that neither the black woman nor Cecilia seemed amused. Cecilia was refusing to look at him for fear, he supposed, of arousing suspicion or perhaps she was now as terrified as he. So much for her understanding of what was really going on! Amado had been doing them a favor! They were all part of the same despicable coven.

But when his nausea abated Michael was momentarily hopeful. He wasn't to be the sacrificial scapegoat for some paranoid maniac's rash impulse after all! Might he be freed at the conclusion of this grotesque *Walpurgisnacht*, albeit that it had come some forty days too early in the calendar? Freed once more to wander wit–forsaken among the broomsticks and the he–goats on the Brocken, a sadder and just possibly a wiser man? He was not the fall guy, no, he was 'Bartolomeo Vespucci'. But who in the world was that? The Vampire Pope? Someone real or a symbolical poppet? The Great Owl Moloch or the Burning Man? A figment of the imagination briefly revered only to be destroyed and discarded in the finale of some fathomless imbecile ritual?

Then he realized with an even more sickening jolt that, patsy or poppet, none of it mattered. Amado could never have intended to let him live knowing what he now knew.

§

Fernando and Enrique and Rafael did not go far. They stopped two blocks away from the hotel at a hole-in-the-wall coffee shop called The Java Bean and Enrique was inside getting them some takeout.

"Why should we stay and risk our necks? Why should we do anything when we have no idea who is doing what to who?" Rafael said.

"I don't think there is much we could do whatever the situation is."

"The only way they'll let us in there now is behind machine guns."

"Forget that."

"No kidding."

"I wish I knew where Chuck and the sister have gone."

"You don't know they went anywhere together. You said he told you he was busy this evening. Maybe he just left."

"He saw me. He wouldn't do that."

Enrique returned with three coffees and six assorted doughnuts in a bag and passed all but one coffee through the window and stood for a while leaning on the door sipping thoughtfully.

"Maybe we could get tickets for that show somewhere," he said.

§

The way the seventeenth floor had been restructured, with the three suites wrapped around and divided by the fingers of the terrace and with Cecilia's and Amado's quarters being slightly larger than what once had been Vicente's and was now the guest apartment in the middle, it was possible for Chuck to watch the French doors of the other two suites from behind the curtained windows of Cecilia's living room.

He had seen the Russians walk from the helicopter and Amado and the black woman greet them and everyone go in. The guards had all remained on the terrace and a minute later he had seen four more come outside and another four appear on the television that provided a partial view of the common area but it was now twenty to five on the day after the spring equinox and the omnipresent desert sun was beginning to dip toward the haze of the western mountains and half an hour had elapsed with nothing happening. The guards were shuffling about on the terrace and some were smoking but no one spoke and the waiting and the eerie quiet were making him seriously regret his decision to come up here. How could he have been so stupid to let himself get hogtied and helpless because of a woman's charms once again?

§

But in the still darkened room that Chuck couldn't see beyond the French doors and the idling guards a great deal was happening and happening rapidly.

After the tape and applause and back-slapping there was more pouring of drinks and a speedy agreement about something that revolved around the words Uzbekistan and nuclear and Al Qaeda, which was not then the all-encompassing catch-phrase it is today but Michael knew of it and gathered the Russians were asking Amado to partner with them in stashing a huge quantity of apocalyptic contraband, three hundred, or maybe even thousand, kilos had been mentioned, somewhere in the Chihuahua desert until the highest bidder could be found and Amado turned to look at him four times and to his shame he had four times dutifully nodded his blessing and said, "*Sí.*"

And now, wonder of wonders or horror of horrors, Cecilia and the black woman were both in the middle of the room taking their clothes off. It was not being done in a seductive way but in the manner of well-understood ceremony. The black woman, though stern and rather plain of face, had a body as beautiful and smooth and shapely as Cecilia's. Once they were completely naked they both took a chair and stood on it with their arms upraised and the three men came to them and Amado cut both women very lightly under the left breast with a small knife and the Russians stepped close beneath and stuck out their tongues to lap the few red droplets without touching them in any other way.

And now it was the Russians' turn and they each put out a hand to help the women down and the women slowly removed all of their clothing, in silence and very deliberately, and the men sat on the chairs. All four were now as God and their own proclivities had made them but the men were no such lovely sight. One was ashen–skinned and almost unbelievably hairy, the second swollen to bursting by decades of indulgence. Both bore tattoos on the right shoulder of a large eight–pointed star.

Once seated the women straddled them, the black woman easily engulfing the smaller man and Cecilia split wide astride the bear, and Amado came behind the men and took the knife and made a similar tiny cut into the lower left side of the men's necks and the women likewise licked away a harmless trickle of blood. Michael was astonished that two aging butchers with countless murders to their credit, who could only have survived so long by constant vigilance, would allow themselves to be as vulnerable as innocent autumn lambs and it occurred to him that it was once again his presence that provided the warrant for their safety and was indeed, in some impenetrable way, the sanction for the whole idiotic ritual. But what did he know about the inner life of vampires? What did he know about anything?

Then all four of them stood up and the women placed a hand on the men's penises and stirred them to tumescence, then came behind the chairs and leaned far forward with arms outstretched over the chair backs.

'Oh no,' Michael said to himself, wanting desperately to look away, 'Not zee performink vampire doggies of Chihuahua, Chattanooga and Chelyabinsk!'

But he was not be spared and, yes, the Russians walked slowly around to the rear of the waiting sphinxes and grasped their hips and, after a few grunts and fumbles and a ladylike tweak of assistance to find their way, they entered and in less than thirty seconds both were spent.

Michael could barely hold in his laughter. What a pathetic spectacle! If this was truly some pseudo-vampiric rite for the international set it was pretty tame stuff in comparison to the antics of the Portillo clan.

And there was more to come. Before the Russians had time to catch their breath or extract their rapidly shrinking members Amado came to them carrying four exquisite crystal shot glasses filled to the brim with vodka and four warm white washcloths for mopping up on a silver tray and they took one of each and the black woman and the two men made a toast.

"Bessmertnaja smert' nash vladelec!" they exclaimed in earnest unison and as soon as they had all knocked back the vodka, which was rather awk-

ward for the women since they were still bent forward on the chairs, the Russians slapped them both on the rump as if they were carthorses and backed away. Then, in a final flourish, all four dutifully applied the washcloths to their privates, thereby avoiding excessive drippage.

Michael didn't have the foggiest idea what the words of the toast meant and he repeated the sounds to himself over and over in the hope that he might remember and live to ask Anna if she recognized them.

'Bessmertnaja smert' nash vladelec! Bessmertnaja smert' nash vladelec!'

Wait a minute, the syllable *'smert'* was repeated in the phrase and wasn't that Russian for death? Yes, there was a character in some absurdist play he had read years ago called 'The Schmurz' who haunts a French upper middle class family. The creature is covered from head to toe in bandages and though the family all beat it unmercifully it never goes away and they retreat from it higher and higher in their house until they are cramped together with it in the attic. Michael had always thought the character represented death but maybe it was more related to the German for pain as in the *'Weltschmerz'* he was certainly feeling at that moment. And what about *'vladelec'*? '*Vladelec* the Impaler', by any chance? No, not very likely either.

Cecilia hadn't shown any particular discomfort or indeed reaction of any kind during this grimly clinical display but when they were all dressing Michael noticed that, despite having used the washcloth, shiny little rivulets of blood were running down the inside of both her thighs and made the same incorrect interpretation of it as he had about her comment on the previous night.

Once everyone was, as the cliché goes, decent again the two Russians quickly polished off another drink and came to Amado and hugged him and kissed him on both cheeks then turned to Michael with a total absence of either self–consciousness or embarrassment and bowed and Michael was aghast to find himself nodding at them and smiling seraphically and playing out the charade to the bitter end with a tiny wave of his pseudo-papal hand.

'I'm sorry, mother, acting was in my blood repress it as I always tried!'

CHAPTER TWENTY-ONE

It was just after five as Chuck watched the Russians walking away across the terrace shadowed by four of their burly henchmen and past the pool to the waiting helicopter. They had been there fifty–seven minutes. The pilot started the rotors and the guards backed away and in a matter of moments the chopper had disappeared behind the sun's blinding reflection from the windows of the Wells Fargo Bank tower heading southeast.

The Russian guards went immediately through the French doors of the guest suite in order, Chuck assumed, to gather up their suitcases and depart and at the same time he could see the black woman crossing the common area and arriving at the elevator.

Inside Amado's suite Michael was standing stock still beside his chair and by the door where Amado had not two seconds previously bade farewell to the black woman his now much less than beloved sister was holding a double–shot Derringer pocket pistol with a blood red designer handle-grip hard behind his right ear.

"Don't make a sound or I'll kill you," she whispered as she closed the door again and gently locked it.

She pushed Amado away and hissed at him to sit down on the seat where she had serviced the obese Russian. Michael could see that it was spotted with a mixture of blood and orgasmic goo because she had perched there briefly to put her panties back on and Amado stopped when he saw it.

"Sit or I will make you lick it clean."

Amado reluctantly obeyed but the expression on his face made Michael shudder. No death would be slow or painful enough for such an insult.

"Now is your chance, Englishman," Cecilia said quietly, "There is someone you will be glad to see in my suite on the far side beyond the elevators. Go and bring him here. If you look casual his men will not stop you."

Michael did as she asked, though he half expected to be mown down in a hail of bullets as soon as he stepped out, and Chuck could barely believe it was him sauntering across the common area and smiling at the green-suited guards who nodded respectfully to him as he passed.

Michael knocked at the door of Cecilia's suite and was equally amazed when Chuck opened it. They looked at each other in total silence until Michael crooked an index finger in the universal gesture that says 'follow me' and turned to lead Chuck back.

As they ambled past the elevator doors each had the very sensible thought of telling the guards to take them down but they didn't. Michael was feeling a rather ludicrous old Saxonish debt of honor to Cecilia for temporarily saving his life, even though he knew she was the heartless bloodthirsty bitch–queen of the vampires and doubtless should best be thrown on the nearest bonfire, and Chuck didn't know any such thing but figured he had come too far to turn back now. And, beyond that, their natural attraction to her was playing a not insignificant part in the foolhardiness even if neither of them would ever have admitted it.

Even more absurd, in the midst of what felt to them like a running of the gauntlet but during which none of Amado's men made the slightest move to stop or search them, eight Russians, all of whom had spent time playing poker down in the bar with Chuck, suddenly came streaming out of the central suite with their luggage and insisted on shaking his hand and saying goodbye to him and wishing him luck. In contrast to this hearty camaraderie they gave Michael a wide berth and averted their eyes, almost bowing and walking backwards away from him as they passed.

He was dying to ask them the meaning of *'bessmertnaja smert' nash vladelec'* before he forgot the phrase but the moment was decidedly inopportune.

Chuck was able to extricate himself at last and they continued on across the area and Michael let them into Amado's suite without knocking and closed and locked the door again behind them with a soft click.

Amado showed no surprise at seeing Chuck though Michael could tell he was uncomfortable because he didn't speak. It reminded him of the moment they opened Vicente's coffin. Clearly he wasn't very skilled at covering his emotions or improvising when his carefully laid plans went awry.

"I told you I'm not here to kill him," Chuck said to Cecilia, who still had her little Derringer cocked behind Amado's ear, "But then it doesn't look like you need me anyway. Go ahead, if that's what you want."

"Can you suggest anything more satisfying?" she replied.

"I think so."

"Unless he is dead he will not rest until we are."

"No doubt. But I'd like to try for something bigger."

Cecilia snorted derisively.

"If it doesn't work you can kill him later," Chuck said.

Suddenly there was the sound of a commotion from the common area and an unmistakable high–pitched voice shrieking, "Take your fuckin' hands off me, you little greaser!"

The snuffling buzz–saw whine came rapidly closer.

'Oh joy, what now?' Michael thought, wincing at the noise.

"Get your hands off me and get out of my fuckin' way, I'm his fuckin' fiancé, dontcha prickless wonders know that! I'm gonna tear your fuckin' runty little boss's fuckin' runty little Mexicano bone right fuckin' off!"

They could see the handle being twisted violently back and forth and then she was hammering on the door.

"Open up you stinkin' nacho cheeseball or so help me god I'm gonna tell the whole fuckin' world what a mealy-mouthed pigfucker you are!"

"Let the little bitch in," Cecilia said with a grim smile.

Michael unlocked the door and opened it a crack and was nearly knocked flat as Beverley burst into the room full–throttle.

"How the fuck dare you!" she screamed at Amado at the top of her lungs, "How dare you move me out for a bunch of fuckin' Russkies!"

She had obviously just seen them leaving.

Amado, on the other hand, seemed for the first time faintly pleased to see her but though Cecilia had hidden the Derringer from view as the door opened she was still holding it pressed between his shoulder blades and he didn't make a move and Michael was able to close the door again in the guards' apprehensive of punishment faces.

Beverley noticed him doing it and instantly changed demeanor, becoming coy and winsome and coquettish all at once.

"Oooh, Mr. Davenport," she purred, "Excuse me, sir, I didn't see you."

Then she whirled around and saw Chuck and let out an involuntary little moan, assuming he too must be part of the Hollywood connection.

"Aren't you going to introduce me, Amado?" she gurgled, "You must be the producer, good sir, are you not? Or another one of the stars, you're so tall and handsome. No, wait, no, you couldn't be, no, but are you . . Gene Hackman?"

Neither Michael nor Chuck had the least notion what she was blithering about.

"This is Chuck," Michael said and smiled at him apologetically.

"Don't you have a last name?" she said, sidling up.

"Bowman," Amado cut in, "Chuck Bowman. An old friend."

Chuck caught his eye with an icy stare.

"Pleased to meet you, Mr. Bowman," the hopeful starlet gushed.

All was forgiven and she fluttered across the room to Amado and alighted on his lap quite blissfully unaware of the situation. Cecilia had the chance to gut them both with a single bullet and very nearly took it.

"Please don't let me interrupt, gentlemen," the insufferable twitter went on and the admittedly pretty features from whence the thwarted warble had the ill grace to emanate tried their best to feign an attentive expression.

"Please go on with whatever you were saying before I was foolishly rude and impulsive enough to butt in," she cooed unmellifluously and was unable to resist adding with an idiotic schoolgirl giggle, "Y'all weren't just talkin' 'bout li'l ol' me now, were ya?"

Amado smiled and chucked her indulgently under the chin. It occurred to Michael that even if he didn't know what he now knew he would have found the simple little gesture extraordinarily sinister.

"They are expecting us downstairs in fifteen minutes," Amado said calmly, testing for a reaction, "To greet the governor's wife. Also Miss Tanya Tucker who headlines the evening's entertainment with Miss McIntyre. We are sharing a light supper with them before the show. I would ask you to join us but I'm not sure I could get the security clearance in time."

"We'll accept a table nearby," Chuck responded without a pause.

"Oh, that would be sooo great, Amado honey!" Beverley said, squeezing Amado and sticking her tongue in his ear, "Come on, boojy–boojy, you can make it happen!" and then gave a big hammy wink at Michael and Chuck in the broad equivalent of a thumbs up signal.

"Come on, coojy-woojy. For me? Pwitty pweeze?"

§

Five minutes later Beverley was happily with her entourage again in the palatial suite of rooms the hotel management had provided on the eleventh floor getting changed and freshened up for supper. She was singing, interspersed with much throat clearing and random warm-up arpeggios, "One way or another I'm gonna getcha, getcha, getcha, getcha . . " as Amado was donning a white tuxedo in his bedroom on the seventeenth floor and Cecilia sat cross–legged on a corner of his California King water bed humming the same catchy little number. She was sipping another martini, puffing clouds of smoke from a fresh cigarillo in his direction and pointing her dainty Derringer at his groin.

Chuck and Michael were in the living room and Michael had quickly told him the main events of the past thirty–six hours, thus far leaving out the vampire stuff and the horror of the tapes, and then they more or less said at the same time that they had seen Fernando and his friends downstairs.

"So why did he dress you up like this? Who did he want you to be?"

"Someone called Bartolomeo Vespucci, I think."

"Doesn't ring any bells."

"It did with the Russians, I can tell you. They cowtowed and kissed my hand like I was Ivan the Terrible."

"What were they doing here?"

"As far as I could make out they were making a deal with Amado to hide stolen nuclear material of some sort in the desert near here."

"Holy shit. Nothing about drugs?"

"I don't think so."

"Not surprising. The Mexicans are pretty much a one product outfit and the Russians are into everything and anything."

"It's been more than slightly weird."

"Good material for your magazine."

"Yes, I feel I might even survive now."

"Don't count on it."

Chuck went and took a look through the curtains onto the patio. Amado had made the mistake of leaving them closed when the Russians left but Michael didn't think the doors were locked and two guards were just outside with their backs turned. A shaft of golden sunlight flickered briefly across Chuck's face.

"Any idea why he and his sister want to kill each other all of a sudden?"

"Not a clue. They're both stark staring bonkers if you ask me. Absolutely the looniest pair I've ever come across with the possible exception of the young Miss Texas monstrosity. They insist they're vampires," he whispered, "A family of vampires, did you know that?"

Chuck looked at him a little suspiciously, as if he might be the crazy one.

"No kidding?"

"No kidding! You wouldn't have believed the charming little ritual they performed just now with the two Russians. Right in front of me! You wouldn't believe any of the horrific stuff they've shown me."

It reminded him of the cassette still digging into the small of his back and he retrieved it with considerable relief.

"You won't believe what's on this tape."

"Oh, I probably would."

Michael suddenly remembered what Amado had done to Chuck's son and quickly put the tape in his jacket pocket but Chuck was too preoccupied to ask more about it and Michael went on.

"He insisted on taking me to see his brother Vicente's corpse. It arrived by plane in a colossal silver casket. At first I thought it might be his brother who he wanted me to impersonate for some reason. Whoever put the body in the coffin had done it very carelessly. The suit was filthy and crumpled, no shirt or socks or shoes, and there were a pair of dentures tied around its neck."

"Dentures?"

"Yes. He got very upset when he saw them."

"Well, the body came from an official autopsy in Mexico City. The new guy down there, Medina, must have been sending Amado a message. Beats me what though."

"All I could think of was vampires. Cecilia told me she and Vicente used to have big vampire fangs but Amado had them yanked out."

"Jesus."

They both grimaced at the sheer madness of it.

"So what's the bigger thing than killing him?" Michael asked, "Personally, I'd be relieved if you'd just shoot him like she wants. And then lock her up. I can't think how to tell you what inhuman sadists they both are."

"Killing him won't solve anything. I want to expose him."

"How are you planning to do that?"

The bedroom door opened and Amado strolled in looking as cool and collected as a member of Sinatra's Rat Pack. Cecilia followed a couple of paces behind with the pistol once again hovering at his ribs.

"Yes, Mr. Bowman," he said quietly, "My sister would like to know too. You are making her nervous."

§

The 'new guy' was not the kind to roll over in the face of political pressure. Hernano Salvador Medina fully realized the delicacy of his president's position and knew he could not expect any kind of reasonable behavior or assistance from his counterparts in Washington but he didn't feel these things should necessarily force him to give up all hope of exposing the true identity of 'Florio Bastida Morales'. He was not without resources or spies of his own and had that very morning dispatched two of the latter to Guamuchilito to report on the funeral which he knew was to be held there tomorrow and another on the ground in Juarez had at three o'clock that afternoon telephoned him about the blaze above the Portillo compound, which he suspected might be a panicked response to the message contained in the dentures, a suspicion in which he was partially correct but not about the identity of the unfortunates being cremated, and as well the less than surprising fact that the local fire department commander had made no attempt to investigate the matter. And yet another had just relayed the much more surprising information, which the American authorities also knew but were not under any circumstances willing to divulge, that a few minutes after four Semion 'the brainy don' Mogilevich and his stateside second–in–command, Vyacheslav 'Yaponchik' Ivankov, had landed in a small helicopter on the roof of the Barragan Hotel.

This last was indeed puzzling. Ivankov had been convicted of extortion and given a nine–year sentence and as far as Medina knew was still being held secretly in the high security wing of the Metropolitan Correctional Center near Foley Square in Lower Manhattan. More than that, there had never before been any particular link between the Russian kingpin Mogilevich and Amado Portillo because their criminal empires neither overlapped nor conflicted. It was a shame but Medina decided he'd better put off the much–needed relaxation of spending Sunday with a favorite niece and their plan to visit the zoological gardens and take a stroll round the lake of San Juan de Aragon and instead fly immediately to El Paso to see what he could find out for himself.

§

News of the black cloud that had billowed up threateningly for two hours on the parched mesquite fastness above the penurious sprawl and the indifferent river had also reached a cell phone attached to the belt of the yellow plaid golf slacks of General Larry McWhirter. He was just whacking his fourteenth ball off the tee at the Beverley Beach driving range south of Annapolis, Maryland, which afforded a fine patrician vista over the upper reaches of Chesapeake Bay and the springtime regatta that was at that moment gracing its sparkling blue waters, and the sudden vibration behind his left hip as he swung a new titanium–headed five iron with all his stringy might at the unsuspecting little orange sphere had caused him to slice.

"Yeah, what?" he slurred unpleasantly into the offending mechanism.

"Something's going on down there," a deep voice said.

"Down where for Chrissake, Connie?"

"Juarez."

"What?"

"A fire."

"Yeah, so?"

"On the hill."

"So?"

"They got the body this morning."

"So fucking what?"

"I think Medina may be playing games."

"How so?"

"Letting him know he knows."

"How would he do that?"

"Don't know. Just a hunch."

McWhirter paused.

"Who gives a Jesus Christly shit what any one of them thinks he knows!" the general barked and grunted as he leaned over to place another orange Titleist on the rubber tee, "Have they had the meeting?"

"That's done."

"Well, so, good."

"Yeah, but something's going on at the hotel too."

"How do you know?"

"The manager called for backup."

"Why?"

"Three *chicos* recognized someone Portillo brought in with him and got pushy about it."

"Who?"

"We haven't got that figured yet."

"So, if it wasn't one of the Russkies, what's the problem?"

"Don't know. Something."

"Well, tell me when you do. Screw your hunches, Connie, I'm working on my swing."

§

Seven members of the cleaning staff had arrived on the seventeenth floor as Chuck was listening to Michael's revelation about the vampire cartel and were hurrying to make the very messy guest suite immaculate for the First Lady of the Lone Star State but her handlers had never intended that she arrive by helicopter nor take advantage of their efforts.

She was running late and at that very moment still in Austin kissing her twin fifteen-year-old daughters goodbye in the broad central vestibule of the 'most historic house in Texas', the Governor's Mansion at 1010 Colorado Street. Originally constructed in 1856 by master builder Abner Cook, who successfully adapted the popular Greek Revival style to the hot arid climate of the frontier, it had been refurbished and expanded many times since courtesy of legislatorial expropriations of taxpayer money as well as the lavish donations of 'friends' and was famous as the oldest continuously occupied executive residence west of the Mississippi with an outstanding collection of 19th century American antiques.

It was taking all her motherly patience and ex-elementary schoolteacher's skill to resist their last minute pleas about coming with her to the pageant and thereby avoiding some important ninth grade English homework but she stayed firm as they followed her across the spacious veranda pouting and whining and with a final "No means no!" walked briskly away between the Ionic columns and down the marble steps to a waiting chauffeur–driven black Cadillac limousine.

She didn't turn to wave as the car passed through the high wrought iron gates and was soon traversing the Congress Street Bridge over Lady Bird Lake, which due to the structural renovations of the 1980's that unwittingly provided a vast number of suitable new crevices was the summer home to a modest–sized colony of two million Mexican free–tailed bats, they wintered south of the border so their unsightly droppings which had to be pressure-washed annually weren't yet in evidence, and from there to Bergstrom Air Force Base where she was to catch a private jet and alight a brief forty minutes later at Biggs Field in El Paso.

§

Robert 'Bob' Oliver and his protégé 'Hap' North, 'Hap' in this case being the necessary contraction of Hippolytus, not the more commonly used nickname for Henry, Harry, Harold, or Harrison, which makes sense only if one imagines the full word uttered by a less than classically-minded young Texan father, were the current chief and deputy chief of the branch of the Drug Enforcement Administration that lurked in the bowels of Fort Bliss Military Reservation just south of Biggs Field. Both were decent honest men but from an army background which had instilled in them an unfailing obedience to the manifold eccentricities of their superiors so they didn't much ponder the matter nor hesitate when the call came from Washington telling them to get some surveillance photographs of an unknown 'subject of interest' who had been seen entering the Barragan Hotel with its owner, the philanthropist Amado Barragan Fuentes.

The subject was wearing a blue Italian–cut suit, had dark brown hair and was thought to be using the alias 'Michael Davenport'.

§

"Maybe I'll just step up to the mike and tell everyone," Chuck replied, "The whole thing's going out live tonight, isn't it?"

"Tell everyone what, Mr. Bowman?" Amado asked, a smile still curling his lips, "Expose what?"

"Who you are."

"Perhaps I am not who you think."

"Could be. Michael tells me you're a vampire."

Amado looked at Michael with an ironic expression of disappointment at the betrayal.

"Michael is correct."

"So I guess you should be able to turn yourself into a frog or a wolf or a bat or something when I call you out. That'd be a good trick."

"Those are foolish medieval legends and superstitions, Mr. Bowman. Old wive's tales. We have no such special powers."

"So what's the point of it?"

"Yes," Michael added, "I'd like to know that."

He turned to Cecilia.

"You said you were born vampires but that you only knew for certain later on when you and Vicente started to grow fangs."

Amado gave a mocking mirthless laugh.

"My sister is a child, Mr. Davenport. So was her brother. I told you not to believe her lies. For them the world of vampires was a game. They played in it but never understood it."

"What more is it to you then?" Michael asked, "This 'world of vampires'. I have seen only the most horrific sadism. What more is it than a twisted excuse for your heartless cruelty?"

Amado was silent for a moment and then spoke with grave earnestness.

"It is best described, I think, as an ideal."

It was Cecilia's turn to laugh.

"You fucking toad," she hissed in his ear, "You cheap pathetic little flunky. You fake. You ass-licker. Our world is no 'ideal' and you know it. It is necessity!"

Michael looked at Chuck as if to say, 'You see, I told you they were out of their minds.'

"What, in the same way you could call Adolf Hitler a necessity?" he asked incredulously, "In the sense of being some sort of inevitable outcome?"

"No, Englishman," Cecilia answered, "In the sense of blood."

"Being *in* the blood?"

"Not only *in* the blood. We *are* the blood."

"Oh, I see, and what blood is that?"

"The blood you lack."

She spoke quite matter-of-factly and neither Michael nor Chuck made any response. What the hell could one say to that more than had already been said? It suddenly occurred to Michael that these two were not the worldly sophisticates they might appear to be at first sight. Latino, yes, bilingual, even multilingual, yes, articulate, yes, well–dressed and groomed and trim, yes, all cliché attributes generally provoke knee-jerk reactions if left unchallenged. But what if they were really quite uncomplicated? Yes, look at their mother, a barely literate farmer's wife. What if they were a perfectly ordinary self–educated country boy and girl who had been totally unprepared for so much money and luxury and power and it had debased and corrupted them and sent them off the rails in this appalling manner. It would have been comforting to entertain the conjecture they were not of the human species but, alas, he couldn't delude himself thus far.

Amado broke the silence.

"It is never easy to give such things words. Even vampires differ in their understanding. It may not be so simple as you think, Mr. Bowman, to define precisely who I am."

"Defining you won't be the problem," Chuck said.

They eyed each other steadily.

"So it isn't true you had their fangs knocked out?" Michael asked.

Amado didn't look at him nor answer.

"There were no teeth in your brother's mouth and Cecilia showed me the awful gaps in hers. The extractions were recent. What was the meaning of the dentures? Why did they upset you?"

Again there was no response.

"Why do you think you never grew fangs?"

"Ask my dentist," Amado answered curtly, then addressed Cecilia without turning to her, "If you have decided not to kill me now, dear sister, please tell these gentlemen that despite the charming diversion of their company it is time for us to go."

Cecilia looked at Chuck and shook her head in disgust, then pushed her brother forward with the barrel of her pistol and concealed it in her purse. They left the suite and walked to the elevator in silence and Amado made no attempt on the way to communicate with his guards.

As they descended he smiled and said, "What would you give for a film of what you have just witnessed, Mr. Davenport?"

Michael fingered the tape in his pocket and ventured a glance at Cecilia.

"I'm not much on that sort of thing," he replied, returning the smile, "But a film of the film you showed might come in handy."

They held each other's eyes.

"All in all," he continued amiably, "I'd rather be on my way with the tapes you promised to return."

Amado shrugged and went on smiling.

"You will introduce them as the famous Hollywood producers your little blow-face thinks they are," Cecilia cut in, "You will stay close by my side and hope Mr. Bowman finds some way to make his foolish plan happen. If you try to whisper or gesture commands you know I will not hesitate. "

Amado turned his smile on Chuck but said nothing.

CHAPTER TWENTY-TWO

Highway 54 north of Fort Bliss leads straight as a die twenty miles across the deserted chaparral into the state of New Mexico and the bulk of the Military Reservation itself and then, just a hundred miles farther, via the forgotten ghost town of Orogrande, where the moonscape road is still sometimes closed for short periods of artillery practice, and passing the Sunspot Solar Observatory and on through the bleached city of Alamogordo and beyond the vast sizzling waste of the White Sands Missile Range, if one had the courage to venture on foot, as once, so legend has it, a German fugitive was forced while fleeing the Inquisition many centuries ago, over the ancient lava flows of the *Jornada del Muerto* due east from Truth or Consequences, finally, nestled between South and North Oscuro Peaks, one would arrive at . . not the Seven Cities of Cibola but the true holy of holies . . Trinity, test site of Fat Boy, the world's first implosion atomic bomb.

§

As they sped in their Hummer down Pershing Avenue and then turned south Hap mused idly about who this 'Michael Davenport' might be.

"Just another pumped-up, pampered, heartless crud like Barragan, that'd be my guess," Oliver opined.

His mother was a Quaker and even in late middle age could never bring himself to swear.

"You just don't like rich people," Hap teased.

"Don't like having to look out for them that's for dang sure."

"You think they think this guy Davenport might be some kind of danger to him?"

"Don't know they think so. Like always they were short on reasons. Bunch of dumb photographs," Oliver snorted, "What are we working at, a gosh darned fashion magazine? Sure ain't what I signed on for."

Hap was silent for a moment in solidarity and then asked, "Think it might have something to do with the First Lady being there?"

"Could be but I doubt it."

"She's everyone's high school sweetheart," Hap drawled and followed the observation with a faint but audible sigh, "A genuine Texas peach."

"Careful now, boy," Oliver warned sternly and they chuckled.

§

Fernando, Enrique and Rafael were still outside the coffee shop debating whether to try and get tickets or go back to Juarez when Ethel and Dickie came huffing and puffing round the corner.

"Look, Dickie, there they are!"

The old couple toddled up and Fernando got out of the cab.

"We hoped you hadn't gone too far. We knew there was more you wanted to tell us about Mr. Davenport," Ethel said.

"It was better to make a little distance. For us the American police can be a problem," Fernando explained.

"Oh, don't worry about that. We understood perfectly."

"We're glad we found you," Dickie added, still somewhat breathless, and then stifled a small belch and added apologetically, "Ooops, sorry, pardon me."

"Do you need one of your pills?" Ethel asked but he ignored her.

"Have you tried this little coffee shop?" he went on, still struggling slightly for control.

"We've had both breakfast and lunch here today."

"The only reasonable place for miles."

"An oasis in the desert, I can tell you."

"Ethel's even taught them how to make a passable pot of tea."

"These American cities can be frightfully barren, can't they?"

"It's far too expensive for us to eat in the hotel. Pensioner's budget, you know."

"But we did manage to get quite a good rate for the room by booking from England. Well, you can, can't you?"

There was a brief pause as they both smiled and nodded and then said the single word, "Yes", in unison and then looked at each other and chuckled at the coincidence.

"We were just going to have a cup of tea now," Dickie said.

"Would you care to join us?"

"We've been bloody clever, I'll have you know."

"That smarmy manager offered us tickets for the Miss Texas thingy but we told him we wouldn't leave his office until he gave us five."

"They can't very well turn you away if you've got seats, now can they?"

"Besides that, you'll be with us."

§

It was twelve minutes to six as the two DEA agents entered the crowded Barragan lobby and the elevator doors opened.

Everyone except Michael noticed everyone else. Amado and Cecilia saw Oliver and North and Chuck did too and Oliver and North saw them. They also saw Michael and both figured right away he must be their 'subject of interest' but neither gave voice to it because of the bigger puzzle. What the heck was their old colleague, that loose cannon Bowman, doing in his company? Washington hadn't said anything about that.

Michael was only aware of a tiny hesitation in Amado's movement before he turned away from the crowd and the flashbulbs and two green-suited guards ushered them through a door into a private corridor that led to the ballroom.

To one side was a large elegantly furnished chamber used for meetings of the hotel board among other things and they entered it.

Brewster Jordan was waiting for them with a troubled face.

"Have Miss Tucker and the governor's wife arrived?" Amado asked.

"Not yet, sir, we've got a problem," he replied nervously, "Miss Tucker sent her apologies but her connecting flight out of Nashville has been delayed indefinitely because of tornado warnings in the area and there's no way she'll be here until after we've started."

"She was to share the opening song with Miss McIntyre."

"Yes sir, I told her and Miss McIntyre says she can handle it."

'Good god,' Michael thought. What next did he have to endure?

"The First Lady has departed Austin and they're estimating her convoy'll be outside the doors around 6:45."

"And Miss Kellerman and her co-host?"

"Miss Kellerman and Mr. Schoendienst are in Miss McIntyre's suite."

Gaylord 'Red' Schoendienst had been nicknamed 'Red' by his parents, not only for his once unruly carrot-top but also in not-so-subtle homage to the great St. Louis Cardinals' second baseman and Hall of Famer of the same surname. He had spent his childhood in the 'Gateway to the West' and had fond memories of summer afternoons in Busch Stadium but his father had moved the family to the Permian Basin Oil Patch in the high optimism of the late fifties and Gaylord was now well-loved state-wide as a sportscaster and TV personality. He had attended senior school in Midland and was a close personal friend and one-time drinking buddy of the present governor before the latter's much-publicized conversion to sobriety and spiritual rebirth in 1986 following a heart to heart, so the PR hype went, with the creamily-coiffed evangelist Billy Graham. He still sat on the board of the Texas Rangers baseball team and it was frequently rumored that he once had a brief teenage romance with the First Lady.

"Let me know five minutes before the convoy arrives," Amado instructed his sweating manager, "And make sure they are on their way down. When she is called have Miss McIntyre escorted directly to her dressing room backstage. The hosts may join us here and come with us to the lobby if they wish."

Jordan nodded and went out leaving two underlings inside the door.

There was a tall white-jacketed waiter in the room standing behind a long table with a huge crystal punchbowl at the center and piled high with plates of hors-d'oeuvres and he came forward to ask if anyone would care for a cocktail and Cecilia lit a cigarette and said she'd have a martini. This time she had the upper hand and Amado didn't try to stop her. He asked for a Perrier and Chuck did the same and Michael settled for beer. The presence of the waiter and the guards caused a strained silence until they had their drinks.

Finally, Michael broke the ice.

"Do any of you happen to know John Donne's holy sonnet number four?" he asked.

They stared at him blankly as if they somehow half expected the question.

"No?" he went on, "Well, not to worry. It begins with the line, 'Batter my heart three-personed God for you as yet but knock.' I can't think why that should be running through my mind just now but it is."

He could see he hadn't really set any balls rolling.

"It ends something like, 'For I shall never be free, nor ever chaste, except you ravish me.' If I recall correctly. Interesting, don't you think? That sense of the Almighty as a sort of dominatrix who, paradoxically, is capable of violating one back into a state of innocence and purity. Of freedom from sin."

The others remained understandably non-committal.

"No, I can't quite grasp the burden of what I'm saying either."

He tried another subject.

"So, Señor Barragan, do you think Miss McIntyre can handle it?" he asked cheekily and launched into an unsuccessful attempt at Beverley's inimitable tone and accent, "The opening number, I mean? All by her li'l ol' self? Shall I expect to be ravished?"

Cecilia was lolling provocatively on the other end of a leather couch from Amado and laughed.

"I think you may be surprised, Mr. Davenport," Amado replied coolly.

'No soap there either,' Michael thought, 'Very well, let's try another.'

"All right then, anyone want to tell me who the two cute guys were in the lobby?"

Chuck took a swallow of his Perrier before answering.

"They were DEA. Bob Oliver and Hap North. I used to work with them. Good men, but blind."

"Any idea why they showed up?"

"Yes, Mr. Bowman, any idea?" Amado said, smiling again.

"I've got a few," Chuck responded drily.

§

Night had already fallen over the clubhouse on Chesapeake Bay and the general was nestling his wiry frame in the embrace of a stuffed arm-chair among a circle of his cronies suffused by the warm glow of the fire in their accustomed bay-window nook, which afforded an unobstructed vista over the darkening water and the twinkling lights of Shady Side and Romancoke and Wittman and all the way to the flash of Sharp's Beacon south of Fairbank, slowly stirring a perfectly chilled double Manhattan with two Maraschino cherries impaled on the swizzle and just on the point of bringing the delectable potion to his expectantly moistened lips when his cell phone rang again.

He squinted at the caller ID and thought momentarily to ignore it, then snapped it open and growled, "What in hell is it now?"

§

Michael surprised himself by the speed with which he put this particular two and two together.

"They came to protect him?" he ventured with a tiny nod toward Amado, speaking very quietly so the waiter and the guards wouldn't hear, "Doesn't he already have all the protection a man could need?"

"You can never have too many friends in high places," Chuck replied.

"Who do you mean exactly?"

"The names are unimportant," Amado chimed in, still calmly smiling, "As my dear sister said, it is a matter of blood. We are a brotherhood."

Michael leaned forward, almost whispering.

"*Nosferatu?* Is that what you're saying?"

Amado shrugged.

"If you like."

"They have no blood!" Cecilia shouted, sitting up and crawling unsteadily over the couch to spit the words in his face, "Their motives have no nobility!"

He took the cigarette from her hand and held it away from his nose and she snatched it back and a spot of ash fell and smudged the pristine whiteness of his jacket and Michael saw the same terrifying look as he had upstairs.

"For them it is nothing but the money and the power," she went on, "And you are the same. Despite what you used to pretend you never had the heart for more, confess it! Vicente and I were the only true ones."

She turned to Michael. The venom in her eyes seemed to make them glow hypnotically. A vampire Medusa with writhing snakes for hair. The guards and the waiter were staring at the floor attempting invisibility.

"What this piece of excrement is blubbering about is nothing but a club. Like your fucking Boy Scouts but deadly. A smug elite of thieves and liars. An empty world that he is panting to be part of. But no matter how much he grovels they will not let him. He will never be one of them."

"Why?" Michael asked.

"Because he cannot be washed clean."

"You mean his money laundered, is that it?"

"No, Englishman, not his money, his skin."

Amado stopped smiling but not because her words had upset him.

"You have always been full of childish foolishness," he said, "It is you that has never understood. They do not care that I am *mestizo* or that my skin is dark. They are themselves of all races and colors. Not only white but African, Chinese, Tatar, Israeli and Turk. We are an attitude of mind."

"No kidding," Chuck concurred.

'And all vampires?' Michael thought with a shudder.

He suddenly recalled an interview he had done the previous year with an ex-footballer who he had dismissed at the time as comical and sophomoric and paranoid but whose theories were now gaining a certain sickening credence. This earnest young man had proclaimed to him in a thick Midlands accent that the world was primarily populated by human robots ruled by a small master race of shape-shifting alien reptiles from the constellation Draco. Good lord, maybe he was right.

§

Rafael had decided he should wait outside in the cab and in the Java Bean as Ethel and Dickie sipped their tea and munched on a heaping plateful of their newly-discovered favorite spicy cheese nachos Fernando and Enrique had been careful not to alarm them about the real identity of Amado Barragan Fuentes.

The old couple were full of surprises and somehow they had got onto the subject of Native Indian Art.

"Yes, that's really why we came," they said with enthusiasm.

"We're off into the Samalayuca tomorrow if all goes as planned."

"We're very anxious to see the petroglyphs."

Fernando didn't know what to say.

"Surely you know the works of von Daniken?" Ethel went on.

"Absolutely marvelous books," Dickie added.

"Yes," she said, "He puts forward a very convincing argument that some of those petroglyphs are actually a primitive depiction of space-men."

"That the big round heads are part of their space suits, do you see?"

"We'd love to visit the Plains of Nazca."

"Von Daniken says that was most likely their landing strip and the Indians made those big outlines of animals and birds to welcome them."

"Over two thousand years ago."

"Before Jesus, just think. Who knows, maybe the man everyone reveres as the Son of God was an extraterrestrial."

"Gently now, Ethel. The lads here are probably devout Catholics."

Ethel gave them a straight look.

"Are you?"

Fernando shook his head 'no' but there were many layers of unexpressed complexity beneath the gesture.

"You see, Dickie dear, they don't mind. There's a fascinating theory that the big halo behind Jesus' head in all those medieval paintings is a representation of his spaceman's helmet. You know, skewed by the passage of the centuries. Well, you have to admit it does look like it."

Fernando and Enrique didn't respond.

"We're died in the wool atheists," Ethel sighed.

"Well, we don't see the sense in anything else."

"Fancy being able to visit the spot where Jesus touched down."

She nudged Dickie and they laughed out loud.

"But we haven't sufficient resources to travel all the way to Peru, not by a long chalk, I'm afraid."

"We'll have to settle for the petroglyphs and the *Zona del Silencio.*"

Ethel gave a self-deprecating grimace at her bad Spanish pronunciation.

"Aren't you worried it may not be safe?" Fernando said at last.

The octogenarian intrepids looked at each other in mock dismay.

"Why wouldn't it be safe?"

"Who'd trouble a pair of harmless old crocks like us?"

§

By a strange coincidence, at precisely 6:22 PM, two government jets were coming in to land from the northeast on parallel runways at Biggs Field, one proudly displaying the emblem of the Lone Star and the other from the Mexican Attorney General's office and unmarked, one carrying Laura Bush and six Secret Service agents and the other the slight and vulnerable-looking figure of Hernano Salvador Medina, newly appointed director of FEADS, the *'Fiscalía Especializada en Atención de Delitos contra la Salud'* or Special Prosecutor's Office for Crimes Against Health, the much more subtly entitled Mexican equivalent of the DEA.

As they were both being met on the tarmac, the First Lady by a cavalcade of five long black Cadillac limousines each sporting two state flags on either side, Hernano Medina by a single nondescript Chevrolet sedan, a great deal was being transmitted about one of them in a hastily arranged three-way call between Bob Oliver, in his Hummer again outside the Barragan Hotel, Director Consterdine, still in his office on Army Navy Drive puffing nervously on a Cuban cigar, and the general who was now slumped irritably in the rear of a chauffeur-driven Lincoln Continental on his reluctant way to yet another silent supper with his estranged and sadly arthritic wife Alice in the oak-paneled dining room of her mid-nineteenth-century Georgetown colonial classic via the relatively traffic free side route of Highway 214.

"First Bolen or Bowkin or Bogden or whatever the fuck his name is and now Medina!" the general groaned, "He just got clearance at Biggs and he's going to the Barragan? What the fuck is going on?!"

"We don't know yet, sir," said Oliver, somewhat confused by McWhirter's angry exasperated tone.

"See, Connie, didn't I tell you? I told you he'd come on as some Zapatista paladin. New boys always do. Or does he have a little chickie-chickie in the bikini brigade?"

"I doubt that," Consterdine answered with a scornful grunt, "Far as I know he's not of the persuasion. But about Bowman, you think there's any chance he may have gone over to the other side?"

"How do you mean?" Oliver asked.

"Oh, for Christ's sake, whaddya mean whaddya mean?!" the general barked, "Connie, how come your goddamned Chief of Operations for the whole south-western area doesn't know his balls from a pair of book ends?! Are you trying to tell me, son, that you don't know who Amado Barragan Fuentes is?"

"Chuck Bowman was right all along, Bob," Consterdine said quietly and then, lying through his nicotine-stained teeth, "I thought you knew."

There was a brief silence as Oliver digested it.

"You're saying Barragan is Amado Portillo?"

"That's right."

"So who died in Mexico City?"

"His brother."

"OK," Oliver sighed unhappily.

"And Connie, please don't feed me any crap about Bowman going over to the other side. Portillo boiled his son in a barrel of hydrochloric acid, for fuck's sake. He can only be there to kill him."

The general thought for moment.

"Or worse."

"Yup, my concern too," Consterdine concurred.

"And what, is Medina some way in bed with him on this? What the hell do Sam Wanless and the rest of your dumb-asses do down there in Mexico? Squirt tequila and blow burritos? Why don't they know what's going on?"

There was silence again and Oliver broke it.

"Anyone care to tell me why any of this is a problem? If he's Portillo why don't we just walk in right now and arrest him?"

"Jesus, son," McWhirter said, cackling mirthlessly and almost choking on the relentless flux of his spittle, "You really don't know shit from Shinola, do you. Portillo is our fucking asset!"

"It would mean big trouble if he was outed, Bob," Consterdine said.

The other two could plainly hear the general sucking his gums.

"So what do you want me to do?" Oliver asked resignedly.

"See if you can get to Bowman and sweet talk him out of there and then lock him up."

"What about Medina?"

"Be polite to him. Find out why he's suddenly in El Paso. We know he knows about Portillo and is itching to go public with it some way or other but Zedillo's told him to keep his mouth shut. And find out if he's got anything to do with Bowman being there or even knows who he is."

"What about the other guy, 'Davenport'?"

"Forget about him."

"Anything else?"

"Talk to me every ten minutes."

§

There was a knock on the boardroom door and one of the green-suited guards answered it and walked quickly to Amado and whispered in his ear and he gave his permission and Gaylord 'Red' Schoendienst and

Cindy 'the fox of KFOX' Kellerman, glowing co-hosts of the Final Night Competition of the 1997 Miss Texas Scholarship Pageant, were ushered, with all their show-bizzy aerobic *frou-frou*, into the distinctly turbid atmosphere and the fictive introductions were free-wheeled through.

"Miss McIntyre couldn't stop gushing about y'all upstairs," Gaylord confided to Chuck with a blinding flash of freshly-whitened laminates, "She kept declaring that you really are Gene Hackman and are just gaming with her, sir. The stars in her eyes must have temporarily blurred her vision but I'd say y'all have a heavy responsibility now putting such grand ideas in a young girl's head."

Chuck shrugged, considering a poker face the only possible gambit, and Michael thought to himself, damn and bugger it, if he could master such a hokey twang he could make millions too.

"What studio are y'all with?" Cindy enquired casually, but the adamantine malevolence lurking behind her glistening brown eyes made Michael cringe.

"Ah, well, now you're asking," he mumbled.

He turned to Amado and caught him looking sly. What was the point of this latest madness? Did the little horror simply get off on messing with people? It was almost impossible to muster the energy for more improvisation.

"We're, um, well, we're saying, it's better really for all concerned, if we say, at least for the moment if you get my drift, that we're, ah, strictly Indy."

'Wow, good boy,' Michael thought, 'Where did that come from?' and then added unnecessarily, with a clumsy movement of one eyelid more twitch than wink, "That's our story and we're sticking to it."

"You Hollywood boys keep everything under wraps," Gaylord said and laughed, knocking back a second schooner of champagne cocktail and chomping energetically on a sixth savory corn cracker heaped with guacamole shrimp, "No telling when someone'll snag an intercept and beat you to the end zone!"

"And y'all are really going to cast little Beverley?" Cindy asked and then added with a tiny involuntary snort, "Isn't she just a tad green?"

"Green can be good," Michael replied, unflinching at her death ray stare.

"And I'm sure the Barragan billions have nothing to do with it."

"No, no, she could be just the ticket for what we have in mind."

"But you're not telling what that is."

"Gotcha," Michael said and attempted to wink the other eye, "Roger, over and out."

'Dear mother scowling in heaven, this is even worse than pretending to be 'Bartolomeo Vespucci', whoever he was!' he growled to himself and glowered at Amado. 'What Barnum and Bailey Spielberger am I supposed to be now? This is worse than being reamed with a caber-sized swizzle stick, more surreal than life itself!'

Mercifully, Brewster Jordan came in before Michael's discomfiture could be pricked to critical mass and told Amado that the First Lady was three minutes away and it didn't take the glittering co-hosts a nanosecond to forget about him and Chuck and even their drinks and the buffet of goodies and make an instant bee-line for the lobby.

Amado quickly followed with Cecilia close behind but turned to Michael in the doorway and said without a trace of irony, "You may leave whenever you wish, Mr. Davenport."

CHAPTER TWENTY-THREE

For various reasons, none of them very honorable, Bob Oliver decided not to share the information he had just been given about the true identity of Amado Barragan when he returned to Hap North's side in the hotel lobby.

"What'd they say?" Hap asked.

"They want us to get Bowman out of here."

"What about the other guy?"

"Told us to forget him."

North could see his friend was even more pissed off than before but didn't press the reason.

"Did they say why Bowman was with Barragan?"

"Said he's gone nuts."

As he spoke, 'Red' and 'the Fox of KFOX' swept through the private door into the lobby and were immediately confronted by a barrage of flashbulbs and reporter's questions. Then Amado and Cecilia appeared and, after a polite pause while the co-hosts deftly turned aside a couple of snide barbs concerning Tanya Tucker's unfortunate lateness and the rumor of Beverley's forthcoming solo, Amado led the way through the crowd and out the revolving doors as the First Lady's flag-bedecked convoy glided to a stop under the grand archway.

§

Chuck and Michael were still in the boardroom and even though Michael had the tape in his pocket, a tape that would more than do all that Chuck wanted about incriminating Amado and giving the lie to his false persona, he could not bring himself to mention it again because of what had happened to Chuck's son.

"Look, old chap," he said, below the hearing of the waiter and the guards who remained somewhat ominously behind, "Perhaps we should, um, do as he suggested and leave."

"Go ahead if you want," Chuck replied.

"It's obvious they're both certifiably mad. They believe they're vampires and their actions prove it. If not as fact then as metaphor. As far as

I can tell they are responsible for everything Fernando has on the walls at his gallery and then some. They are utterly evil. They will certainly kill us. They've shown me things, gut-wrenchingly awful things that I could attest to later on if you think it will help but what would be the point? She's right. The only way to put a stop to it is to kill them. We'll probably need stakes and mallets for all I know."

Chuck was silent but Michael could see he was thinking it over and went on.

"What kind of a world is it when two of your own colleagues are sent to protect such a man? How can you expose him when very likely they've been told to kill you first? Let's get out of here while we've got the chance."

"Like I said, go if you want. This is nothing to do with you. But it's too late for me. Too late for you too, I'd guess, no matter what he said."

Michael could see the probable truth of that and swallowed.

"Mm. Well then, how are you going to achieve what you propose?"

"Don't know. Play the cat and mouse game and see what happens."

"Do you have some sort of weapon at least?" Michael whispered.

Chuck nodded.

"Pleased to hear it."

Michael finished his beer and looked at the waiter and cleared his throat, gesturing for a refill.

"It's comforting to know you've got such a clear plan."

§

The six Secret Service agents had leapt from their limousines fore and aft and while two of them conversed in muffled tones on walkie-talkies with unseen others in the breathlessly officious manner of all such men the remaining four made a phalanx on either side of the rear door of the gleaming central Cadillac. The hotel green-suits had been stationed outside for the last half an hour and had already created a wide passage through the crowd.

There was a fractional moment's hush and then one of the agents said for all to hear, "Ladies and gentlemen, please give a big Texas welcome to our First Lady," and opened the door and Laura Bush stepped demurely out of the car and smiled and blinked her famously Chinese eyes into the cameras' glare.

The applause from the crowd was tumultuous and no one heard Amado as he came forward and said, "How nice to see you again, Laura," and held her hand and gave her a familiar little peck on the cheek.

"This is my sister Cecilia."

Cecilia was standing glued to his shoulder, still wearing her tinted glasses and carrying her martini, and didn't even offer a hand in friendly greeting but if her presence or behavior puzzled the First Lady there was no outward sign of it.

"And, of course, you know Miss Kellerman and Mister Schoendienst."

"You look fabulous as usual. I love your outfit," Cindy gushed.

"Howdy, honeybunch," Gaylord said, grabbing his erstwhile girlfriend a little too tightly around the waist and, ever the wag, planting a definitely too big kiss on her mock-embarrassed lips, "How's everyone's favorite delinquent?"

The crowd was hooting and hollering a mix of shock and approval.

"He's fine, Gay," she said, still smiling, "And he's watching."

Suddenly, as the whistling and applause subsided, Beverley burst through the revolving doors and everyone within two city blocks could have heard her bray, "Amado, you stinkin' little snake, why didn't anyone let me know she was here?!" but then turned on such a winning smile that the whole crowd laughed and cheered and clapped some more. Jollity, Lone Star style. The good Lord's luck to 'em but it was gonna be one heckuva marriage!

Amado had to grin and bear it as Beverly came and hugged and kissed the governor's placidly malleable better half and they all proceeded back through the revolving doors and across the lobby, the First Lady politely declining on the way Amado's offer of a comfort stop in the now spotless suite on the seventeenth floor, and then on past a bevy of green-suited guards into the Dome Bar which had been temporarily evacuated for security purposes and continued without breaking stride to the Grand Ballroom where, elevated above the others to the left side of the stage like a kind of Royal Box, a large circular dinner table was laid ready for them and all the while during their passage Beverley barely made pause in her rapturous description of the wonderful movie people who were here to watch her perform and the fabulous career they were planning for her once she had gratefully relinquished her diamond-studded tiara.

"So where is Bowman now?" Hap said to his boss after the First Lady and the whole gabbling entourage had disappeared through the doors, "He was with Barragan and this 'Davenport' character a minute ago. You said they say he's gone crazy. What do they think he's gonna do?"

"Figure it out. Chuck always kept telling everyone Barragan was really Amado Portillo. That Portillo killed his son. What do you think they think?"

Hap gave a little whistle under his breath.

"How do we know he's still here?"

Oliver didn't bother to answer.

"So, um, whoever Barragan is he doesn't know who Chuck is, is that it?"

"How the Sam Hill would I know?"

Then Oliver began to get an uncomfortable idea.

"You ever see a movie called The Manchurian Candidate?"

"Laurence Harvey and Frank Sinatra, yeah, sure, what are you thinkin'?"

"I'm thinking we need to get ourselves a good view over that ballroom."

But, even as the thought moved him, Oliver checked himself.

"I better call first. They want ten minute updates."

As they hurried back through the revolving doors to return to the Hummer, Hernano Salvador Medina walked in and neither of them noticed him.

§

Ethel and Dickie had heard something of the commotion outside the hotel as they were leaving the Java Bean with their three new Mexican friends and as they approached the Barragan Fernando gestured them to stop and they watched Oliver and North cross the street to their vehicle.

Fernando spoke to Enrique and Rafael in Spanish.

"They're DEA. I'm pretty sure the shorter stocky guy with the gray crew cut was Chuck's boss."

"Who is Chuck?" Ethel queried and smiled triumphantly at their surprise, "Dickie and I got quite good at Spanish before we left Bournemouth."

"An old friend," Fernando replied.

"Does he have something to do with Mr. Davenport?" asked Dickie.

"They know each other. Chuck is somewhere inside too."

"Does he have a last name?"

"Bowman."

"What does the acronym DEA stand for?"

"The American Drug Police," Enrique answered.

ADP didn't quite tally in the old couple's minds but they let it go.

"Why would they be here?"

Fernando and Rafael and Enrique looked at one another and, finding no easy way to answer, simply shrugged.

"We're not sure," Fernando said, "Let's wait and see if they go back in."

"Isn't this fun, Dickie? I feel like Agatha Christie."

"Rath-er!" her partner of fifty-seven years concurred excitedly.

§

The moment Hernano Salvador Medina walked through the revolving doors he was stopped by the green-suits and asked if he had a ticket for the gala and he showed them his FEADS ID card which didn't mean anything to them even though it had *'Procuraduría General de la República'* written on it in bold embossed letters and so he told them in his excellent English that he was an official of the Mexican government and was here to see Señor Barragan about a private matter and they decided they'd better escort him to the manager's office.

§

"What have you done with them, boojy-boojy?" Beverley said as two of the Secret Service men retreated to standing positions in the relative darkness behind the table and the others spread out around the ballroom and they were seated by four white-jacketed waiters.

"Who do you mean?"

"Come on now, don't be coy, you little rascal," she cooed, "Mr. Hackman and Mr. Davenport, who else."

"Aren't they going to join us?" Cindy said.

"You'll love them, pet," Gaylord said with his left arm draped around the chair of his old squeeze, he had virtually shunted Cindy out of the way with a right hip block in order to sit beside her, "Though her Mr. Hackman is surely not Mr. Hackman, the other has that quaint English sense of humor and his accent is just adorable."

The First Lady had been given the seat with the best view of the stage and the runway and also the place that would give the audience the clearest sight of her as they came in. Amado would have sat on her left had Cecilia not been there and Beverley not thrust her way into their midst and, after being body-checked by her co-host, Cindy decided to sit directly across the table with an empty chair to either side.

"Come on, Amado, send someone to get them, there's plenty of room."

"The extra seats are reserved for Ms. Tucker."

"Well, she's not here, is she?"

"They say she's back on the booze," Cindy confided with an expression of deepest concern, "I tried to tell everyone we should have a back-up. The rules say there have to be three judges."

"Oh now, I'm sure she'll be fine," Gaylord offered gallantly, "But, what the heck, have them join us. You said she's not going to make it until after curtain up and we three'll be called to our duties way before then."

Cindy turned to Beverley with the innocent sincerity of a pit viper, "And you're OK about carrying the opening number?"

"Oh, yeah, no problem," Beverley replied smoothly, not rising to the bait, "The director told me he couldn't tell us apart. Everyone's always said we look just like twins. It's true, dontcha think? Did you see the video of 'Soon'? She is soooo sexy! Come on, hurry up, boojy-boojy, I only got a minute and I need to tell them what's going on!"

Cecilia cackled.

"What are you waiting for?" she said, "They're your partners, no? You're supposed to enjoy their company."

Amado was cornered. He was about to tell one of the waiters to go and fetch them when a green-suit came up to the table and whispered in his ear that someone named Medina was here to see him and that the hotel manager, being temporarily over-burdened with last minute details for the gala, had thought it best if the gentleman waited in the boardroom. Amado blanched noticeably at the news and considered for a moment.

"What is it, honey pie? You've gone white as a ghost."

"It's nothing. A friend has arrived unexpectedly," Amado said and rose to his feet, "You will have to excuse me, Laura. I apologize but it will not take more than a few minutes. I will ask the movie men to join you if that is all right."

The First Lady smiled and shrugged her assent and Amado walked away abruptly and Cecilia lurched after him without a word.

"Strange lady," Gaylord said with a wry grin as he watched them go.

"She's a total bitch," Beverley added unapologetically.

§

Michael was fully expecting one of the guards in the boardroom to draw a silenced sidearm and shoot them or to already have had his beer poisoned by the waiter or eventually to be garroted by the implacable green-suits when Hernano Salvador Medina strolled in. Chuck could barely believe it. Had the 'new boy' been so quickly and easily corrupted or was the reason for his appointment that he had been part of the whole slimy mess all along?

Medina didn't appear to know who they were. He gave them a polite nod and made his way to the bar where he asked for a Coca-Cola with ice and a slice of lime and started to fill up a small plate with hors-d'oeuvres.

Michael caught Chuck's reaction and when Medina's back was turned he asked Chuck with his eyes and a gesture of his head who the man was.

"New boss of the Mexican DEA," Chuck whispered.

The plot was getting murkier and murkier. Michael gestured again with the obvious question, 'What's he doing here?' and Chuck shrugged.

Then Medina turned and looked straight at Chuck and said, "Your name is Bowman, is it not?"

Chuck was too surprised to answer for a moment.

"That's right," he said cautiously, "And yours is Medina."

"I think we are both wondering why the other is here."

They didn't have time to pursue the matter because Amado came briskly in with Cecilia on his heels. She looked at the assembled company blearily and seemed faintly pleased to see that they were still there and was just about to call for another drink when Amado snapped his fingers and made a motion for the waiter and the guards to leave the room so she went and helped herself instead.

Once they had gone Amado turned to Chuck and Michael and said, "Miss McIntyre would like you to join her party in the ballroom."

"Oh, I think we'll stay," Chuck answered.

"As you wish," Amado said coldly and then went on in Spanish without a pause, "It is a pleasure to meet you, Señor Medina. President Zedillo is a friend of mine and I congratulate you on your recent appointment. Unfortunately, I am otherwise engaged for the next few hours so if your business with me is more than trifling I'm afraid it must wait. If you do not mind that inconvenience I will be happy to meet with you in my suite at, shall we say, half past ten? If you would enjoy the diversion of the gala that will soon be in progress it can easily be arranged."

Medina answered in English, "I will wait."

Amado nodded curtly, almost clicking his heels, and then turned again to Chuck and Michael, holding an outstretched arm to the door, and said, with his gimlet eyes shining murderously, "I'm afraid I must insist, gentlemen. The First Lady is also asking."

'Oh my fucking oath,' Michael thought, 'More charades.'

"Come on, boys," Cecilia said with a smirk, "Where's your loyalty?"

It was clear they didn't have much choice if Amado decided to force the issue and anyway Medina had agreed to stay so they acquiesced. The questions hanging in the air would have to wait for resolution.

CHAPTER TWENTY-FOUR

As soon as the First Lady's table had been served the doors opened and the rest of the ballroom began rapidly filling up with the crème de la crème of El Paso society, a few of whom came over to the Royal Box and reached up to shake Laura Bush by the hand and kibitz with her for a moment and many others made a show of waving to her from a distance. The sixty-six identical circular tables set with twelve places each on the dance floor surrounded a runway for the contestants that led from the stage to the center of the room. Between the tables wide aisles had been created for roving television cameras which were already in evidence and the camera operators and cable jockeys were listening on headphones and practicing their moves. There were also eight rows of bleacher seats beyond the tables capable of accommodating at least another five hundred spectators who would be allowed in once the gala meal was finished.

A twenty-four piece orchestra was playing a potpourri of Texan favorites and a selection of the hit songs of Tanya Tucker, star of the Tuckertime, Liberty, Capitol Nashville, Arista, MCA and Columbia labels, born to humble beginnings in Seminole, on the outskirts of the Oil Patch but as well known for its peanuts and cotton, the teen sensation who stunned the world in 1972 with her version of 'Delta Dawn', which rose to number six in the Country Top Ten while she was still, according to some, the too-tender age of thirteen, and went on with a string of memorable successes like 'What's Your Mama's Name?', 'Blood Red and Going Down', 'Would You Lay With Me In a Field of Stone?', 'Lizzie and the Rainman' and 'Strong Enough to Bend' and who, despite some well-publicized mid-career lapses with cocaine and alcohol, was now back on top again with her new album, 'Little Things'. The doggedly upbeat music filled the air, mixed with a hubbub of loud voices and laughter and clattering dinnerware.

Michael and Chuck had traversed this minefield following Amado as he did his best to avoid shaking too many hands and brush off well-wishers with a knowing smile and nod. They had reluctantly taken their places on either side of the breezy-mannered dragon lady from KFOX and were now being forced to suffer through Beverley's breakneck low-down on how Tanya Tucker's delayed arrival could be about to give her the chance of a lifetime.

"Just think, if the tornadoes completely stop her from showing I get to sing all four numbers by myself!"

'Oh joy, oh rapture unforeseen,' Michael thought sourly.

"A lucky opportunity," he said.

Amado was understandably morose, not even nibbling at his food, and Cecilia sat like a blind sphinx, clearly beyond eating. The fuse that had been lit between them was burning down ever more rapidly and Michael could feel an implacable subterranean vibration approaching beneath the vapid counterpoint of the orchestra, the ominous thrum of dark Hadean chords.

Gaylord was oblivious and went on shamelessly monopolizing his high school flame's attention as Beverley's idiotic monologue continued without pause or mercy.

"The opening is sooo great. Most of the girls are standing way up behind me in a beautiful dim blue light and they kind of hum along, y'know."

Michael had taken note of the stage décor as they had walked through the room. A trifle garish but thoroughly professional. It hadn't been possible to rig a curtain and the setting was there for all to see. Two long flights of stairs rose up on either side behind the inlaid floor to an upper platform with hundreds of tiny twinkling lights outlining the entire structure. Dangling perilously above them, and shimmering in front of a plush purple starlit cyclorama, were seven massive sequin-studded designs of indecipherable meaning and standing proudly on the forestage, five huge gold glittering letters, T, E, X, A and S.

Beverley sang the first line softly, almost shyly.

"'When I die I may not go to heaven', do you know it?"

Michael didn't.

"'I don't know if they let cowboys in . . '" she crooned on helpfully.

"Everyone here does," Chuck told him, "It's called 'Texas, When I Die'."

"A few of the girls are really good dancers and they've brought in a bunch of guys too. I wind up with four of them."

"How's your high-steppin' coming along, dearie?" Cindy enquired.

"It may not be my strong point, Cindy, but I've been working really hard," Beverley replied in kind and then asked, turning to Michael and

Chuck with a goofy teenage face that was almost endearing, "There isn't any dancing in the movie, is there?"

They leaned forward to look at each other, part question, part accusation. What are we, some preposterous parody of the Smothers Brothers? How did you let this happen? Cindy was squinting at them narrowly as she knifed up a mixed forkful of pork tenderloin, braised apple-and-walnut cabbage and maple-glazed sweet potatoes.

"No," they answered in unison.

"Well, not yet," Michael added, making it sound like a compliment.

"What about your plans to study with Dr. Dobson this summer?" Cindy went on, "I guess that's on the back burner now, mmm?"

"Oh, he would understand better than anyone. He would never want me to miss out on such a great chance," Beverley countered, "His whole philosophy is opportunistic."

Michael had never heard of the 'doctor' in question but if he had he might have laughed along with Cindy's dry cackle.

"A truer word, sweet thing, was never spoken," she said, twitching with enjoyment at Beverley's mangled meaning. The expression lighting up her Queen of the Night features was the closest Michael had seen to a genuine smile.

"But listen, honey," she continued, gently dabbing the corners of her lips with the monogrammed napkin, "We all know the opening number's a snap but what about 'Little Things' and 'Two Sparrows in a Hurricane', do you think you can hack those, too?"

Even Beverley was at a momentary loss for words.

"I think so, yes," she said, regaining her composure, "Do you think you can hack it if I rip your falsies off?"

Despite their intimate colloquy, Gaylord and the First Lady could hardly have remained unaware of the sudden Antarctica that was upon them.

"Now girls, girls, we've got a show to do," he remonstrated softly.

And then one of the gathering funnel clouds struck.

The director of the gala, a small balding homosexual who was the current artistic head of Houston's Alley Theater, came around the corner of the stage onto the Royal Box with a deeply furrowed brow and, after being stopped and discreetly frisked by the two Secret Service men, walked rapidly up to the table between Michael and Cecilia and leaned on the back of their chairs.

"Sorry, everyone, to interrupt but we've got a crisis," he announced in a dramatic sotto voce, "We've just been told that hailstones the size of baseballs are coming down over the airport in south Nashville and she's not going to make it at all."

It wasn't necessary to ask "Who?" but Amado did.

"Tanya Tucker."

Beverley was beside herself and couldn't restrain a tiny squeal of triumph.

"I've got to go," she said and stood up and spun about in a sudden dither of excitement and panic, "Wow. Oh boy, you guys are gonna have to come up with a third judge pronto. And, oh no, I don't think it should be me. No, no, that wouldn't be right and anyway I've got sooo much to do! What about you, Mr. Davenport? You're a famous international movie director, after all. I think you'd be perfect. Oh, wow, wish me luck," and she took a big deep breath and made a daft little curtsy and dashed away blowing kisses around the corner.

The commotion in the Royal Box had drawn the attention of the nearby tables and two of the cameras from the dance floor were taking a rehearsal slide toward them.

"The rules are clear," the director went on quietly, doing his best to appear calm, "We have to have three judges."

"I told you," Cindy said to nobody in particular and then turning to her co-host, "Come on, you big lunk, we better go too and make sure they change the right stuff on the autocue. What movies have you directed, Mr. Davenport? We'll need an intro in case you agree to fill in."

Michael was utterly flummoxed but Amado came to the rescue.

"I think it's a very good idea, Michael," he said.

It was the first time he had addressed him as anything but Mr. Davenport and to say that Michael found it creepy would be the understatement of the Transylvanian New Year.

"Why not?" Amado went on without missing a beat, as though the whole situation had infused him with some bizarre new energy, "It's an emergency. Be a sport. We need you. Please say yes."

"A nice cameo for your demo reel," Cecilia offered from behind the dark recess of her glasses, puffing on her cigarette with an unhelpful smirk.

Michael still found himself unable to respond. Chuck didn't want to add fuel to the fire and had to look away, barely managing to contain his laughter.

"I'll take your silence as agreement. Thank you, my dear friend," Amado concluded with a winning smile.

'Life is a dream, they say, waking to die.'

Why did this obscure line of manic-depressive Victorian poetry throb like an impending aneurysm in Michael's brain? If the King of the Bloodsuckers was calling him 'dear friend' he surely hadn't long.

"Do you want to tell her about the movies, Michael, or shall I?" the little madman sailed on in a kind of improvisatorial mania, "They have been making box office history all across Europe."

Michael could only stare in awe. It came to him that Amado's real talent was not being mastermind of a billion-dollar drug cartel nor his conscienceless cruelty nor his childish ambition to become High Archon of the Cacodaemons, no, none of the above. His real gift was bullshit. Pure bullshit.

"There are two in particular, both very recent. Michael, you'll have to fill in some older titles. 'The Enigma of the Aran Islands', a truly great movie. And, I'm sorry Michael, I don't think this one touches it despite the accolades, 'Murder in Mexico'."

Cecilia's amused guffaw caught her the wrong way and devolved into an unhealthy smoker's rattle but Gaylord seemed genuinely impressed and took a silver pen from his jacket pocket and actually began scribbling the titles down on a napkin.

"Can you give me a couple of older ones, Mr. Davenport?" he asked.

Michael cleared his throat. What had he got to lose? This was America, Tinseltown, Disneyland, Hollowwood, the Land of the Free and the Home of the Brave, the Republic of Attention Deficit Disorder and unreasonably white teeth, where anything and everyone was 'do-able'. What the hell did piddly little things like truth or reality matter?

"Um, yes, all right then," Michael croaked, his eyes watering, "Let me see, there's 'The Peddler of Dreams' and, um, 'Wake Up and Die', yes, they did rather well, come to think of it."

Only Cindy's frigid unbelieving gaze, that was literally causing a cyclonic squall line down the side of his collar and raising an Adirondack of goosebumps on his neck, stopped him from bursting into hysterics.

"I think I remember those last two," the First Lady affirmed sweetly.

§

After their brief report to Director Consterdine, who had almost yelled at them, "Yes, I meant every ten minutes but not if you clowns have got nothing to say!" but who had nonetheless concurred with their 'Manchurian Candidate' assessment of the situation and reiterated that it was absolutely imperative for them to apprehend Chuck Bowman as soon as possible and get him the hell out of the building as well as reminding them to keep an eye peeled for Medina and to try and discover what he was up to, Oliver and North had gone immediately back inside the hotel and through security again to the manager's office and though Jordan couldn't really see the sense of it they had obtained his permission to observe the gala from the lighting booth which was perched high above the bleacher section at the rear of the ballroom.

It afforded an unobstructed view of the stage and the dance floor and the Royal Box but not the tiered seating directly below.

The stage manager, a tall tanned Amazonian body builder well over two hundred pounds with tattooed arms and shoulders like Hulk Hogan but with an incongruously delicate pretty face beneath her tousled streaked-blonde hair, was already in the booth and about to speak into a microphone which communicated to the PA system in the dressing rooms and inform the cast and crew that it was half an hour to show time when they arrived in her aerie with their green-suited escort. She wasn't any too pleased at first but once she found out they were military she pointed them to a couple of hard fold-down seats on the back wall where they would cause the least distraction from her weighty responsibilities. She could easily have been mistaken for the twin of the recently dethroned WWF champion Bret Hart as she pored over her prompt book with broad hands poised above a dimmer board to one side and a sound console on the other and her colossal bulk seemed to swamp them in its embrace and teeter on the verge of shattering her swivel chair.

"Hey look, Bob, they're both with Barragan again," Hap noted once they were settled, whispering and not wishing to disturb the gigant overseer.

"Yup."

They watched as the co-hosts departed the Royal Box leaving only Amado and Cecilia, Chuck and Michael and the First Lady, who was now concentrating on consuming her coconut milk poached salmon and quail egg purple potato salad with the appropriate politesse and struggling not to appear bereft.

"How're we supposed to get him out of the building from there? They got TV cameras all over the place."

"Gonna have to wait is all," Oliver replied morosely, "If he tries anything we'll just have to shoot him. Think you could get him clean from the catwalk outside?"

"Oh sure."

"Go back down and get the rifle."

"Security ain't going to let me bring it in here."

"If they give you any grief, tell 'em to talk to Washington."

"You better come."

"You'll be all right. Here, take the phone."

Oliver handed it to him.

"Sure wouldn't mind a plate of that food," Hap sighed as he left the booth.

A few moments later Queen Kong lifted her face from mission control and turned to Oliver and said softly, "He's cute."

§

'Thank the Great Plumed Serpent, the Smoking Mirror and He from the Innermost Twist of the Conch Shell,' thought Michael as the First Lady delicately chewed and swallowed and chewed and swallowed, 'The sweet woman is so shy she isn't going to ask me to remind her what those effing movies were about!'

The director had tried to inject a note of caution, saying they really ought to consult with other members of the Pageant Committee before making a final decision about a replacement judge, but Amado and Laura Bush had looked at each other and smiled like naughty schoolchildren and that was that.

And now they sat in silence as two waiters cleared the table and a laconic curly-haired young man wearing headphones who said he was an assistant to the director came onto the Royal Box with some forms and lists for them to use in making their decision. Michael was grateful to learn that since this was the culmination of the contest most of the hopefuls had already been winnowed out and they were only going to have to choose a winner from the Final Ten.

These were, though the assistant director told them that the semifinalists themselves didn't know it yet, Miss Dallas, Miss Rio Grande Valley, Miss Collin County, Miss Burleson, Miss Lake o' the Pines, Miss Hurst-Euless-Bedford, Miss Garland Area and Misses Arlington, Texarkana and Oak Cliff.

Since it didn't involve him Chuck was free to have a good look around the great room. The control booth was partly obscured by the intense light from the warming follow-spots on either side but he could see some wisps of cigarette smoke from the operators on the catwalk leading to it high above the bleachers and he thought he could just make out the figure of a man making his way along it carrying what he was pretty sure was a rifle bag.

"OK," the assistant director was saying in his unpressured drawl, "They do the evening gown walk first and then the talent show and then it's swimwear all up and down the runway and after that you have to whittle it to a Final Five. Then those five get into a kind of panel-type discussion with Mr. Schoendienst to see if they can put two words together without falling over and from that you choose the winner, runner-up, second runner-up and on down the line. You'll have plenty of time to talk things over if you need to because there'll be breaks before the two announcements when either Miss McIntyre'll be singing or Miss Kellerman and Mr. Schoendienst gabbing. OK? You've got the forms and names and some pens and pencils and beyond that you can handle it however you want. Obviously I'll come out and get your decision on the Final Five and again at the end. Any questions?"

They had none. At least none on that topic.

Despite his relief at the governor's wife's lack of inquisitiveness, Michael's sensitive maternal upbringing nonetheless made him feel he ought to engage her in some polite conversation but he was fearful of where it might lead. Inevitably to those movies and he didn't have the strength for yet more fabricated drivel and anyway Amado was doing brilliantly with small talk.

In fact, Michael was suddenly aware of feeling quite crushingly exhausted but things perked up because the doors opened again and all those who had not had tickets for the dinner portion of the evening came flooding in and began taking their seats in the bleachers. They weren't allowed to get near the Royal Box but somewhere in the last hundred or so Michael saw Dickie and Ethel and then, much to his and

Chuck's surprise, Fernando and Rafael and Enrique.

Ethel and Dickie were peering around the room intently as they entered and Michael could see that she was saying, "Look, Dickie, there he is!" and they both waved and turned to the three Mexicans and Ethel said, "Look, he's all right. There he is on the platform with Mr. Bandicoot," and the five of them got seated.

Fernando was relieved that Chuck and Michael were still in one piece but he couldn't figure out how Chuck was sitting up there because he knew Amado had to know who he was.

Chuck was glad to see some friendly faces and Amado watched him for a moment and then looked at Cecilia.

"What do you think of these movie people, hm, Chichi?" he asked with a wicked smile, "Are they your kind, or no?" then turned his crocodile grin on the First Lady and added, "My sister thinks they lack . . what is the word she is so fond of using, Michael? Ah yes, she thinks they lack . . 'blood'."

Cecilia didn't deign to move a muscle in response to his goading.

"I think I can understand what she means," Laura Bush said and then after careful consideration, "It's fantasy, isn't it. It's a make believe world."

§

"Any problems?" Oliver asked North as he came back into the booth.

The titanic stage manageress was busy sotto-barking one instruction after another into her microphone and her thick tanned fingers were playing the dimmer board and the console with the sensitivity of a Rubinstein but she found time to glance in their direction and saw the rifle bag and let out a little whistle.

"You boys planning to use that thing?"

"If need be," Oliver answered, "But most likely not."

"Too bad. I wouldn't mind a few pops at little Miss McIntyre."

She couldn't elaborate because the show was beginning and she had to go on fast and furious with her cueing and Oliver and North didn't know what she was talking about but gave a little chuckle of appreciation anyway because they could tell she was a kindred spirit.

"No problems?" Oliver repeated.

"Nope. The lobby was empty and they more or less took it in stride."

Oliver made a kind of loopy surprised face and shrugged with his head.

"I think Chuck might have spotted you," he said, once Hap had stowed the rifle bag and was sitting beside him again, "He was looking up here."

As the lights dimmed and the orchestra launched into the overture Oliver and North realized they weren't going to be able to see the Royal Box quite as well as they hoped and the great double doors which had been closed by the ushers opened again and a last spectator entered the ballroom and walked under them out of their line of sight into the bleachers.

"Son of a gun," Oliver said, "I'll bet that was Medina."

"Do you know what he looks like?"

"Only from the TV but I just bet that was him."

"Guess he took a detour from Biggs."

"Maybe."

"Think we should put in another call?"

"No, sirree," Oliver replied stubbornly, "If we gotta sweat this thing out, so can they."

The lights came up again slowly on the stage and purple sky surround to reveal all forty-six of the original contestants swaying to the music on the stairs and upper platform and then four of the girls came down and joined four young men in tuxedos and shimmering rhinestone vests in a lively dance and they swept to the left side of the stage and brought Beverly on, now dressed like some inept designer's rodeo version of Annie Oakley complete with white Stetson hat, super-short white pleated skirt, cowhide vest with small white lone-star patches, white high-heeled snakeskin boots and a pair of ivory-handled silver six-guns in spangled white leather holsters. The audience broke into whistling and applause and the huge gold letters T, E, X, A and S magically moved away and Beverley raised her mike, flashing a sea-to-shining-sea smile, and began to sing.

"When I die I may not go to heaven,
I don't know if they let cowboys in.
If they don't just let me go to Texas,
Texas is as close as I've been . . "

It was true, she did look exactly like Tanya Tucker and even Michael had to admit she wasn't half bad. It may have been pure imitation, cracked country cadences and all, but by some blessed miracle the sound was emanating from a completely different corpuscular zone to her speaking voice. And it wasn't that she was lip-synching, oh no, it was one hundred percent her.

As the song went on Hap sat deep in thought and finally he leaned back and scratched his head and said, "You know, Bob, this ain't right somehow."

"What ain't?"

"In The Manchurian Candidate Laurence Harvey was the one up here."

Oliver stared at him blankly.

"Chuck can't do anything where he is," Hap went on with irrefutable logic, "Sitting with the First Lady. They got those two Secret Service guys right behind him."

"I'd ride through all of Hell and half of Texas
Just to hear Willie Nelson sing a country song.
Beer just ain't as cold in old Milwaukee.
My body's here but my soul's in San Antone . . "

By the end of the number where the main verse repeats a second time just about everyone in the ballroom was standing swinging their hips and clapping out the rhythm and singing along and a triumphant Beverley was almost carried off to the right of the stage by the four male dancers and Oliver and North got the stage manageress's attention with a little wave and gestured that they were leaving the booth and she took the barest sixteenth-note rest from her concerto, snapping her head toward them like a soldier on parade, and gave Hap a tiny wistful wink, so fleeting is the promise of true friendship in the helter-skelter of modern life, and now they were both making their way step by careful step back along the catwalk.

Chuck had been wondering whether to try and make it around the corner of the stage before the Security Service men could stop him and was watching their progress as the lights changed and came up on the contestants again. They were still swaying to the vamp of the orchestra and snapping their fingers and grinning like an army of lunatic mannequins as the amplified singsong twang of an unseen female announcer filled the ballroom and addressed the TV audience.

"Ladies and gentlemen, live from the grand ballroom of El Paso's Barragan Hotel, it's the 1997 Miss Texas Scholarship Pageant, official preliminary to the Miss America Pageant in Atlantic City. Tonight starring Miss Texas, Beverley McIntyre, Miss Texas 1994, Aryanne Archer, former Miss Texas finalist, Vanessa Hunt-Witwell and the Miss Texas Dancers. Plus Dallas's famous Turtle Creek Chorale, the Fort Worth Men's Chorus, the Bruce Lee Dance Factory and Rick Stitzel with the Miss Texas Orchestra . . "

Michael's need for sleep had become irresistible and he was nodding off.

"And now, welcome the Miss Texas contestants as they let the celebrating begin!"

The forty-six young hopefuls launched instantly into a puzzling sequence of calisthenic arm movements, smiling broadly all the while, and sang together in a not entirely inharmonious piping tremulo.

"The air is deep tonight as we walk into the crowd
My heart is pumping and my feet don't touch the ground,
There's no resisting but tonight we're on the cloud,
Oh, let the celebrating begin! Living it up!
We're living it up because we got to be proud
And we're going to say it out loud . . "

And these deeply meaningful lines repeated several times until suddenly the singing ceased and all forty-six walked forward one by one and energetically announced their names and the place where they had been lucky enough to meet with their initial success and then retreated to their previous positions and went on swaying and snapping and smiling as the disembodied voice continued.

"The Miss Texas Scholarship Pageant is brought to you by Chevrolet Trucks, the most dependable, longest lasting trucks on the road . . Nice 'n Easy, it's Nice 'n Easy to be natural, only from Clairol . . Lancôme, Paris, the name that means beauty and innovation in any language . . and Eckert, proud to be part of the Miss Texas Pageant. Eckert reminds you to try Eckert first for what you want most from cosmetics, designer fragrances, sun care and all your photo processing needs. It's right . . at Eckert."

The saccharine tsunami segued without a pause into the introduction of Cindy and 'Red' Schoendienst and the audience applauded loud and long as they came forward to their podium near the Royal Box and the lights changed again and the judges' table became illuminated in the bounce.

By the grace of some weird instinctive mechanism, no doubt mostly to do with the increased intensity of photons on his eyelids though a cynic might say it was the ovation, Michael let out a snort and returned to consciousness.

"Well, Cindy," Gaylord began, "It is so great to be back in El Paso and with you again. I understand that congratulations are in order, you've added a new family member."

"Yes, that's right and thank you, Gay, we've just celebrated my son John Michael's first birthday."

'Good lord,' Michael mused blearily, 'That creature is someone's mother?'

"Well, we truly are excited for you," Schoendienst went on with studied ease, "And I'm sure you can really feel the excitement in the air here this evening in El Paso."

"You bet I can, Gay, and we'd like to give a very special welcome to our wonderful First Lady, Laura Bush . . "

Cindy had to wait for a full minute while the shy ex-schoolteacher stood and acknowledged the thunderous outpouring of affection from the crowd.

" . . who has graciously agreed to be one of this evening's judges. Good luck, Laura, it's not going to be easy. And, of course, we'd like to thank our great philanthropist and friend, Amado Barragan Fuentes, for the use of this gloriously renovated and historic ballroom."

"Señor Barragan has told me," Gaylord confided, tongue-in-cheek, "That it will be his love for the high-rolling world of international finance that will guide his judgment here tonight."

Hearty yuk-yuks all round as Amado smiled and waved but didn't get up.

"Now we know y'all were expecting our beloved Tanya Tucker to be the third judge but . . "

Again Cindy had to wait while the whoops and hollers abated.

" . . but unfortunately Tanya's connecting flight from Nashville has been grounded by a tornado warning and she's stuck there and can't be with us this evening . . "

"Praise the Lord for our great American weather."

More cackles and whistling.

"She's our good ol' gal from Seminole, we'll miss her, God bless her, but . . but . . and hey, isn't Beverley doing just a fantastic job!"

Yup, they all sure thought so.

" . . but, as the Lord taketh away so does He give, and it so happens we are lucky enough to have in our midst a brilliant movie director from the fabled isle of Great Britain, Mr. Michael Davenport!"

Ethel nudged Dickie and said, "I didn't know anything about that."

"It appears our Mr. Davenport is a very dark horse," Dickie replied.

"Please stand, Mr. Davenport," Gaylord requested, "So the audience can see which one of our honored guests you are."

Michael was horrified but Cecilia nipped him savagely on the crotch with her painted nails and he wobbled blinking to his feet.

Gaylord had to pull out his napkin and read from it.

"Mr. Davenport has two box-office smashes currently playing in theaters across Europe, um, 'The Enigma of the Aryan Islands' and, um, a title that will no doubt soon be released on these shores, 'A Murder in old Mexico'."

He pronounced the 'x' as an 'h'.

"I've never heard of them, have you, Dickie?"

Dickie thought for a moment and shook his head.

There was embarrassingly little applause until the First Lady stood again and clapped which brought on a confused smattering that she almost outlasted. Michael smiled wanly at her in gratitude and slumped back down disconsolately in his seat. Not only was it all bullshit but, even more galling to his scrupulous Saxon nature, in Gaylord's glib mouth it had become inaccurate bullshit!

"Mr. Davenport has responded to the call and has agreed to fill in for Miss Tucker and, by golly, we thank him for being such a darn good sport!"

"Yes, and there is even greater cause for excitement here tonight, Gay. The Miss America organization is the largest source of scholarships for women in the world and before tonight is over every contestant on this stage will be offered in excess of one million dollars in scholarships and awards."

"In fact," Gaylord said, taking over seamlessly, "For the second year every single contestant will be offered a cash scholarship."

"Didn't she just say that, Dickie?"

"Yes, I thought so."

"They don't think people listen."

"Stay tuned for the announcement of the top ten semi-finalists after this word from Chevrolet Trucks, the most dependable and long-lasting trucks on the road," Gaylord concluded the segment with a megawatt smile and strolled over to the Royal Box as the assistant director came quickly onto the stage carrying a white cardboard sign informing everyone that the broadcast had cut to a five minute commercial break.

Chuck had decided he was better off staying put because if he ran into Oliver and North anywhere else in the building he knew they would try and strong-arm him out.

§

But they had returned to the Hummer.

"We know where he's sitting!" McWhirter shouted, "We saw him just now when those two air-brushed hicks were introducing everyone!"

The general had bailed on supper with his invalid wife, churlishly getting his driver to call and tell the maid there had been an emergency, and he was once again in Consterdine's office in Arlington, where they had been watching the live feed from KFOX in El Paso, drinking a cup of coffee and munching noisily on a slice of pineapple pizza.

"Your boss is trying to find out more about this Davenport joker."

Consterdine was at his desk punching data into a computer and talking to them on speaker-phone.

"What were the names of those movies again?" he asked.

"What movies?" Oliver said.

"The ones the red-haired dipshit said when he introduced him."

"Didn't hear it. We must've been on our way down."

"I told you what they were, Connie," the general sighed impatiently, "'The Stigma of Error in Iceland', some kind of boring Nordic social documentary, and the other one was 'The Murder of an Olmec *Hijo*'. Mesoamerican history epic'd be my guess. No doubt Davenport's a Jew. Abraham and Isaac but retold with flashing knives and feathered head-dresses on the temple altar. Thought the Injuns only sacrificed girls back in the day but, hey, what do I know."

Consterdine observed him with a peevish squint.

"Yeah, great, but I can't find anything like that and I can't find him either."

"So quit fucking with it. There's nothing we can do about the sonofabitch until after the show anyway."

"And how do you want us to proceed now?" Oliver asked, concealing his growing anger and frustration with difficulty.

"You say you saw Medina?"

"I think so. Came in at the last minute. But I can't be a hundred percent sure."

"Well, ask hotel security, maybe they know."

"OK, and then what?"

"Maybe send Bowman a message that Medina wants to speak to him and when he comes out, grab him."

McWhirter almost choked on a pineapple wedge.

"Christ on a fucking crutch, Connie, that is about the stupidest thing I ever heard you say!"

"Oh? Why?"

"Bowman won't believe the little greaser knows who he is even if he knows who Medina is and more than that, if he's in there like Bob said he thinks he is, Bowman can see him!"

"I still think it might work."

"No, no, no, look, what's the problem with you two geniuses down there? At the next break just go right in and sit down with them. What can they do? Introduce yourselves to the governor's wife as friends of Mr. Barragan. He'll get what you're doing and play along with it. Then all you gotta do is sit tight and, when it's over and the cameras are off, knock him on the head."

"What about Davenport?"

"We'll find out later. How do we know he and Bowman even know each other? Maybe he's just a friend of Portillo's who makes stupid movies."

CHAPTER TWENTY-FIVE

Michael was not making a movie of the tiger now and had he been by the wolf enclosure on the mountaintop above Juarez an hour before he would probably not have been cold-blooded enough to bring the lens to his eye.

When Amado and he had driven away from the compound that afternoon *'El Tigre'* was still enjoying his siesta on the grand couch in the villa and the great beast had been left in peace there as the sleepy sun went down and his handlers and most of the other guards dealt with the last of the blaze in the pig barns but at about twenty-five minutes after seven o'clock that evening, the normal time for him to awake and begin imagining barbecued hind quarter, as the welcome cool of night swept in over the desert of the Samalayuca and the Franklin Mountains and darkness began to surround the luminescent fragility of the twin cities in its motherly embrace and just as the Royal Box was being informed of the hailstones crashing down in Nashville, a very different kind of storm was approaching up the winding road from the valley.

'El Tigre' had been perplexed as he sat waiting on the villa steps for the handlers to take him back to his jungle grotto, which normally took the form of a leisurely un-coerced evening stroll, that they came with whips instead and forced him up a ramp inside an armored van and had driven it past the comfort of his sanctuary to the wolf-pen and opened the gates and prodded him with sharp sticks to get out, then hurried away without a word, nervously locking the gates again behind them.

He looked about to get his bearings and heard the sound of many trucks roaring into the circle around the bronze fountain and screeching to a halt. There were a few shouted orders and pops of muffled gunfire and then silence and he watched with a blank expression as the wolves materialized out of the darkness and came closer.

Inside the floodlit marble mansion Doña Aurora woke from her slumber in front of the television to the sudden sound of women screaming in the hallway and the door to her cozily-lit apartment was thrown open and seven men burst in brandishing weapons and one of them, a tall handsome young man sporting a floral shirt with a golden chain visible beneath the wide collar, spoke in guttural Spanish and said,

"Kill her." She hadn't time to pull herself to her feet before her sturdy peasant neck was slashed to the bone.

"That will teach your animal son to kill my brother," the leader said.

The wolves seemed almost to grovel on their forepaws before the tiger's majesty, whining and whimpering in feigned obeisance, as they surrounded him. He snarled and bared his fangs and had to spin like a Dervish to swat them away as one after another began darting in to tear at his flanks or leap upon his back to sink their teeth and rake his flesh and eyes with savage claws. Their mouths were frothing red as he caught one in his jaws at last and broke its back and flung it like a child's poppet squealing lifeless to the ground.

From the murder of the mother, the seven men had been led down to the cold room where Amado's brother lay jumbled in his silver coffin. They had opened it and though they chuckled with false enjoyment at the sight they were all secretly afraid to touch it and anxious to get away from the smell. The leader was sweating too but sneered at them and called them cowards and snatched the long knife from the man who had cut the old woman's throat and went to work hacking the head clean from the body. It took a full minute to achieve his aim and cupfuls of embalming fluid oozed slowly onto the plush cream upholstery of the coffin, staining it like green sweat. As a last gesture, he plunged the knife into the cavity where Vicente's heart had been and then, letting go of the handle as if it were a live wire, stood back and said quietly, *"Vámonos."*

The unaccustomed necessity of defense had made the tiger frantic as well as furious and though he had been able to inflict wound after punishing wound on his persecutors he was flagging and they felt it and redoubled their attack.

The roundup of servants and guards in the villa who had not been part of the conspiracy was complete and all had been herded outside by the sparkling dolphins and three of the men were shot point blank in the temple by the man in the floral shirt to make sure the others paid attention. Vicente's head dangled in his other hand grasped by the hair as he told them they could trust in continued employment if they chose and they chose so.

The sound of the three gunshots made the wolves pause and some instinct in the tiger's wounds if not the pain told him to break from his torment and run.

The electrified chain link fence was fourteen feet high including the coils of razor wire at the top and though the wolves continued their assault as he ran and easily kept pace yelping and leaping and biting all the while they couldn't stop him and were left with crimson tongues lolling and circling in haphazard disappointment as the tiger cleared it with room to spare and disappeared like a bleeding ghost into the chaparral.

CHAPTER TWENTY-SIX

Michael was again fast asleep with his head lolling on Cecilia's shoulder as the second segment of the Scholarship Pageant came to an end and they went to another commercial break.

It had begun with the forty-six back on the risers in brand new outfits and Beverley being re-introduced and taking a meaningless walk across the stage in a sparkling red gown and she waved to Chuck and pointed at him. Then Cindy and Gaylord had gone through the interminable process of naming the Top Ten who all had to come forward to hugs and kisses and fanfares, the last one fairly jumping up and down in adolescent excitement. Then they had all gone off and the co-hosts had waded through the rules and the percentages of what segment was worth what and then the remaining girls had sung an awful choral number called 'Before You Forget, Kiss Her Now', or something like that. Beverley had joined them round a playerless grand piano to render 'Beyond the Blue Horizon' and only then did the evening-wear segment start and that took forever as the Top Ten made awkward individual parades up and down the runway in their floor-length designer dresses and the Turtle Creek Chorale for some inexplicable reason sang 'Secret Love' lightly in the background, the song Doris Day made famous, 'Now I shout it from the highest hills, even told the golden daffodils', so it was understandable that Michael was in the Land of Nod when the assistant director announced the break.

Not more than thirty seconds later Oliver and North came in the double doors and walked through the tables to the Royal Box and began mounting the stairs. The Secret Service men had seen their arrival and moved briskly to stop them before they reached the top of the platform which caused the decibel level which had gone sky-high with chatter to subside a bit as they questioned them and checked their ID. Amado looked at Chuck with a bland smile and reassured the First Lady they were friends.

Once satisfied, the Secret Service men retreated to the anonymity of the shadows and Oliver and North introduced themselves.

"Hello boys," Chuck said.

"Hey there, Chuck," they replied.

"Are you in the movie business too?" the First Lady asked them as they sat down. Michael's groggily re-awakened mind found it to be a perfectly reasonable assumption under the circumstances.

Fernando and Enrique and Rafael, on the other hand, were watching with concern.

"Didn't you say those men were Drug Police?" Dickie asked Enrique.

"I think so, yes."

"Whatever are they doing here?"

"I don't know."

"Maybe the movie is about drugs," Ethel suggested, "I mean, Mr. Billabong is Mexican, isn't he?"

"Bit of a cliché there, Ethel, my old girl," Dickie countered with a covering chuckle, glancing humorfully beyond her shoulder at the other three.

"I don't mean he has anything to do with them personally, silly, but it is a big problem in his country, isn't it?" she said and turned to Fernando.

"Yes, very big," he agreed.

"No, ma'am, strictly friends is all," Oliver had answered.

"Come to enjoy the show?"

"That's right, ma'am."

Cecilia knew differently because she had caught a glimpse of their ID and could always tell when Amado was lying. Since he very seldom did anything else it was much more difficult to guess when he told the truth.

The band struck up again and the lights dimmed and the conversations and laughter fell to a murmur and they sat without a word for the next half an hour as the Top Ten ploughed through the talent section of the contest and by the end of it even Chuck was starting to fade despite the undiminished danger of the situation.

They had to endure ten lengthy numbers beginning with a pretty blonde singing and dancing a quasi-balletic version of 'Don't Cry for Me, Argentina', then Billie Holliday's 'It's Easy to Lie to Strangers but What Will I Tell My Heart', sung by one of the two black contestants, and there were two girls whose forté was baton twirling, complete with cartwheels, flips, spectacularly high throws and finally juggling three batons at once while doing the splits, who Michael had to admit were both very impressive and a blessed relief from the querulous tones of two others who had martyred themselves upon the unscalable precipices of Whitney Houston's 'I Will Always Love You' from The Bodyguard and 'I Believe in You and Me' from The Preacher's Wife, and then Cliff Richards' shameless schmaltz 'It's in Every One of Us to be Wise', which was bad enough without being hopelessly flat, and a country favorite 'You Hurt Me' sung by a lovely plump girl who probably didn't have a chance of winning but who Michael found much more than tolerable. It was followed by a shriek-making thing called 'Via Dolorosa', Christ's mythic passage to Calvary trivialized by lyrics like 'but He chose to walk that road out of love for you and me', repeated in Spanish, *'y fue Él quien quiso ir por su amor por ti y por mi'*, in a fruitless and hypocritical attempt to give such mawkish nonsense dignity, and rendered with a kind of stuffingless religiosity by a starry-eyed, gloss-lipsticked, gangly yet matronly born-again girl, with a first name that was the surname of the actor president who believed in the 'Evil Empire' but swore he never dyed his hair, who Michael could sense from the audience's rapturous response would beyond a doubt have captured the crown that night if the contest had ever been allowed to come to a close. Last, and thankfully by far the best, was a Charlie McCarthy ventriloquist act with a lively back and forth of 'Row, Row, Row Your Boat' and Michael had to smile at the line about life being but a dream and he actually laughed out loud and long and caught the audience's attention at the old vaudeville joke, 'I was gonna be a fiddle but I wasn't cut out for it', after which he gave Amado a meaningful look but Amado seemed not to get the connection.

And then the whirling maelstrom of fate made another unpredictable shift in direction as Beverley appeared again with microphone in hand. She was still wearing the red clinging floor-length gown which now sported a yellow rose to the left of her ample cleavage. She should have gone straight into Tanya Tucker's first big hit, 'Delta Dawn', but when she saw Oliver and North in the Royal Box instead of starting the number she broke from the script asking, "Ain't you gonna introduce your new friends, Amado honey?"

And then she forced Rick Stitzel and the Miss Texas Orchestra into what turned out to be an abortive intro vamp as she walked over to the table with the spotlights and the cameras following her and put her hand on Chuck's shoulder and said to the audience, "I don't believe y'all were properly introduced to Mr. Gene Hackman!"

A few in the distant audience applauded but most were puzzled.

"Course, I know he's not really Gene Hackman but don't he sure look like him? Stand up, sir, and take a bow!"

Chuck stood and seized his opportunity.

"Well, Beverley," he began, stooping to get his mouth to the mike, "There's someone else here tonight who isn't who people think he is . . "

Oliver and North were about to leap to their feet and smother him but Cecilia was instantly holding her Derringer hard against her brother's throbbing left temple and, as the follow-spot widened to include them all, she said quietly and very firmly, "Let him speak."

Several women screamed and the music tailed away and Beverley initially thought it was a gag and started to giggle.

"Is this a part of the show?" Ethel whispered to Fernando.

Chuck pointed at Amado and had to shout over the growing uproar, "This man is a fake. He's not Amado Barragan Fuentes. He is Amado Portillo!"

He didn't have time to elaborate because the two Secret Service men were coming forward and he thought they were making a move on Cecilia and went for his gun but they were only interested in protecting the First Lady and waved him off and he let them hustle her backstage and out of harm's way. Gaylord and Cindy had long since vanished in the same direction.

Chuck could see an army of green-suits surging towards them from every corner as the show lighting was snapped off section by section and the crystal chandelier in the center of the ballroom was brought rapidly to full blaze. Oliver and North glanced up at the booth to see the Incredible Hulkess standing by her console and staring down like some Olympian goddess awaiting developments.

People were frantically rushing for the double doors but Beverley hadn't moved. The adoring smile was gone from her face and whether her sudden fit of trembling was rage or terror or something worse, one couldn't say.

The TV crews had quickly turned away and were already shutting down their equipment. Chuck had a pretty good idea who would have given the order and though quite a few enterprising audience members were busy capturing the pandemonium on hand-held camcorders it was obvious to him that something even more dramatic was needed to capitalize on this first lucky blow.

He could see Fernando and Enrique and Rafael pushing their way toward the Royal Box across the stream of patrons making for the exit through a maze of tables and tipped-over chairs and strewn cutlery and a strange old couple who were valiantly attempting to keep up behind shouting, "Wait for us!" and beyond them the isolated figure of Hernano Salvador Medina calmly observing the chaos from his seat in the bleachers.

"We're going upstairs," Chuck said to Michael and Cecilia and then to Oliver and North who were also still in their seats because he had them covered, "I told you all along who he was. Now I'm going to prove it. Do your job for once and get the hell out of my way."

§

"It's too fucking late!" the general roared, "The damage has been done! It went out live! The clip will be picked up on every fucking late night news report nation wide! 'This man is a fake! He's not Barragan, he's Amado Portillo!' It's too fucking late to suppress it!"

Consterdine sat glumly behind his desk as the spitfire commander of the 24th Mechanized Infantry Division during Operation Desert Storm, and recipient of the Distinguished Service Medal for his speed and boldness but who, if one were temperamentally more inclined to believe the testimony of someone like Private First Class Charles Sheehan-Miles, was also described as overseer of 'the biggest firing squad in history', paced furiously up and down before him.

"We'll say he was mentally ill and get Oliver to kill him."

"What about the other jerk? The movie man."

"Kill him too. Who cares if he's a friend of Portillo's."

The general suddenly stopped dead and sucked his teeth.

"Shit. What if he's with the Russians?"

Consterdine didn't have an answer and the retired chief of SOUTHCOM, which was headquartered in Panama and oversaw all U. S. military activities in Central and South America, resumed pawing the carpet and growling.

"Why haven't those two imbeciles called in?!"

§

They hadn't because they were hovering amongst a circle of green-suits, like an army of frustrated spermatozoons spinning around a rapidly moving and thus difficult to penetrate ovum, who were being forced to follow the tight knot of their boss and his sister, still wearing impenetrable dark glasses and holding the Derringer glued firmly to his head, and Chuck on the other side wielding a Glock 9mm Compact and Michael and Fernando, Enrique and Rafael trying to shrug off Beverley and close behind them a very excited Ethel and Dickie as the whole gaggle struggled across the now sparsely populated but seriously distressed ballroom to the door under the bleachers that led into the private hallway where the enclosing walls increased the pressure on their collective momentum and squeezed them, like the glistening spurtle from a freshly opened tube of KY Jelly, past the boardroom and out the door at the other end of the corridor into the panicked havoc of the lobby, all miraculously without anyone stumbling or getting trampled but with almost everyone shouting at once.

There were more screams as they emerged to face, unlike in the ballroom where the stage manageress had, following instructions, been able to exercise a modicum of control, a barrage of lights and not-to-be-denied news' cameras.

The First Lady had been instantly whisked away by her handlers via the service entrance and Gaylord had beaten a hasty retreat by a similar exit and they were both well on their way to Biggs Field and El Paso International in their respective limousines but the indomitable 'fox of KFOX' was waiting in the lobby with her crew.

"Hey there, cutie-pie!" she shouted above the din, "Is this any way to hold an engagement party?!"

At which Beverley, who was still holding the wireless show microphone, exploded and, stabbing the bulb of it high into the air, screeched at the top of her young lungs, "Why dontcha twirl that dry gulch between your legs on this, you fuckin' cunt!" and was upon the instant immortalized in cyberspace thereby forever queering her pitch with 'Focus on the Family' and the smugly rectitudinous Dr. Dobson.

Chuck looked at Fernando as they moved toward the elevators and said, "We've got to lose the old people," but it turned out to be easy because there truly wasn't any room for them and, as the guards backed away from the doors at the sight of the Glock, the rest somehow managed to jam themselves in and set off for the seventeenth floor. Chuck did his best to prevent Beverley from joining the crush but it was totally impossible and they had to suffer a deafening stream of vitriol about Cindy Kellerman and every other fucker who'd ever crossed her all the way to the top.

§

A minute later when Oliver and North got back to the Hummer and called in there was no response and though Oliver patiently listened to it ringing for a full minute expecting his boss to hear the call waiting signal and pick up it didn't happen.

§

Ethel and Dickie were understandably out of breath and more than a little out of sorts but had kindly been offered a pair of armchairs to flop down in by a polite young Texan couple as Cindy Kellerman and her crew approached.

At least a dozen of Amado's green-suited guards had already departed for the seventeenth floor in two separate loads and a dozen more remaining were stopping anyone at all from using the other elevators at the manager's orders so the lobby was packed with curious gala ticket-holders, random onlookers and no doubt soon-to-be complaining hotel guests as well as an ever-increasing media presence, some of whom had noticed what Cindy was doing and hastily cut off their own interviews to follow her.

"May I talk to you folks for a moment?" she said sweetly.

Ethel and Dickie looked at each other. They had both been engaged in the sometimes tricky process of removing the clear cellophane wrapper from Barley Sugar candies, boiled sweets were an old favorite of theirs and a marvelous cure for a dry mouth if a cup of tea wasn't handy, and Dickie said, "We'd be honored, wouldn't we, Ethel?"

"Mmm, rather," she agreed, sucking the brown circular lozenge away from the last of its now slithery enclosure, "It's all been very exciting, hasn't it?"

"Would you like us to stand?"

§

Two guards were normally sufficient to protect the common area on the seventeenth floor when nothing special was afoot but they had been immediately alerted and were standing ready on either side of the elevator with guns pointed stiffly in outstretched arms but Chuck knew they would be and had already told Amado to order them to lower their weapons which he did as soon as the doors were opening and they all backed rather awkwardly away to his suite with the guards shadowing them but hamstrung to intervene and Michael was last in and couldn't resist a little waggle-fingered wave of farewell and a whispered, *"Buenas noches"*, before he locked the door behind them.

§

"No, no, please stay comfortable," Cindy told the still hyperventilating old pair as if butter wouldn't melt in her mouth.

"You're visitors to El Paso, aren't you?" she began.

They both nodded, working the Barley Sugars in their mouths to gather some necessary moisture.

"From England?"

More nodding.

"And guests here at the hotel?"

"Yes, pushed the boat out a bit," Dickie said, "Pensioners, y'know."

"We're leaving tomorrow," Ethel added.

"And you were at the Miss Texas Pageant just now."

"Yes."

"We wouldn't normally enjoy that sort of thing but we were worried about Mr. Davenport."

"The film director. Yes, I believe you know him."

"Well, no," Dickie said.

"We don't really know him. As a friend, that is."

"No, we only knew him as an actor."

"On Coronation Street."

"Yes. I don't suppose you've heard of it. It's a wonderful program."

"We've had it in England for years and years."

"But you don't seem to get it over here, more's the pity."

Even Cindy was finding it hard to interrupt their flow.

"You say you don't know him as a film director."

"No."

"What is his connection to Mr. Barragan, do you think?"

"We haven't the faintest idea."

"We thought at first he might be taking part in a movie of some sort."

"Because he was acting so strangely."

"And then some friends of his told us he was a journalist."

"And you didn't know that?"

"No."

"Which friends? Was the big man with the gun one of them?"

"No, not exactly."

"How do you mean?"

"Well, the big chap who shouted out that he wasn't Mr. Barrenboom..."

"For the last time, Ethel, it's Barragan."

"Yes, yes, alright, keep your shirt on. As far as we know, the big chap is a friend of one of the men who told us."

"Who also happens to be a friend of Mr. Davenport," Dickie clarified.

"Where is this man now?"

"He went up in the elevator."

"He was from Mexico."

"And ever so nice."

"Well, we thought he was until he pushed us away."

"What was his name?"

"I'm afraid we never enquired," said Dickie, rather shamefacedly.

"What about the big man? Did they mention his name?"

"Hackney," said Ethel, "Wasn't that it?"

§

As soon as Michael had closed and locked the door he heard the first load of guards arriving in the common area and everyone talking in loud voices. He was certain they would storm the suite and that in moments he would be dead. Why hadn't he gently extricated himself from the whole business in the lobby while he had the chance? No one would have shot him if he'd kept his hands up. Yes, surely, he would have been apprehended and questioned by the authorities but at least he would have been alive and once he had been able to prove his identity they would have eventually let him go and he could have worried about whether Amado was really going to go to all the trouble of having him tracked down and executed later. He could have phoned Los Angeles and told Gottfried and Anna that he had been delayed a second time and would not be arriving on the 11:17 and in due course he might even have made it back to the bliss of Chalk Farm and Helen and Marta and, oh sweet, sweet remembrance of things long past, Flossie. But the truth is one doesn't always think clearly in the heat of action and, anyway, it would have been cowardly and disloyal and he wouldn't have liked himself very much afterwards if he had.

All those thoughts took less then a millisecond and as he turned from the door he became aware that Beverley had collapsed on the sofa and was sobbing uncontrollably. No one seemed interested in comforting or answering her as she wailed, "Why? Why is this happening, Amado? Would someone please tell me what, what, whaaaat is going on?"

Amado had seated himself on the throne chair and Cecilia stood over him with the Derringer and said, "Michael, get me a drink."

Not a bad idea he thought and went to do it.

"Anyone else?"

There were no other immediate takers.

"What now, old friend?" Fernando asked.

Chuck looked at the three Mexicans with gratitude and apology.

"I'm sorry, *amigos*, to have got you into this."

"The only important thing is how to get out," Enrique said.

Chuck nodded.

"I guess none of you are carrying."

Fernando and Enrique and Rafael all shook their heads 'no'.

"Stupid question."

Chuck handed Fernando the Glock.

"I'll be back," he said and went off into one of the bedrooms.

Amado cleared his throat and smiled lightly.

"I would like a soda with ice, Michael, if you don't mind."

"Why should I mind?"

He brought Cecilia her martini and the soda for Amado and a large snifter of cognac for the blubbering beauty queen but she waved it away with another wail and so he kept it for himself.

Chuck came back from the bedroom with a cream-colored top king sheet and spread it out full on the carpet. They could hear the thump of running feet as guards deployed on the terrace beyond the thick curtains and an anxious voice shouted through the door from the common area, "Señor Barragan, what do you want us to do?"

Chuck looked at Amado.

"Nothing. Wait there until I call you," Amado shouted in return and then added quietly, "Mr. Bowman is serving a picnic."

Chuck ignored him and asked Cecilia if she had some lipstick but she had ditched her purse by the table when she drew the Derringer.

"Try the bathroom," she said, "The little bitch may have left some in there."

At which Beverley ceased her lachrymose display and hissed, with hatred boiling from bloodshot mascara-flooded eyes, "Who are you calling a bitch, you fuckin' *puta* spicaninny, you're nothin' but a fuckin' *bruja* pig fucker!"

She was fortunate Cecilia had a better use for her bullets.

At a momentary loss for words because Cecilia hadn't responded Beverley rose unsteadily to her feet and struck a pose of bruised dignity.

"What am I doing here?" she chided herself, her voice almost calm, "Fuck you, Amado. You've ruined everything. You don't care now but you'll see, you'll see. I don't need you, you know."

Amado was staring at her with glacial indifference.

"And I don't give a hot flyin' fuck who you really are, you little shit!"

Michael had known it couldn't last.

"I don't need this! How dare you treat me like this!"

Amado's rattlesnake immobility caused tears to well up again and she was forced to turn her rage on the others.

"Fuck you, Mr. Bowman, and fuck you, Mr. Davenport! You can take your movie and shove it! I don't believe there was a goddam movie anyway! Fuck you all, I don't need any of you! Fuck the whole stinkin' world six ways to fuckin' Sunday, I'm outta here!"

She made for the door but Rafael and Enrique stopped her and she started whacking at them with the microphone and kicking out viciously at their shins with her pointed high-heeled shoes and screeching, "Let go of me!" but Enrique didn't wait two seconds before slapping her so hard across the face that she shut up and was instantly motionless and Rafael led her back to the sofa where she sat twitching in shock but mercifully silent.

Amado was smiling again at some private enjoyment as Chuck returned from the bathroom with two lipsticks and said, "Someone come and hold this," and Michael and Rafael came and pulled the sides of the sheet tight and Chuck knelt down and started greasing big red letters on it.

§

The two artful bastards in the plush office in Arlington were well aware of Oliver's repeated attempts to make contact but during the whole frantic passage from the ballroom to the elevator McWhirter and Consterdine had received a call from an operative in New York. It had taken the operative less than a minute to impart some totally game-changing information and, being who they were, they were not about to share it.

On Oliver's fifth try Consterdine answered.

"I've been pushing buttons for the last ten minutes," Oliver grumbled.

"Sorry, Bob, we had another call and I couldn't let it go."

"What could be more important than this!"

"Lots of things, Bob, now don't get huffy. What's the situation? We lost the live feed but I'm sure you know that. It's gone national since, of course, and everyone's scrambling for clarity."

"Bowman muscled Portillo onto the elevator and he's taken him hostage up to the seventeenth floor."

"And you couldn't stop them?"

"Portillo's sister is some kind of weird partner in this. She put a gun to his head. You didn't see that?"

"Yeah, we saw."

"And Bowman had an ankle-arm."

"Figures."

"You said Portillo's an asset so we couldn't risk a shoot-out."

Suddenly Hap was tugging on his sleeve. Dozens of people who had been milling about under the great archway had spilled out into the street and were pointing upwards.

"Holy Toledo, wait a minute," Oliver said, "There's something happening up there."

"Up where?"

"Off a balcony on the top floor. They're dropping a big white flag, I think. No, wait, it's got lettering on it. It's a sign."

"What does it say?"

"I can't tell. It's blowing around."

Chuck and Fernando were working to steady the sheet by tying Amado's shiny black Italian shoes into the lower corners and Enrique and Rafael held the vampire drug lord firm as Cindy Kellerman came through the revolving doors from the lobby followed by her crew and then several others who had also been conducting eye-witness interviews. They all looked up at the sign and the crews started pushing the crowd aside and rolling out follow-spots.

Cameramen were already focusing on the unfurled message and the faint wash of beams from the camera key-lights as well as the ambient city spill were just enough for Oliver to make out the lettering even at that distance.

"I can see it now. There's a short arrow at the top pointing upward and underneath it says, 'If you want Portillo come and get him'. Yeah, that's it, in great big capital letters."

Oliver could hear the general's voice asking for the words to be repeated and his boss saying, "If you want Portillo come and get him," but then there was some muffled conversation between them that was too faint.

Spotlights were turning on and illuminating the balcony and Hap pointed to a CNN van that had just arrived and was double-parking itself in the hotel drive.

"Sir? I can see people up there now," Oliver cut in.

"Yes, Bob? What did you say?"

"I can see Bowman and Portillo and another Hispanic-looking guy. I saw him in the ballroom. He sort of appeared out of nowhere with two buddies. I think the other two are standing behind them. They're holding Portillo and leaning his head and shoulders out over the edge of the railing so the arrow on the sign is pointing right at his face."

"Is that so? Son of a bitch just doesn't know when he's licked."

Oliver was puzzled. Why did his boss seem unconcerned all of a sudden?

"Did you make contact with Medina, by the way?"

"No."

"He's not up there too, is he?"

"Don't think so."

"Well, see if you can find him. We still want his take on all this."

It had been fully seventeen minutes since all hell had broken loose at the pageant but it was only now that the El Paso police arrived with sirens blaring. At least, in any quantity. There had been a squad car with lights flashing outside the revolving doors when Oliver and North had first come back to the Hummer but they hadn't seen any officers inside.

"That the EPPD showing up?" Consterdine asked.

"Yeah, sure took them a while. CNN beat them to it. You'll be getting this live in moments."

Oliver could hear the general speaking again but not the words.

"So how do you want us to play this thing?" he asked.

"Hang on a second, Bob."

Oliver waited, looking at Hap with a scowl. There was no sound for a long time and then a loud click and finally Consterdine came back on the line.

"Bob?"

"I'm still here."

"We think you should let the EPPD do their job."

"OK."

"But if they don't and it looks like it's getting out of hand you guys better take care of it."

Oliver was silent for a moment, staring up at the sign.

"OK, you're calling the shots. And the party line on Bowman?"

"No change there. He's insane."

CHAPTER TWENTY-SEVEN

Chief Harlan Walters, the stocky and well-liked veteran of the EPPD and a native West Texan, walked calmly into his old pal Brewster Jordan's office and found Hernano Salvador Medina sitting by the desk.

"Jordan not here?" he asked.

"I think he went outside."

"Didn't see him."

"I'm sure he'll be back in a moment."

"Hm," Walters grunted but as he turned to go Medina stood up and said, "May I introduce myself? I am Hernano Medina. From the Attorney General's office in Mexico City. I have just been speaking with Mr. Jordan. He doesn't think so but I'm sure I can be of help."

"How?"

"I also believe that Amado Barragan is Amado Portillo."

"Portillo's dead."

"I know he is supposed to be but our investigation has proved otherwise."

"Is that so? Well, all I know is Chuck Bowman, the guy up there who has Barragan hanging over the rail, was fired by the DEA because . . "

"Because he wouldn't stop speaking the truth?"

At that moment the telephone on the desk started ringing and Brewster Jordan hurried in sweating like a pig. He nodded to Walters and said, "Helluva situation, hm, Harley?" then took a deep breath to control himself before picking up the receiver.

"Jordan here."

He listened for a minute, mopping his brow with a tissue.

"Are you kidding me?" he exclaimed, listening some more and looking at Walters, and then said, "Holy shit," and put the handset back on the hook.

"What was it?" Walters asked.

Jordan glanced at Medina.

"Nothing. A message for Señor Barragan about his mother. She's not at all well."

"That's too bad. Señor Medina here seems to think Chuck Bowman's right. That Barragan is Amado Portillo."

"Yeah, I know. He told me. It's ridiculous. Excuse us, *señor*," Jordan said to Medina and walked out the door with Walters following.

"What are you going to do about this, Harley?" he whispered urgently as they reached the lobby, "You gotta put a stop to it and I mean now."

§

The private line was also ringing in the suite on the seventeenth floor and Cecilia answered it. She listened and Michael could see her face turn white and after a moment she sank down on the couch and the receiver fell from her hands to the floor. Michael could hear the otherworldly tremor of Hadean chords again and felt suddenly nauseous as if the whole hidden substructure of the room was losing its coherence. The sensation made speech impossible.

And then it stopped and Cecilia got to her feet and walked unsteadily to the bar and filled her glass twice to overflowing with vodka and swallowed both at a gulp. She wiped her mouth on the back of her hand and stood examining her reflection in the ornate Venetian mirror above the rows of bottles for a full thirty seconds before picking up her Derringer again and striding out onto the balcony. Michael knew something utterly dreadful was about to happen and stayed close behind in case he had to shout to Chuck in warning.

Amado wasn't struggling and Cecilia motioned Chuck and Enrique aside saying, "I have something important to tell him," and she leaned in very close to her brother's cheek and whispered in Spanish.

"Jorge Arellano has taken the villa. Mother is dead."

Amado stared at her in horror and the air froze between them. Michael thought he could see the space itself go taut and shatter and in that twinkling as Amado let out a terrifying howl of pain and Cecilia emptied the Derringer point blank into his gut some bestial superhuman power visibly crackled through his tiny frame and he grasped her by the groin and neck and lifted her high above the railing and before Chuck or anyone else could move to prevent it he hurled her off the balcony.

Michael rushed to the edge and watched her descent. It seemed almost in slow motion with the loose silk of her suit flapping in the updraft like the wings of a dark purple bat until she smacked face first into the diving board at the deep end of the hotel pool nine floors below with a nasty juddering clang. As her limp body sank languidly to the bottom a cloud of blood spread outward in the green shimmering floodlit water.

'The blood you lack,' Michael said to himself.

And as they all stood momentarily stunned at the rail's edge he saw the flash of a rifle from the street below and then an infinitesimal blink of time later his ears heard the report and in that briefest second, while the echo of Amado's agony still reverberated from the canyons of the surrounding city and even the inky mountains beyond, Chuck staggered from the railing and fell dead. There was a trickle of blood from a black indent above his left eye.

Amado's shirt was sprouting crimson patches and he howled again and backed away from them toward the door. His eyes were blazing like a wild thing and Enrique, who was now holding the Glock, didn't try to stop him.

Fernando was on his knees beside Chuck's body and Michael could see Beverley still perched motionless on the edge of the couch in her sparkling red sheath as the apartment door smashed open and a mix of Amado's green-suits and EPPD poured into the suite followed by Jordan and Chief Walters.

Amado was heading for the bathroom clutching his belly and he spun around to face them and bared his teeth and snarled and then let out another long despairing howl that stopped them in their tracks. Michael was looking on from the balcony door and fancied he could feel the sound vibrating all the way down to the hotel basement and rumbling deep into the dry desert soil beneath and then Amado's eyes rolled suddenly heavenward and he lost his balance and collapsed reeling to the carpet.

§

Oliver and North and everyone else outside the hotel heard the rifle shot and looked around to see where it came from. A tiny puff of smoke was rising above two of the EPPD cruisers on the outskirts of the crowd and some of the cameras caught it but the shooter and his weapon, if that was indeed where they were, remained hidden from view between them.

Consterdine was still on the line even though they were now picking up live coverage of the unfolding scene on CNN.

"That wasn't Hap, was it?" he asked, half joking.

"No, sir," Oliver replied, "Looks like it came from the EPPD."

"Did anyone get hit?"

"Don't know. There was a quick burst from a weapon on the balcony and then the sister fell but as soon as the rifle fired everyone up there stepped out of sight."

There was more muffled conversation on the Washington end.

"Tell you what, Bob. The general and I think you should get yourselves back on out to Bliss and call us later."

Oliver knew the sound of fishy when he heard it.

"Why the change?"

"Well, as things panned out you were both turned away from the cameras when Bowman stood up in the ballroom and we think maybe it's better we stay with the low profile. If it comes up we'll say you were shadowing him because you knew he was unstable but then you handed everything over to the EPPD."

"What about Medina?"

"We don't think he's that important any more."

Oliver could hear sirens approaching along North El Paso Street and two ambulances came racing around the corner onto West Mills and even though the crowd parted for them they had to draw carefully up to the front of the hotel to avoid crushing anyone. Once they had come to a stop the paramedics jumped down and three gurneys were quickly pulled out from the rear and some valets held open the double doors for them and they were wheeled inside at the run and clattered across the now empty lobby to the elevators.

"Somebody must've got it," Oliver said, "Paramedics just arrived."

"No need to hang around, Bob. We'll fill you in."

Oliver shut down his cell phone and sighed.

"They know something we don't that's for darn sure," he muttered and then looked at his young partner with guilt in his eyes, "Hap, I owe you one heck of a big apology."

§

Two of the gurneys were taken up to the seventeenth floor where one medical team pronounced Chuck dead and, while the other team hurried to get Amado on life support, Michael, Fernando, Rafael, Enrique and even Beverley, who remained staring at the officers with a blank expression and didn't seem to comprehend what was going on, were hand-cuffed and Walters informed them they were all under arrest as possible accessories to murder.

The team working on Amado said they needed a few more minutes to stabilize him before taking his gurney down so Michael and the others went first in two separate loads but they had to wait in the lobby while their transport was being organized. Chuck's body was brought with them and they stood together beside it in respectful silence, too numb to speak.

The crowd was being kept outside and Michael could see Ethel and Dickie through the glass pointing at him. The whole horrifying event had happened so quickly, and he was in such a state of shock, the welcome realization of survival didn't truly penetrate until hours later.

He looked on in a kind of trance as the elevator doors opened again and Cecilia was brought out on the third gurney. Her face was covered but he could see a trailing end of wet purple sleeve and her left hand and the blood red nails. It was romantic silliness he knew but he found himself a trifle disappointed the police and paramedics had actually found a body in the pool. And perhaps even a little bit surprised. Her fall had seemed so much like flying away.

And to add to the weirdness of the moment Beverley came partially back to a state of conscious awareness and raised the dead mike to her lips and began singing very, very softly.

"Hey, Delta Dawn, what's that flower you have on.

Could it be a faded rose from days gone by . . ?"

Ah yes, the yellow rose of Texas. She was so completely lost in her fantasy Michael was hard pressed not to dissolve in tears.

The paramedics trollied Chuck and Cecilia out to the waiting ambulances and Michael saw them being loaded in and driven away.

And just before Amado's gurney came down, Hernano Salvador Medina strolled casually out of the manager's office and because that was where he had come from none of the officers or green-suits bothered to accost him or move him aside and, when the elevator finally arrived and Amado was wheeled past him, Michael watched in astonishment as Medina took out a set of cheap Halloween plastic dentures with pink gums and long Dracula fangs from his jacket pocket and, holding them between his fingers and thumb and smiling down at Amado, clacked them open and closed two or three times. It was clear Amado had seen the gesture because his hand rose up weakly from the covers and tried to snatch them as he passed and then Medina was pulled away from the gurney's path and quietly admonished by a guard.

Michael knew exactly the expression that must have crossed Amado's face beneath his oxygen mask because he had seen it before at Vicente's open coffin. Now he could be certain Medina was the one who had put the dentures around Vicente's neck but what on earth did they mean? And what a strange thing for the polite little man to do! Michael knew the importance Mexicans attach to the Day of the Dead but practical jokes? If Medina was invoking La Catrina, the death-mask harbinger of things to come, it was nearly Easter not All Hallows.

He was still puzzling over it as the officers moved them outside and told them to wait again while Amado's gurney was being lifted into the back of yet another ambulance which had just arrived and then the most astonishing and bizarre thing of all happened.

There were sudden screams and the crowd parted in panic like the waters of the Red Sea before the Hand of God and Michael watched in trembling awe as the great white tiger materialized from the street like vapor in a cloud chamber and flowed like a shining Niagara of spume through the gap. The nimbus of its fur was streaked with matted blood. Its movement seemed to ripple the night air as the majestic beast floated to the gurney and rose on its hind legs to tower over Amado like an avenging mirage. Then placing one massive paw on his forehead it grasped its erstwhile master's throat with the other and tore the life away with a single wrench of its huge claws. Amado didn't even have time to cry out. Then, clenching the skull of the grotesquely squirting corpse between its colossal teeth, deeply piercing the temples and crushing the occipital bone, it attempted to carry him away.

But Amado's body was strapped to the gurney and it tipped over and the tiger shook the entire apparatus up and down and swung it around in a circle causing the intravenous needle to pull free from Amado's arm and the drip stand to fly off into the crowd like a spear. Then it circled again, slamming the gurney into the side of the ambulance like a matchbox toy and the severely weakened neck of the corpse was the first thing to give way as the vertebrae separated and the remaining vessels, tendons and musculature stretched and snapped and the tiger vanished by the same route from which it came with only a mangled head for its prize.

So intense was the spell cast by the great cat's presence that no one fired a shot and the entire crowd stood transfixed for a full five seconds when it was all over.

Michael had thought to cover Beverley's eyes as she was close beside him but she remained locked in her own saddened world and sang again in that tiny plaintive voice, this time without even raising the mike.

" . . And did I hear you say he was a-coming here today
To take you to his mansion in the sky."

It was the only sound in the silent plaza.

CHAPTER TWENTY-EIGHT

As the CNN reporter at the scene recovered his wits sufficiently to begin describing the event, the equally jaw-dropped McWhirter and Consterdine realized what they had seen had truly happened and both burst out laughing.

"What is that Latin phrase?" McWhirter managed at last, still catching his breath, "*Deus ex* what?"

"Machina. Deus ex machina."

"And what does it mean?"

Consterdine didn't really know.

"Ha! I knew you wouldn't. It means literally something like 'God from the machine' but it covers all completely unpredictable circumstances."

The last word was a slush puddle and McWhirter had to spit an excess of saliva into his handkerchief and then wiped his eyes with it before he was able to continue. Consterdine looked at him in disgust and lit up another Cuban.

"And, boy oh boy oh boy, if ever there was one of those this was it! That cat'll bury his head in the desert and then let Medina talk to us about his damn teeth!"

He began laughing again so uncontrollably he nearly lost his upper plate and had to press his thumb into his mouth to adjust it.

"What does it matter now?" Consterdine said and turned away.

§

And no one noticed until the next morning, when one of the hotel cleaning staff sweeping up the parking spaces under the great archway found something he thought was curious, that a pair of dentures had been flattened and almost obliterated beneath the wheels of a departing ambulance.

§

It was still not quite ten o'clock when Michael and the others arrived at the EPPD Central Command, which was only eight short blocks from the Barragan, where they were fingerprinted and asked to show some ID and neither Michael nor Beverley had any with them. Not that the officers were in any doubt about Beverley and because she was clearly either suffering some kind of breakdown or under the influence of drugs it was decided to whisk her out to the Psychiatric Hospital on Alameda for observation.

Michael's case was not so simple. He explained patiently that his billfold and a few pieces of identification that bore his name were with some of his other belongings in Fernando's cab which was parked near the hotel and Fernando was dispatched with an escort to fetch them but, though Michael was delighted to be in possession of his camera and shoulder-bag again, the items turned out to be less than satisfactory because, the same as at the border, they were only credit cards and a business card from Enigma magazine and a dog-eared card for the Chalk Farm Library and a long, long expired membership card for British Actor's Equity and none of them had a photo. Michael had tried his best while they were waiting to make the story of the passport theft short but that turned out to be impossible and, even though he told his interrogators the requisite document was very likely still packed with his clothes and shoes and two videotapes, tapes that he was exceedingly anxious to reclaim by the way, in a small white duffel bag in the driver's compartment of the now deceased Señor Barragan's limousine which in all probability was still in the vicinity of the hotel, after more than an hour of trying to make heads or tails of the eccentric Englishman's disjointed narrative the brain-taxed officers finally decided to put it all off to the morning.

The accused were each allowed one phone call before being taken over to the county jail across the street and Fernando called Marta, who was incredibly relieved that he was all right but wept when she heard that Chuck was dead, saying, 'I knew it would happen, I knew it the moment I looked at him', and Rafael and Enrique called a lawyer friend in Juarez who said he would come early the next morning.

Michael called Gottfried and Anna in Los Angeles and found out they had seen a great deal of the whole bizarre event on CNN and knew he wasn't going to be on the 11:17 already and, *macht nichts*, it wasn't even time yet for them to leave Silverlake and drive to the bus station downtown to meet him anyway so they hadn't been at all inconvenienced. He asked them to call Helen in London and tell her he was fine and they said they would and he was about to say he was going to change his itinerary and fly directly home in a few days instead of coming all the way west to visit them because the experience of the last thirty-six hours had left him more than slightly frazzled when the officer beside him said to hang up and that was that.

The way to the jail was a bright fluorescent tunnel beneath the street and as he was being taken through Michael was overcome by the terrifying thought that home might never happen. It was all too possible he might join the ranks of the disappeared and spend months or years or indeed, horror of horrors, the rest of his natural life incarcerated in some forgotten corner of the vast faceless maw known as the United States Federal Correctional System. The separation from everything one held dear would be unendurable!

The three Mexicans had already been transported to a different section of the jail so Michael was even denied the solace of conversation and lay alone with these fears during the almost sleepless night to come.

§

The dawning sun, however, brought another cloudless Texan sky.

After they had been individually walked back over to Central Command and had brief statements taken they were told no charges were to be laid against them. The three Mexicans in particular could barely believe their ears. There was to be no further investigation and they were free to go. The morning duty officers didn't even mention Michael's passport. What blessed relief!

They waited for each other on the gusty steps and by half past nine they were driving together the few blocks back to the hotel in the retooled Citroën sedan of Enrique and Rafael's lawyer, a dapper, relaxed and surprisingly young man named Jim Garcia who told them their release had been a *fait accompli* before he arrived. It was obvious to them all that wherever the order had come from it was somewhere much higher up the food chain than the EPPD.

Garcia brought the morning papers and a glance at the headlines supplied some of the reason if not the source. They proclaimed almost unanimously that ex-DEA officer Charles 'Chuck' Bowman was a hero who had given up his life to prove that Amado Barragan Fuentes, the real estate tycoon, friend of presidents and noted philanthropist, had a double identity and was, in fact, the infamous *narcotraficante*, Amado Portillo Perez, who had been incorrectly reported dead after surgery to change his appearance at an exclusive Mexico City clinic just one week ago.

There were photographs of Chuck and Vicente before his death and the man who had fooled everyone as Barragan Fuentes and several also carried an old head and shoulders picture of General McWhirter in his army uniform. He had been contacted at the DEA office in Washington well after midnight on the previous evening and his brief statement was quoted.

"There's no doubt our intelligence was wrong," the general had admitted, "We thought Chuck Bowman was crazy. We had information that he was at the hotel and sent two agents from Fort Bliss to find out why and now we know. The American public should be very grateful to him. He has performed an invaluable service for our country. Let his courage and determination be an example to us all. Our deepest sympathies and prayers are with his family."

Many articles were reporting that Amado had killed Chuck with Cecilia's Derringer as he valiantly tried to stop her being thrown from the balcony.

"That's utter tripe," Michael exclaimed when it was read to him, "I saw the gun hitting the water. It bounced out of her hand and splashed on the other side when her head struck the diving board."

"And we all saw the muzzle flash in the street," Fernando added.

"It is why they do not want your testimony," Garcia told them, "They want nothing to contradict the official story."

"Shovel one manure pile, another always takes its place," Rafael said.

They fell silent for a moment.

"What a shame he's not alive to see his victory," Michael said.

Enrique turned around in the front seat to look at him.

"For us there are no victories. Nothing will change."

"Was it the tiger that forced them to admit it?" Fernando asked Garcia.

"Maybe," he replied, "But look inside the Mexican papers and somewhere you will find that last night while Portillo was here the Arellano-Felix took the villa above Juarez and killed his mother. That is the real reason. Whoever set you free knew before the tiger came that Portillo was finished."

"Who was it, do you think?" Michael asked.

"It was someone. Someone who was protecting him for years, someone for whom he was useful. There are so many. What does it matter?"

"So Chuck's death was pointless?"

"Not entirely, no. But it is only what the ancients called a Pyrrhic victory. He proved he was right and that others, who believed what they were told, were either fools or liars. And he might have caused some minor problems we don't know about. But he didn't change anything."

"Maybe he stopped the murders," Michael said, "That's not nothing."

"No," Fernando agreed and then added, "If they stop."

"You said you thought they were responsible."

"Yes, I believe they were. But I think there is also something more."

"What?"

"I think the murders are born from the seeds of hopelessness. That has not changed."

Michael made no rebuttal. The truth was the truth.

He had refrained from any talk of vampires but couldn't resist bringing up the subject as they said goodbye beside Fernando's cab.

"You know, both Portillo and his sister told me they were vampires."

The Mexicans all smiled.

"They are," Rafael said.

"They're not dead, believe me," Enrique concurred.

"They are like poisonous mushrooms that connect unseen beneath the surface," Garcia added.

Michael nodded and smiled ruefully and asked, "Did they find the tiger?"

"Not yet. Not as far as I know anyway," Garcia answered.

Michael and Fernando then spoke about Chuck's family and agreed that they would try and take Chuck's body home to Sweetwater and explain as best they could what had happened to his sister Laurie and Fernando said he would phone her as soon as he got home and come to the Republic tomorrow morning and they could go to the police station together and see what could be arranged.

"Good luck finding your passport," Fernando said, "And the videotapes. Do you want me to come and help?"

"No, thanks. I'm sure I'll manage."

"Try and stay out of trouble."

"Who me?"

They both smiled and the two cars drove away, Enrique riding with the young lawyer and Rafael with Fernando in the cab, and Michael walked across South El Paso Street to the Barragan. 'Well, it won't be called the Barragan any more,' he thought, 'What was the original name they mentioned, Camino Real?' The Royal Way or the Real Way? The title of a peculiarly shapeless drama by Tennessee Williams. He had been in a student production of it at Rose Bruford all those years ago and played a number of small supporting roles, one of which was the corpse of Kilroy, the perennial innocent, in the scene where the surgeons discover his golden heart. At the beginning of the play Don Quixote arrives on the Camino Real and his squire Sancho Panza reads a direction to him from their crumpled map, 'Turn back, Traveler, for the spring of humanity has gone dry in this place.' Michael smiled ruefully at its aptness.

A teenage Hispanic garage attendant was just parking a newly washed Volkswagen Beetle outside the revolving doors and before Michael could turn around and try to escape Ethel and Dickie came out followed by a black valet hefting a copious array of plastic bags and small hand luggage.

"Good heavens, Dickie, it's Mr. Davenport!"

"Good morning, sir, what a happy surprise," Dickie said jovially.

"We thought you had been taken into custody."

The valet was still holding the bags and cleared his throat meaningfully.

"Oh yes, sorry," Dickie said to him and pointed to the Volkswagen, "Just see if you can get it in there somehow. Good lord, Ethel, they've washed it. Look, it's all shiny again."

"Yes, yes, how nice of them," she said dismissively, barely giving the car a glance, "Tell us what happened."

Oh my dear mother in heaven, hell has many forms!

"Um, nothing," Michael said and cursed his upbringing. Why couldn't he just tell them to bugger off and be done with it? "They let us go. We weren't guilty of anything after all."

"Yes, we bought a copy of the Dallas Morning News."

Well, at least they already knew some of it.

"Poor Mr. Bowman," Dickie said.

"Yes," Ethel agreed, "I never did quite understand why he called himself Hackney. But the papers weren't very clear about your involvement."

"No," Michael said.

"We've decided you're a bit of a dark horse," Dickie chortled amiably.

"A very dark horse," Michael agreed and spied his out.

"So there never was a movie?"

"No, I'm afraid not."

"No, we can see that now. We were fooled at first."

"How did you come to be mixed up in it all then?" Ethel asked, unable to let it go.

"I'm not at liberty to say," Michael answered.

"Ah yes," Dickie said with conspiratorial jollity, "Oh ho, hush hush, all that. Ho ho. Wasn't the business with the tiger extraordinary?"

"Yes, quite extraordinary."

"And rather gruesome."

"Yes, extremely gruesome."

"The paper said the beast was his pet."

"Yes, I believe it was."

"Strange thing for it to do then."

"Very strange."

"Well, you never can tell with animals of that sort, can you?"

"No, you never can. Look, if you'll excuse me, I'm in rather a hurry."

"Oh yes, yes, don't let us keep you."

"We're off to the *Zona del Silencio.*"

Michael restrained himself from the obvious, 'Aren't we all?'

"We want to see the petroglyphs."

"Ah, yes, I'm told they're very interesting."

The sweating valet had finally managed to jam all the bits and pieces of their paraphernalia into the cramped little vehicle and still leave room for them to sit. Michael saw him hesitate but then decide not to wait for a tip and he said, "All set now, folks, have a good trip," and went back inside.

"Well, toodle-oo," Ethel said cheerily without having heard or noticed the valet, "It's been tremendously exciting." She began adjusting herself carefully into the driver's seat. "Ever so much better than that dreadful pageant."

"Good lord, yes," said Dickie, attempting the same on the passenger side, "Wasn't that typically American!"

"Absolutely ghastly," Michael agreed.

"Wait a minute," Ethel exclaimed, "I don't have the keys."

"The boy left them in the ignition, Ethel."

She looked and saw them dangling there.

"Oh yes, well, he might have said so."

"I suppose there's no chance we might see you again at The Rovers."

"No, a thing of the past, I'm afraid."

"What a pity."

"Well, good luck."

They were almost set.

"Bon voyage," Michael said and started walking away.

"Arrivederci," Ethel reciprocated with a girlish little wave, trying to help a struggling Dickie with his seat belt.

Just as Michael was disappearing through the doors he turned back to see Dickie thrust his thumb in the air through the car window and wink.

"Love your suit!" the old man shouted.

Good lord, could he really be quoting Hannibal Lecter? Michael certainly knew the old couple must be moviegoers. But what is it about the British male, he mused as he hastened across the lobby to the manager's office trying his best to look unapproachable since quite a number of hotel patrons were watching him curiously, how was it possible this well-traveled octogenarian had retained such a boyish sense of humor?

Michael rapped on the door and a voice said, "Come". He entered and found Brewster Jordan sitting behind his desk, looking as if he hadn't slept much either though he was freshly scrubbed and perhaps a wee bit more relaxed than the night before but Michael knew that lurking beneath the false bonhomie must lie a gaping chasm of doubt about his job security.

"Morning, Mr. Davenport, what can I do for you?"

Michael had rightly suspected he wouldn't be surprised to see him.

"Is Señor Barragan's limousine still here?"

"I believe so. Why?"

Good news!

"There's a small white carry-on bag in it that contains some things of mine. The driver had it with him."

"Have a seat, Mr. Davenport. We'll check it out."

"Thank you."

Jordan picked up the phone and Michael felt he was looking at him with a kind of relief as he spoke with the underground garage.

"Diego's not still around, is he? No, I figured not. Listen, can you take a boo in the limo and see if there's a white bag on the driver's seat. Yeah, you know, like a sports bag. If it's there, bring it to my office right away."

Jordan hung up and looked at Michael with a smile, then leaned back in his chair and folded his hands on his tummy and sighed.

"It's real sad about Chuck Bowman," he said.

"Yes."

Michael eyed him carefully and decided to go on.

"The newspapers didn't report his death correctly. Barragan or Portillo or whatever you want to call him didn't have a weapon. Chuck was shot with a rifle from down here."

Jordan did his best to appear shocked.

"You don't say. You ought to tell someone."

"I did."

"Who?"

"I told the officers who questioned us."

"And what did they say?"

"They said they'd look into it."

Jordan clicked his tongue.

"Son of a bitch, ain't that something? Well, whatever happened, you can bet Harley Walters and his boys'll find out."

Michael nodded. 'Turn back, Traveler,' he thought, 'And run.'

The teenager from the garage knocked on the door at that moment and Jordan said, "Come," and the boy wandered in chewing a wad of gum and, joy of joys, he had the bag in his hand.

"It's the property of Mr. Davenport," Jordan told him with a gesture.

The young attendant handed it to Michael and went out again.

"Take a look inside," Jordan cautioned, "Make sure it's all there."

Michael did and it was. The troublesome passport, the treasured and oh so nearly fatal videotapes and, almost best of all, his own clothes.

"The bag is not actually mine," he admitted.

"Take it, what the hell," Jordan said and then added, "You have someplace to stay in town or are you leaving?"

"Both," Michael answered and stood.

"Thank you very much," he said and then asked almost without thinking, "What will they do about completing the pageant?"

Jordan chuckled.

"Bowman sure made a mess of the whole thing, didn't he? It's not my call. They've got a committee. I can guarantee it won't be here though. My guess is they'll regroup and move it to Austin, someplace like that."

"Any word about Miss McIntyre?"

"How do you mean?"

"I believe she was taken to a Psychiatric Hospital."

"Really? Can't say as I knew. But I wouldn't worry about it. Her old man's sitting on a pile of dough. I figure she'll be OK."

Michael couldn't resist a trace of imitation drawl.

"Yup, I figure so too."

Jordan looked at him and his eyes went cold and humorless.

"Well, if I can be of any further help, Mr. Davenport, don't hesitate."

"I won't. Thanks again."

Michael didn't look back as he went out. He could sense the reptilian stare following him and didn't want to see it. He was feeling so drained and so completely demoralized all he wanted to do was collapse into that awful bed at the Republic and sleep for a week, even the hippopotamus concierge would be a welcome sight, but, as his luck would have it, Hernano Salvador Medina was just stepping out of the elevator and saw him and waved at him to stop.

He was dressed as nattily as ever and strolled up to him and said, "I am very glad to see you, Mr. Davenport. Have you had breakfast?"

It occurred to Michael that, despite his fatigue, this polite little man might be able to fill in some of the many blanks that were rattling around in his brain.

"No, I haven't as a matter of fact."

In truth, he was famished. He had not had more than a few mouthfuls in the nearly twenty-four hours since breakfasting by the pool at the villa.

"Will you honor me then and be my guest? They begin serving Sunday brunch, as they call it, in a few minutes. They claim it is famous throughout the Southwest. I have not eaten yet either."

"I'd be glad to."

CHAPTER TWENTY-NINE

A battered pale blue 1990 Dodge Dakota was kicking up sporadic clouds of dust as it bounced and zigzagged across the Samalayuca that morning. The wilderness it traveled was even beyond the endless network of sandy tracks that laced web-like through the sparse and spindly vegetation and two men standing in the rear of the truck were doing their best to stay on their feet and tossing out big chunks of something reddish from a long rectangular box that glinted in the relentless sunshine.

The lid of the silver coffin was banging up and down on the side of the cargo deck away from the men and the roast-sized lumps they were ditching in the desert were all that remained of Doña Aurora Perez Fuentes and her beloved youngest son.

When the men had finished emptying the lavishly ornamented casket they dumped it down a deep ravine and went home.

§

"I have many questions," Medina began as he and Michael walked toward the restaurant, "I'm sure you have many also."

"Very many."

"You spent the night as a guest of the El Paso police."

"Yes."

"I hope it was not too unpleasant. What did they say when they let you go this morning?"

"That no charges were to be laid against us."

"None of you?"

"No, they let us all go."

"Where are your Mexican friends?"

"They have gone home to Juarez."

"And, of course, the police did not say why."

"No."

The queue for brunch was quite long but Medina had pre-booked a relatively private corner table and they were seated immediately. They agreed that Medina should order for both of them since Michael was not familiar with almost all of the dishes on the menu and once the waitress brought coffee and a quite promising smelling pot of tea Medina went on.

"Do you know why?"

"I believe a rival gang took over Portillo's villa and so perhaps covering up his identity was no longer pointful."

"Pointful for whom?"

"I haven't the faintest idea. A faction in the American government?"

Medina took a thoughtful sip of his coffee.

"I must confess I am not perfectly sure either. Tell me this, you are not involved with the *narcotraficantes*, you are a journalist, are you not?"

"Of sorts."

"And once you were an actor?"

"Alas, yes."

"And you were kidnapped by Portillo to portray some sort of role?"

"Yes."

"How did that happen?"

"I filmed his tiger at the river and then the tiger getting into his limousine and not long afterwards two of his men knocked me over in the street and took my camera. The tape inside was very important to me and I foolishly went to his night club in Juarez to try and get them back."

"You are very lucky to be alive."

"I know. I have Chuck Bowman to thank for that."

"How did you know Mr. Bowman?"

"We met by chance at a bar."

"Here in El Paso?"

"Yes. Called 'Pantera's' funnily enough. I have a strange fascination for all members of the cat family."

The waitress came with their breakfast. Medina had asked for a plate of seafood for himself, six oysters on the half shell, delicate slices of smoked salmon and some extremely jumbo 'peel and eat' shrimp and Michael, being more in the Englishy breakfasty mood, had agreed to try *'tortilla de huevos'*, a Mexican-style omelet, as the closest available thing. As the smell of jack cheese, red and green peppers, cumin, garlic, onion, sour cream and fresh tomatoes rose to his nostrils he was reminded of chili burritos and Cactus Cooler and a grateful smile came to his lips. Glory of glories, it was a blessed spring morning, he was alive and no longer suffering the slightest trace of that hideous English winter bug and he tucked into it with gusto.

As they ate, Medina continued with his questions and Michael told him all that he knew about the meeting with the Russians and the black woman and the talk of nuclear contraband, and though the name 'Bartolomeo Vespucci' meant nothing to Medina he wrote it down in a notebook, and about the gut-wrenching tape Amado had shown them and even the disgusting vampirish ritual he had been forced to watch. He stopped short of offering Medina the tape of the same event that he still had in his jacket pocket because for one thing he was not one hundred percent sure he could trust him and for another it might turn out to be useful in some macabre way. Images from it might possibly accompany an article about his experience for the magazine or even a book he was now contemplating.

"The tape is probably still in the VCR in his suite," Michael said, trying to assuage his slightly guilty feeling.

"No. The hotel manager allowed me to look through the rooms early this morning and everything personal has been removed. But, strangely enough, I do have a tape of what you describe. After the chaos I was able to retrieve Cecilia Portillo's purse from the platform where you were sitting. She dropped it when she pulled out the gun. There was also a young girl who was being treated very cruelly. I wonder why the sister had a copy of it with her."

"She thought if she showed it to the Russians they would be angry with Amado and it might help to save her life."

Michael was relieved to be off the hook.

"Yes, I see," Medina said, "And unfortunately she was wrong."

"Yes."

Medina took a moment to suck down an oyster.

"The ritual of blood and semen that you witnessed is very interesting. We believe this family was responsible for many, many disappearances and deaths of young women."

"My friend Fernando thinks so too. He is a photographer. His gallery in Juarez is entirely dedicated to the women. He calls it *'Nada Que Ver'*. The images he has captured are quite astounding. And Cecilia Portillo showed me a tape of her brother Vicente and herself and a group of friends and helpers, both men and women, crucifying three helpless girls in the desert. I found it almost impossible to watch but she wasn't in the least affected by it."

"Did you know they were vampires?"

Michael was surprised by the apparent sincerity of the question.

"They weren't shy about telling me that they were."

"No, I imagine not."

"On the tape of the crucifixion they frequently displayed large fangs to the camera but do you seriously believe it?"

"I am not sure what to believe."

"Last night you clacked some cheap plastic dentures in Portillo's face as they wheeled him out. You caught my eye after you had done it. I thought it was odd because he had shown me his brother's corpse at the villa and a pair was also tied around its neck. He became extremely distressed when he saw them."

"I must confess I put them there, yes."

"Chuck said he thought so. Why?"

"It is rather a long story but in a nutshell it was my way of telling him that I could prove the body of the patient named 'Florio Bastida Morales' was not him but his brother Vicente. The gums of the corpse were raw. It was obvious that the teeth had been recently extracted and it had been done crudely. The logic behind the removal was obscure. You see, we had known from the very beginning that Amado Portillo was born edentate. It is an extremely rare occurrence but his jaw was formed in the womb without the necessary structures for developing teeth. This defect caused considerable facial deformity and when he was a child he had to undergo many surgeries to correct his appearance and he was forced to wear dentures ever after."

"His sister told me she and Vicente began to grow vampire fangs at some time during their teenage years."

"I believe that is a fable."

"She showed me huge holes between her molars and incisors where these dogteeth would have been. She told me Amado had pretended outrage at their recklessness when really it was jealousy and he had drugged them, both she and Vicente, and had some ham-fisted dentist carve them out. The excavations in her mouth were certainly real and recent and looked very painful."

"And then he gave instructions to finish the job on his brother as part of the cosmetic surgery. As I said, one can only conjecture at the reason behind it. It did nothing to help the charade. It appears to have been pure malice. But to go back to the enlarged Dracula teeth you have seen in the tape she showed you, I think they were attachments only. As far as we know they all used them."

"Then why did he have their real canines removed?"

"Simply as a punishment, I imagine."

Medina had eaten his fill and wiped his lips.

"But you know," he went on with an ironic smile, "None of this can any longer be proved. No one has found the tiger and I doubt they will. The sister's face was broken beyond recognition on the diving board during her fall. I visited the morgue very late last night and was allowed to see the corpse."

The expression that flickered across his delicate features told all.

"And the Arellano-Felix will assuredly dispose of Vicente and the mother. Not that any autopsy remains necessary. Whether or not they were vampires is truly of marginal importance. Except perhaps to the curiosity of people like us. But I think it will be sufficient satisfaction for me that one small fragment of the wider truth has finally come to light. It is bad sportsmanship to be greedy."

Michael too had finished and sat for a moment silently digesting both the eggs and the story. They had been equally delicious.

"What will happen now with the Russians and the stolen plutonium?"

"I suspect," Medina answered, "That Jorge Arellano will not be unwilling to make the same arrangement. He and his brothers are, if anything, even more brutal and heartless than the Portillos."

He caught the quizzical look in Michael's eye.

"You are right. It is foolish to make such distinctions. Once the spring of humanity has run dry all hope is lost."

EPILOGUE

Three days later, Michael and Fernando stood in the early spring grass outside Chuck's house in Sweetwater watching Laurie and the silent old man and a small gathering of friends as she slowly poured his ashes around the base of a towering honey locust tree.

After the official funeral ceremony at Fort Bliss his body had been cremated according to his wishes. The photo of the corpse provided to the media showed no visible mark on the forehead.

§

As the desert wind scattered all that remained of the 'national hero', General McWhirter and DEA Director Consterdine were once more in the latter's office in Arlington congratulating themselves on their good fortune.

"You know what," the general said, "I think we should go totally hands off and let Arellano and the Russians make their own deal. It'll be safer and better that way. The whole suitcase nuke idea seems kind of passé right now."

"How so?" the director asked, failing to mask his irritation at being made to feel he was out of the loop.

"Well, I had a call from one of the good doctor's people this morning and he intimated consensus was moving away from that option."

"To what exactly?"

"More along the lines of the Yousef thing. You know, completing it."

The director's eyes behind his glasses widened slightly in surprise.

"With more powerful explosives?"

"Yeah, sort of. Planes first, I'm guessing. Then explosives."

Consterdine let it sink in for a moment.

"Well, if they want to get complicated that suits me. I'm sick of working on their damn stuff anyhow. I'll be happy to get back to the old-fashioned business of making money."

The general chuckled. He was standing by the window, staring out from moist gray eyes at a sprinkle of late falling snow.

"It's all connected, Connie. What's the difference?"

There was a knock on the door and Consterdine looked at his watch.

"Time for the meeting."

He walked the twenty or so paces from his desk across the plush carpeting and let in five men of mixed middle age, three dressed in senior army uniforms and two in dark blue suits, preceded by a tall fleshy woman outfitted in flowing floral silk who, despite her ample figure and the conspicuous femininity of her garb, was much more mannish than the men.

Last to enter was the black woman, wearing a conservative medium-blue skirt and matching jacket with a discreet yellow patterned scarf tucked in around her neck, and she locked the door behind her.

They came in without speaking and, assisted by the serious-faced director and the still lightly smiling general, moved all the chairs in the room into a wide circle and stood one behind each.

They kept their eyes averted and began taking off their clothes.